UCE Tales

Philip T McNe

First Edition – September 15
Cassie Edition – October 15
Football Accuracy Edition – January 16

Also available separately as:
Caedo Tu
Kill-Soc
The Stereotypes

To whoever – I'm tired

CAEDO TU

TOM

I remembered being happy that night as I skateboarded down that street in the balmy May humidity. I had just come from uni and was desperate to get home, as it was my birthday. Twenty one years old – old enough to do whatever I wanted, but still young enough to wear the badge that came with the card I got from my mum that morning, along with the brand new Darkstar Skateboard I was furiously blazing along on. It was all black gloss and flames – clichéd I knew, but I didn't care because I'd wanted it for ages.

I was always knocking about campus in my torn three quarter lengths and blacks, tunnelled ears and beanie hats, and now the board completed the image.

Overall, it had been a pretty solid week. Lectures had been easy, homework had been minimal, and I'd received the welcome pack for the UCE Kill-Soc widegame I'd applied for – basically, life was good. In hindsight, I should have expected what came next.

The manicured lawns and low walls blurred as I shot past, pumping my legs, furiously spurring the board along. Too fast to recognise the figure across the road in combats and the tight t-shirt giving me the eye, and definitely too fast to avoid almost crashing into one of the UCE football jocks walking the other way, boots slung over his shoulders and a dejected scowl slung over his face.

"Watch it, idiot!" he yelled as I swerved around him, my rucksack just grazing his side as I leaned across.

"Whoa," I grinned, revelling in the adrenaline rush and the fact that I would be long gone before the crew cut grunt could get me. "Sorry mate!"

I skated on, flickering in and out of the streetlamp halos, riding past one of the pretty boys decked out in designer jeans and a shirt. As I streaked past, I caught part of what he was shouting exasperatedly into his iPhone.

"For God's sake Marie, you do this every time. How am I supposed to know where your bastard hairdryer is?"

Nice.

A few minutes later I hopped off, flicking the board stylishly into my hands. I was at the end of the street, which now melted into a dimly lit country lane. It would wind through a couple of cornfields before emerging onto the estate where I lived. I could have taken the main road around, but that would have added another twenty minutes onto my journey, and I knew for a fact that my mum would have made a cake for me. Now I know what you're probably thinking – going down a dark lane at night is a recipe for disaster, but what could I say? My mum made awesome cake.

I walked into the darkness, the gravel too rough for the board – I didn't want to ruin the trucks on the first day. The lights of the street behind me soon faded as I rounded the first corner, amazed at how quickly the sky opened up until I felt like I was miles from civilisation, just me and the stars. I continued, only faintly aware of the humming sound that was growing steadily louder. It sounded like a car engine, but there were no headlights on the lane in front of me, and besides, the track wasn't really intended for traffic. The odd tractor was usually as busy as it got, and never this late. As the noise got closer, I still couldn't see anything so I stepped out and turned around, thinking that maybe the car was coming from behind. Still no lights. I turned once more, just as two tons of steel smashed into me. I was weightless for a second as I flew into the air, and the car pulled round wildly beneath me, screeching to a halt amidst a fine powdery gravel dust.

The initial impact was too much of a shock to hurt me, but when I finally came back down to earth, it felt like every bone in my body shattered at the same moment.

Naturally, I blacked out but oddly could still hear what was going on around me. I could hear the papers that had spilled from my split rucksack fluttering gently in the breeze, and the tinkling of glass bottles before the slamming of doors and hurried footsteps.

"Oh my God, what the hell were you thinking?" the first voice said in disbelief. This one obviously had a conscience.

"I... I didn't... Nobody comes down here," the second voice tried to reason. I figured this guy was the driver. "What was he doing in the road, huh?"

Great. So now it was all my fault that I was lying slumped in the hedgerow at the side of the lane.

"Is he...?"

"I don't know."

"What are we going to do?"

"I don't know! Just let me think for a minute."

Um, call an ambulance maybe? I didn't doubt that these guys were in shock too, but hey, I was the one potentially dying here. I heard the sound of a bottle landing dully on the ground and the whimpering of a frightened young man.

"Ok nobody saw us, right?" This was the driver, and I didn't like it. I could see where this was heading and I found myself screaming in my head for him not to finish the sentence the way I knew he was going to. "We just get back in the car and pretend this never happened."

"But?"

"No buts! I didn't have the headlights on and you were drinking - that's not gonna earn us any points. Now come on, before someone else gets here."

Once more there was the sound of footsteps and slamming doors, but in reverse order. The engine growled to life somewhere near my head, and then faded into silence as I was left for dead, the two halves of my brand new skateboard lying at my feet and the pin from my badge sticking into my ribs.

The next time I woke up was later that night, after a burst of intense violet light. Except I wasn't awake. Not really. I knew this because I could see myself lying in a hospital bed in the centre of a bland room, connected to a dozen machines branching out of me at all angles like I was Frankenstein's monster. The sheet was folded down over my waist, which was heavily bandaged, and my chest was a mass of purple bruised tissue.

Looking down at myself, I almost seemed peaceful although I could tell there was something going on behind my eyes – probably the weird out of body thing that was happening. On the side least cluttered by beeping monitors, my mother was sitting, sobbing as she clutched her handbag to her lap. She was still wearing her coat, so she must have just arrived, but even with the extra layer, she looked smaller than I'd ever seen her. Her face, which usually beamed with rosy cheeks at the slightest thing, was now drawn and tired. Her hair was hastily pulled back, and I thought for the first time ever, I could spot a few greys. It seemed that with me lying there before her, part of her had slipped into the darkness with me.

A doctor came bustling in, a clipboard clutched to his chest. My mother looked at him hopefully, but he merely shook his head.

"I don't understand, it's not fair," my mum cried to herself. "He's such a hard working nice boy."

Aww mum – always got my back. It was a pity that being a hard working nice boy had no bearing on my current predicament though – it wasn't as if I could have deflected the car with some A Grade coursework.

"Don't worry," the doctor said unconvincingly. "The body is a delicate thing. He's been knocked out of balance, that's all."

Knocked out of balance? And the award for worst doctor ever goes to… although maybe he did have a point. Perhaps it was all about balance? Didn't they say that everything in life is balanced, and that energy is neither created nor destroyed? As I gazed at my still body, the undeserving victim of a hit and run, I wondered. On every TV soap ever, a baby is supposedly born every time a person dies to maintain this equilibrium, so why couldn't I do something similar? How many lives would it take to buy back my own? After all, my mother was right - what happened to me wasn't fair. I wasn't lying there because of nature, I was lying there because of *human nature,* the conquering desire for self-preservation, and that was what was now driving me to attempt this trade. I could already sense that somehow I had been granted the power to change my awful situation. I just hoped that the world would understand.

I thought back to the last people I saw before the blackness, and I swear I saw myself smile slightly as I lay comatose in the bed. They were ripe, I could feel it. It wasn't as if I was going to trade off some innocent babies or anything – these guys were practically there already. Years of stress and tension simmering, waiting for me to bring them to the boil. Each one of my saviours ran on a different fuel, whether it was depression or heartbreak, but I vowed then that I would do whatever I could, I would strike whatever bargain to retrieve my life from the bedridden state it was currently in, if only to dry my mum's tears. And so I planned their downfall…

ADAM

As usual, I was awake and ready well before I had to leave for uni, and that was even including my daily ritual of posing in front of the full length mirror, deciding which outfit to wear. In the end, I had settled for a pair of simple black combats with a check shirt - fitted of course.

I was lying on the bed flicking through the latest copy of *Attitude* with Lloyd my cuddly shark tucked under my arm. He'd been a present from my aunt when I was born, and I'd slept with him ever since. I tried to think what I would do if I ever got a boyfriend, but every time I looked at Lloyd's twenty year old patchy fur and his one eye hanging out on a bit of thread, I always chose him. My nonexistent boyfriend could sleep on the floor.

There was a light knock at my bedroom door, and I quickly shoved the magazine under the mattress. That was another thing standing in the way of my eternal happiness. I still lived with my parents, who didn't know I was gay. I just hadn't found the right moment yet, but I was well aware that every day I left it was another chance for them to find out some other way – and that wouldn't be fair. Not that I was too worried, as my older brother Andrew had just been promoted, so the spotlight was on him lately.

"Adam?" my mum asked, her voice slightly muffled through the wood of the door. "Are you up yet? Don't forget you have lessons today." *Lessons.* She was always calling them lessons instead of lectures or seminars. She made it sound like I was still at primary school, not studying a Psychology degree at university.

"I know, I'm ready."

"Will you see Tom today?"

"Yes mum." A couple of nights ago, my best friend had been hit by a car and left by the side of the road. It was his birthday, and they'd just left him for dead. I'd been to see him in hospital every day since it had happened, but so far nothing had changed – he was still in a coma.

"Check the news before you go."

I flicked my TV on as I heard my mother's footsteps descending down the stairs. The news was still going, the presenter speaking hurriedly against a woodland background. The scrolling banner at the bottom of the screen mentioned a dead body being found in the forest. I rolled my eyes and turned the screen off. My mum was always panicking about stuff like this, even though she knew I never went anywhere near the woods. During the Bird Flu crisis, she wouldn't even let me leave the house. It was even worse lately after Tom's accident - she somehow seemed to think that the same thing would immediately happen to me if I wasn't careful.

I rolled off the bed with a sigh and hefted the rucksack I'd packed the night before. To complete the final part of my morning routine, I went to the window and opened the curtains, looking out across the city, a cover of rainclouds reflecting in a thousand puddles embossing everything with silver. I always checked before I left, just to make sure aliens hadn't invaded during the night, or we hadn't suffered some major god-wrath or something.

In the western section of the metropolis, the ancient castle sat upon its raised mound, jagged ruins breaking the skyline. The four oaks of UCE bloomed above the rooftops in the centre, and just behind them rose the bland grey concrete tower of Morgan's Car Park. I always liked to start by looking at the castle then scanning across – it felt like travelling through time just by moving my head. The vision was completed by the motorway and the river lacing out of the corner, two lifelines pulsating from the urban heart.

Everything was as it should be.

With one final glance to make sure my magazine was hidden, I made for the door, being sure to reassure my mum before I left.

ALEX

I opened my eyes reluctantly, the morning light flooding into my face and making me growl angrily. I didn't do mornings. Once my vision had cleared, I rolled over and looked at my alarm clock, which was helpfully blank. Did I dream the little snippet of radio earlier whilst I was dozing? *Please, please, please,* my mind begged as I fumbled about on the floor for my phone. It was 9:45 - almost an hour later than it should have been.

"Awww, shit!" I hissed as I flopped out of the bed in a tangle of duvet and landed on the floor amongst heaps of discarded clothes and lecture notes. In a normal sized room, the floor would have been completely covered, but in the small halls room, the clothes had actually taken a couple of inches off the total height of the place. If I didn't clean up soon, my head would end up scraping the ceiling.

After angrily slamming the stupid clock into the bin, I crawled about, throwing clothes across the room until I found a pair of jeans that didn't smell too fusty. I hurriedly yanked them over my shorts. Next, I hooked any old t-shirt from the top of the nearest pile and jammed it unceremoniously over my head. No doubt looking like a homeless, I shoved a stack of papers roughly into my bag, slipped my trainers on and ran out the door, hoping that I hadn't missed too much of whatever seminar I was heading to.

Seconds later, I was running down the steps into the foyer of O'Connell Hall. The soft faux leather seats, potted plants and payphones made it look more like a hotel lobby, but the students slouching about gave its true purpose away.

I slowed down a little as I hit the bottom, trying to catch my breath. If I was too red in the face, the others would probably think I'd been up to something questionable, especially with my creased and mismatched ensemble.

Standing by one of the exotic looking potted ferns was one of the girls on my floor, Marie something or other. She was one of the beautiful people with chestnut hair cascading down her back, and a trust fund probably stashed away somewhere.

"Jack, it's me," she spoke softly into the latest model of smartphone. I couldn't help overhearing as I slouched past. Jack was her boyfriend. I'd never met him but I'd heard the two of them arguing a couple of times out in the corridor. "Listen, we've had some fun, but this isn't going to work."

Ouch, I thought as I pushed open the glass doors and jogged out into the quad.

JACK

"Jack it's me. Listen, we've had some fun, but this isn't going to work. I just don't feel for you any more. I guess I'm saying it's over. Goodbye Jack." The voicemail beeped as the message ended and I stared at the phone, speechless, the tears already stinging the corners of my eyes. How could she do it over the phone like that? I wasn't sure which hurt more, the fact that she'd done it, or the fact that she hadn't even told me in person.

I'd always thought Marie had been out of my league, and sure we'd argued a bit, but it was always just petty stuff. I honestly thought things were working out. And then this.

I tried to remember all the good times we'd had: our trip to the beach during Reading Week, the Winter Ball and that first night we'd snuck into the park, but all of it was marred now. Was she thinking of ending it, even during those memories I'd cherished?

I pressed the play button again, then turned away from the treacherous phone. The tears fell freely as I came face to face with her smile. The framed photo I kept on my bedside table seemed to be taunting me, the way she was flicking her hair back and looking at me with those deep hazel eyes, as if she'd already moved on. Bitch. I tried scrunching my face up in an attempt to squeeze the tears back inside, but they just wouldn't stop. No way I could go to lectures today – she'd probably told her brood all about it by now, and they were all bound to be on their various perches waiting to hit me with some snide remark. Like me, Marie's friends also didn't think I was worthy of her company, and they'd told me so on numerous occasions when Marie had been at the bar or the bathroom on nights out.

I slumped back into my pillow as the message beeped once more.

ADAM

I took my usual seat at the back of the room and got my pad out. The lecturer, Mr Davis wasn't there yet and other students were steadily flowing into the room and unpacking their things.

With a loud serenade of cackling giggles, a trio of girls flounced into the room, all similarly dressed in the latest fashion and makeup. Honestly, who went to that much trouble just to go to a seminar? I narrowed my eyes, willing them to sit somewhere else, but they continued along the aisle between the tables until they reached the row directly in front of me, their perfume hitting me in the face so I had to cough to clear my throat. One of them made a point of glaring at me for existing before they dropped their bags and continued their gossiping. I couldn't help listening as I opened my pad and began doodling half-heartedly.

"So I finally did it…" That was Marie, the leader of the little troupe. She obviously wasn't talking about losing her virginity, as I imagined that had happened quite some time ago. I smiled at my own scathing humour as the girls erupted into laughter.

"Another one bites the dust," one of the minions said. "Not that we disagree with your decision, but why this time?"

"The usual," Marie said with a playful shrug. "He couldn't even drive."

"You know, that could develop into a serious problem." This was the other drone, but to me they all sounded the same, the Maries, the Kellys and the Sarahs.

"You're never going to find Mr Right if you keep dumping them for stupid reasons like that."

"But I've already found Mr Right. He has his own car, house and credit cards."

I have to admit that I pricked my ears up at this point. After all, if there was such a perfect guy out there, I wanted to know who it was!

"No!" one of the others shrieked. "Who is it? I can't believe you didn't tell us!"

Marie paused for a second, dragging out what I can only imagine must have been excruciating suspense for her friends. "My dad of course!"

I rolled my eyes and went back to my scribbling as the girls once more erupted in high pitched giggling that halted just as abruptly and falsely as it had begun.

"So, back to Jack. Poor, useless Jack. How did you…?"

"I phoned him up this morning and told him straight. Well, I told his answering machine straight anyway."

"You're such a cow! You're like the cruellest girl I know. You can't just leave them normally can you?"

"What can I say? Image is everything." A typical response from somebody who quite frankly looked perfect. She should try saying that when she had terrible acne or a moustache. Not that I had those things, but it was fun to wish inflictions on those who were better looking than you.

"So how did he take it?"

I looked up to see what Marie would tell her friend. Did she have a heart after all? No – she just shrugged.

JACK

"I guess I'm saying it's over. Goodbye Jack." I couldn't stop listening to it. The message was like a judge pronouncing a life sentence that kept echoing in my head. My room, despite being covered in framed art and classic movie posters, seemed leeched of colour as if the message was sucking all the warmth out.

I lay there waiting for the beep to come. It seemed to take longer this time, but perhaps I was just losing track of things. It wasn't like I checked my watch after each re-run of my ultimate failure. I had lost count of how long I had been lying there, still in my shorts, eyes now red and puffy.

Something crackled and whispered on the end of the message.

"Caedo Tu…" And then the beep. I was sure that hadn't happened before, and it didn't even sound like Marie's voice, it sounded deeper, like a boy's. What did it even say? Some sort of Latin? Confused, I leaned over and jumped the message back a few seconds.

"Goodbye Jack." The message beeped once more without the whisper. Maybe it had been a noise from outside? Either way, the creepy sound had told me it was time to at least put a top on and get up out of my room. Perhaps I was going stir crazy stuck up there, dwelling in my misery.

I walked over to my drawers, took out a freshly folded polo shirt and put it on before shuffling out of my room and down the stairs.

The living room was slightly messier than my bedroom, a constant reminder that I shared my student house with people who were less meticulous than I was. There were still glasses from a couple of nights ago, as well as a pizza box poorly hidden under the table. I moped in dejectedly, slumping myself across one of the sofas that had seen too many years of student living. It had once been a crisp bright blue, but there were now darker patches and threads sticking out.

I turned the television on and flicked half-heartedly through the channels, but it was all doom and gloom. Dead bodies in the woods weren't exactly going to cheer me up.

Before I knew it I was crying again. I ended up curling myself into as small a ball as possible, like I was trying to disappear into the sofa. At least as a piece of furniture, I wouldn't be concerned with heartbreak.

The tears continued, each one wracking my chest until my ribs began to ache. No matter how hard I tried to stop them, they kept coming, my body convulsing silently as I tried to hold my breath. Finally, I was struck by a thought – a silver lining, tarnished as it was. Perhaps this dumped feeling was like being sick after too much boozing. Once my system was purged, I'd be ok again. With that, I released my breath and stopped trying to prevent the onslaught of misery, hoping it would run itself dry.

ADAM

The room had filled up and students were now lounging in their seats, waiting for the seminar to start. Luckily, Marie and her cronies had shut up long enough for me to notice the sheer perfection that was Luke Ashford come in. He sat a few rows in front of mine, two places to the right, not that I was counting or anything. Luke was your typical football player – tall, athletic, attractive, and even though he had probably just thrown on whatever he could find, he still looked amazing in faded jeans and a creased t-shirt.

Whilst I was shamelessly ogling, Mr Davis strode in and sat at his desk. He was one of the more relaxed lecturers, choosing to dress casually rather than wearing the outdated suit and tie combo that older educators clung to. After a brisk shuffle of his papers, he started taking the register, calling out the list of names, most of which I couldn't give a crap about. It wasn't like I was a loner or anything, but I wasn't one to surround myself with hordes of sycophants like Marie did.

"Tom?"

Silence. I looked awkwardly at the empty place next to mine and I could feel a dozen pairs of eyes facing my way like sniper sights. Obviously Mr Davis hadn't heard about Tom's accident. I found myself feeling grateful that we were at uni, and technically classed as adults. If this had been school, some idiot would have blurted it out and I would have had to endure the mock concern of everyone in the room. At least students were generally too self-absorbed to even pretend they cared.

There was a moment more of muffled whispers before the register continued. I felt glad when the heat of the others' eyes left me, satisfied that I hadn't broken down. Yes, I was concerned about my friend, and I missed hanging out with him, but getting soppy wouldn't help him get better.

"Ok," Mr Davis said once he had read the last name. "We need to continue with our work on Displacement Theory. If you turn to page thirty two and read the following chapter, then we can discuss some of the ideas."

Relieved that the tension was finally broken, I flicked open my text book and began to scan the page, occasionally peering over my book to watch Luke, lips moving slightly as he read.

ALEX

The corridor was empty – a sure sign that I was drastically late. I snuck forwards across the uni standard grey tiles, my heart sinking as I saw that the classroom door was shut. There went any chance I had of creeping in quietly. I took a few deep breaths, hoping to disguise the fact that I had just ran here, before donning my confident couldn't care less face and pushing open the door.

As I feared, everybody's heads snapped up in my direction. I could hear stifled whispers as the door closed softly behind me. I turned towards Ms Wells, my defiant swagger crumbling beneath her cold glare. Without a word, I crept awkwardly to my seat at the back, trying not to knock anybody with my bag. My face flushed red as anger fought inside, trying to burst out and burn all the sniggering morons that were judging me. I couldn't decide if I was more angry at the alarm clock for making me late, or myself for actually thinking I could salvage something from a lesson I'd pretty much already missed. I should have just stayed in bed.

Forcing the rage back, I sat down as quietly and inconspicuously as I could, fishing out my crumpled papers and looking dejectedly at the board, which was already full of complicated notes and diagrams about Sociology of some kind. I scrabbled for a pen and began to hurriedly jot them down, hoping that I would be able to make sense of them later despite not having had the explanation.

I glanced to the side and noticed that the guy next to me had already finished copying. He was leaning back in his chair, a smug grin plastered across his face. Bastard. If I didn't hurry up, Wells would clear the board and I would miss out. I squinted hard, my pen moving swiftly across the page – I didn't even want to waste time checking if I was writing in straight lines or not.

I began to imagine lecturers and professors reading the notes to me in stuffy voices – I guess I must have still been half asleep.

"According to Philippe Aries, children in the past…"

"The absence of the notion of childhood…"

"The state versus the parents will always be-"

"Do it!"

I frowned. That voice was younger, like my age. I was still furiously scribbling but out of the corner of my eye, I could see the guy next to me hadn't moved, let alone said anything.

"Childhood is a social institution…"

"Do it now!"

The voice rose to almost a scream, causing me to jump out of my seat slightly, my pen skittering away across the desk. And then nothing. The room was silent once more. I could feel the sweat beading on my forehead and I looked around nervously, making sure nobody had noticed my minor freak out. Not even Ms Wells was looking my way this time. I glanced down at my notes, my mouth hanging open in shock. I hadn't written down any of the notes from the board, just the words Caedo Tu, over and over again. I didn't even know what that meant! I gulped, worry seeping into my mind. I definitely needed to stop drinking on weeknights.

"Alright guys," Ms Wells said warmly, breaking the panic I was slipping into. Her voice seemed to anchor me back into the classroom. "Well done. If you carry on with that and have it done for next week, I'll see you then."

As one, the class started to throw their things into their bags and get up to leave the room, but I couldn't bring myself to move. I kept reading those words, trying to make sense of them. If it was some sort of subconscious memory thing, I couldn't think of where I had seen the phrase before.

I became aware of footsteps and the scraping of a chair on the lino floor, and I looked up to see Ms Wells, eyes searching mine, intense concern written across her face.

"Alex? I've been meaning to have a word with you."

I hastily screwed up the useless notepaper and scooped it into my bag before giving her a lax shrug.

ADAM

Mr Davis had called a ten minute break - something he frequently did so he could slip out for a smoke. Most of the class were gossiping about the two main events: the body in the woods, and the Kill-Soc widegame, neither of which I was that bothered about. I was just glad they weren't going on about Tom's accident.

I was pursuing my usual pastime of trying to sketch Luke from various angles. My notebook looked like a stalker's collection, as each time I would see him doing something different. Today, he was talking to one of his mates, arm draped casually over the back of his chair – a perfect profile picture.

Nobody usually bothered me and Tom during breaks, our usual back and forth banter seeming like a secret code to them. However as he wasn't here, I kept my arm curled over the paper just in case – not that my pictures were good enough for people to guess who it was of. They all just looked like random guys, but it was enough that I knew it was Luke. Just seeing a particular sketch could transport me back to that exact lesson, or that specific time we had walked past each other in the corridor.

I cringed as the harpies in front began to giggle again, but I was fixated on my doodling. Even when one of them coughed to announce her presence, I still didn't look up.

"My pen's run out. Do you have a spare?"

I looked up to where Marie was hovering eagerly over my desk. I quickly flashed through my repertoire of put-downs before deciding on an answer. "Doesn't anyone else in your coven have one?" I tried to give her my best 'not impressed' face, but she didn't seem to be put off.

"I need a pen..."

Reluctantly, I fished into my pencil case and held a spare out to her, which she grabbed, immaculately painted nails clacking against the plastic. *Go away, go away, go away!*

"What are you drawing?"

I sighed as Marie craned her neck, trying to see over my arm. Why is she suddenly so interested? She had pretty much never spoken to me before, and now she was a budding art critic? With a pointed glare, I flipped my pad over so she couldn't see. It was oddly satisfying to deny something to the girl who had probably got everything she ever wanted whilst growing up.

"What do you want?" I asked, annoyed but basking in my small sketch-hiding victory. She gave a hopeful smile, and tilted her head slightly. I swear she was one step away from the dreaded bat of the eyelashes.

"Well I'm free and-"

"A bitch?" I cut in with lightning fast scathing. "Looking for your next victim?" She clenched her jaw and I knew I'd scored another one, despite her silence. To my surprise, she forced a smile and ploughed on.

"No," she said, extending the syllable as if she was talking to a small child who had learning difficulties. "I'm wondering if you wanted to do something sometime?"

Ok, I thought. *I* definitely wasn't the one who had the difficulties.

"You're asking me out?" My voice rose in pitch with disbelief, but luckily nobody else was watching this tableau of horror.

"No," she blushed. "I just thought we could, you know, talk and stuff."

I admit it, I laughed. I couldn't help it. She couldn't be serious surely? Why would she want to talk to me? I could just imagine the two of us hanging out, swapping gossip and comparing outfits... yeah right.

"Trust me," I said. "I'm not interested."

"It's not like that. I want... I need..." She sighed in defeat. "I need a pen."

"Well you got what you came for then."

Marie clenched her jaw angrily again, and I could see that whatever line was keeping her from lashing out was breaking.

"You know what, fine," she hissed. "Be a wanker."

"Whatever. Now do you mind? I was busy ignoring you."

"Try out for the team this year, Adam?"

I snapped my head up but she had already flounced off, seamlessly ingratiating herself back into the conversation her peons were having. She'd riled me, and it wasn't fair. What did she know about it anyway?

I looked over to Luke once more, knowing that just the sight of him would make my anger melt away. One of his friends was coming to the end of some epic story, and the boys broke into laughter. It wasn't harsh and grating like Marie's gang - instead Luke's laugh was soft, warm and deep. I could fall asleep to that laugh...

I turned to a clean page and began to draw, intent on adding 'Laughing Luke' to my collection.

ALEX

My face was red as I sat at my desk in the now empty room. The walls seemed to have shrunk inwards, boxing me in with the lecturer. I was staring intently at my lap, but I could feel the potential telling off I was going to get emanating from Ms Wells and washing over me. She had pulled up a chair and was now sitting opposite, staring questioningly at me. Her dark brown hair was pulled back into a tight bun, the black framed glasses she wore making her look like a stern librarian.

"Do you know what this is about?"

I didn't want to admit any guilt by saying yes – it was a classic trick my mum used when I was growing up. She'd pretend she knew something and then I would end up confessing to all sorts of misdemeanours when all she really wanted to talk about was homework or something.

"Alex?"

"No..."

"Alex, you were forty minutes late. For a seminar that only lasts an hour, that's pretty disgraceful."

I looked up, injustice boiling in my brain. "My clock stopped, it wasn't my fault." A feeble excuse, but at least this time it was the truth. I thought back to the numerous times I had skanked off because I was too hung over, or had extra football practice, and realised that I didn't really have a leg to stand on.

"It's never your fault," the lecturer sighed. "Yet it continues to happen. You've spent more time on your way to my lectures than you have actually in them."

"But..." I hadn't actually planned what I was going to say, but I wasn't going to hold my silence either – that would be like giving up and waiting for punishment.

"Last week you didn't show up at all. I have to ask Alex, is everything all right at home?" *Great*, I thought. She was going to play the caring and concerned adult. In some ways that was worse than just giving me a straight off bollocking.

"No, my cat died," I said with dripping sarcasm. I was tired of this now. If I could make her think I was an obnoxious brat, then hopefully she'd just tell me to get out of her sight, end of. She sighed, not impressed with the joke.

"You live in halls right? Do you get on with your flatmates? Do you go out much?"

It's none of your sodding business what I do, I thought venomously.

"I got rid of my mother when I moved here," I snapped. "I don't need you checking upon me." I could have left it there, and deep down I knew I should have, but something inside me wanted to push. How dare she pretend she cared what I did with my life? "Of course, if you want to come over and cook me dinner, you're more than welcome. There's laundry you could be getting on with if that's more your thing."

I watched in satisfaction as she sat back, affronted. She wasn't the only one who knew stuff – it was a well-known fact that Wells was one of those feminist women's rights bitches. I knew how to push those buttons.

"This isn't the time to make jokes Alex," she continued, straining to remain calm. "You're failing Sociology."

I stopped smiling as the news sank in. To be honest, I hadn't realised it would be that serious.

"Badly failing," she went on. "I'm guessing you haven't finished the assignment that was due for today?"

I looked down – she had me there.

"For God's sake Alex, did you even start it?"

Again, she had me. I meant to start it, I really did, but then the match against BMU came up and it kind of just got pushed to the back of my mind. The back of my mind was more like a bottomless pit – once something had slipped in, it was never coming back.

"Um…" I faltered, all excuses dissipating before reaching my mouth.

"That's what I'm talking about. If your work was good enough it would be able to balance out the lateness and the lack of participation, but you don't try."

If this was a football match, I would be about 20-nil down by now.

"You don't do the reading or the assignments - you don't do anything." She struck the final blow and I saw red. I wasn't going to sit here and be called lazy and useless, even if most of what she'd said was true.

"That's great, Lizzie, but where is this going?" I said, knowing how much she hated being called by her first name, especially the shortened form. I remembered the only time a student had been foolish enough to do it. He never did it again.

This time, Ms Wells leaned forwards, planting her hands firmly on the shiny grey tabletop. I could almost see the steam rising from her ears. "Fine. Walk out of here. Go and play football with your little friends." She emphasised the word *little* just to make me feel childish, but to be honest, I was expecting more fight from the legendary Elizabeth Wells.

"Is that it?"

"I'm not a babysitter, and quite frankly you're acting like you need one."

"Yeah well. What are you gonna do?" I could instantly tell that I'd pushed her too far. Her expression became a grotesque sneer of contempt and disdain.

"Do you know how many times I've dealt with people like you? Arrogant middle class little shits sent here to see if they can manage in the real world without mummy and daddy. From my experience, most of you can't. You think I care if you fail? It's not my job to pick up the pieces after you wreck your life. I give you the information you need to get a degree - it's not my problem if you choose to mess around. Go on then, play football if you think that's more worthwhile, but just get the hell out of my room."

For a few seconds, I was stunned. It was as if years of resentment had just poured out of this woman, and I was on the brunt of all the animosity she had been feeling.

"You can't say that," I managed weakly.

She leaned in and did her best to impersonate my arrogance. "Yeah well. What are you gonna do?"

She sat back triumphantly and I fumed in silence, fists clenched as my face got redder and redder. She was supposed to be a professional, used to dealing with students like me. I don't care what I'd said to her, she shouldn't have erupted at me. I stood up with such force that the chair overturned and skidded back along the floor. To her credit, Ms Wells didn't flinch as I snatched up my papers, swung my bag over my shoulder and stormed out of the room.

As soon as I was in the corridor, the door slammed behind me. I stood there, chest heaving, my breath escaping with difficulty through gritted teeth. I yelled to myself, slamming my fist into the notice board that hung on the wall. A cascade of party notices and Union promos fluttered to the tiles as I stared in satisfaction at the ragged dent I had made. There was a collective gasp from a group of studious looking girls who stared at me with open mouths. With their thick rimmed glasses and notebooks full of visibly protruding post-its, they obviously thought I had committed sacrilege by damaging UCE property. I growled at them until they hurried around the corner, leaving me on my own.

My breathing slowed as I watched the trickle of blood snake its way around my knuckles.

ADAM

Lunchtime at last. The seminar had overrun slightly and I had run through the rain to the cafe just outside campus, but my brother still wasn't there yet. It was one of those ultra modern places, walls covered in urban graffiti and nothing but ridiculously expensive fair-trade food on the menu. I'd ordered the simplest and cheapest thing I could see, but even my cheese sandwich came with grapes for some reason. I had taken a seat in one of the corners and was watching the world go by outside. It was a slow day and the waiting staff were all standing idly by the counter.

The bell rang and I looked up to see Andrew strolling into the building. He was twenty six and a taller more built version of me. He used to tease me when we were younger, saying that he got all the good stuff and all the dregs went into me, and looking at him in his suit and tie, I could well believe it. The light shower outside that had made me look like a slimy mess had only seemed to make him look even better, as if he was master over the elements. The eyes of the waiters lit up when they saw him, each jumping up and grabbing a menu, vying to be the one to break the monotony of the shift by serving one of the few customers, but their excitement was soon quashed when Andrew signalled to me and came over to the table. The waiters slumped back against the counter shaking their heads with disappointment. Sorry guys, maybe next time.

As he approached, I felt myself warm up and I broke into a smile. We used to fight viciously when we were smaller, but now we'd both grown up, Andrew was the only member of my family I felt that I could really talk to. He ruffled my damp hair and ruined my spikes before sitting down opposite.

"So how's my favourite little brother?"

I grinned. I was his only brother, but he always said it to make me feel special. "Yeah, I'm good thanks. You eating?"

He shook his head. "Nah, there was a big executive lunch thing earlier. It was very important, or so I'm told."

I laughed at his sly grin. I couldn't believe how he could be such a slacker and still keep hold of his office job.

"Alright, so I may have been a little hung over... slash drunk."

I rolled my eyes, never knowing when he was being completely truthful or not.

"Anyway, enough of this flirting!" he announced loudly and theatrically, earning a glare from one of the waiters. "What's going on with you? Still after what's-his-face?"

"Luke," I said, cheeks immediately flushing. "And yeah – but I haven't actually spoken to him properly."

"Ah, you youngsters. Still so naive! When we get older, we have to actually talk to people we like instead of chasing them round the playground."

"I'm working on it."

"Well work harder. How are the rents?"

"They're good. I thought you were going to see them?" Andrew had his own flat in some high rise in the middle of town, and his visits had become less and less frequent. I think that's why mum was so keen to have me go to uni here rather than move away. She wanted to keep at least one bird in the nest for as long as she could.

"Ah, I didn't have time. I was busy training my secretary." He said this with a wink and he smiled again.

"I don't want to know." I took a bite out of my sandwich, the grapes going unexpectedly well.

Andrew leaned in conspiratorially. "But seriously..."

I hated it when he started a sentence with that.

"Have you told them yet?"

Luckily I managed to swallow and not choke on the fresh bite I had just taken. "No way! Dad would do his nut!"

Andrew shook his head. "He's not that bad."

That was easy for him to say, he hadn't lived there for three years. Our dad didn't talk about feelings or any other 'pansy crap' – that pretty much said it all really.

"Don't think, just do it," Andrew continued. "The sooner you get it out in the open, the sooner you can start working your magic, right?"

He had a point but I wasn't sure that I wanted the upheaval just yet. I was waiting for the right time, preferably when I could get my mum on her own and then get her help to tackle dad. I changed the subject craftily.

"I'll tell them I'm gay when you tell them you didn't really get a first, and the only reason you got promoted was because you lied on your application."

My brother laughed loudly and unashamedly. "Alright, alright. You got me."

"Honestly, I don't know why they still think you're the golden boy. You could kill the Pope and they would still love you."

Andrew smiled knowingly, tapping his nose. "Now *that's* why I got promoted, but shhh, it's a secret." We laughed together for a few moments before I checked my watch.

"I have to go. Sorry man."

He stood up and I ran round the table clamping him in a tight bear hug. "It was good to see you." I meant it. I knew he didn't get long for lunch, and he really did care about his job despite what he said, but he always made time to catch up with me. "Come home one weekend soon, yeah?"

"Will do," he said with a nod and a salute. I started to walk towards the door. "Be careful of the UCE killer!" Andrew warned in an overly loud and spooky voice.

I turned back to where he had already helped himself to the rest of my sandwich. "Not you too," I said with a shake of my head.

"Yeah, mum phoned me this morning. She was most insistent that I stay away from the forest." Andrew couldn't help chuckling as he said it. "Anyway, what have you got to go for?"

"Football practice." I said it like it was the most obvious thing in the world.

"You don't play football."

"I know I don't..." For my older brother, he really was slow sometimes.

JACK

I can't remember when the sound of the raindrops outside lulled me into an uneasy slumber, but it was bright and sunny at the dream playground. It was loosely based on the Queen's Park in town, but everything seemed brighter, like I was looking at it in hypercolour. I stood with my bike, looking out across the playground. The swings were occupied and children were charging across the grass, tumbling and cartwheeling over each other amidst shrieks of joy. Others were chasing each other round a tall statue, a Greek gladiator brandishing a spear and a shield, watching them with cold indifference from beneath his stone helmet.

I walked past the slide, not really sure why I was there. I looked down and grimaced at the shorts I was wearing. Short shorts. I turned, eyes searching out something familiar, something that could tell me what had happened to my flat and also my fashion sense. That was when I saw her. Marie. She was sitting on the roundabout wearing a red checked frock, white cotton socks and those shoes that everybody gets from *Clarks* - bluish leather with a little red flower stitched over the toes. Her long hazel hair was tied up in pigtails and ribbons, but she didn't look happy.

As I approached, I saw that she was holding an empty ice cream cone, the rapidly melting vanilla blob on the squidgy tarmac at her feet explaining her tear streaked features. I stepped forwards.

"What's up?" I asked, although it was obvious. I just wanted her to talk to me again. She stopped sniffling, but didn't look up.

"I threw away my vanilla so I could have strawberry, but the man had run out..."

Ha! That served her right. But truthfully, I didn't like to see her cry, no matter what she'd done to me.

"Do you like mint?" I asked. "How about I buy you a mint ice cream instead?"

Marie looked up, eyes still shining. "You'd do that?"

I reached into my pocket, searching out every corner for loose change. I held my palm out and counted it, which seemed more difficult than usual. "Oh," I gasped once I'd sorted through all the lint and sweet wrappers. "I only have forty three pence, and I don't know where my mummy is." Despite a vague knowledge in the back of my head that she was on the other side of the country, I looked around, scanning the park for my mother, who I knew could give me more money to buy ice cream.

"It doesn't matter," Marie said dejectedly, already beginning to sniffle once more. Before I could stop myself, I also began to cry, slumping down onto the roundabout next to her. I felt the soft touch of her arm on my shoulder as she leaned into me. "I don't even get pocket money," she said. "My daddy said it will spoil me."

I was still crying, not cheered any by her admission.

"Tell you what, I'll spin you..." She jumped off and gripped the bars, tensing her arms. "Ready?"

I nodded and she pushed with all her might. Soon, the roundabout was spinning wildly, my vision blurring through the bars. I started to laugh and I could hear her whooping with excitement outside the whirling cage. Round and round I went. I saw Marie step back from the roundabout and watch me, but on the next rotation there was somebody else with her – a boy. He was also wearing stupid shorts and a t-shirt. He leaned in as if to whisper to Marie but the roundabout spun again and they slipped out of sight. On the next pass I saw him hand her something pink – a strawberry ice cream. By the time the slowing roundabout got there again, both of them were gone.

By the time I'd clambered off the roundabout and run back to my bike, I could see Marie and the mysterious boy over by the duckpond. It took me another couple of minutes to strap on my knee pads, elbow pads and my helmet – my mum insisted I wore them or else she wouldn't let me out with the bike. I pedalled as fast I could, the spokey-dokeys rattling as I went over the uneven path. I eventually caught up with them as they were staring at the ducks and whispering to each other, Marie licking her strawberry ice cream, over exaggerating her movements as if to really savour the moment. The sunlight was glimmering off the gentle ripples as various waterfowl paddled across the mirrored surface.

They started walking again, but I managed to keep up with them as I wobbled precariously.

"I thought you were going to have a mint one?"

She looked at me with disdain. "You couldn't afford it, and you can't even drive!" Marie snapped before taking a big chunk out of her ice cream. "Tom has his own Go-Kart." She patted her new friend on the shoulder appreciatively and he smirked at me.

Still trying to ride my bike along the path, I looked him over. He was taller than me, wearing a black t-shirt with some weird language on it. *Caedo Tu*, it said. The phrase seemed vaguely familiar, but I couldn't work out what it meant. We didn't do Latin at my school. As I was squinting at the words, he pushed out hard, catching me in the shoulder. The handlebars twisted out of my grasp and the bike lurched sideways, taking me with it. I landed in one of the bushes that lined the path, somehow managing to hurt everywhere that didn't have a pad over it. My backside stung and I'd grazed my ribs on the thick, knotted trunk of the bush. Luckily, I'd avoided landing on the empty whiskey bottle and the discarded pill packets that littered the ground around the bush, but even so I started to cry again. I seemed to be doing that a lot.

Marie and Tom looked down at me pityingly, their faces contorted into dark menacing grimaces as the sun shone behind them.

"Lame!" Tom sneered harshly. "Do the world a favour and just end it, yeah?" I lay there, stunned, amongst the litter and my overturned bike, Marie and Tom walking off into the afternoon sun. Tears were pouring down my face, and I kept gulping, straining to hold them back.

"I was told to kill myself by my girlfriend's lover. That's the problem our next guest today had to face. Find out all about his shocking story, after the break." A woman's voice boomed out across the park and I looked up, wiping the stinging liquid from the corners of my eyes.

My eyes snapped open and I sat up. I blinked a couple of times, adjusting to the gloom of my front room after the golden light of the dream playground. Outside the window, the sky was still grey, raindrops streaking across the glass.

I was curled on the sofa, the television blaring adverts at me, the memories of the dream rapidly fading into the random mush that was the waking mind. Already, I'd forgotten the exact words said by Marie and her friend… what was his name? I shook my head and rubbed my eyes wearily. I had no concept of time, no idea how long I had been sleeping the fitful vision laden sleep that overloaded minds fell victim to.

Keys rattled in the front door and I scrambled, trying desperately to make it look like I hadn't just been face down on the sofa. I was still in my shorts, but I'd just about managed to look respectable by running a hand through my hair and wiping my mouth when my housemates bustled into the room, their arms laden with bags from pretty much every high street shop in existence. *Nothing like spending your student loan on the latest brands,* I thought with a hint of jealousy. Normally I would have been with them, no doubt lugging some new purchases of my own.

Kieran walked forwards and dumped his bags on the floor, whilst Will and Ben hung in the hallway, kicking off their shoes. Kieran was the talker and could win any argument or avoid any punishment just by using his charms and wit. He was the entertainment of the English seminars, always mastering debates and cutting lesser mortals down with scathing comments. He would make an excellent lawyer, I had always thought.

"Hello mate!" Kieran yelled theatrically as he saw me slumped in my underwear. "No offence, but where the hell were you, having a wank day? English was shit without-" He stopped and I saw his eyes narrow as he also took in my red puffy eyes, and the fact that I hadn't even bothered to do my hair this morning. He turned back to the others who gave him weak shrugs. When Kieran faced me again, his expression was a mask of sincerest sympathy. "Do you wanna talk about it?"

TOM

In my slumber, I kept reliving the morning of my birthday, clinging onto the happiness I'd felt that day as if it would somehow feed my body and bring it back to life.

I'd been woken up by my mum knocking on the door of my skate themed bedroom. There were Tony Hawk posters covering every patch of wall space and my old Skull and Crossbones board was lying on the floor. Health and safety would have called it a trip hazard, but I liked having it in view all the time, ready to hop on at any moment.

"Tom, are you awake?" my mum called through the door.

I shoved the pillow roughly over my head. "No."

My mum laughed and opened the door, carrying a bright blue envelope. "Happy birthday darling."

I rolled over and sat up against the wooden headboard as she handed me the envelope. I ripped it open with a smile. Inside was a card with a picture of a skater pulling a grind, the '21' badge pinned to the front. I opened the card, my cheeks flushing slightly as I read the message.

"Happy Birthday my Little Man"

Mum had always called me her little man for as long as I could remember, even though I was now a good foot taller than her. I leant over and stood the card on the bedside table as my mum ducked back onto the landing. She returned almost instantly, a small, carefully wrapped package in her outstretched hand. I eagerly grabbed it and pulled the paper off, deflating slightly at the sight of the safety pads inside.

Nobody cool wore safety pads – it took the whole element
of risk out of a pulling a totally awesome jump.

"Thanks mum," I said, trying to sound as grateful as I
could. I hoped I hadn't hurt her feelings, but she smiled
mischievously.

"I thought you could wear them with this," she added
with a wink before heading for the landing once more. This
time she emerged holding a much larger box, and I knew it
had to be a new board. I ripped the paper off hungrily,
taking in the black gloss and the neon orange flames of the
Darkstar board.

"Oh, yes!" I cheered. It was the exact board I'd been
staring at in the window of *Deckers* for months. "Thanks
mum, seriously." I opened my arms and she practically fell
into the hug before kissing me on the forehead and standing
up again.

"Now come on," she called over her shoulder as she
left the room. "Just because it's your birthday doesn't mean
you can skive off."

"Oh!" I complained with mock petulance. "Me and
Adam were going to pick up some hookers."

"Well you can do that *after* your lectures."

I laughed as the door closed behind her – as if I would
miss the chance to show this baby off at uni, not to mention
that I was fairly certain my best friend Adam would have a
present of his own for me.

I set the board carefully on the floor and climbed out
of bed, heading to the wardrobe but always keeping one eye
trained on my new toy – if I took my eyes off it, it might
somehow stop being real. I pulled on my three quarter
lengths and then chose one of my slogan t-shirts to wear
before turning back to the bedside table and proudly pinning
the birthday badge onto my chest. With only a slight feeling

of guilt, I hastily shoved the safety pads under the bed before leaving.

I couldn't stop thinking about how everything could have been different if I had worn the safety pads. Maybe I would have escaped serious injury instead of being here now, somehow watching my mother break down into wracking sobs as she hunched over my still body. In heaven, or hell or wherever, if any of that stuff was real, people were probably thinking about how terrible I was, subtly forcing my saviours to make the bargain of life that would save me, but I wasn't terrible really. Surely it wasn't so hard to understand?

Wouldn't anyone in my position do the same if they could? I didn't know why I was able to think and act as if I wasn't lying in death's shadow, but I could. So I was going to use it. I could feel my mother's pain, and I was doing it for her as much as for me. And if they still thought I was a monster, well... I would live with it.

ALEX

The sun was shining weakly through the rainclouds onto the university football pitch. It wasn't much, just a patchy rectangle of waterlogged grass surrounded by half height stands, but it was the home of The Centaurs, my team. We weren't that special, and in fact the campus joke was that we played as if we actually did have horses' backsides, but the exercise helped me burn off a lot of steam. Considering a teacher had just destroyed me, I felt like I could have boiled water just by looking at it.

The rest of the team were already on the pitch, warming up as I jogged out of the changing rooms. The Coach's favourite, Luke Ashford was leading the drills, bending and flexing athletically as the indigo and gold-clad team copied his movements a second later. Coach Williams himself was standing at the corner, smiling as he watched his prime striker taking charge.

I scanned the pitch as I approached the team, noting the one lone person sitting up in the stands, blue and gold scarf wrapped around his neck. I also noticed Coach Williams' smile drop as he registered my presence. It appeared I didn't have a good track record with members of staff.

Luke and some of the others turned to face me, many of them echoing the Coach's less than welcoming expression. Just because I didn't go out on the lash every single night with them, setting fire to my chest hair on the Union stage, they seemed to think I wasn't a team player. It was pack mentality, with *mental* being the operative part.

"What took you so long, Marshall? Been up the woods?"

I had no idea what that was supposed to mean, nor could I tell which of the cretins had said it. I tried my best to ignore the glares as I jogged forwards and belted one of the waiting footballs with all my strength. The guy in the stands tilted his head as the ball sailed over it and into the car park beyond. No doubt the Coach would blast me for that later.

I turned back to my loving teammates and smouldered, smirking slightly as I saw Luke shake his head and turn back to his knee lifts. He was such a pet – always following the Coach's orders and motivating the others. Not that it won us any games. Luke might have the dedication, but he was still a Centaur.

Coach Williams blew his whistle and beckoned us over. I smiled again when nobody stood near me, thinking how *Primary School* they all seemed to be. Well fine. As long as they passed me the ball then I didn't care.

"Alright lads," Coach began in his gravelly barking voice. "That'll do for warm up. I want you to split into two teams and get a mini game going, and remember, I'm going to be watching for any mistakes. We came *this* close to beating BMU yesterday, but we've got to be perfect for the next match. I want a tight game."

I rolled my eyes at the motivational speech. He always said we were *this* close to beating whoever we played but it never helped. Whatever *this* distance was, it was always just a little bit too far. "Hemmings, try not to get attacked this time. Luke, Dan? You're Captains." This last comment caused a ripple of laughter in the overcast air. At yesterday's game in town, one of our mid-fielders had a boomerang chucked at him, and Glen was still glowering about it.

Coach Williams backed off as Luke and Dan began picking their teams and, not surprisingly, I was last pick with

Dan ending up having to take the sacrifice and let me play on his side. We squared off and the Coach rolled one of the balls into the centre. With another blow of his whistle, we charged at each other, ducking and dodging in and out to gain possession of the ball. I knew I should have been concentrating, but all I could focus on were the snarling features of Ms Wells accompanied by the condescending revulsion that my teammates threw my way. As a result, I hoofed the ball straight past one of them, missing an easy wide open pass. I looked down at the ground, feeling every shaking head and sigh of lost potential burn into my shoulder blades.

I had to prove to them that I wasn't a waste of space – that I really did belong on the team. Naturally, they weren't passing to me so I hung back, waiting for the right moment.

Eventually, Dan blasted a long kick from the goal line, sending the ball sailing halfway up the pitch, and well over the crowd of players that had congregated at his end. In my head it seemed simple – I would jump and scissor kick round, sending the ball blazing through the top right corner of the net. The goalie would be powerless to stop the shot and they would all have to acknowledge my power and accept me as a Centaur. The ball flew closer and closer, dipping now as it lost speed.

I launched myself off the ground, pushing backwards with my studs. The angle was wrong. The ball whistled past my head as I spun around, leg outstretched. I crashed hard onto the turf, rolling through the mud and onto my chest, breathing deeply as I watched the ball roll harmlessly away.

I lay there, ignoring the muffled sniggering as I watched through a forest of moving legs. The rest of the team were running back and forth in front of my vision as if taunting me that they were upright and I wasn't. Through the blur, I noticed that someone else had come to watch us practice, a skater guy that looked vaguely familiar, although I couldn't place where I had seen him before. There was nothing special about him, but he seemed to hold my gaze, drawing me to my feet. It was only when I was standing that I realised what it was. There was a slogan across his chest. *Caedo Tu* – the same thing I had somehow scribbled all over my note paper back in class.

Awash with curiosity, I picked my way forwards, ignoring the game going on around me as I stepped over one of the larger puddles. All sounds and sights seemed to fade into the background until it was just me and this random guy. He stared mournfully forward as I approached. The stranger lifted his arm and pointed ominously at me before, out of nowhere, a black car slammed into him and carried on. I cried out loud as the skater was thrown into the air, papers spilling out of his backpack. With a sickening crunch, the boy landed back on the grass in a crumpled heap, legs twisted at impossible angles.

I stood there gasping, frozen by shock. After a few seconds, my legs seemed to reactivate and I ran forwards, slamming straight into Luke as he was making a run for the opposite goal. In a rush of sound and colour, my senses jolted back into full function as Luke and I tangled around each other and went down. He quickly rolled off me, cursing under his breath, but I didn't care. All I could do was look to the side of the pitch. Everything was gone. The skater, the tyre tracks gouged into the wet grass and the scattered paper - all of it was gone, and in its place, a crowd of awkward looking football players. They shuffled nervously, flicking their eyes between Luke and me, anxious to see what their star player would do at this upset.

Luke rolled to his feet, glaring venomously in my direction. "What the fuck is wrong with you?" he spat. "Are you blind?"

"I thought I saw…"

What exactly was it? Obviously it couldn't have been real, and there was no way that anybody would choose my side over Luke the Golden Boy, even if a car really had just ploughed into some poor kid right in front of us.

Luke started shaking his head in disbelief. "Freak," he muttered, turning away and rubbing his elbow where he had landed on it.

Suddenly I snapped. None of this was my fault and here he was, Mr Perfect calling me a freak as if he had never had a bad day in his life. I leapt forward just as he turned back towards me. I caught him in a flying tackle that sent him crashing once more onto the ground. Mud splattered and within seconds I was straddling his stomach, my fists curled in his shirt collar. I slammed his back into the sludge hard, satisfied when he coughed and winced. The others edged forwards, still unsure whether to jump in and help or not. I knew that if they decided to rescue Luke, I wouldn't stand a chance, but I didn't care.

"Say that again," I growled.

Luke paused for a second as if weighing his options. Of course, he knew that everybody would have his back in this. He raised his head until our faces were mere centimetres apart.

"You stupid *fucking* freak." He spoke slowly, wrapping his lips around every syllable as if to hammer the message home. In response, I screamed as loud as I could and slammed my fist into Luke's face. I felt his teeth graze against my knuckles as I pounded again and again, seeking out the softest flesh, the strongest lines – I knew all the girls were crazy for him, and in that instant, I wanted to ruin his pretty little face.

ADAM

I jumped up from my cold, damp perch in the stands when I saw Luke get punched. I'd been watching The Centaurs practice for long enough to know most of them, and I wasn't surprised that it was Alex Marshall, the hot-headed midfielder that had caused the trouble. He carried on punching with wild ferocity.

Hands to my mouth, I scrambled down the next couple of rows of seats until I reached the steps, hurtling down them until I was hovering at the sidelines. As soon as the blows had started, the rest of the team rushed forwards to haul Alex off their Captain.

Coach Williams was jogging towards the fracas, his cheeks red with the effort. By the time he reached the action, Luke was standing once more and Alex was struggling against the two footballers that were holding him back. I craned my neck anxiously trying to see if Luke was all right. Was that blood I could see? Luke spat into the mud, and it was definitely red. As he turned in my direction, I could also see the unmistakable trail of crimson tracing down from his nostrils and snaking across his chin and down his neck. All I wanted to do was rush onto the pitch and give him a hug, but of course I didn't. I remained where I was, whimpering every time I saw the pain on Luke's face.

ALEX

The hands clamped around my shoulders held me firmly in place, despite how hard I squirmed. It was two against one, and all I could do was watch. To my dismay, Luke still seemed to be coherent and stood holding his sleeve to his nose, trying to shrug the injury off heroically.

"You two!" Coach Williams barked after catching his breath. His face was a deep red, making him look like a giant angry egg. "What the hell is going on?"

He looked at me questioningly but I remained silent. I didn't want to tell him what I had seen at the side of the pitch. With an exasperated sigh, he turned to get Luke's version of the story.

"This fucktard wasn't concentrating," he began. "We collided and then the next thing I know, he's laying into me." Saint Luke, of course he was completely innocent.

"I saw… I was looking at… I was looking the other way," I said half-heartedly, already knowing that the Coach was already blinded to everything except Luke, complete with his golden halo and pure white feathery wings.

"At what?" the Coach exclaimed. "There's nothing there." Whilst the others were looking at the side of the pitch where I had seen the car crash, I seized the opportunity to shuffle free of my captors. Luke's fists were instantly raised as I stepped forwards angrily.

"He called me a freak!" I shouted, immediately aware of how stupid that sounded. The Coach seemed to share my sentiment.

"I don't care what he called you!" he roared. "You're supposed to be an adult, not some twelve year old in the playground. You need to grow up, son. By the looks of it, you've a long way to go." I scowled and watched mutinously as Luke sidled up beside the Coach, sycophancy plastered all over his bloodstained face.

"He's a compromise to the team sir," he said, narrowing his eyes at me once Coach Williams had turned away from him. "I don't want him messing up the next game this weekend. As you said sir, we were *this* close last time."

I could almost hear the screeching of the long disused cogs in Williams' mind as he mulled over what Luke had said. An air of silent expectancy enveloped us as we all awaited judgement. For everyone else, it was whether they would have to suffer another defeat as a result of my playing with them, but for me it was much more. Being kept off for a game was like a criminal record – people looked at you differently.

"He's not going to mess up the game," Coach Williams announced. I sighed, knowing what was coming next. "He's not going to play."

"You're benching me," I muttered dejectedly.

"Benching you?" the Coach exclaimed incredulously. I looked up, wondering where he was going with this. "I'd bench you if playing shit was your only problem. You, you're off the team for good."

A hammer blow to my stomach. The pain continued as the Coach laid into me. "I can't have you attacking people on the pitch. Go and get yourself changed, then leave the kit in my office. I'm not having you ruin everything for those who do put the effort in. If you want to piss about, that's your choice, but don't waste our time."

"Just like that?" I stammered.

"Just like that? Luke's lucky his nose isn't broken! I'd ask you to apologise if I thought it would do any good."

"It wouldn't."

Once more I could feel the anger bubbling up inside me as another so called 'responsible adult' treated me like shit. The Coach shook his head and turned away from me, obviously eager to put me out of his mind as soon as possible. I looked into the sea of scowling faces, trying to find a friendly one, but I was disappointed. Luke's immediate henchmen wore the same mask of contempt that he had, and even those who weren't that close to him were frowning, reluctant to show any allegiance in case it cost them valuable status points. I was alone, isolated behind enemy lines, so furious that my limbs were trembling. After another second of excruciating rage and embarrassment, I turned on my heels and ran off the pitch.

JACK

The first thing Kieran had done was crack out the beer – that was his primary step to solving any problem. We were now sitting on the musty sofas, cans in hand, ready to talk about my feelings. It was as if the beer made it ok – normally, four guys would never sit down and discuss stuff like this. Also, to further enhance the manliness, we'd left the television on some sports channel, but with the volume down low. To the casual observer it would look like a completely normal no feelings guy hang out session.

I started by explaining the situation to my housemates, and by the time I had finished the brief tale, there was already a small monolith of beer cans forming on the coffee table. I scanned the room, taking in the mixed looks on my friends' faces. On one hand, there was some sympathy, but none of them looked entirely surprised which made me feel even worse. It was as if I was the last to know that my relationship had died. Will cracked open a fresh beer and slurped up the froth before it spilled onto his designer jeans.

"So let me get this straight," he said. "She dumped you over the phone?"

"Yeah. I don't even warrant a face to face."

Ben snorted into his can halfway through taking a sip. "What, never?" he asked, trying to stifle a laugh. Kieran thumped him casually on the shoulder.

"Dude, not the time."

After rubbing his shoulder, Ben looked at me apologetically. "Sorry mate."

I shrugged, not really knowing what to say. Why waste time getting in his face about a good burn? Compared to my current problems, getting a little rip from Ben seemed insignificant. "I just don't understand why she did it, you know? I didn't do anything wrong." I looked up, hoping to see the confirmatory nodding of my housemates. Instead, Kieran was frowning slightly.

"Wait a minute," he began. "No offence mate, but didn't you two fight all the time?"

"Never about anything major, just stupid stuff." As I said this, I realised how my relationship with Marie must have looked from the outside. We did shout at each other a lot, but it was always about meaningless petty things like hairdryers, money, or me spending too much time with my mates. We'd always worked it out eventually, but all everyone else would see was us yelling and fuming.

"Hmmm," mused Will as he flicked the ring pull on his can idly. "Sounds to me like you're better off without her. She doesn't sound that great to me."

"She was perfect," I snapped quickly, still ready to defend her even though she'd broken my heart.

"All I'm saying is if you two can get into slanging matches about stuff that isn't even important, what would have happened if something that actually mattered came up?"

Kieran gave Will a glare that blatantly said 'shut up' and he quickly went back to his beer.

"There was more to us than arguing," I said lamely. There was no way I would be able to convince the others if I couldn't convince myself. I had to keep telling myself that I did have some good times with Marie. To my surprise, Kieran smiled mischievously.

"I think I know what you're saying dude. She was great in bed?"

"Well… yeah." I could feel myself squirming into the cushions. Marie had made it very clear she didn't like me discussing anything like that with the boys.

"There you go!" Kieran roared, slapping his knee. "That just proves you shouldn't be with her." I shook my head, unsure of what Kieran was getting at. This house meeting was rapidly going the wrong way. Where were the consolations? Where was the support? Instead it was like they were telling me it was doomed from the word go.

Will and Ben were looking at Kieran expectantly, and I knew what was coming, but I couldn't help myself. I had to ask him, even if it did lead to one of Kieran's famous philosophical rants.

"What do you mean?"

Kieran cleared his throat theatrically before speaking. "Nice girls," he began. "You know, relationship material, partners for life even, are good in bed. Nothing wrong there. But - and here's the magic - slutty girls are *great* in bed. That's how you know if she's a keeper or not."

We collectively looked at him, nonplussed.

"On the first run, take notes," Kieran suggested. "If the sex is good, then all systems go. But if the sex is *great,* and I mean nasty, filthy sex, then that's when the warning light comes on. Where did she get all that experience from eh? She must be a full blown whore, and let's face it, most whores have been. So gentlemen, to summarise, if the sex is that amazing then she's a slag and not relationship material. Therefore use her, abuse her, and get the hell out. It's what I call the good sex/great sex hypothesis."

Kieran stood up and took a bow whilst Will clapped enthusiastically. Ben looked less impressed, however.

"You know," he reasoned. "You can't just put the word 'hypothesis' on the end of something and expect it be universally accepted."

"That's what I call the denial of greatness hypothesis."
My housemates fell about laughing, and I admit even I
cracked a smile. It felt good to be focusing on something
else, and what better to distract me than getting sucked into
banter with Kieran, even though I knew I would get totally
destroyed just like everybody else who verbally duelled with
him.

"Well thanks for that Kier, but it doesn't really help."
I was baiting him now. "It's not all about sex. There's
personality and going out - you know, normal stuff."

"Yeah," Kieran said with a dismissive wave. "But all
that boring stuff leads to sex anyway. You take a girl out for
dinner then to the cinema, it's almost guaranteed sex
afterwards. Everything might not be about sex, but it usually
ends up with it eventually."

"A noble victory," I said, admitting defeat. It was
pointless arguing with him. The camaraderie I'd thought I
was feeling was rapidly fading into a mixture of self-pity and
beer headache.

"Jokes aside mate," said Will. "It sounds to me like
Marie wasn't that bothered about dumping you. It's not like
she would take you back if you asked." I raised my eyebrows
at the notion, seeing Will raise his hands defensively. "Which
I'm not saying you should," he added quickly. "All I'm saying
is she's not gutted so why should you be?"

I jumped to my feet with new found energy. "You're
right."

"There you go," Will said with a satisfied nod and a
smug sideways glance to Kieran. Will thought he had
triumphed over our eloquent friend.

"I have to call her," I stated. Now it was Kieran's turn
to smile as Will opened his mouth in surprise.

"No, that wasn't what I-"

"What if she *is* gutted?" I reasoned. Perhaps Marie was feeling just as bad as me? Marie might be regretting what she did and thinking I would never forgive her! "She's probably sitting at home crying her eyes out!"

"She's probably sitting on the first piece of man she saw after hanging up the phone, more like," scathed Ben. I'd always known he didn't like Marie so I dismissed his comment. I think he asked her out in first year and she said no.

"I have to!" I told myself as much as I told them. I had to congratulate them on what happened next, although it annoyed me immensely. As I strode forward to the hallway, my housemates simultaneously jumped into action without a word to one another, as if they instinctively knew what to do. Ben jumped up and ran into the kitchen, whilst Kieran and Will clamped themselves onto my arms. With two built guys dragging me backwards, I was never going to make it upstairs where I'd left my phone. By the time they had wrestled me back onto the sofa, Ben had reappeared with a fresh can of beer – the medicine of all the student ailments. He popped the ring pull and shoved the can into my hand, physically wrapping my fingers around the cold aluminium.

"Don't be her bitch, man," Ben muttered before Kieran silenced him.

"There's only one word this boy needs to hear now," Kieran said authoritatively. "Drink."

ALEX

The tranquil atmosphere of the park was shattered as I stormed alongside the iron railings, banging a stick as loudly as I could against each post. Small children stopped swinging to observe the red faced, puffing-through-gritted-teeth monster I had become as I stomped back to halls from the football pitch. It was taking all my strength to keep what little composure I had left, and the worried parents could sense this. Out of the corner of my eye I saw one mother hurriedly scoop up her child and carry it away.

An empty drinks can stood before me on the pavement, taunting me as it blocked my path. I growled as I transferred every ounce of hatred and anger I had into the can that now wore three faces simultaneously like some hideous mythological beast. It was Ms Wells, Coach Williams and Luke Ashford all at once, all of them sneering at me with disdain and contempt.

I kicked the can as viciously as I could, just as a car drove past. The can glanced off the side of the vehicle and the woman driving beeped the horn loudly, shaking her fist for emphasis.

"Piss off!" I yelled loudly as she drove away down the street. I added her face to the can as I stomped on it repeatedly until it was nothing more than a crumpled flat disc moulded to the contours of the tarmac.

ADAM

After the trouble on the pitch, the Coach had called an end to practice and the team had shuffled back inside. As soon as they had disappeared, I had jogged round the building as quickly as I could, heading in through the main entrance and doubling back until I was hovering outside the door to the changing rooms.

The sports corridor was just like any other, dull and grey, except all the notice boards and posters were showing upcoming fixtures or advertising the latest sports brands.

I reached into my backpack and fished out a small notebook, tucking a pencil behind my ear. This was my 'reporter' look – when I had the pencil and the pad, it meant I was on official Rag business. I'd even contemplated buying a pair of geek specs, but the practicalities of carrying them around just in case were too difficult. I collected stories for the Uni Rag because it gave me a chance to practice my writing skills, and also on occasions, I would get the inside scoop on some of the lesser known goings on inside the establishment.

I don't know where my courage came from. Usually I would report on the exam results or the chess club, but a fight on the pitch was too good an opportunity to pass up. I took a deep breath and pushed open the door, immediately feeling the heat as the steam from the showers hit me.

The changing room was tiled to about waist height in indigo, then becoming yellow paintwork from there to the ceiling – the team colours. In one corner was the Coach's office, and lockers and benches formed rough aisles that led down to the row of showers at the end of the room. The individual cubicles were emitting great billows of steam mixed with the scents of Lynx and sweat. Paradise.

Most of the team were in there, in various states of undress - some wrapped in towels, some in their underwear. They were all typically well built and athletic, but I was searching for one particular body. I moved into the room, casting my perverted gaze left and right, eyes widening at each piece of candy I spotted.

"Can I help you with something?" Luckily I managed to stop before I actually walked into Coach Williams. He was staring quizzically at me, sizing me up and knowing that I couldn't possibly belong in a sports changing room.

I coughed lightly, preparing my 'professional' voice. "Yes. I was wondering if you could give me any details about the fight. For the Rag?"

Coach Williams continued to stare at me thoughtfully. "I've seen you on the stands, son."

"Everybody loves footballers… I mean football." Shit! I glanced over the top of my notepad, but luckily Coach Williams didn't seem to pick up on my slip.

"Well I suppose so," he grunted. "Alex Marshall attacked Luke Ashford so-"

"Unprovoked?" I cut in, hastily scribbling words onto the paper that was rapidly becoming damp. I doubted I would even be able to read the scrawl - it was hard concentrating on literacy with so much flesh about.

"Yes. Definitely unprovoked."

"And is Luke all right?" I asked, aware that my voice was rising slightly. "I mean, he's one of your key players isn't he?"

The Coach nodded over my shoulder. "No major damage. See for yourself, he's still fighting fit."

I turned around and stared, mouth gaping wide. Luke was walking right towards me, wearing nothing but a pair of tight black hipsters that accentuated everything they needed to. A towel was slung over his shoulder and his whole body glistened and shone as he passed under the misted lights. There was only a slight amount of bruising on his face, like a shadow over his eye socket and cheek, but apart from that, he looked more than fighting fit.

As he got to his locker, he flicked his head and sent flecks of water onto the floor and walls. My mind fluttered with depravity as for a second I wished I was standing within spraying range. He stretched his arms behind his head teasingly before pulling a jumper out of his locker and sliding it over his head.

"So are you done?" The Coach asked, drawing me away from the vision of rippling muscle I was drowning in. *Any longer and I would be,* I thought.

"Um, just one more question," I stammered, adjusting my stance so I could keep Luke in my field of vision. "What did you do about Alex?"

"I had to kick him from the team."

I raised my eyebrows. "Like, forever?" It seemed a little harsh even for someone who had punched the object of my affection in the face.

The Coach looked thoughtful for a second as if mulling something over. "Yeah..." he mumbled, trailing off. I sensed my grace time in the changing room was drawing to an end.

"Well, thanks a lot Coach Williams." I clutched the notepad to my chest once more and hurried towards the door as The Coach strode into his office, closing the door. Seconds later, I was leaning against the corridor wall trying to recall as much of what I had seen as possible. There was valuable sketch fodder that needed to be committed to memory. I sighed contentedly as I relived the curves, the steam and the heat. Suddenly, the door next to me opened and I jumped forwards away from the wall. Before I could turn away and pretend I was just passing, Luke stepped out of the changing room, now fully dressed, his still damp hair mussed into rough spikes.

My heart jumped as Luke nodded at me before strolling away down the corridor. Once he had disappeared round the corner, I fell back against the wall once more, cheeks flushed. He noticed me! He acknowledged my presence! I was getting closer...

ALEX

I'd burst into my room and chucked my bag unceremoniously on the floor, not caring that the contents spilled out. Next, I'd thrown myself face first onto the bed. Fists clenched into the duvet, I had plunged into a fitful sleep – a lion of a catnap.

I found myself standing in the park I'd blitzed past earlier, except all the colours were brighter, like someone had turned the contrast up to maximum. The sun was shining and the smell of freshly cut grass hung in the air. All around me, children were playing, running about with finger pistols, shrieking and whooping.

Standing a little way off, huddled around the warrior statue on the wide expanse of grass were my teammates, wearing shorts and blazers with socks pulled stupidly high. It was as if I was dreaming one of the *Just William* stories I used to read when I was younger. As I approached the others, I was about to laugh when I looked down. Oh God, I was wearing the same ridiculous grey socks hoisted up to my knees.

Luke stepped forwards, naturally wearing the most expensive blazer with some sort of crest on the front. I squinted, then scowled when I saw that the crest had the words Head Boy embroidered through it. *Dickhead Boy,* more like. He picked somebody else to be the rival captain, and they began picking their teams. Each time, the captains hovered over me whilst I looked eagerly up at them, but they always passed me by – Luke even chose Murray over me, and he was fat!

Eventually, I was the only one left. I scanned both teams and noticed they both had the same amount of players – there was no room for me. I looked expectantly at Luke, hoping he would make a decision.

"Right, that's everyone," he said, staring right through me.

"Hey!" I shouted. Luke continued, seemingly oblivious to my presence.

"You guys run. We'll give you to a hundred. One... Two... Three..." Luke and his team sat cross legged on the grass as the others ran off in all directions yelling and cheering. I walked slowly up to Luke just as he was reaching fifteen.

"Hey, you stupid twat!" This time, I leaned so close that I could see the tiny hairs on his ear move when I shouted. Luke still didn't move – he didn't even blink.

"Twenty two... Twenty three..."

Next, I grabbed him by his fancy jacket and shook him violently, but still nothing. I looked around furiously, but none of the others were reacting either, they were all sitting with their heads down, some of them tearing up clumps of grass and throwing them casually at each other.

As I cast my eyes around, I noticed a small figure standing in the shadow of a large tree, its branches hanging low with verdant leaves. He was holding his hand in front of his face and giggling conspiratorially. He could see me! I let go of Luke's lapels and marched over to the tree, taking in the boy's black hair covering one eye. It was the skater I'd seen earlier on the pitch! Anger flared up inside me as I was suddenly thrown back into the football practice that had ended in blood and violence – and me getting kicked from the team. It was his fault: after all I'd been watching him when I messed up.

I stepped into the shadows of the tree and he lowered his hand, stifling more laughter.

"What are you laughing at?" I demanded, annoyed that he thought the whole situation was funny. I hadn't laughed when I thought he'd been hit by a car.

"What you said just then. Twat!" He spoke timidly, almost guiltily as if he wasn't usually allowed to swear. "That's naughty isn't it!" He started to laugh again, and I couldn't help but smile.

"I learnt it at school," I said, chest swelling with pride. "It's the most baddest word I know. Did those hurt?" I asked, pointing to the black piercings in his ears. I could see the sunlight shining through from behind.

"Uhuh," the boy nodded, his turn to feel proud. "They go all the way through, like tunnels!" He thought for a moment, as if sizing me up. "You're cool. You want one?" He held out his hand with a roll of sweets in. Love Hearts. I tried not to dwell on the fact that I was getting a Love Heart from a boy as I took one. I clutched it in my hand, turning to give a mournful look at my teammates, half wishing that they would suddenly break out of their practical joke and welcome me back into the game.

"Ninety eight... Ninety nine... A hundred! Let's go!" As one, the boys jumped up and sprinted away, spreading across the park, eager to hunt down their prey. I turned back to my companion, trying to pretend I didn't care, but the look on my face must have given my feelings away.

"I wouldn't worry about it too much," he said consolingly. "I'm not allowed to play either. My mummy says I get knocked down too easily."

Too right, I thought grimly as I remembered the phantom car on the football field.

"Well, you are a little small for your age."

Suddenly, the boy's face lost all traces of childlike innocence and became deadly serious. "Anyway, you have much worse things to worry about."

I was confused. What could this total stranger possibly tell me about my own life?

"What do you mean?" I asked sceptically.

"Catch me!" The boy shrieked as he suddenly burst into life, sprinting away across the grass. The boy was mental, no arguments there, but I admit I was baited. After a brief pause, I jogged after him, watching him disappear into the bushes on the other side of the playing field.

When I arrived panting, the boy was nowhere to be seen. I was standing at the edge of a hedge maze, the walls towering about a foot over my head. The entrance went on for a couple of metres before ending in a T-junction.

"Come on, I want to show you something!" His voice floated over to me from deep within the maze, and without a second thought, I ran inside.

As soon as I turned the first corner, the sky seemed to darken as the hedges loomed over me. From a distance, the walls looked smooth and lush, but close up, the hedges were patchy and full of spiky branches that jutted out into the pathway. I had to duck and weave just to avoid cutting my shoulders. I could tell I was gaining on him though, as I began to hear his footsteps running ahead of me. Eventually it got so that I could see quick flashes of his feet disappearing round the next bend and I found myself wishing the race would end – I couldn't run forever.

The paths got narrower, the turns more frequent and the obstacles more prominent. On numerous occasions, branches flicked into my face from where the other boy had just displaced them seconds before me. I raised my arm to protect my eyes, taking turns blindly and bouncing off the hedges until I half ran, half fell into a small clearing. The centre of the maze. Along one side was the crumbling red brick wall that surrounded the back of the park, and set into it was an old wooden door covered in flaking green paint.

The boy was leaning against the wall, and didn't appear to be out of breath at all. I'd been sprinting as fast as I could, but he'd always seemed to keep one step ahead.

"What did you want to show me?" I panted. "If it's the dead cat, I saw it ages ago."

The boy pointed solemnly at the door, his face still completely humourless. I stepped forwards and grabbed the handle, fine red rust powder drifting to the grass as I dislodged it. "What's through it?" I asked.

"It's what will happen unless you-" he began to explain, but I had already pulled the door open and stepped through into the darkness beyond.

I found myself standing in the foyer at halls. Ignoring the obvious fact that the park blatantly didn't join on to my Halls of Residence, a number of things had changed. For one thing, it was now night, and I also seemed to be the right age again, dressed in jeans and a jumper. In front of me, the foyer was deserted. On one wall, a huge banner was hanging lopsidedly with the words *"Drink 'Til You Drop – B5 Today! Almost Everyone Invited"* painted crudely on. All of the payphones were dangling off their hooks and papers were scattered across the tiles – it looked like it had been an awesome party. At that point, I remembered what the boy had been saying when I stepped through the door.

"Unless I what?" I turned around, but I was alone. The boy was nowhere to be seen. I peered out through the glass doors, but the world seemed to have become a pool of ink – not even the campus lights were penetrating the darkness. I realised I was clenching my fist tightly around the Love Heart the boy had given me. I uncurled my fingers and there, sitting in my sticky palm was the message. *Caedo Tu.*

Half of me flared with anger again, as if this phrase was taunting me somehow, whilst the other half sighed like I was expecting it. I still had no idea what the words meant, but this was the third time I'd seen them.

I don't know why I did what I did next, but I ate the sweet. It felt like I had conquered something. As I crunched the sugary tablet into sweet paste, I imagined that it had Luke Ashford's name written on, for he was a much more palpable enemy.

I walked over to one of the phones, casually picking it up and listening to the receiver. The line was dead.

"Hello?" My voice echoed through the foyer, but there was no reply. No sound at all, not even music. Perhaps the party had finished? After all, I had no concept of what the time actually was, just that it was night. As I walked over to the staircase, I began to think about what the boy had been saying to me. This was what would happen unless *I* did something to prevent it. Well if a little foyer mess was the worst of my worries, I wasn't exactly going to break a sweat over it. That was when I saw the stain.

It was unmistakable – a deep crimson blotch soaked into the fabric of one of the chairs. It had spread from a spot on the back but was now almost soaked through to the floor. Whilst the edge of the blemish was dry and dull, the centre of the stain was glossy and glistening. It was blood. In my mind, the idea of a great party was rapidly melting into something more sinister. Perhaps there'd been an accident that I could have stopped – maybe that's what the boy was talking about?

I slowly walked up the stairs, trailing a finger along the banister as I went. As I emerged onto the landing, I noted more crimson splodges pitter patting along the corridor – a trail of ruby breadcrumbs leading me to God knew what.

The landing split off into three separate branches labelled A, B and C. Considering the banner downstairs said the party was in B5, this was the branch I took - my choice confirmed by the continuation of the blood droplets. I counted the doors as I passed, trailing my fingers across the wall as I went. With each door, I could feel the complete lack of life behind it, like a poison spreading through the building and sucking out all of the energy.

Eventually I reached B5, and still there was no sign of a party. There was no music, no lights, no laughter and no warmth. The door was off the latch, so I gently pushed it open, suddenly anxious that something might jump out at me from the pitch-black interior.

The sight that met my eyes could only be described as a massacre. Students were curled on the floor or sprawled across chairs. They could have been sleeping save for the copious amount of dark shadowy stains that I knew was more blood. The lights were off, and the whole scene was blue filtered as the moonlight shone in through the window. I was grimly transfixed for a second, mouth wide in horror before I finally snapped to my senses and ran forwards into the flat. With any luck, there might be survivors.

I knelt by the first body I could see, slumped against the wall of the hallway. I gingerly placed my finger on his neck before flinching away from the cold and clammy flesh. The body was long dead, numerous splodges marking the places he'd been brutally stabbed. Again I thought back to the boy's warning. This definitely hadn't been an accident, this looked like murder, and how could I possibly have prevented that?

I advanced into the living room. In there it was worse. The room had been decorated for the party, hung with banners and streamers, but they had either been ripped down or now hung in tangled clumps, congealed with blood. It was the student version of sacrilege. The floor was carpeted with bodies, the furniture draped with luxuriously reclining corpses, throats cut, their springs of life long since run dry. The coup de grace, the centrepiece as it were, was a lone guy strung up from the light fitting, his noose a cheerfully blinking trail of fairy lights.

I couldn't look away from his face. His eyes had rolled up into his skull and his mouth hung open, a slick of viscous fluid dribbling down his chin. His skin was pale, almost bleached white as the blood had drained out of him from the many slashes in his chest. Morbidly, I couldn't help wondering if he had been stabbed before or after he had been hung. I couldn't work out which would have been worse.

It was too much for me and I bent over, throwing up onto the already soiled carpet. I hoped that when I woke up, I wouldn't find myself covered in sick.

Suddenly, the door to the flat slammed back against the wall and a swarm of black figures spilled into the dimly lit room. Between the flickering of the fairy lights and the post-vomit tears in my eyes, I could only just make out that they were armed police officers. Without seeming to react to the carnage everywhere, the men flicked on their torches, bathing me in roving spotlights, which all eventually focused on my face.

I felt a wave of relief sweep over me as I blinked in the harsh brightness. Finally somebody was here to help. The skater boy was wrong – this wasn't anything to do with me, and now the police could take care of it.

"Ok mate, take it easy," the lead officer began, his voice muffled through his helmet. Unable to see their expressions, I could have been listening to robots. "There's nowhere to run now. Just drop the knife."

I didn't have a knife! I was just about to tell them as much, when I caught a glimpse of my outstretched hand, now gripping a large kitchen knife gilded in blood. The touch of it disgusted me, as if I could feel the blade slicing through flesh and jarring against bone. With a scream, I flung the blade away from my body, sending it thudding across the floor.

As soon as I was unarmed, the policemen flocked towards me, arms outstretched like zombies. One of them grabbed me and roughly spun me around, forcing my arm behind my back, whilst another hit me with a gut punch, winding me. The last thing I remembered was trying to yell through airless lungs as the policemen dragged me out of the room.

I woke up face down on my bed, just where I had left myself. The duvet was soaked with sweat and my eyes were stinging. The sheet was bunched up where I had been clenching it and my entire body felt tense as if at any moment, the policemen from the nightmare would burst through the door and drag me away. The message of the dream however, was awfully clear. Some part of me seemed to think that if I couldn't control my anger, I would psych out and kill a load of people, but surely I wouldn't let that happen? And who was the mysterious skater dude with the echoing phrase of *Caedo Tu*? I sat up and tried to avoid my gaunt reflection in the mirror, haunted and confused as it was. Perhaps the skater was like my conscience, or my spirit guide? Well so far, he'd done a bang up job – getting me kicked from the team and then setting me up as a mass murderer. I shook my head, running a hand through my hair.

"Not gonna happen," I muttered resolutely.

ADAM

The sky outside was getting dark as I walked into my room and flicked the light on. After the excitement of the football practice, my return home seemed to be incredibly dull, but at least the rain had let up. I dumped my bag in the corner and kicked off my shoes, smiling at the trouble I always used to get if my mum saw me doing so without untying them first. I walked over to pull the curtains shut, casting a thoroughly unimpressed eye down on the street below with its perfectly manicured lawns and company cars – all status but no substance.

"Adam, is that you?" This was my mother's voice through the door.

"No it's a burglar."

I heard her tut quietly as she entered the room. "You shouldn't joke like that." I gave her my most contrite look, earning a smile. "I've cooked dinner," she said. "Have you got time to eat before work?"

"I suppose," I replied wistfully. It wouldn't take me long to get ready for my high octane job as Student Union barman. "Gimme a few minutes to get changed, then I'll be down."

My mother shifted awkwardly on her feet, as if deliberating whether to say something else or not. I noticed she was wringing her hands – something she only did when she was nervous. "Your father's here," she half whispered. That was no big deal. Often, my dad didn't make it home in time for dinner, so mum would always put a plate aside for him. It didn't really make much difference to me whether he was there or not - we hardly ever spoke.

"Ok?" I waited, seeing if she would elaborate, but she seemed to hang there frozen with her mouth open between words. "Right then, I'll be down in a minute." Mum nodded silently and then left the room. I figured she had obviously had a long day or something.

With a shake of my head, I switched the stereo on, pumping the volume until the room seemed to be throbbing with pop. All my troubles seemed to melt away in a whirlwind of harmonies and dance routines.

I pulled my clothes off until I was standing in front of the mirror in my shorts, ready to begin the routine of flexing and posing. I wasn't obsessed with my weight like some people, but I liked to have a bit of definition. Satisfied with the shape as I sucked in my stomach, I turned and flexed my arms – they could do with a bit more work. All the time I had spent lifting beer kegs and shoving tables around didn't seem to be showing in the bicep department. I stood front on, critiquing myself against the Adonis form of Luke I had seen earlier in the changing rooms. That's when I felt the tingle. I glanced guiltily at the clock. Did I have time? Yeah I had time. I double checked the door was closed and slid my laundry basket in front, just in case.

It's not just in my sketch pad that I collect images of Luke – I have a lot stored in my head that are slightly more risqué. This time, he was standing in a yard, all red brick and chain link. He was dressed in a white shirt and grey shorts, complete with a cap, tie and blazer, and a torrent of water was pouring down on him from a broken gutter somewhere above. It was a simple cross of images from the changing rooms and the vintage *t.A.T.u* I was listening to.

With smouldering eyes, Luke ripped off his tie and threw his cap onto the concrete, the water cascading over his head and turning his shirt tight and translucent. I made him tilt his head back and revel in it – it was easier for me if he was enjoying himself.

Next, he pulled his shirt open and slid it down his arms until it floated away from him. He began massaging his chest, working his hands lower and lower until he was at the waistband of his shorts, easing them down...

And I was done. I'll admit that it didn't take long with Luke as the material. Face flushed and heart slamming against my ribcage like a wildcat, I wiped my hand on my thigh (no one would know!) and I stared at my reflection for a second before turning to my wardrobe and my work uniform. Black trousers and a yellow polo shirt wasn't the most flattering of outfits, but the Union seemed to be extremely resilient when it came to suggestions. Also, the colour had earned us the nickname of Fireflies as we were always visible shining in the gloom.

By the time I made it downstairs, the dinner was only just getting lukewarm. *Like me,* I thought, smiling at my genius pun. To my surprise, mum had set things up in the dining room. We usually ate at the kitchen table, saving the polished wood and china filled dresser for special occasions. Had something happened that I didn't know about? Maybe dad had got promoted?

My parents were both in there, and thankfully they had started on their food without waiting for me – that would have been embarrassing. My dad was still in his work suit, and he fit in well with the general dining room theme - unlike me with a plastic name badge on, and 'Bar Staff' emblazoned across my back. As I sat down, I felt as if I should have been serving them rather than sitting with them.

I helped myself to potatoes, only acutely aware that my dad seemed to be huffing and puffing under his breath. *Bad day,* I told myself naively, although I should have by now realised what was going on. My mother's small talk only made it worse.

"How was school today?" she asked without looking at me. My father and I scowled at her, although his was out of genuine disgust. Despite the warning signs, I carried on the joke, pretending to be offended.

"It's uni, not school," I bantered. She looked taken aback for a second, before realising I was joking. Why was everybody on edge today?

"Did you get a chance to see-"

My father's fork clattered onto his plate and my mother's sentence faded into silence. Dad was glaring at her, his face darkening as anger polluted his features. His greying beard made it look like a storm cloud had settled around his head.

"How can you talk to him like nothing's happened?" he growled.

Mum waited until she had cut a very precise piece of meat with her knife before replying. "Can't we just leave this?"

I looked back and forth between my parents, who were glaring tensely at each other. I might as well not have been in the room. "What *has* happened?" I asked, my appetite rapidly dropping and reversing until I felt slightly nauseous.

My mum turned to me, an unconvincing smile hastily plastered over her face. "Nothing Adam, you just eat your dinner before it gets-" Again, my father cut her off.

"I'll tell you what's happened, you little pervert."

My cheeks reddened as I thought of my little self abusive misdemeanour upstairs. Perhaps I hadn't been as stealthy as I thought...

"Your mother found some of your dirty queer magazines this morning."

So this was it – crunch time. Caught out by my mother suddenly deciding to be thorough. I allowed my hurt expression to show for one second only. That was all my dad was going to get, before I set my jaw defiantly, suppressing the urge to retaliate, or even worse, burst into tears. I had been half expecting this sort of fallout for a long time, but I think I had managed to convince myself it wouldn't hurt so much.

"Please!" My mum's breathing increased as she raised her hands defensively, but it was too late. His face almost a cherry red, my father wasn't going to let up now – he'd just got started.

"If I'd known my own son was..." he floundered, searching for the right word. I found myself wondering whether he was searching for the least or most hurtful term he could use. "If I'd known you were backwards, I would have beaten it out of you years ago."

I didn't doubt that, I thought, remembering some of the times me and Andrew had been punished when growing up. My fists were shaking, but I wasn't sure if it was through anger or pain. I focused my gaze on a single spot on the tablecloth, imagining my father's words bouncing off me and fizzling into nonexistence.

On the other side of the table, my mother began to cry, and I hoped it was because of my father's grand overreaction to my situation, and not to my situation itself.

"How long has it been, eh?" my father continued, droplets of venomous saliva visibly flying from his lips as he spat each word at me like I was some *thing* that had turned up and ruined his dinner. "When did you lose my respect?" I wanted to stand up and shout into his face that I'd never had his respect, but instead I furiously maintained my calm. I wasn't going to give him the satisfaction. Instead, I crossed my cutlery and pushed my plate away.

"Mum, I've had enough." I stood up and turned towards the door. My dad instantly raised his fork and waved it, no, *brandished* it in my direction like a lion tamer at the circus.

"Don't you walk away from me, queer boy! Come on homo, defend yourself." Part of me wanted to rush over there and smash his face into his dinner, but then I would be no better than him. I turned to give him one last look, hopefully to give him some sort of clue of the damage he was doing. Instead, all he did was lean forward, his mouth curling maliciously.

"Does it hurt? Taking it all the way? I hope you scream."

That was when I let the tears fall. My father sat back triumphantly as my mother sat sobbing next to him. I turned on my heels and ran for the door, snatching my coat from the banister.

"You're nothing compared to Andrew!" he shouted after me, aiming the comparison like a kick to send me on my way. Again, I was tempted to stoop to his level, to grass Andrew up so that my stupid ape of a father realised that neither of us were perfect, but it wouldn't achieve anything. It was selfish to bring Andrew down with me. I decided to run to work and lose myself in the bustle of the Friday night rush – with a bit of luck it would take my mind off the horrors awaiting me at home.

JACK

We were all slumped on the sofas in an alcohol induced lull. I had reluctantly taken Kieran's advice and drank a few beers with my housemates – the evidence of which was now formed into an elaborately balanced beer-can tower on the coffee table. The TV was still on, but none of us were paying any attention to it.

To be honest, Kieran's booze therapy had worked briefly, but now I was beginning to sink again. I kept hearing those final words echoing in my mind, and it always ended up with the reverberating realisation of how alone I was.

There was the creaking of fabric as Ben rose from the other sofa. He wobbled slightly before straightening up and traipsing into the kitchen. I saw his back as he opened the fridge and knelt down, almost sticking his whole torso inside. After a few moments, he re-emerged and stuck his head back into the front room.

"We're out of beer," he said flatly.

Kieran sat up awkwardly. "What?"

"I said," Ben repeated, halting to lean onto the doorframe. "We are out of beer."

Kieran rolled his eyes and then nudged Will next to him, who looked like he had fallen asleep.

"Wha?" Will managed, focusing bleary eyes on Kieran. Kieran tilted his head in my direction, and they both scrutinised me. It was obvious what they saw, as I could feel myself slipping into more tears, and therefore losing myself some major reputation points. My friends staged a pretend secret conversation in front of me, raising their hands in front of their mouths as if this magically prevented them from being heard.

"I don't think those beers worked," Kieran said in a loud whisper.

"What can we do now?"

"There's more out there than beer you know!"

"Like what?"

"Cocktails! Shots! Pitchers!"

Kieran burst into a wide grin and jumped to his feet, clapping his hands. I rolled my eyes – I could see where this was going.

"Children," Kieran announced, pointing at me. "We are leaving. We are taking this poor fallen one to the Union. We will unite! If we cannot take his mind off that which has wronged him, then we will destroy it with many harmful toxins! Who's with me?"

Will stood up, and he and Ben both raised their right arms in salutes. I couldn't help smiling, but partly because of how ridiculous they all looked, half drunk already and campaigning for more. Ben and Will cheered, but Kieran wasn't satisfied. He thrust his own fist into the air and yelled. "I said who's with me?"

They cheered again. Kieran grinned triumphantly before lowering his arm and offering me his hand, his other hand pressed firmly behind his back in a mockery of a Jane Austen gentleman asking for a dance.

"Come on mate, my treat?"

After a second's pause, I sighed and took his hand. He hoisted me off the sofa and marched me out of the room. So we were going to the Union...

ALEX

After the nightmare, I had needed the shower to cool down. I imagined all of the fear and confusion from the dream vanishing down the plughole. I came back into my room, got changed and made the bed. It almost looked half respectable, and thankfully all evidence of my freak out had been cleared up.

Next, I made myself a cup of hot chocolate, remembering how my mum always used to make me some when I was feeling upset at home. Compared to how I had felt when I woke up, I was much calmer. It was just a dream after all - it wasn't like I was Cassandra of Troy.

Footsteps shuffled past my door as I took a sip of my drink, breathing in the sweet scent. I was used to hearing a bit of noise outside in the corridor, and this was a quiet day, unlike last week when the guys on A corridor were playing corridor hockey - a game which had quickly been stymied by the halls attendants.

The footsteps gave way to scratching, and I looked up curiously. I couldn't think what new game they might have invented that would sound like that. I set my mug on the desk and stood up as the sound got increasingly louder. I looked at the sliver of light coming in under the door. It was smooth and unbroken by the shadow or outline of feet – nobody was standing outside my door, so where was the noise coming from? The scratching was frantic now, almost desperate, and the image of somebody scratching away at the inside of a coffin sprung to mind.

I reached out a hand tentatively towards the door handle, and I was less than a centimetre away from the cool metal when my phone beeped. Despite the fervent scraping, it was still loud and pierced the air, grating against my eardrums. I fished my phone out of my pocket and opened the text message I had just received. It was blank – not even an insult, which struck me as odd. Recently there had been a spate of random abuse texts that some jokers were sending around campus, usually single word insults or random phrases, but this had nothing.

The scratching began to mix with the faint sound of sniggering, as if somebody was watching me, giggling at how confused I looked. Turning back to the door, I realised it was actually vibrating now, the force of the scratching too much.

Without hesitating this time, I lunged forwards and grabbed the door handle, ready to pull it open and hurl some verbal fire. Even when I hadn't just had the worst day of my life, the students on my corridor generally accepted that I wasn't to be messed with. Somebody was going to get it big time for this severe lapse of judgement.

There was nobody there. I thrust my head into the corridor, looking in both directions, expecting to see the back of some miscreant disappearing around the corner, but it was empty on both sides. The only thing to be seen was an envelope lying directly outside my door. My name was written on it in curly handwriting. I stooped to retrieve the envelope, no doubt wearing a look of extreme confusion. I half felt like I was still dreaming and that I hadn't woken up at all. I was almost expecting the nightmare police to jump through the window at any moment and drag me away again.

I turned back to my room and froze, eyes not quite comprehending what I was seeing. Somebody had scratched the words *Caedo Tu* into the door. The blue paint was flaking away from the gouges that formed the angular letters, and as I leaned in closer, they looked to be at least a centimetre deep. My mind became a whirlwind of thought, half revolving around the idea that somebody had actually had the audacity to vandalise my door, and half dwelling on the fact that it was those particular words. I ran my fingers over the rough edges to confirm their existence then stormed inside and slammed the door.

I sat on the bed, my hands furiously clenched around the envelope. I thought my fingernails would tear through the paper and ravage my own palms, I was clenching so tightly. It had to have been somebody from Sociology who had seen my notebook - that was the only explanation wasn't it? The other stuff was just a dream. And as for the *Caedo Tu* phrase itself, I must have just seen it somewhere – maybe it was a band or in a song or something? I realised I was getting paranoid. I needed something to focus my mind on, to stop it from spiralling off in all sorts of crazy directions. The phrase "that way madness lies" was coined for a reason. I turned my attention instead to the envelope, admiring the curled writing that I could now see was written in some sort of glittery gel ink. Definitely written by a girl, I thought. At this notion, my spirits began to rise. Obviously as part of the football team, I got my fair share of action, but there had been a bit of a break in the romance department lately. Perhaps some female company was just what I needed to ground myself?

I tore the top off and pulled out the folded paper inside. As I unfurled the contents, my eyes widened. It was a flyer. *Drink 'Til You Drop – B5 Today! Almost Everyone Invited!* It was the exact same party from my dream, and it was happening tonight! I had dreamed the exact name of a party that I hadn't known about at the time. Suddenly, my throwaway comment about Cassandra echoed back to me - surely that couldn't be it? I kept trying to reason with myself – telling myself that again, like the phrase *Caedo Tu*, I must have seen the Drink 'Til You Drop party advertised somewhere else, but as I was unable to pinpoint exactly where, my arguments of rationalisation didn't do much to comfort me.

I tore the flyer up and dumped it in the bin. As I sat back down, I noticed my hand was trembling. If my dream was correct, then this party was supposed to be where I killed most of the students in my block. Before I could stop myself, I jumped up and screamed, sweeping my hand across the desk and sending everything smashing on to the floor. My lava lamp cracked and the slime inside oozed out, soaking all my papers. It felt good to release my anger again.

"I'm not a killer," I muttered as I surveyed the damage.

JACK

The Union was alive, a seething mass of bodies, pulsing with neon passion. To one side, the dancefloor flashed with strobes and hummed with bass, slowly melting into the slightly calmer and more chilled section with the comfy chairs. Running through the centre was the backbone of the Union – the bar. The Fireflies in their bright yellow shirts were surrounded by the rectangular counter making it look like they truly were fireflies trapped in a jar. On either side it was packed with people elbowing and clawing their way forwards, eager to grab a sip of whatever they'd chosen to poison themselves with, either happiness or forgetfulness.

We had all made a slight effort to dress up for the evening, although my slack attempt paled in comparison to Kieran's designer shirt. There was also the faintest hint of some sort of aftershave, which was no doubt one of the top brands around – Kieran probably owned them all. Usually me and Kieran would compete on things like this, but this evening I just wanted to sit around and wallow, so all I'd really done was put on some chinos. I didn't even know why I had let them talk me into coming out.

Kieran's eyes lit up as he surveyed the scene – this was his ideal night out. He barely even hesitated before plunging into the thronging masses and shouldering his way towards the bar. I reluctantly glanced at Will and Ben, but as I feared, they were with Kieran on this one and followed suit.

Embarrassingly, my complete fear of being left alone conquered my total lack of enthusiasm for partying and I followed my housemates into the crowd.

ADAM

I looked out at the sea of faces, in varying degrees of rosy cheeks depending on how many they'd had. I was thankful for the polished counter that separated me from them. It made me feel like I was better than those on the outside, desperately reaching for drinks as if their lives depended on them. The constant rush was enough to take my mind off what had happened at home, barely giving me enough time to dwell on my father's acidic barbs.

Whilst my colleagues dived into the whirling mass of orders being shouted over the music, I hung back. I was a more discerning Firefly, choosing the cute ones first. It wasn't as if anybody was sober enough to pull me up on it.

A group of four lads approached the bar, the one in front obviously taking charge. He gently slid around some skeezy girl and clicked his fingers theatrically. Ok, so he was probably arrogant, but he was well dressed, and if my nose wasn't deceiving me, he was wearing Gaultier. I quickly checked my reflection in one of the fridge doors and then leaned in, satisfied that it wasn't too apparent that I had spent the entire walk to work crying my eyes out.

"Good eve, Firefly!"

I tried a half-hearted grin. "What can I get you?"

"It's quite severe I'm afraid," the guy said earnestly. He looked back at one of his companions who didn't seem to be enjoying himself. "We'll start with four double blue Aftershocks, and four pints of the proper Bow please."

I filed the order in my mind and noted that he had at least said 'please', even if his order read like a train wreck.

I made the drinks on autopilot, casually scanning the reflections again to see if I could pick out my next cute serve, or whether I would have to go on some menial journey to the stockroom until some more attractive prospects turned up.

JACK

Kieran dumped a handful of cash into the Firefly's hand and scooped up a tray laden with pints and shots. Without stopping, he spun away, expertly lifting the tray over people's heads and weaving in and out until we had followed him over to the comfy chairs. I breathed a sigh of relief that he hadn't immediately taken us over to the dancefloor. At least at the chairs I could take my time over my drink and try to pace myself. The last thing I wanted was to get wasted on the first pint and make a complete arse out of myself.

We sat down and Kieran handed out the drinks. We each appeared to have a pint and a shot of something that was luminous blue. I looked expectantly at Kieran, waiting for him to explain what the game was. There was always some sort of rule to follow or game to play – it was never simply just sitting and drinking.

"Well come on then!" Kieran challenged as he poured his shot into the pint. Before the drink had settled, he took a deep gulp and smacked his lips. "I call it the Blue Tit."

I mixed my own and watched as the drifting tendril of blue gradually mixed with the amber coloured cider.

"It looks more green to me," Ben muttered.

"Shut up and drink it," Kieran snapped playfully. "I've decided we're getting wrecked. Next bar stop is in fifteen – synchronize watches. No exceptions!" Kieran made a big show of checking his watch, which was a chunky silver thing that probably cost the income of a small African country.

I hurriedly took a sip of the Blue Tit, aware that Kieran would be making sure I kept pace.

ALEX

It turned out I had gone a little psycho on my bedroom. When I'd finally managed to restore my breathing to a steady pace, I was leaning against my bed, surrounded by wreckage. Everything that had been on the desk or stuck to the walls was now lying broken and torn on the floor.

I looked around, the anger rapidly melting into regret as I began to spot tattered edges and broken corners of things that I actually liked, or worse, needed. A lot of the lecture notes I could do without, but there were a few text books that were now missing a few pages, and I was pretty sure that the Uni Library wouldn't look fondly on that.

There was a knock on the door. Instinctively, I looked at the light shining through from the corridor, and thankfully there were two very clear shadows that indicated somebody's feet. I hauled myself off the floor and stepped cautiously over all the debris, opening the door a tiny fraction. I didn't want anybody to judge me on the state of my room.

A girl was standing in the corridor, roughly my age. I had seen her around halls a couple of times, but I wasn't sure if she lived on my corridor or not. She was wearing an extremely short skirt and a halter top, but for some reason it didn't make her look slutty. In any other situation, I would have said she was hot, but obviously I wasn't in the mood for scouting for girls. In the end, I just glared at her.

"Hey," she began lamely. "I'm Gemma. You're a Centaur right?" I continued to glare, wondering how many of my team mates she'd tried before coming to my door. "Are you coming to the Drink 'Til You Drop tonight?"

"No," I snapped flatly. "I'm not going." That was the party where I was supposed to stroke out. Gemma looked taken aback and disappointed, like she actually thought she could turn up at my door and ask me out like some stupid Richard Curtis movie.

"Oh. Ok then." Just then, she seemed to notice the graffiti scratched into my door. She reached up and ran her finger along the grooves. "What's *Caedo Tu*?"

"I don't... I mean, it's nothing." I changed my mind about telling her I didn't know – that would just add to my retarded room smashing image.

"Well..." She paused to see if I would say anything else, but I didn't so she shuffled away down the corridor. I didn't feel too bad for her. After all, anybody looking like that wouldn't have trouble finding a date for the party - preferably one that wasn't supposed to be a murderer.

I looked once more at the words scratched into the door, then it hit me all at once. I cursed myself for being so narrow minded. I hadn't even considered that *Caedo Tu* might actually mean something. Maybe it was the Latin word for nightmare? Or some sort of mental illness? I could just about handle being a spaz as long as I wasn't going to kill anybody.

I hurried back into my room and fell to my knees, pulling tattered posters out of the way and chucking odd socks across the room. Finally I found the familiar smooth rectangle of my laptop, which I had carelessly thrown from the desk along with everything else. At first glance, it looked intact, but I still held my breath as I turned it on. I was reassured by the soft humming and whirring that emanated from within as the screen flickered to life.

The browser immediately went to the UCE homepage, where the main story was about some body in the woods. *The woods,* I thought, remembering the jibe from the football pitch. Even then, they were teasing me about being violent. I scowled as I opened up the search engine.

Although my fingers were trembling with anticipation, I carefully typed *Caedo Tu* into Google and hit enter. I clicked the first result – *The Caedo Tu Chain*…

JACK

The pile of empty pint and shot glasses was reaching critical mass, and still Kieran and the others didn't show any signs of stopping. I myself had been pretending to drink for the last half an hour, sneaking most of my shots to Will under the table so Kieran wouldn't see. To Will's credit, he wasn't complaining, nor did he show signs of being drastically more wrecked than the others.

Honestly, I did appreciate what they were trying to do for me, but it was working about as well as playing a cheerful song at a funeral – the timing was wrong. In a couple of days maybe, I would love nothing more than to go out and get blitzed, but now I simply wasn't feeling it.

I turned to casually scan the crowd whilst Kieran launched into another epic tale. A group of lads had just walked in, and it seemed as if everything had gone into slow motion. They were movie star cool, dressed in the finest shirts and jeans that rivalled anything I had stashed in my wardrobe. They were a pair of sunglasses away from being total dicks, but as it was, they had the right amount of style to own the place without appearing like slimeballs. The girls eagerly watched them pass, flicking hair and batting eyelashes whilst the boys they were with watched in envy or tried haplessly to regain their girlfriends' attention. As the alpha male got to the bar, the people already there parted to let him in immediately, like he was royalty.

ADAM

I was still on autopilot, already beginning the barman speech before I had turned back to the crowd. I had caught a glimpse of gelled hair and broad shoulders in the mirror, and at this time of night, that was enough for me to count as worth serving.

"What can I ge-" I paused dumbly. It was Luke, surrounded by his footballers. He didn't seem to notice my awkwardness as he leaned in to make himself heard over the din of the music. A waft of aftershave washed over me – I inhaled deeply.

"Ten Snakebites, on the team." He didn't say please, but I didn't care. I'd accept any words that came out of the boy's mouth as long as they were directed at me. Of course, the football team rarely paid for anything here. The idea was that their drinks would go onto the team tab, which was paid off every month from the uni sports budget, but as long as I'd been a Firefly, we had never received any such payment. The golden boys' tab was miraculously wiped clean every month, no questions asked.

Luke rested against the bar and chatted idly to his companions whilst I tore myself away from him to make the Snakebites.

JACK

I turned back to my housemates, noticing that Will had followed my gaze. He was staring at the boys at the bar with a look of distaste distorting his features.

"Look at them," he scathed, the extra alcohol lending his speech a measured quality. "Walking around like they own the place." Ben and Kieran followed his eyeline and smiled.

"Everyone knows the sports teams split funding with the Union, so when you think about it, technically they *do* own the place," Kieran said with a shrug.

Will frowned as he took another sip of his drink, generously topped up from my glass. "Well it's not fair." I couldn't work out if Will was actually sulking or whether he was pretending, but either way, he didn't look happy. He was a Drama student, obviously accomplished at his art.

Ben leaned in, a sly grin on his face. "So this has nothing to do with the fact that again you didn't get on the team this year?" I couldn't help smiling at the look of outrage that flickered across Will's face. Kieran snorted into his pint as Will replied.

"No! But incidentally, I caned at tryouts this year. I was totally robbed."

"If you were that good, why would they rob you? It's not like the Centaurs couldn't do with a boost," reasoned Ben.

"I dunno," Will said slowly. "They call me Drama Boy. Maybe they think I'm gay?"

At this, Kieran cracked his knuckles and made a show of clearing his throat. Once more, I could tell we were in for another dose of Kieran's self-proclaimed wisdom.

"It's not how you play, it's who you play," he began.

"Are you saying Will *should* go gay?" Ben laughed.

Will rolled his eyes, smacking Ben on the shoulder. "Go on then," he said to Kieran. "Explain everything away with some magical theory."

"Think about it," Kieran continued as we listened intently. "The whole team know each other, right?" We nodded. So far, we were all following along. "Not just from playing football though – at least five of them went to the same secondary school and got into uni through scholarships and stuff. Did you know that Coach Williams went out with Glen's mum?"

"I heard *everyone's* been out with Glen's mum," cut in Ben, unable to resist the lure of a good mum joke.

"All I'm saying is," Kieran went on, "it's a chain. Probably one or two of them have decent talent; they get their friends on the team, then those guys bring their friends too and then on and on until the whole team is closer together than Mary's knees. That's how chains work – it's usually just one thing passed on and on. You could play like shit, but if you knew Luke or that other one, then chances are you would have made tryouts."

"Hey, I saw Alex once in JJB," Will said thoughtfully, actually considering Kieran's theory. "He bought some socks…"

"Oh my God!" Ben exclaimed, holding his hand to his mouth in mock shock. "You should have mentioned that at tryouts! You would have definitely made it on the team with connections like that!"

I smiled again as Kieran and Ben fell about with laughter. Even Will's face was cracking whilst he tried to maintain his displeasure, complete with folded arms.

"Enough!" Kieran commanded, wiping his eyes and regaining his composure. "Jack, go and get shots. We're playing Truth or Dare." I sighed, stoically refusing to move until Kieran physically shoved me out of my seat and chivvied me away with a wave of his hand, like he was shooing a puppy. As I moved towards the bar, I could hear the sounds of the table being cleared ready for the game. Knowing Kieran, he could probably turn even Truth or Dare into something increasingly epic.

TOM

My few brief appearances and influences with my prey had worn me out – weirdly, because it's not like I had physically gone anywhere, but still – I was knackered. I couldn't help feeling a small amount of regret about what I was doing, but I was resigned to it now I'd started. I kept telling myself that my boys were heading that way anyway, I was just helping them along for something in return. It didn't sound so bad worded like that. I decided to allow myself a short reprieve into my dreaming body.

My senses revelled in their new surroundings, and although I was dreaming of a graveyard, it was definitely better than my hospital bed. I breathed deeply, taking in the scent of the freshly cut grass, tilting my head back as the breeze played through my hair.

The only building in sight was a small chapel, grey brick and vintage looking. It was enough to create a sense of freedom – I truly felt like I was in the middle of nowhere, cut off from civilisation, the people and the cars. *Especially the cars.*

The sky was a complex mixture of greys, with a tinge of blue creeping out from behind the clouds. I think it had just rained and I could *smell the ozone,* as my best friend would have said.

I held out my arms as if to embrace the nature and noticed for the first time what I was wearing. It was a smart black suit jacket, with equally suave trousers and shoes. It was a far cry from my normal attire but once again, I wasn't about to complain, considering my alternatives. Judging from the setting and the outfit, my mind immediately focused on one word. Funeral.

A little way off, a group of mourners were huddled together against the cold, all heads bowed in either respect or to keep the breeze off tear stained cheeks. I figured that seeing as I was dressed appropriately, I must be part of the service that was taking place, and I just hoped it wasn't anybody that I was too close to.

As I picked my way around the graves, I could see that the minister was standing at the front, his white robes whipping about his ankles like some flapping swan amongst a crowd of subdued ravens. He was holding the Bible, and every so often when the breeze changed direction, I caught faint snippets of his voice as he read. To one side was a large pile of dirt, a shovel sticking out of the top expectantly as if waiting for the service to end so it could begin working once more.

Nobody heralded my arrival, and I was greeted by an impenetrable wall of black clad shoulders. I tried to squeeze my way through to the front but nobody was moving. The woman closest to the morbid pit was my mother, and my heart gave a flutter both of comfort as I hadn't really seen her in ages, and of relief – it wasn't her funeral.

I stretched out my hand, desperate to reach her, but still nobody would let me pass. Every gap I found, the mourners always shifted their stances at the last moment before I could slip through. Frustrated, I took a step back. I couldn't understand why they were being so unreasonable. That was when my childish streak kicked in, after all they would hardly make a fuss at a funeral would they?

I took another couple of steps backwards, then charged full pelt at the crowd. There wasn't even the slightest outcry or objection as I barrelled past the grievers and finally made it to the side of the grave and my mother. Even the minister continued to read as if nothing had happened. All triumph however, was knocked out of me as I looked down into the hole.

The coffin was in the grave - a light coloured wood, pine or something. A plaque was in the centre of the lid, and it was shaped like a skateboard. I peered harder, although I knew what it was going to say.

"Thomas James Ferrier – Beloved Son"

Clenching my jaw resolutely, I turned to my mother, hoping to see some light of denial in her eyes – anything to tell me it wasn't so, but she was still staring intently at her feet, face shadowed by a black veil. I scanned the crowd of mourners, recognising Adam in a snappy suit, as well as a couple of other guys from uni.

"I'm not dead," I stated defiantly. Nothing. "I'm still here, I'm alive!" Without realising it, my voice had risen to a yell, but still the crowd remained unfazed. I grabbed my mother by the shoulders and shook her violently – even a reaction of pain would be a comfort to know that she could feel me. She rocked awkwardly, but as soon as I released her she resumed her previous position. Before I knew it, I was crying, pressing myself into her shoulder like I used to when I was younger, hoping I could somehow break her stillness with the warmth from my body.

I clung to her until the lapel of her jacket was wet and sticky, and when I finally pulled away, a snivelling mess, I realised she was looking directly at me. It had worked!

"Time to go, Tom," she breathed. Her eyes were shining with regret, but at least she could see me now.

"Mum?"

"Forgive me, my little man." All of a sudden, my mother jerked into life, marching forwards until I had to edge away from her. As I looked around me in confusion, I saw that the others were moving too, even the minister, crowding around me, hemming me in and forcing me back and back until my heels hung on the lip of the open grave. I hovered there, arms flailing with my mother hanging on to the collar of my jacket.

"Please..." I whimpered pathetically, but I could tell that her mind was made up. She had already said goodbye.

She gave me a sharp push and I tumbled into the hole, landing with a harsh crack on top of my own coffin. Without hesitating, my mother seized the handle of the shovel and dumped the first load of soil onto my chest. I tried to scream but another lump of dirt landed in my mouth, cold and gritty. The last thing I saw was the other funeral guests reaching eagerly into the pile of mud, all helping to do their bit in burying me alive.

In a flash, I was back in the hospital room, caught once more in the transient state of being able to see and hear all that was going on, as well as seeing my own prone and broken body lying below me.

Somebody had brought a university yearbook and set it on the bedside table – I didn't remember it appearing, and I was beginning to question the rules of my out of body experience. It seemed as though every time I closed my eyes, hours would pass.

An orderly was checking the charts at the end of the bed, and my mother was sitting in her usual place – a sentry watching her son with empty eyes. For a brief moment I wondered which existence was better – this one where I could see her, or the nightmare where I could touch her. Either way, she would not acknowledge my presence.

Suddenly, my body started to tremble in its sleep, eyes rolling beneath the closed lids. My mother lunged forwards and grabbed my wrist, looking questioningly at the orderly who had barely glanced away from the charts.

"I wouldn't worry," he reassured my mother, "he's just dreaming." The orderly replaced the chart in its holder and left the room whilst my mother gently put her hand on my brow – another simple soothing action I remembered from my childhood.

I'm not dreaming, I know that now. If that was dreaming, then people would never sleep at all. The truth was that I was finding it harder and harder to stay grounded. You'd think it would have been easy, my body lying in state as it was, but now the darkness seemed to be closing in. I hadn't noticed it before, yet now there was a slight shadow that outlined everything. It was as if the light was physically fighting to break through. Death was obviously anxious to claim me, regardless of how deserving I was.

It was time to make the final push. Lives were hanging in the balance, but for mine to survive, I needed to tip the scale. My poor camels were standing unaware as I loomed over their backs with the last straws.

ALEX

The website seemed to take forever to load as I sat leaning against the wall, surrounded by the wreckage of my bedroom. I wasn't sure if it was down to the crappy UCE intranet, or whether I actually had done some damage when I chucked the laptop.

Finally, a logo appeared against a black background. There was a picture of Death, complete with skull and cloak, except he was standing with his arms outstretched. Instead of a scythe, he was holding a sword in one hand and a set of scales in the other. The image vaguely reminded me of something but I couldn't place it. Underneath the figure was a golden banner that read 'Caedo Tu – Victim's Justice Everlasting.' *Oh, right.*

My curiosity was piqued and I clicked the picture, wondering what I was getting myself into. Victims and Justice sounded like one of those personal injury adverts that were all over the television, but the figure of Death added an extra layer of creep to the situation.

The next page was nothing more than a set of links, white on black: *Find out more, Press, Message board* and *Contact us.* Not that I was an expert in web design, but the site was very simple – almost amateurish. I clicked to find out more, hoping that I wouldn't have to sift through endless amounts of useless crap to get the information I needed. I had visions of myself following a stupid trail of links for hours on end, going round and round in circles.

I frowned as the new page loaded up. Again, it was the set of links but this time accompanied by a small passage of writing in the centre. My eyes stung as I read the glaring text.

There are currently sixteen Caedo Tu chains in the world today, the oldest one dating back to 1912 and involving over 20000 people. At one time, there were as many as 42 chains but many of those ended during the Second World War.

Caedo Tu originated in ancient Rome, but the first documented case was not until 1867, and even then, the survivor was hanged, accused of devil worshipping.

I shook my head, not quite sure what I was reading. Chains? Devil worshipping? I began to feel the flares of anger once more, suspecting that I was being led into a load of nonsense, but something kept me from closing the browser. For whatever reason, this phrase seemed to be following me around – the more I found out about it the better. I clicked on the *Press* link.

I was taken to a page of newspaper cuttings that had been scanned in. There were headlines such as *'Eight strangers die together in mysterious circumstances'* and *'Alleyway black spot for teen suicide'*. I didn't bother to read each story fully, but my eyes were drawn to the numerous grainy pictures of bodies and crime scenes.

My stomach knotted as I scanned the page, remembering my dream. I had seen violence and death, and once again my path had led me to a place of morbid fixation. Was this some sort of underground group set up to solve crimes? To get justice for the victims as the slogan suggested? But why was I involved? I didn't know any victims and I hadn't committed any crime more serious than the occasional joint and punching the odd pretty-boy.

At this point, my mind began to spiral off in all sorts of crazy directions. I was thinking of premonitions and time travel. The dream had seemed to suggest that I was going to end up murdering a lot of people, and I supposed they would be the victims. What if the boy from my dream was a messenger from the future sent back to stop me?

I laughed to myself and looked around cautiously to make sure nobody was watching. I blushed, ashamed at where my mind had taken me. Time travelling! Next, I would be suggesting that the kid was a robot! There had to be a logical explanation for what was going on, and this website obviously wasn't the place to find it after all.

Before logging off, I decided to check out the message board and see what some of the nutjobs had been saying, for I was now convinced that this was probably one of those conspiracy websites that claimed aliens were real, and that the government knew. Those people were so serious about it that I was sure it would make for some light entertainment.

Sure enough, there was a full page of comments. I started to read through them, a slight smirk on my face.

May 13th 1996 – Schindler, Bridgwater – Caedo Tu hits Britain! Three of my work colleagues all died on the same night. It has to be!

May 14th 1996 – Matty G, Chichester – Another chain here in Chi. A mate's cousin was saved by some of the girls in her aerobics class. Anyone in the area, watch out if you've been hanging with Beth, Stacey or Big Em!

Saved? Saved from what? This was getting weirder and weirder... I scrolled down to the bottom of the page to read the most recent posts.

April 27th 2006 – Hogan's Hero, Tangmere – Tina, Phil, Liam and Matt, rest in peace guys. Without your help, I'd still be in that place. Gs till the end. Caedo Tu...

May 7ᵗʰ 2006 – TJ Ferrier, UCE – So there are 16 chains in the world, and at least 7 in Britain. How do you start a new chain?

I snapped to attention suddenly, my eyes focusing solely on the final comment as I re-read it. A comment from UCE! So whatever this was, it was definitely here. The comment was a couple of weeks old, but that wasn't what was bothering me. The name TJ Ferrier was ringing a bell, but I couldn't quite remember why.

I scanned around my room, suddenly feeling a pang of regret at the destruction I had caused. There had probably been some things I'd smashed that I really would have prefered to keep hold of, but for now, I was searching for a particular item.

At last I noticed a corner of paper sticking out from under a cracked mug that bore the swirling red UCE logo, like an out of control ball of wool. I deftly fished the Uni Rag up and flicked through until I saw what I was looking for.

In a yellow box and bold print was an appeal asking if anybody had witnessed an accident involving one of the students. He had been knocked down the other night, and was currently lying in a coma in the City Hospital, but that wasn't the worst thing. All of that information, I glossed over – stuff like that was always happening to students as they stumbled home from whatever dive they'd been hanging out at, pissed off their heads. The bit that was causing my blood to freeze was the guy's name. Tom Ferrier. TJ Ferrier, the guy who had been looking at the *Caedo Tu* website.

I was certain now that Tom had been the one I'd seen on the football pitch before my fight with Luke. I was also sure that he had been the guide in my dream. Whatever was going on here, he would know something about it. He had to.

JACK

"You see, it was because she had taken the wrong bag. She had all of my stuff, and I had all of hers. Well I had to get home somehow, and I couldn't do it naked could I? And that, my friends, is why I turned up one morning wearing a very strappy top and a lovely summer skirt."

Kieran and Will burst into applause as Ben finished his story. I was only half listening, and in any other situation I probably would have found it hilarious, but tonight the lads' efforts to cheer me up were sadly failing.

There was a lull in the laughter as Kieran turned thoughtfully to his next victim. "Will?"

"What the hell, gimme a dare."

I couldn't help pricking my ears as Kieran and Ben whispered to each other, no doubt trying to come up with a horrifically humiliating task for Will to attempt. After a moment, Kieran cleared his throat.

"I've got it. William, I dare you to drink one of these *foulcopops* without using your hands... or a straw." He waved his hand over the various bottles of luridly coloured drinks with a smirk. Will stood up, clasped his hands resolutely behind his back, and shuffled closer to the table.

"Ready?"

I turned to watch, unable to resist the temptation of seeing one of my friends spill cheap booze all over himself. The others leaned forwards in their seats as Will bent down and clamped the bottleneck between his teeth. Rising seal-like and tilting his head back, Will began gulping the contents until the bottom was empty. He didn't even release his hands until the bottle was safely returned to the table. Raising his arms in celebration, Will sat back down as Kieran shook his head.

"Well I wasn't expecting that," Kieran said with a hint of disappointment.

"Learnt it at the Drink Olympics," Will replied proudly. "What about you then Casanova?" he continued after wiping his mouth.

"Don't call me that," I snapped.

"Jack'll take a dare, won't you Jacko?" Kieran grinned, slapping me forcefully on the back.

"Guys, I'm still not really in the mood for this, ok?" I raised my hands defensively. "By all means, you carry on, but I'll just sit this one out." The last thing I wanted was to be drinking out of an ashtray on top of all the shit I'd had this morning.

"What's that?" Kieran exclaimed, looking right at me. "Dare, you say? Let's see what my associates and I can come up with." Once again, my hands went up in protest, but it was no use – the others were already in a huddle plotting my inevitable embarrassment. All I could hear over the music was the occasional whisper accompanied by malicious sniggering, until finally Kieran cleared his throat and stood up like a judge about to pronounce the sentence. "Jack Aaron Dyer," he began as I cringed at the use of my full name. "We hereby dare you to go onto the dance floor and work your funky mojo until a female specimen becomes entangled in your web of charms."

What?? I guessed that was Kieran speak for 'dance with a girl'.

"You may only return when you have retrieved said ladyfriend's phone number. What say you?"

I glared at my friend indignantly. "I say-"

"Jolly good! Off you go then!" Kieran waved his hand before picking up his drink and downing it in one. To cement the decision, he banged the empty bottle on the table like a gavel. For him, the matter was obviously settled. I briefly looked to Ben and Will for some sympathy, but they were already deviously plotting the next dare for Kieran. Well, I hoped it was something horrific. I know Kieran's supposed to be my friend, but sometimes his arrogant, know it all, take charge persona was grating, especially at a time like this.

I turned away from them and cast my eyes over the writhing dance floor, a couple of hundred people grinding their cares away in a torrent of sweaty bass. Well, not for me. My heartbreak wasn't something I could just cancel out by talking to the next pretty thing that twisted across my vision. How could my friends put me in this position? Did they honestly think this would help me? Or were they just trying to amuse themselves with my torment? Well, you know what? Screw them! I had made up my mind. I was going to leave them to their stupid game. I would be much happier at home anyway – it was a mistake to get lured into a night out.

I slipped down into the sea of bodies, the exit doors my only focus. I thought I had convinced myself I was leaving, but as I pressed my way through the clammy flesh, a new idea came into my mind. If Kieran and the others wanted me to be happy, then I could at least trick them into thinking their plan had worked.

I changed direction and swung around to a dark and deserted corner behind the bar. Once I was certain my housemates couldn't see me, I fished out a crumpled piece of paper from my pocket, and liberated a pencil stub from one of the Fireflies.

Leaning against the wall, I began fervently scribbling a random phone number down. I was so absorbed that I didn't notice the girl until I had practically knocked her over in my eagerness to shove the fake number in Kieran's face.

"Are you ok?" she asked, even though I'm sure she was the one who took most of the force of the impact. I tracked her eyeline to my scrap of paper, which I hastily stuffed back into my pocket before giving her a flustered nod. Dressed in a skirt and halter, she looked like a typical party girl, although her face was a lot kinder than some of the usual bar-hags that dominated the Union scene.

"Err, yeah. I was just... I'm fine," I muttered, aware that my cheeks were burning. I hoped that she wouldn't be able to tell in the gloom.

"When I saw you leave your table, I thought you might have fallen out with your friends."

I frowned slightly, taking a few seconds to process her words over the thumping music. "You were watching me?"

"So it's the Drink 'Til You Drop at halls tonight," she said with a coy smile, deliberately avoiding my question. I stared blankly at her until she shifted awkwardly. "It's a huge party," she continued. "I don't have anybody to go with."

Suddenly it was like the haze lifted from my mind. This girl was hitting on me! Really? I looked down briefly at my less than well planned outfit and wondered for a second what possibly could have drawn her to me.

"Oh," I flustered. "I err... I just got out of a long term relationship. I'm not sure if I want to be going to parties with girls just yet."

The girl's face instantly fell, a dark flash of annoyance tainting her once smooth features, and I found myself wondering if I was the first knockback she'd had this evening. She turned to go, and that was when I saw it. A flicker of a top that I recognised, heading into the centre of the dance floor. Just that one hint of pink and silver was all I needed, because it was a top that I had bought. Marie was here.

"Do you know what?" I exclaimed, grabbing the girl's arm a little harder than I needed to. "Let's dance."

"Cool. I'm Gemma."

"Jack," I muttered, eyes scanning the thronging masses in front of us. She smiled softly as I practically pulled her forwards, taking the rough direction I had seen Marie take. As I disappeared into the crowd, I was vaguely aware of Ben hooting at me from up on the seating gallery, but I ignored him, knowing that if I paused even for a moment, my resolve would crack.

Within seconds, we had found the beat and had become part of the twisting ritual of club dancing. Barely paying attention to Gemma, I was constantly turning my head, trying to sneak a glimpse of Marie. She came into view and I desperately tried to catch her eye before the rhythm tore us apart once more. I had to know how she was doing, who she was with, why she was here. Was she trying to get over it too?

I purposefully steered Gemma around until Marie was in my field of vision once more, but this time she wasn't alone. She was caught up in the dance, hardly touching or acknowledging the guy next to her, but he definitely seemed to be *with* her. The stranger was dressed in a black tee and combats, kind of skater-ish, and he certainly wasn't one of Marie's usual friends. I had never seen him before, nor heard her mention anybody like that. If this guy was what I thought, then she was rebounding *hard.*

As if sensing my gaze, the mysterious guy started dancing closer and closer to Marie, though she still didn't react. He spiralled in, looking as if he was going to glance against her bare arm with the softest touch before spinning away again behind and around her, encircling her, surrounding her. As he turned, I noticed he had some sort of phrase written across his top – some sort of Latin. I was just getting my head around it, when I was yanked forcefully around and brought face to face with my now quite angry looking dance partner.

"What's wrong with you?" Gemma demanded. "You won't even look at me!"

"Caedo Tu..." I muttered, completely absorbed by the stranger's t-shirt, rather than the furious girl.

"What the hell?"

I watched as Marie and her tall, dark and handsome twisted out of sight. Gently, I lifted Gemma's hand off my arm and began to fight my way through the crowd after them. "Sorry," I said over my shoulder.

"Isn't there anybody here that's just normal?" Gemma called after me. Define normal. Is it not normal to go after the one you love?

I pushed my way through yet another human barrier, and there she was standing with her back to me. I reached out, making her jump with surprise before spinning round. It was an expression of curiosity that greeted me.

"Oh," she murmured, clearly disappointed. "Jack. Hi."

"I didn't think you would replace me so quickly," I challenged, the words physically stinging as I vocalised what she'd done to me.

Marie looked confused. "Replace you? I haven't replaced you."

Anger boiled up as she lied right to my face. "Oh so you dance like that with everyone do you?"

Now Marie's face began to match mine, her nostrils flaring. "First of all," she stated indignantly. "I wasn't dancing with anybody." I craned my neck to see over her shoulder, and sure enough the enigmatic skater was nowhere to be seen. "Secondly," she continued. "Dancing like *what?*"

"You were all over the place like some kind of-"

"Some kind of *what?*" Marie's nostrils flared again, dragon-like now. "You're calling me a slut!"

"I didn't mean…" I stuttered. Technically she was right, but I hadn't planned on wording it quite so harshly. I honestly hadn't intended to upset her.

"You know what Jack, just fuck off! I'm not stupid ok? I get it. You're upset that I finished with you, who wouldn't be?" I rolled my eyes as the egotism poured out of her mouth. "It's only natural you'd want to hurt me as some sort of revenge," she continued. "But if that's all you've got to say, then just fuck off. I don't need you anymore."

With that, Marie turned on her heels and stormed through the crowd, me trailing a split second behind.

ALEX

I walked apprehensively through the sliding doors into the hospital's ultra-modern foyer. There were rows of seats in front of a large reception desk, where the receptionist herself sat amongst towers of files and monitors. Dotted around the seating area were various patients waiting to be seen and despite there being no obviously visible wounds, an air of misery hung over them.

As I moved forwards, a couple of nurses passed through from one corridor to its identical twin on the other side, heads bowed. It was obviously a quiet night for the hospital – either that, or every episode of crappy medical drama I'd been forced to sit through with my mum had lied.

When the receptionist looked up, I fed her some bullshit excuse about being Tom's cousin and she idly pointed down the corridor to a sign for the intensive care ward. I thanked her and moved on.

I paused outside the double doors to the ward. This was the deep breath moment. What would I find on the other side? Would I find some grinning kid having a laugh at my expense? I looked cautiously back up the hallway to where the receptionist seemed to have already forgotten me, her head once more hidden behind a stack of folders. I had to take advantage of the slow evening – who knew if I would be able to get in as easily another time. Mind set, I pushed the doors open, a waft of sterile air escaping with a faint hiss.

The corridor beyond was lined with doors and large observation windows like the kind you looked through to identify some mugger at the police station. Next to each one was a chart outlining the patient's name and condition. A strong mix of guilt, pity and disgust washed over me as I couldn't help staring into each window I passed. There were people who looked close to death, gaunt skeletal arms draped over pristinely starched sheets, sunken eyes and translucent skin, and also patients that seemed to be more machine than flesh, hooked up to various monitors, pumps and tubes. All looked hopeless.

I finally reached the chart I was secretly dreading. 'Ferrier, T' followed by lines of horrific sounding medical jargon. As I was squinting, the door opened, a woman I assumed to be Tom's mother stepping out. Her coat was undone and her eyes had dark rings around them. I cringed as she stopped in front of me, and I rose onto the balls of my feet, in case I had to run. Instead, she smiled.

"You are sweet," she said softly. "He'll appreciate the company. Did you come with Adam?"

Who the hell was Adam? "Um, he couldn't make it tonight," I lied.

Tom's mum nodded before patting me gently on the shoulder. "Thank you," she said before heading up the corridor.

I stood astounded for a moment, my heart racing. Could I really go in there now? I had to didn't I? I steeled myself before looking through the glass.

It was amazing how young and vulnerable he looked, surrounded by his machines yet completely alone.

Technically, Tom was the same age as me, but just to look at him shrinking into the mattress he could have been years younger. I half expected him to sit up as I opened the door, but the only movement was the soft rise and fall of his chest as he slept. He was frowning, and I was glad that his eyes were largely hidden behind his emo-fringe.

Without taking my eye off the sleeping man, I edged around the bed to the single plastic chair and sat down. Up close, I could see the bruising poking out from beneath tightly wrapped bandages, and I wondered what a mess he was in internally. If the bandages split, would he spill out?

Once more, I looked around to make sure I was alone, my cheeks burning with what I was about to do. I was aware of all the research that had gone into the benefits of talking to unconscious people, but I still felt like an idiot trying it. I leaned forward, my breath dislodging Tom's fringe. I tried not to flinch as his eyes were revealed, dark rimmed and haunting, despite being closed. I was so close now that I could see the tiny hairs on his cheek rippling as I breathed, yet still no reaction. I put my lips to his ear and whispered.

"Caedo Tu..."

Nothing. I don't know what I was expecting, but I was hoping for *something*. I knew that the phrase wasn't going to be some sort of magical revival spell: that was stupid – there was no such thing as magic - but I knew the words were important somehow. Why else would I be seeing Tom wearing the phrase on his t-shirt?

Suddenly, the hopelessness of it all swept over me, igniting in my chest and flaring back up as flames of anger. It was as if my predicament was mixing with that of the boy lying next to me, creating a nadir of despair. Like back in halls, I felt my rage building, rising until it was threatening to pour out through my fists. Breathing deeply, I fought to control it.

"I see you, and I don't know why," I whispered, despite knowing Tom couldn't answer. "I've never even met you before, but every time I close my eyes, you're there with the same message. Caedo Tu, Caedo Tu, Caedo Tu. Why are you doing this to me?" The fury was literally pulsing against my knuckles now, and I reached out for the only thing I could see to grab that wasn't Tom himself. A tattered copy of the UCE Yearbook had been left on the bedside table, and I now scrunched it forcefully into the palm of my hand. "Why can't I get you out of my head?" I breathed, my voice rising. I was racking my brain for any possible explanation. Was it a warning? Was I supposed to somehow save this kid? Then it hit me... what if it was the opposite? "Maybe you *want* to die. Did you walk in front of that car on purpose? And now you're somehow sending me messages to help finish you off?" For some insane reason, it made perfect sense. I was already seen as the renegade Centaur - maybe Tom came to me because he thought I was the only one who would dare.

I leapt to my feet, punching the comatose body in the chest. Still Tom did not move. The monitor that had solemnly been counting away Tom's heartbeat rose in tempo, a frantic indication that the boy himself could not show. "Is that what you had in mind?" I roared, no longer caring about remaining hidden. "Is it? How about this?"

I was punching him wildly now, raining a flurry of blows into the chalky flesh, not registering how easily my fists struck against the bones beneath. I barely heard the crack of Tom's nose beneath my knuckles, but I did hear the yell of the nurse who had just seen me through the window. I ran, frantically pressing my face against the glass, only to see a white plimsolled foot vanish through the swishing ward doors.

My breathing finally beginning to slow back down to sub-psycho levels, I made my way back to the prone figure on the bed, blood trickling down from his shattered nose. I thought about how my whole day had spun off course because of him.

"I control my life," I whispered menacingly. "Not you, understand?" With that, I ran out of the tiny room and sprinted down the corridor away from the foyer. I would have to find another way out.

Five minutes later, after crashing through a fire escape, I was crouching against the red bricks of the hospital, panting into my hands. I was fairly certain that I had taken a route that had meandered through the hospital just enough for nobody to have followed me, but I had stopped running when I had seen the police car pull into the car park. Cautiously peeking out from behind one of the benches, I watched as the flustered nurse came out of the building, gestured to the police officers and led them back inside.

I paled and looked down at my hands, still stained with Tom's blood. The severity of my actions crashed over me and before I could stop myself, I was crying into my scarlet palms. I wasn't usually a violent person, but in the same day I had somehow got into a fight with one of my teammates, then gone mental on a coma patient. What the hell was happening to me? Why had I become so angry? It all boiled down to that phrase, Caedo Tu – just thinking about it made my heart beat faster again, and I struggled to force the words out of my mind.

It was then that I realised I still had the crumpled yearbook from Tom's hospital room. In an attempt to distract myself, I began to flick through the pages, my tears finally diminishing into a string of pathetic sniffles. As I was expecting, each page was filled with rows of student photos – all pulling the cringiest poses and grins to make them look as cool as possible. Underneath the typical quotes ripped straight from famous actors, philosophers and characters, some students had written personal messages to their sick friend. A lump rose in my throat as I read the *get well soon*s and the *miss you*s, each one burning the severity of my actions into my conscience.

I turned the page and saw my own goofy face looking back at me, a genuine smile on a carefree day. It had been a

long time since I had felt like that, but obviously Jonny the
yearbook photographer had put me at ease.

*Alexander Marshall – First year rules! Although next year
BMU are going down, Centaurs for the cup!*

Feeling the threat of tears again, I hastily turned to the
next page, where I found Tom's picture. He was also smiling,
a warm and friendly expression that was a million miles from
the prone form lying in the hospital bed. Despite wearing a t-
shirt with the dreaded words on it, there was nothing else out
of the ordinary. As I stared, the picture seemed to move,
Tom's happiness falling away as his face contorted into a
scream. I blinked the image away, pushing my guilt back
below the surface. I read his comment to try and focus on
the boy he was, rather than the boy I had just attacked.

*Thomas Ferrier – Forget the skate park. I pull my 360s up at
Morgan's Car Park, where the answers lie...*

My eyes widened as I read. Where the answers lie? I
turned to look across the skyline of the city, where Morgan's
tower stood out above the trees and surrounding buildings,
already lit up by powerful floodlights in the fading sky. In his
own way, Tom had given me an answer after all. Dropping
the yearbook, I ran across the hospital car park and headed
for the tower.

JACK

"Marie, wait!" I had followed her into the UCE quad, a large grassy area set between the main teaching blocks. Pathways criss-crossed over the grass, and a large oak tree stood in each corner. The music from the Union was now a faint thumping in the background.

She whirled around, her teeth visibly gritted. "What exactly do you want, Jack?" She sighed, sounding fed up now more than anything else. "I'm not your girlfriend anymore."

"You were yesterday." I couldn't help myself. "I just don't understand what could have changed overnight. What made you suddenly hate me?"

"I don't hate you Jack," she said, rolling her eyes. "I just don't need you right now." I guess I deserved that, after pulling a cliché on her just a moment before.

"That's not an answer," I muttered, before remembering the real reason for my frustration. "And I can't believe you bin me this morning, and now you're out here as if nothing has happened."

"You're out too," she snapped. "What did you want, me to be sitting at home crying into my pillow?"

"Of course I don't want that," I said with a shake of my head. "And anyway, I'm not out by choice, the guys dragged me here." I felt my cheeks flushing even before the lame excuse had finished coming out of my mouth.

"You're telling me this like I actually care," Marie said, glaring at me with exasperation. "What do I have to do to get you to leave me alone, Jack?" It sounded as if she was trying to force me away on purpose. Perhaps that was it? Suddenly my mind was filled with all the crappy TV dramas I'd watched on Sunday afternoons, nursing a Saturday night hangover. Overly tanned Americans were always breaking up with each other to avoid revealing some big piece of news. Maybe Marie was ill?

"I'm not going to abandon you just because you think you don't want to be with me." Judging by Marie's mouth, now wide open in aghast, this was evidently not the best thing to have said.

"Are you saying I'm some sort of drone that can't make her own decisions?" she yelled. "I don't *think* I don't want you, I *know* I don't."

"You don't mean that."

"Try me."

I couldn't believe my ears. The bitchy side of my ex-girlfriend had been close to the surface for a while now, but I still had to plough on, as long as there was any small hope that she was making a mistake.

"No," I said flatly. "You've never had a boyfriend for longer than this because every time you start to feel something, you get scared of the commitment." I paused, waiting to see if she would refute my psychoanalysis. She scowled lividly but remained silent. "You loved me, Marie. I know you did. I felt it, and so did you. But now you're afraid. So now you'll do anything you can to get rid of me as long as you don't have to sign your life away to one guy. Even if you have to lie about it, I know Marie, and I don't care! We can work this out. Together."

I paused triumphantly, convinced that I had verbally beaten her into submission. As an English student, I had finely honed skills in character analysis, although I'd never used them on a real person before.

A brief flicker of surprise passed across Marie's face, and for that split second before she returned to fierce indignation, I thought I had won her over.

"You couldn't be more wrong," she snorted. "You really want to know why I split up with you?"

I looked into her eyes to see if there was any clues as to what might come next. It was either going to be 'Jack I'm dying,' or 'Jack I wish *you* were dying.' Would it make me a bastard if I hoped for the first option?

"The truth is I *do* hate you," she stated brutally. "All of your predictable little ways, your life just makes me sick."

I felt the familiar sting of tears building in the corners of my eyes, and I wondered if there was anything left inside to pour out.

"You're pathetic. Everything has to be perfectly planned out for you, and when something doesn't go exactly right, it ruins everything. You have no capability to understand freedom, spontaneity or experimentation. You're the drone Jack, not me."

She paused, as if daring me to defend myself, but I knew that if I opened my mouth, I wouldn't be able to hold back the sobs.

"At first I thought I could still use you," Marie went on with a fresh wave of destruction. "A girl doesn't just need personality, but you're not even good for that, are you Jack?"

I winced, willing her to stop, but she was warming to her tirade now and I knew she wouldn't relent until I was reduced to nothing.

"I think you managed it maybe once but that was all, and I was so drunk I barely noticed. What could anyone see in you?"

Again, she paused and again, I couldn't answer. It was as if her venomous insults had erased all the positives I knew I had. My mind went blank and I couldn't remember a single redeeming quality.

"Now do you get it?" she asked. "I couldn't stay with you, not the way you are. You're such a fucking parasite, sucking the life out of everything. After about a month, I felt just as dull and predictable as you, so I had to do something Jack. Something to relieve the boredom. Know what I mean?" She smiled harshly and I knew exactly what she meant. I was crushed. If what she was saying was true, then she'd spent more of our relationship cheating on me than she had being faithful. Despite every instinct telling me not to, I finally found my voice, at the same time relinquishing my hold on the tears that were now falling freely down my cheeks.

"Who?" I managed, forcing myself to look at the grin Marie was wearing. She was obviously relishing the prolonged pain she was causing me.

"Luke Ashford."

"No," I winced. Of course it would make sense that one of the popular girls would end up with the football star – my life *was* becoming crappy American drama after all.

"Yup," she nodded triumphantly. "You must have seen him."

I had.

"He's probably the exact binary opposite of you."

He was.

"Tall and gorgeous, packed full of rippling muscles, exactly where it matters. And the football!" she exclaimed loudly. "It's certainly taught him some useful manoeuvres – although after being with you, sleeping with a corpse would be a refreshing and exciting experience."

I looked down at my feet, my resolve crumbling with every barb she lashed at me.

"So you see why I had to leave you? I had to get out before I went mad and killed myself. Now fuck off Jack, before I call the police."

There was an awkward pause as we both waited to see if the other would speak. I couldn't think of anything to defend myself with, as if the barrage Marie had dealt me had destroyed my ability to structure a response.

Obviously not needing to add any more insults to her artillery, Marie turned and continued out across the quad.

ADAM

The Union was looking a lot emptier now. There was no queue at the bar, and I could actually see empty patches of dance floor. Most of the remaining students were either lounging on chairs, with puffy eyes and rosy cheeks, or were still out on the floor, their movements reduced to a half-hearted shambling wobble.

Without warning, the house lights flared up, illuminating everything in stark white. I called this moment of the evening the 'harsh reality' as this was when you saw what the people you were dancing with or recklessly groping truly looked like. In my tenure as a Firefly, I had seen many an awkward unclasping of hands and mouths once the truth had been revealed.

The DJ made his closing speech, wishing everyone well on their way, with an extra reminder to be safe in light of the recent news about the death in the forest. The random clusters of people turned into a steady flow towards the exits. The Gaultier guy and his mates were passing by when they stopped, their leader pulling his phone out of his pocket. He dialled whilst his companions stood there bleary eyed, hands stuffed into their pockets.

"Alright Jack, you skank. Obviously got more than a phone number eh mate? We're homeward bound now so we'll get the details tomorrow. Have a good night, see ya!"

"Use protection!" one of the others shouted over his shoulder as he hung up. All three of them erupted into laughter and I couldn't help but smile. One of their number had obviously got lucky before the dreaded lights-on moment. Not to be outdone, I noticed Gaultier spy a lone girl leaning against one of the walls. He sauntered over to her and they started to talk, and I could tell the night wasn't going to end badly for him either.

I sighed as I turned away from the last few leavers and grabbed a broom from against the wall. This was the least favourite part of the job – the cleanup, yet I'd still volunteered for it in an attempt to prolong my return home. Sometimes it was ok, but other times there was all manner of hideous substances to clean up. Luckily, as I swept my way around the bar, tonight was looking fairly standard.

I waved goodnight to the other Fireflies as I finished the sweeping. They'd already cleared the tables of all the empty glasses, crisp packets, spilled peanuts and chewed up straws. All that remained now was to lift one set of tables onto the other to make room for the morning cleaner's buffing machine.

I'm the first to admit that whilst not exactly scrawny, I'm not a meathead either, and lifting the first table was enough to make me grunt with effort. After a few moments of struggling, I managed to slam it roughly onto its counterpart. Already weakened, I moved over to the next table, getting ready to brace myself against the wall this time.

"Hey Firefly."

I turned around and came face to face with Luke. "Um, hey Centaur," I replied before realising how dumb that sounded out loud.

"Have you seen my jacket? It's black." He was wavering slightly, obviously feeling the toll of the many snakebites he had bought. It was funny how he looked cute even when drunk, not deteriorating into a sweaty blotchy mess like some of his teammates. I stared at him for a second, weighing my options. Normally I would never have dared to speak to him, but I could clearly see he was still riding the booze high, and after my horrendous family dinner, I thought I deserved to try. The final decider was remembering what my brother had said at the cafe. More than anything else, it was about time I talked to Luke properly.

"A black jacket?" I ventured. "That doesn't exactly narrow it down."

Luke narrowed his eyes for a second as if trying to work me out, then laughed. "No I suppose not. Well... I guess I'll leave it." He turned to the door, but I leaned forwards desperately.

"Don't go!" I yelled, louder than I had intended, sending the sound echoing around the empty dancefloor. I was a hair's breadth away from actually grabbing his arm. He looked back at me questioningly as I floundered for something to say that would justify my embarrassingly needy outburst. "Somebody might have handed it in," I reasoned. "I'll go and check for you." Cheeks burning, I left Luke waiting by the wall as I returned to the bar, heading into the cramped cupboard like area where the staff took their breaks. By some bizarre coincidence, there actually was a black jacket there, and I recognised it instantly as the one Luke had been wearing earlier. "Tadaa," I chirped as I reappeared, holding the jacket out in front of me like a victory flag.

With a grin, Luke stepped forwards to take the jacket before swinging it over his shoulders. I figured that was going to be the extent of my Luke adventure so I returned to the odious table lifting, unaware that my idol had for some reason stopped to watch me. I set my hands on the edge, forced my back against the wall and heaved with all my might. The table barely moved and I blushed furiously when I noticed Luke approaching, shaking his head.

"Whoa there, little dude." Condescending, but meh – I'd take it. "You shouldn't be lifting those by yourself. Here, let me help."

"It's ok, you probably have friends waiting," I muttered through my embarrassment.

"Hey, you found my jacket, it's the least I can do," he said with a warm smile. "Besides, I'm sure they won't mind waiting a bit longer."

"Ok," I nodded, trying to sound like I wasn't bothered either way.

It turned out that when Luke said he would help me, he actually meant he would do it for me, as he was easily capable of lifting the tables alone. I was content to lean back against the wall and watch his biceps.

"So you're a football fan eh?" he asked as he moved along to the next table.

In an instant, I was suddenly defensive. "What makes you say that?"

"I've seen you watching us practice," he said with a sly grin. "And I bet you've been to a few matches too, right? It's the thrill of the game, it brings in a lot of fans."

"Something like that," I murmured, avoiding his gaze as he hoisted another table.

"There you go," Luke said contentedly, stretching as he admired the now tidy Union.

"Thanks a lot."

"Any time."

We both stood silently, and although Luke seemed completely at ease, I was struggling. I kept almost looking into his eyes but then bailing out at the last moment. I was afraid that if I looked at him looking at me, I would see how he felt, which was probably indifferent.

"Well, see you at next practice, I guess." I said lamely. He reached out and patted me gently on the shoulder – not the usual fist bumping, back slapping horseplay I would have expected from a footballer. Every muscle in my body tensed under his touch and before I could stop myself, I was blurting. "It's not the thrill of the game."

I turned away again. I'd stepped too far over the line now.

"I know..."

What? I looked up in surprise, our eyes meeting properly for the first time. Luke was wearing a confident smile, like he knew what was coming next whereas I could only watch with wide eyed expectancy. He leaned in, closing his eyes before gently kissing me on the lips. His own lips were soft and cool, but he only held them there for a second, as if testing my resistance. I wasn't going to give him any.

Throwing away all of my shyness, I leaned forwards and kissed him back, bringing every one of my sketches flourishing into life. Luke responded by grabbing me roughly and pulling me into him, jamming his tongue into my mouth, the beginnings of stubble grazing tantalizingly across my jawline.

Soon I was clawing at his shirt, pulling the buttons open and sliding my hands across his smooth chest, searching out every contour. He held me there and let me explore. I felt my confidence growing. I slid my hands down his torso, hooking fingers into the waistband of his jeans. This was rapidly turning into a real life version of my self-abuse fantasy from earlier. Still Luke offered no objection, so I took the plunge and slipped a hand into his shorts. He tilted his head back and both of our bodies seemed to flash with heat.

"Luke?"

Both our eyes snapped open to see one of the other Centaurs staring in confusion. Where Luke had charm and refinement, this guy was a typical dumb jock, his pig-like eyes utterly failing to comprehend what he was seeing. I hastily pulled my hand away and looked up at Luke for guidance.

Was he going to explain? Surely if the Captain of the team was ok with it, then the others would just have to deal.

Instead, Luke rammed me so hard in the chest that I fell to the floor, jarring my elbow as I landed sprawling on the black tiles.

"What the fuck are you doing, you sick bastard!" he yelled. I looked up at him, horrified. What angle was he aiming for? Luke turned to his team mate. "I came in to get my jacket and this guy jumped on me!"

What the hell was he saying? That wasn't how it was!

"He's sober, I didn't react quick enough..."

As I heard my dreams shrivel and die, I felt tears in my eyes and I desperately tried to hold them back. If this was how it was going to go, I was determined not to make a show of myself – not to prove my father right.

Luke turned away, and the other guy's face contorted into a mask of disgust. It wasn't long before I felt his rough hands grab the scruff of my neck and start dragging me across the floor. I couldn't hope to fight back.

I was hauled through the fire exit and dumped unceremoniously on the cold tarmac of the Union car park. Standing in a rough semi-circle were the rest of the pack, huddling against the night's chill, breath rising in ragged bursts. As one, they eyed me with interest, waiting for some sort of explanation as to why this sacrifice had been thrust before them. Luke appeared, hurriedly buttoning his shirt and avoiding the gaze of the others. It appeared he had Judased his way out of the situation inside – my fate now rested solely in the eloquence of the lunkhead who had brought me out here. I abandoned hope as I watched him furrow his brow, trying to work out what he was going to say.

"This fucking Firefly..." he began haltingly. "He was... Luke... He fucking pounced on Luke... fucking molesting him or something... fucking wrong!"

Despite the obvious lack of literacy, the rest of the team seemed to grasp the concept fairly well, some of them looking towards Luke for some sort of verification. Their Captain said nothing, merely wiping his mouth on his sleeve as if disgusted by the taste I had left there. He seemed to have forgotten that he started it.

For the rest of them, the matter was cemented. They started advancing, keeping their semi-circle formation so as to pen me in. Their faces changed as every ounce of predatory training the Coach had drilled into them ignited in their puny minds.

"Please," I whimpered, the desire for self-preservation finally kicking in all too late.

The first blow came as a shock even though I had seen the footballer pull his leg back with almost theatrical grace. In a flash, I was surrounded by howling, jeering and swearing creatures. It was hard to think of them as human as they rained punch after punch, kick after kick down on my curled form, especially when you considered the reason *why* they were doing it with such ferocity. Instinctively trying to protect my face, I rolled over and caught a glimpse of Luke through the legs of my attackers. He was holding back, watching every hit with an unreadable expression. I thought about trying to signal to him somehow, trying to remind him of the spark I was sure he felt back in the Union. If he wasn't ready to admit anything, fine, but he didn't have to sit by and watch me get beaten to a pulp.

A size 12 connected heavily with my gut and I coughed, spitting blood from my split lips onto the grit. Suddenly, Luke launched himself from the wall and strode forwards, a strange look on his face.

"Enough!"

At once, the others stopped and took a step away from me, obeying their leader. I felt hands grab me and hoist me up until I was supported between two of the footballers. By now, one of my eyes was swollen shut, and the other was blurring. I could see the crimson stained ground beneath my feet, and could only imagine what a state my face was in.

A hand gently cupped my chin and lifted my head, and although I couldn't make out the features, I knew it was Luke. He had finally decided to end the torture. He was going to admit the truth and take me away.

I heard my nose break beneath Luke's knuckles, my world spinning as I was allowed to fall to the ground once more.

"Come near me again, and I'll kill you." This was followed by the unmistakable sound of him spitting on me, although I was too numb to feel where it landed. As they walked away without giving me a second glance, I squeezed my eyes shut - hurt, angry, disappointed and ashamed. It was a long time before I awkwardly uncurled myself and scrambled shakily to my feet.

JACK

The glare of the lights in the petrol station shop were dazzling compared to the blackness of the night outside. The attendant had paid me no heed as I wandered in, so I must have done a pretty good job of looking normal. This late, they had to buzz each person in once they'd ascertained they weren't going to cause trouble. Passing the test would certainly make things easier.

I was currently hovering by one of the shelves, piling box after box of painkillers into my arms. I caught a glimpse of my red-eyed reflection in one of the chiller cabinets – weary and haunted, but at least not crying any more. Grabbing one more rattling box and a bottle of water, I made my way over to the counter.

The greying attendant looked up as I dumped my items in front of him. He cast his eyes over the stuff, then gave me the classic up and down look you get when you're about to be ID checked. To my surprise, he merely smiled and nodded slightly, as if remembering some nostalgia from his past.

"Rough night mate?" he asked jokingly. "Stocking up for the rest of your friends?"

"Uhuh," I nodded, glad that he had supplied me with a good enough excuse.

"Well, no point in waiting for the morning after."

"Yeah... no point," I echoed, looking hollowly over the counter at him. He rang the items through the till and I chucked him two twenties, grabbing the bag and turning away before he could even get the correct change out.

ALEX

Eight storeys up, I emerged onto the roof level of Morgan's
Car Park, the cool night air making the hairs on the back of
my neck stand up. A chest high railing ran around the
perimeter, and in each of the four corners was a low brick
structure that I assumed held the mechanisms for the lifts by
each stairwell. Although the car park had long been usurped
by the more modern complex in town, the floodlights still
blazed atop their poles and it was these that gave the tower
its beacon-like glow that I had seen from the hospital.

My eyes roved keenly across the scene. This is where
the answers would be – Tom as good as told me himself. I
made my way over to the nearest brick hut, which was
covered in tattered posters and graffiti.

"Where are they?" I muttered to myself. "Where are
the answers? I have to know..." Nothing else could occupy
my thoughts at this moment – I had to know what *Caedo Tu*
was. I scanned the flyers - endless music gigs and events
plastered over one another. I wondered exactly how many
customers they drummed up from the top of a barely used
car park. That was when I saw it. Sticking out from
underneath a poster about the UCE Kill-Soc game, I could
just make out the words *The Ans,* the second word vanishing
behind one of those arty minimalist fliers that just read *Are
you a Stereotype?* My eyes widened as I realised what that
hidden word had to be. Kneeling down, I began frantically
peeling the posters away, desperate to reveal the one below.
"Come on, come on!" I yelled, aware that I was scraping my
fingers raw on the rough bricks.

Eventually, I had managed to free the hidden poster, and as I sat amidst scraps of torn paper, I got ready to receive my enlightenment.

"No..." My face fell as I scanned the poster. It was a picture of Christ, a halo shining above his head. Underneath was written the slogan *The Answers Lie With Jesus. In Him We Trust,* however somebody had crossed out the word *With* and scrawled *Through* over the top. Whoever had done it was obviously not too impressed with the word of God, but I couldn't think about that now. All I could feel was despair. I realised I was helpless. Tom had got his yearbook slogan from the stupid poster. There were no answers.

"You promised..."

ADAM

As fast as I was able, I was running along the road, passing in and out of the pools of yellow light cast by the streetlamps. I had forgotten all of my restraint and was sobbing loudly as I ran, not caring who saw me, not caring what anybody thought about the bloodstained gay boy as he fled.

I passed a parked car with a dented fender, the two men inside catching my eye as I ran past. I saw them shake their heads before I vanished around the next corner. I stopped, panting through my broken nose and staring up at the multi storey car park looming over me. The floodlights at the top were on and a soft glow was pouring invitingly out of the nearest entrance. I had been up to the top of Morgan's Car Park enough to know that hardly anybody used it. It would suit me just fine. With another loud sob, I started to jog up the grimy concrete steps.

ALEX

I hadn't moved. I was still staring blankly at the Jesus poster, my tear stained features utterly forsaken. What was left for me, if not understanding? If my actions had no reasoning behind them, then what was the point? I wondered aimlessly towards the side of the car park, when I heard one of the doors open. I thought I heard quiet sobs amidst shuffling footsteps, but when I whirled around, I could see no one. I squinted, but the only clue that anything had changed was the nearest door slowly closing, the slice of light from inside growing smaller and smaller. I paused, suddenly afraid. My first thought was Tom, but even I knew how absurd that would be. He wasn't leaving that bed for real any time soon.

"Hello?" I called tentatively. Nothing. *Sod them then.* I took one final look before returning to the railings, gripping them with both hands, the icy metal tingling against my skin. As I looked over the edge, my eyes once more widened with shock. There, daubed on the concrete below in what looked like blood, were those damned words - *Caedo Tu.* I swallowed hard as the words called up to me. I had found my answers. I knew what I had to do.

JACK

I don't know what exactly had drawn me to the car park. Perhaps it was the certainty that I wouldn't be disturbed – after all, who in their right mind would be up there at a time like this? Nobody *in their right mind*, I thought darkly.

Resolved, I started to climb the steps, casting furtive glances through every door I passed to make sure that the car park was truly empty. There wasn't a single car in sight. It didn't help that one of the floors was covered in police tape – I didn't want to think about what had gone on there earlier. I didn't want to be distracted from what I was about to do. About half way up, I stopped, head pounding as the hangover kicked in early. *Perfect*, I thought.

I shoved my bag of treats roughly onto the windowsill and ripped it open, spilling the brightly coloured pill boxes on to the clammy cream coloured tiles. If you squinted just the right way, they looked like sweets. I proceeded to take a pill for every insult Marie had ever dealt me, for every time she had made me feel like crap, washing each mouthful down with a gulp of water.

Once I'd taken them all, I dropped the now empty bottle of water and continued up the stairs, trying not to think of the hopefully now lethal mix of alcohol and painkillers sloshing around in my stomach. The last thing I wanted was an eleventh hour moment of weakness to make me stick a finger down my throat.

I made my way to the top storey, pushing the door open and bracing myself against the cool breeze as I stepped out onto the roof. The first thing I noticed was that I was not alone. There was another guy standing by the railings of the far wall. He had his back to me and seemed to be staring down at the ground below. Stepping shakily forwards, I suddenly noticed that this other man wasn't standing *by* the railings, he was *over* them – and that meant only one thing – he was probably going to jump!

As soon as I realised this, I seemed to snap into sobriety, hurrying across the car park to reach this fellow lost soul.

ALEX

I was leaning as far forwards as I could without letting go of the railings. Caedo Tu almost completely filled my field of vision, enveloping my mind and taking over my senses. The words wanted me - they called to me, and soon I would meet them.

"That's kind of dangerous, don't you think?"

I looked over my shoulder to see a guy about my age watching me with a look of concern. He was relatively smartly dressed, but his flushed cheeks and slight wobble made it obvious that he had been out drinking – had to be a fellow student.

"Leave me alone," I muttered with a helpless glare. I was lost now – there was no hope for me. I turned back to the edge, but still heard him take another step forwards. "I said get lost!" I yelled angrily. I didn't want an audience for this – it was my moment of discovery.

"Look," he began. "I've seen you with the Centaurs. Alex, right? I'm Jack. Let me help you. Nothing's worth this." It was obvious he was trying to sound as reassuring as possible. I turned once more and appraised him in detail. The wobbling was more pronounced now, and now that he was closer, I could see that his pupils were beginning to dilate, his gaze beginning to lose focus. There was more than alcohol here...

"Yeah?" I snorted. "And you got wasted then came up here for the view, I suppose?"

"That's different," he replied with a frown before staring down at his feet.

"Is it? We're both up here aren't we? I know why I am, but what about you?"

"Stop it," he snapped. "You're trying to distract me. Just come back over the rail ok? We can talk about this."

"You sure you'll last that long?" I asked, laughing despite everything.

"How can you be like this? You're treating your life like a game."

"How can I be like this?" I asked, anger bubbling up once more. "I don't want my life to be a game, you hear me? I want to control my own existence!"

JACK

I didn't understand what Alex was talking about. He was obviously mental – at least my reason for coming up here made sense. Marie had made it clear that nobody would ever love me, so why bother? But if I could save someone else, it would certainly make me feel slightly better.

"You're jumping off to prove that you're in control?" I asked, incredulous. Perhaps if I could make him realise how stupid that sounded, he would climb back over. Instead, he shook his head in exasperation.

"I'm jumping off to prove that I'm *not* in control. Don't you understand? This *is* a game, and we're all just pieces being moved. It's too late for me. Caedo Tu."

"What did you say?" My head snapped up and I struggled to align my eyes on his face. That was the phrase I had heard on the end of Marie's answerphone message. The skater she'd been all over on the dancefloor had it written on his t-shirt. Suddenly, it became vital that I saved Alex, if only to found out how he knew those words.

He took a deep breath.

I lurched forwards, arms outstretched but it all felt painfully slow. I wasn't going to reach him.

ALEX

I let go of the railing.

"What does that mean?" I heard Jack shout, but all I could do was smile for him. He would soon learn what Caedo Tu meant.

The last thing I saw was the bright red words rushing up to catch me in their twisted embrace.

JACK

Holding my breath, I leaned over the railings to see Alex sprawled on the concrete below. A single gout of blood came from his head like a crimson thought bubble. He wasn't moving.

I turned away, knowing that if I looked for too long, I would probably end up vomiting my lethal cocktail onto the grit. All I could do was gasp and blink as I staggered back from the railing. Should I have tried harder to bring the Centaur back to safety? I stumbled, the chemicals jolting through my bloodstream beginning to kick their torment up a notch.

I became aware of how hypocritical I must have sounded – after all, we had both come up here for the same reason hadn't we? Our lives had become untenable – he had just ended it quickly, whereas I was going to take a little longer to expire. Thinking of it like that, who was I to stand in his way?

The car park seemed to stretch out in front of me as I looked up, my vision wavering and contracting like I was standing on a boat, rolling across the waves. Arms outstretched, I made for the nearest of the four low brick structures, slumping against it, my head lolling as I slid to the ground. It wouldn't be long now.

A faint sobbing reached my ears, and for that first moment, I was convinced that it was my soul crying just before it was extinguished. As I listened, I realised that the sound was coming from behind the brick square I was leaning on.

"Is someone there?" I muttered, my voice weak and shaking. No reply. I gracelessly flopped onto my side, the impact reverberating through my body. I scrabbled at the grit, pulling myself forwards a meagre amount. I just made out a splash of maroon before I lost the strength to keep my eyes open.

ADAM

I leant against the rough red bricks. Everything was red now. *Incarnadine*, I told myself, my mind dredging up the word from GCSE English. My front was red from the blood that still pulsed faintly from my shattered nose. My arm was red from where moments ago I had carved the words Caedo Tu with the sharpest piece of grit I could find. And now the ground was red, a pool of scarlet, growing with every heartbeat as life fled my body.

A soft thud came from round the corner, and I shuffled around to see what it was. A boy was lying face down on the grit. Something about his shirt struck me as familiar – I was certain I'd served him earlier. I gasped when I saw the thin string of white foam leaking from his mouth. Funny how I had barely flinched when I had hacked into myself, but the sight of someone else was enough to ignite sympathy and panic.

"Hey!" I called. The boy didn't respond, although I could see the laboured rise and fall of his chest as he breathed into the gravel. He was alive at least. Next, I scooped up a handful of the tiny chunks of tarmac that always seemed to get dragged up here, wedged in various tyre grooves. I sent the spray cascading off the guy's back, but still he did not react. "Wake up!"

I don't know what made me do what I did next. In my mind, I told myself it was the desire to save this other guy from the same fate as me, but as I stared at my mutilated forearm, I couldn't deny the faintest glimmer of self-preservation I felt. I fished my phone out of my pocket and dialled 999.

TOM

My mother was sitting at my bedside. Not the cold, cruel woman who had pushed me into my grave, but the caring, affectionate mother who had looked after me for twenty one years. She had stopped crying so much, but the trauma that I had inadvertently put her through was etched into her face. I hoped that time would ease those worry lines. If I woke up.

An orderly bustled into the room to check my charts. She gave nothing more than a casual nod to my mother, revealing nothing about my condition. Has it changed? I can't tell. It's difficult to know these things when I've not exactly been *attached*.

I felt a flutter in my chest, my heart beating slightly faster than the comatose fugue state it's been used to. My mother looked questioningly first at me, then towards the orderly whose face remained blank. I realised that no matter how much planning ahead you do, everything always crashes together at the last minute. Despite my scheming, I could never have planned the end – I couldn't have physically *made* them take the plunge – I guess I just *hoped* it would all turn out okay. But my time had run out.

The steady beating of the heart monitor fused into a single monotone as I flatlined. My mother jumped up, a hand to her mouth, whilst the orderly calmly pushed a button on her pager before guiding my mother out of the room. A fleet of doctors flooded in, dragging the defibrillator with them before placing the cool paddles against my skin...

And suddenly I was out on the car park roof, immune to the icy night time breeze whipping around me. I observed calmly as paramedics burst from one of the stairwells, their eyes widening as they saw Jack lying face down in the grit, his breathing slowing to a halt before they could reach him.

One of the medics ran to the railing, perhaps to check where the ambulance had parked, and then he saw Alex sprawled down below. He yelled, and two of his colleagues returned to the stairwell, but I already knew they were rushing in vain. The eyes of the Centaur stopped blinking blood out of them and glazed over, frozen in a deathly stare.

Another flutter racked my chest, and I was back in the hospital room, the heart monitor beeping steadily once more. I had been granted my reprieve by those at the car park.

My eyes snapped open and I sat up, gasping as if just emerging from under water. I cast my eyes around the room, desperately searching for that one face – and there she was, behind the glass, tears coursing down her cheeks.

I didn't take my eyes away from my mother, even as one of the doctors placed his hand on my forehead, gently forcing me back against the pillow. There was a sharp sting as another man injected something into my arm.

A warm and fuzzy sensation spread through my body, like my insides were turning to cotton wool. I lay back, and nothing seemed to matter anymore. Satisfied that I was settled, the doctors left my room and vanished down the corridor, my mother sweeping in to take their place, gripping my hand with devotion. I closed my eyes.

I didn't know how long had passed when I next looked up at the ceiling lights, but I was aware that now I was awake, *truly* awake, I had lost my omniscience. I had no idea that just a few metres down the corridor, Alex Marshall's parents were standing tearfully over their son's body as a nurse gave them the bad news. I didn't see the next room along, where Jack's housemates were gathered solemnly around their friend, too late to save him. Sorrow seeped through the corridor like rot, but I was content. Their suffering had ended mine.

The next day, the sun shone brightly through the open curtains. It felt like I hadn't seen it for weeks. I stood next to the open window, revelling in the breeze that played across my skin. My mother had brought a fresh t-shirt and clean shorts from home, and I'd finally been allowed in the shower unsupervised. It felt good to be out of the scratchy hospital gown.

Aware that I technically hadn't used my legs for days, I slowly moved towards the door. Now that I was up and about, I was anxious to leave the ward, but the doctors had said there was still a lot of healing to do on the inside.

I stepped into the corridor just as an orderly was pushing his trolley absent-mindedly along. His wrinkled face creased into a warm smile as I approached.

"Looks like you're making a miracle recovery," he noted.

"Yeah," I grinned. "Looks like I am."

"That nose is going to be crooked though."

I shrugged. I couldn't remember breaking my nose in the accident, but nor could I remember anything else happening to it. In the grand scheme of things, it wasn't a deal breaker. I had fallen into step with the orderly, the two of us slowly meandering up the corridor. My speed of atrophy matched his speed of age. We walked slowly past one of the rooms where a girl sat holding the hand of the guy inside. I couldn't help reading the name on the wall chart - L. Brennan. I wondered what had happened to him.

"It's quite a coincidence really," the orderly continued as we walked past a couple more rooms – empty this time. "The same night you wake up, we get a few victims of some weird suicide cult…"

"Oh?" I stumbled slightly, catching hold of one of the many handles protruding from the orderly's cart. I tried to feign an interested expression as I waited for him to continue. There was no way I could be linked to Alex and Jack's deaths – after all, what I had done was pretty impossible.

"Yeah," the orderly wheezed. "They were up on Morgan's Car Park. All three of them were brought in last night. It wasn't pretty, I can tell you..." I froze whilst the orderly trundled a few steps ahead. Once he noticed I wasn't next to him, he stopped and slowly turned around. He looked me up and down appraisingly, as if trying to judge my physical and mental condition with one glance. Instead of speaking, he raised an eyebrow.

"Three of them?" I asked. "What do you mean there were three of them?"

The orderly was shaking his head now, eyes glancing up and down the corridor, no doubt hoping for a doctor to appear.

"There can't be," I muttered, the jumbled thoughts of my convalescence cascading around my head. "I only used... who??"

I was expecting Alex and Jack, but who was the third? Was there someone else that had fallen victim to my manipulations?

The orderly glanced towards the window of the next room along, quickly changing his expression when he saw that I had noticed. Despite my body's protests, I ran to the window and my face fell.

My best friend was lying on the other side of the glass. Adam Lane had bandages wrapped across his wrists and his nose was in plaster. Mrs Lane and Adam's brother Andrew were sitting by the bed.

"No..."

How had he become caught up in all this? I hadn't gone anywhere near him! I appeared to Alex on the football pitch, and I made sure Jack saw me at the Union, but I had left Adam alone. Why was he here? My mind started racing through all the different possibilities – maybe it was just a coincidence? But no, the orderly had said they were all brought in together. Adam must have been with Jack and Alex at the same place, but I was sure they didn't really know each other. Tears began to sting my eyes as I realised that I had caused the death of my best friend. The other two were just randoms – they meant nothing to me, but I had spent so much time with Adam, sharing so much with him that it felt that I had woken up with a bit missing. Had this connection somehow dragged him into it without me knowing?

"Are you alright?" It was the orderly, looking at me quizzically. I didn't answer, lost in memory.

The sun was shining on the bright summer's afternoon. It was a couple of years ago, before UCE and Caedo Tu. Adam and I had opted for our usual routine of skiving off Friday afternoon at college and chilling out on top of Morgan's Car Park. With only a few drivers ever being bothered to make it all the way to the top, it was the perfect place for me to practice my skateboarding. Adam liked to watch me make a fool of myself, and we'd talk. We'd talk about girls, boys, going to uni next year – anything really. It was our place to hang.

The makeshift grindrail I had constructed out of an old clothes rack was set up by one of the ramps. There was no point using the official skate park, as it was always full of total bells. I was considering finally plucking up the courage to attempt a grind, whilst Adam cracked a beer. He was leaning against one of the lift housings, his sunglasses pushed up over his hair. He was watching me expectantly.

It was now or never. I kicked off and skated towards the rail. At the last moment, I jumped, the black skull-print board rising with me, and then – I never was sure how I did it – I flipped the board, landed on the rail and managed to flip off without breaking my neck. Adam erupted into applause behind me.

"Did you see that?" I yelled, exuberant.

"I did indeed."

"I'm never gonna be able to do that again," I panted as the adrenaline faded from my system. "You just witnessed a once in a lifetime event – like Hindenburg or something."

"But with slightly less emotional trauma," Adam rallied with a smirk.

I plastered my face with mock defensiveness. "Only slightly!"

Adam grinned as he took another gulp from his can. I scooped up one of my own, snatched the glasses from Adam's head then sat down beside him, cracking the ring pull.

We sat together for a few moments, simply enjoying the atmosphere. Eventually, Adam turned his attention to the myriad of posters covering the crumbling brickwork. A frown crossed his face as his eyes scanned one of the recent additions.

"Uhoh!" I exclaimed with a smile. "I know that face. What have you seen?"

Adam rolled his eyes. "Have you read that shit? It really winds me up."

I followed his accusatory finger to a poster depicting Jesus smiling benevolently. Underneath was written the slogan *The Answers Lie With Jesus. In Him We Trust.*

"Ah yes," I laughed. "Christ hates the gays, so the gays hate Christ."

"I just don't see why a religion who follows the teachings of a guy who went around the desert in sandals and a dress can be so anti gay," Adam went on indignantly. "Jesus has to be like history's biggest closet case ever."

"You'll go to Hell for that," I warned, a big smile on my face.

"Well if I'm already going…" Adam said smugly, before taking a marker pen out of his bag. He crossed out the word 'with' and wrote 'through' over the top. "There," he said, satisfied. "That's more accurate."

"To Jesus," I cheered, raising my can. "The biggest closet case ever."

Adam rolled his eyes once more, but raised his can anyway. "To Jesus. Where the answers lie, apparently." We smashed our cans together jubilantly, then proceeded to down the contents.

That day seemed worlds away now, and I wondered if we would ever get to spend time together like that again. As I stared through the thick glass at Adam's prone form, another memory drifted to the front of my mind.

As usual, I was lying in the hospital bed, eyes closed, bandages wrapped around my healing ribs. Also as usual, the seat next to the bed was occupied by a sorrowful visitor, but it wasn't my mother this time. It was Adam. He leaned towards my ear.

"I don't know if you can hear me but, well…" He looked around awkwardly, almost as if he was embarrassed talking to a coma patient. I wished that I could have done something – moved slightly, or blinked – to show him that he wasn't wasting his time, but I think at that time my mind was busy elsewhere with Jack or Alex.

Adam lifted up what seemed to be some sort of book. "I got you this," he said quietly. "It's not much, but all the guys have signed it for you." I could see now that it was a UCE yearbook, and Adam began to absent-mindedly flick through the pages, reading out some of the comments and 'get well soon' messages from my coursemates.

After a few minutes, Adam set the yearbook on the bedside table and leaned in once more, placing a tender hand on my shoulder.

"They miss you," he began wistfully. "I miss you. Wake up soon, ok mate?" He squeezed my shoulder gently, sniffing to hold back tears. Adam always was a sensitive guy, and even though I was the one in the coma, I couldn't help feeling sorry for him. He got up to leave, then seemed to think better of it. He returned to my side, a look of desperation flashing briefly across his delicate features. "You wouldn't do anything like this… on purpose just to be part of the chain would you?" He was talking about Caedo Tu – the belief that somebody near death could save themselves by sacrificing others. I had found it whilst trawling the emo and skater sites online, and whilst I hadn't really believed it at the time, I'd still invested enough in it to get the t-shirt. Ironic really, that in the end it had turned out to be real, and had in fact saved me from my own demise.

"You're not stupid Tom, but… No. I trust you. Just… I'll see you soon, ok." He turned and left the room.

Adam's final words were ominous somehow. Was that his goodbye? Had he thought I'd put myself there on purpose, so he felt he had to get me out of it? After all, I was certain that I hadn't led him to his death, but maybe the strength of our friendship was enough to make him sacrifice himself for me?

"I didn't even do anything to him," I muttered, as if voicing it out loud would somehow change the situation we were in. "I made sure I left him out. Made sure I focused on the other two. This wasn't meant to happen."

"Well that's the thing isn't it…" I jumped as the orderly spoke, his voice little more than a croak. I had completely forgotten he was there, but now he was looking at me, nodding with some sort of hidden understanding. Suddenly, he grabbed the handle of his trolley and shuffled back up the corridor. "Nobody gets out for free." I frowned. "Not in Caedo Tu…" The squeaking of the trolley's wheels faded as the orderly disappeared around the corner.

I felt my cheeks redden as anger coursed through my veins. Was he saying that Adam's death was my punishment? It couldn't be. I gritted my teeth and turned towards the door of Adam's room. I had to see for myself. I had to see that I wasn't to blame.

Mrs Lane and Andrew looked up as I entered. Andrew stood to greet me with a nod, whilst his mother looked solemnly back into her lap. I dared not look at Adam's pale face. Just a day ago, I was in that position, and I felt like shit lording my recovery over them.

"I'm glad you're ok, Tom," Andrew said, placing his hand on my shoulder just as his younger brother had done. Mrs Lane let out a quiet sob. I wondered where Adam's father was.

"I'm sorry," I mumbled, inclining my head towards the bed. "What happened?" I was aware that it was probably a tactless question, but I had to know as much as I could. I was desperate for anything that could free me of my guilt.

Andrew looked fondly down at his brother. He was an important suit somewhere in the city, but now his shirt was ruffled and his sandy hair stuck out at awkward angles. His face was pale.

"He lost a lot of blood," Andrew said with a strained voice. "I've given him as much as I can, and the doctors say that it's possible for the body to remake the rest gradually. There's a good chance that Adam will wake up."

My brain stalled. "He's not..?" I couldn't believe it, but as I finally brought myself to look closely at my stricken friend, I could see that his chest was in fact rising and falling faintly.

Andrew looked at me, brows furrowed. "No. A coma. Similar to yours I think." Andrew looked down once more, brushing a strand of hair from Adam's face. "We're still not sure why he did it." This time Mrs Lane cried more loudly, Andrew rushing to comfort her. I turned, not wanting to intrude on the family moment. I was also aware that my cheeks were burning with culpability. I was glad Adam had survived, but that still didn't change the fact that he might have hurt himself to save me.

As I glanced back at the window, I saw a face retreat away from the glass. I couldn't make out who it was, but I thought I recognised a Centaurs football shirt. I put the figure out of my mind and looked back at Adam.

"I'm sorry…"

LUKE

As soon as I noticed Tom looking, I spun away from the glass and leaned against the wall. I hoped he wouldn't come out into the corridor. Before I knew it, I was shuddering violently. I wrapped my arms around myself and squeezed my eyes shut, waiting for it to pass, but I still couldn't escape the knowledge that Adam Lane was my fault. I couldn't stay here anymore. I stuffed my hands into my pockets and hurried from the hospital.

The cold air hit me like a brick wall as soon as I had sprinted through the automatic doors. My stride broken, I glanced around to see if anybody had seen, immediately cursing myself for still being so self-obsessed after everything. Who cared if anybody saw me in a state? As I'd just seen, it could have been a lot worse.

Across the car park, a couple were sitting, and I couldn't help wondering why they were here. Were they about to come in, or just about to leave? Thinking about them helped distract me briefly from the awful mess I'd caused.

Closer to me, a girl was alone on one of the benches, lost in thought. Her elbows were resting on her knees, her head sullenly pressed against her palms. Without quite realising why, I went and hovered next to the seat until the girl looked up. I recognised her, and instantly knew why she was there. Marie shuffled across slightly to let me sit.

"I heard about your boyfriend," I ventured. I didn't actually know Jack, but the guy who overdosed himself to death was the talk of the campus. *One* of the talks of the campus, I corrected myself.

"He isn't... he wasn't my boyfriend." Marie looked across at me, eyes ringed and raw.

"Oh," I mumbled, cursing myself again. "I'm sorry." We sat in silence for what felt like a lifetime before I tried to rekindle the conversation. "So did you see him before...?" Marie started to cry so I put my arm tentatively around her shoulder.

"You know what the last thing I said to him was?" she sniffed.

A hundred different possibilities crossed through my mind, but none of them seemed worse than what I did to Adam.

"I told him to fuck off," she continued. "I insulted him so badly. I lied to him. I told him that I'd slept with... somebody else, but none of it was true. I didn't mean for this."

"Why did you say those things then?" I said, aware of how hypocritical I was sounding to myself.

"You've never said something you didn't mean?" Marie snapped, a flicker of 'spoilt rich girl' emerging briefly. I looked down awkwardly, my cheeks flushing. I was the king of saying things I didn't mean lately. "I was selfish," she continued with a sigh. "I took the easy way out because I didn't want the hassle of explaining myself. But Jack never gave up on me." A crystal tear formed then traced a single streak down her face. "I guess I made him give up on himself." She sobbed harder, tears flowing freely now. "I as good as killed him. I might as well just have fed him those pills myself." Marie sniffled, dabbing at her eyes with the corner of her sleeve. I looked around the car park uncomfortably while she regained her composure. I could tell she was feeling just as guilty as I was. "God, listen to me," she said sullenly. "A couple of days ago, I wouldn't have given a shit. I suppose there's nothing like a tragedy to make you realise what a bitch you are."

I nodded, applying her words to myself and Adam. "How's Alex?"

"Huh?" I asked, confused at the subject change.

"Your team mate. Isn't that why you're here?"

"Oh," I shrugged. "He didn't make it either." As soon as I realised what Adam had done, I forgot all about Alex Marshall's suicide jump. My last moments with him hadn't exactly been spectacular either, but I was fairly certain I wasn't responsible for his death.

"I'm sorry," Marie offered hollowly. We sat in silence again, wallowing in our individual pools of grief and regret. "Well," Marie ventured after a moment, "I better…"

"Yeah…"

Marie stood up, smoothing down her skirt and giving her eyes a final wipe before she set out across the car park. "I'll see you."

"You're right you know," I called after her, wanting her to know that what she'd said was true. She turned inquisitively, awaiting my next words, and I was suddenly torn between confessing what I'd done to Adam, and offering more hollow sympathy. I settled for the middle ground. "It does take a tragedy."

She gave a weak half smile before turning again. I stood up and resolved to go back inside to face the boy I'd ruined.

TOM

After a week had passed, I was allowed home. It had taken a couple of days for my mother to relinquish me from her protective clutches – she seemed convinced that as soon as I left the house, I would get hurt again – but I had eventually managed to escape when she had to go to work.

The first place I had gone to was Morgan's Car Park, newly reopened after the police tape had been removed. It turned out that Friday had been quite eventful – some other kids had run into trouble there in the afternoon, but I couldn't worry about that. I had something important to do.

The sun was out and the breeze was blowing through my hair, much longer following the neglect it had received in the hospital. It was a lot like the days me and Adam used to hang here, and I fancied I could almost hear our laughter echoing forward from a forgotten time.

I had got what I wanted, so why wasn't I happy? Because everyone was right. It was true. Nobody gets anything for free. There's always a price to be paid. Maybe not straight away, but eventually we pay for everything we do. Humanity is so stubborn, calling it luck or coincidence – anything we can invent to protect us from the truth – that we are all part of a worldwide debt collection scheme. The only things that break this resolve are the disasters, the summits of luck or coincidence that smash the very words to pieces. That is when humanity changes.

I thought about how on the other side of the city, a university football star was taking the hand of the boy he'd inadvertently put in hospital. For some people, it was about realising something they always knew, but could never express. The fear of others' opinions had been shaken loose and for the first time, they were free, even if they knew their crimes could never be forgiven.

My mind wandered across town to the graveyard, where the popular girl dropped a single rose at the grave of the boy she treated like dirt. For her, the change came when she realised that image came second to love, and that if she could take back that one defining moment, she would, no question.

Back to me, standing on the top of the world. What had I learned from all this? I thought I could deal with my salvation. But it doesn't matter why you kill someone, you're still a killer, and I'd killed two people, maybe three - people who could have been friends, enemies, companions, lovers or heroes if they'd had the chance, but thanks to me, they hadn't. I was so preoccupied with the fact that I could save myself, I never even wondered if I should. Perhaps that was meant to be my time to die? Maybe I was *destined* to get hit by that car? But we never did hold much stock with destiny. Human nature had done it again, unsatisfied with being out of control. At least now I was sure of one thing…

I pulled off my t-shirt. *The* t-shirt. I held it front of me like a flag, gripping it with only the tips of my thumb and forefinger. It represented this whole experience, and I was loath to touch it now. With my free hand, I pulled a lighter out of my pocket.

"The chain has to end," I stated as I held the flames to the cotton. Once they had taken hold, I dropped the shirt onto the concrete, watching defiantly as the words 'Caedo Tu' curled and smouldered in the fire.

EPILOGUE

ADAM

I woke up. Except I wasn't awake. Not really. I knew this because I could see myself lying in a hospital bed in the centre of a bland room, connected to a dozen machines branching out of me at all angles like I was Frankenstein's monster. My wrists were both bandaged heavily and my skin was pallid.

Looking down at myself, I almost seemed peaceful although I could tell there was something going on behind my eyes – probably the weird out of body thing that was going on.

On the side least cluttered by beeping monitors, Luke was sitting. A rush of warmth flooded through me as I saw he was holding my hand. Better late than never.

They say that everything in life is balanced, and that energy is neither created nor destroyed. As one chain ends, another begins. I was sleeping now, and I wondered. How many lives would it take to buy back my own?

I thought back to the last people I saw before the blackness – two miscreants in the car with the dented bumper - and I smiled.

KILL-SOC

Prologue – One Year Ago

4:50 pm

Jimmy's legs ached as he crouched behind the dumpster. He was breathing shallowly, trying to be as quiet as possible. Silence and stealth would be the key to a successful hit.

Days before, he had scoped out where his target worked, his habits and routines, the routes he took and the people he walked with. Today for instance, his target's colleague had been called away for a family matter – something which Jimmy had gone to great length to organise. Today, the target would be alone.

Jimmy had a small backpack on, in which he carried his spare ammunition and a collection of photos – each one detailing a previous victim, with a cross to signify the kill. He knew his rival would have a similar set although he was certain that most people wouldn't feel the same about carrying them around. For Jimmy, it was a thrill. He liked to stay close to all the victims he had ended, liked to be able to flick through them any time he wanted, reliving each particular kill. He thought about whether they begged and pleaded, whether they tried to run, or whether they went out with dignity.

He glanced at his watch. The target would be rounding the corner any minute now, heading for the back entrance into the restaurant he worked in. Jimmy idly traced his finger around the grenade tucked into his pocket. Not a classy way to eliminate somebody, true, but he was only planning to use it as a decoy - a ploy to get his target to face him before he died.

Normally, Jimmy was crafty. He planted traps and hidden weapons, preferring to avoid confrontations –

however, he always made an exception for the last kill. He wanted his opponent to see who had taken him out. The image of Jimmy's face would be burned into his victim's mind for the rest of their life. That was why he was hiding in the shadow of the huge rubbish bin, overflowing with wasted food, empty bottles and other casualties of decadence. The last kill made all the previous ones worth the effort.

Footsteps echoed in the alleyway and Jimmy tensed. Peering out through the minute gap, he recognised the shiny black shoes and work trousers of his target and, as planned, he was on his own. Seconds passed as the target moved down the narrow corridor of brick. Was he walking slower than usual? Was it simply caution, or had somebody tipped him off? Perhaps the target would have a weapon of his own, ready to blast Jimmy as soon as he jumped out.

The target walked directly past Jimmy's hiding place. With a final breath, Jimmy put his plan into action. He took the grenade out of his pocket, took careful aim, and lobbed it across the tarmac. The grenade rolled perfectly through his target's legs, gently coming to a halt a couple of feet in front of him. The target stopped and stared at it for a second, giving Jimmy the perfect opportunity to clamber cat-like from behind the dumpster. He stood tensed behind his victim, arm outstretched.

As predicted, the victim backed away from the grenade, turning to face Jimmy. He froze, eyes wide with shock.

"Bang," Jimmy said firmly, recoiling his fingers as if the pistol they represented had just fired.

"Aww man!" the victim complained. "If I didn't have to work this shift, I'd have got you first!"

Jimmy shrugged nonchalantly. "You have your targets?"

The victim nodded, reaching into his pocket and pulling out a wad of crumpled photos. Jimmy now owned all one hundred pictures – ninety nine victims that had been eliminated, and one that hadn't. Him. He caught a glimpse of his own picture tight lipped and awkwardly looking at the camera through his blonde mop of hair.

As his opponent shuffled dejectedly towards the restaurant back entrance, Jimmy uncurled his pistol fingers back into a hand, and knelt down to pick up the grenade that was really a tennis ball. This was not murder, this was Kill-Soc, and Jimmy had just won.

<u>Present Day - The Week Before</u>

10:02 pm

Jodie stared intently at the computer screen in front of her, scrolling through pages and pages of emails, selecting those who were worthy. Although the deadline for application into the game had been over a month ago, somehow she always managed to leave the actual selection of the hundred competitors until the last minute. She couldn't believe May had come round again so soon. It felt like only yesterday that her ears had stopped ringing from last year's after-party.

Of course, she could admit some of the contestants simply by looking at their names – this was the fourth year the Kill-Soc of UCE had run its assassination widegame, and in that time as President, Jodie had learned to recognise who the serious players were and who were merely timewasters. The amount they wrote was also a solid indicator. The old hands tended to keep it simple, one or two sentences tops, whereas the newbies seemed intent on writing vast essays about why they should be part of the game, listing their personal qualities and achievements like they were applying for a job.

Jodie rubbed her eyes for a second, looking around the windowless room and taking in the clutter that surrounded her, quite often teetering in unstable towers in corners or leaning against the sides of the actual furniture they had in there. The desk was taken up by the computer and server equipment – Kill-Soc hosted its own website, but the uni refused to grant them a link from the official UCE network, saying that Kill-Soc was 'unsavoury', hence the large black box that flickered with hundreds of LEDs and hummed with the ever present data transfer. Luckily, one of Jodie's friends, Rick, was able to set all this up for her.

Around the desk were stacks of envelopes, a hundred in total, in which very soon she would be placing final copies of the rules along with photos and any other last minute information, ready to be sent out to whoever the final hundred should turn out to be.

On the far wall were two whiteboards. One was occupied with a large map of the whole city. Of course Kill-Soc was only open to UCE students, but there were three different campuses and three Halls of Residence, not to mention the numerous students that lived in their own accommodation across the city. That was one of the reasons it was called a widegame – the players could literally be anywhere within the city limits. The other whiteboard was blank, but in a week's time, it would be full of brightly coloured post–its tracking the progress of every player in the game.

The final feature of the room was a double mattress and a couple of blankets stowed roughly into the corner. Obviously, once the game had started, somebody had to be at the HQ twenty-four hours a day, and the bed just made things easier.

Before returning to her email trawl, Jodie found herself wondering if any of the other university societies worked as hard as they did. All of them were on the same corridor, and Kill-Soc was nestled way down at the end, its closest neighbours being the Frag-Soc and the Harry Potter Soc. Jodie knew the Frag-Soc played nothing but computer games, but she had no idea what went on in the Harry Potter Soc, as every time she'd tried to strike up conversation with them she was met with cold indifference because she didn't belong to Hogwarts.

With a sigh, she turned her attention back to the screen. There were only a few more competitors to select, and Jodie was half tempted to stop reading the applications all together and simply choose people based on what their photo looked like. Each potential player had to include a picture, which could then be printed and used in the game, and quite often you could tell who would last and who wouldn't just by looking at them.

Jodie heard keys rattling in the lock, and she looked up just as her boyfriend Liam entered, two steaming Chinese takeaway cartons balanced precariously in the crook of his arm.

"How's it going?" he asked in his soft Irish accent, setting the food down and cracking a pair of chopsticks.

"Almost there," Jodie said, barely taking her eyes from the screen despite the enticing aroma of chow mein wafting over to the desk. "Did you get the copying done?"

Liam nodded his head towards the rucksack he had dumped. Spilling out of it, Jodie could see various bits of paper and coloured sticky notes. She had trusted Liam with the daunting task of photocopying the sets of rules that would need to be sent to each contestant. Liam smiled at her, mouth full of takeaway.

"Come on," he said warmly. "It's called 'Wok to Walk', not 'Wok to Walk and Wait and Wait… and Wait Until It Gets Cold.'

"Done," Jodie said, clicking a final button. The printer buzzed into life as she walked over and dropped onto the bed next to Liam. It was good to have him there to sometimes force her to stop working. He handed her a carton of food and she took a mouthful, leaning her head against his shoulder and glancing at the clock. "This time next week," she mused, "the game will be just about to start."

Applications

Harper Fleet
Second Year Health & Fitness
I should be in this year's Kill-Soc because: All the running away from my hunter will keep me looking trim!

Jimmy Hale
Third Year Statistics
I should be in this year's Kill-Soc because: I won last year.

Gemma Hart
Second Year Media
I should be in this year's Kill-Soc because: I'm pretty and everybody loves me. I can use my feminine wiles to entrap my victims – it will add an interesting dynamic to the game, plus I might actually find a boyfriend!

Jonny Hayes
First Year Journalism
I should be in this year's Kill-Soc because: I want to make a name for myself at UCE. I'm a maverick. I'm unpredictable. I'll see you at the winner's podium (if there isn't one, there should be one)

Lewis Howard
Second Year Sports Science
I should be in this year's Kill-Soc because: I play for the Gryphons, but this is a different type of game – I want to experience as much as I can during my time here. Uni is the time to make memories right? Kill-Soc seems like a unique thing and I reckon I could be good at it – I've played a lot of Assassin's Creed.

David Hughes
First Year Law
I should be in this year's Kill-Soc because: As a Law student, I'll probably have to research some crimes. I might as well commit some pretend ones to get in the spirit of things. Plus, it would probably annoy my dad.

Sean James
Second Year Photography
I should be in this year's Kill-Soc because: I've already bought an amazing vintage weapon. Trust me, it's a classic – it deserves to play!

Ewan Lloyd
Second Year Drama
I should be in this year's Kill-Soc because: I came so close to winning last time. I just need one more chance to make this my year. I have to win!

Ryan Marino
Second Year Art
I should be in this year's Kill-Soc because: The further I get, the less I'll wear to the after party...

Leo Martin
Second Year Drama
I should be in this year's Kill-Soc because: I guarantee you'll get an Oscar winning performance. I won't just be Leo Martin playing Kill-Soc, I'll be James Bond infiltrating Spectre.

Mark Miller
Third Year Engineering
I should be in this year's Kill-Soc because: I'm a badass. The guns might be fake but the screams will be real.

Victoria Newton
Fourth Year Communications
I should be in this year's Kill-Soc because: OMG I'd be just perfect for the game! I'm stylish and sophisticated, and Daddy says I'd do really well at it!

Rick O'Reilly
Third Year Computer Science
I should be in this year's Kill-Soc because: I'm just a regular stereotypical Geek. Chances are you'll get a load of posers and assholes applying, so you need a few normals to balance it out. Plus I totally did you a favour Jodie, so you owe me ;)

Two Days Before

12:59 pm

The lecturer's final words were nothing but a dull droning as Ewan Lloyd sat staring at the clock, physically willing it to turn faster. *Come on, come on!* he urged silently, having long since packed away his notebook. He was barely touching his seat, ready to spring away and out of the door before being caught in the usual end of lecture crush. Usually, he enjoyed his Theatre Studies classes, but today his mind was elsewhere.

Before the bell even finished ringing, Ewan was halfway down the corridor, dodging and weaving through the emerging crowds, spouting insincere apologies as he went. He raced out across the quad, hopping lightly over some of the bike rails and ducking round one of the four oak trees as he left the campus.

The stretch of street between UCE and the Halls of Residence was a blur, and eventually Ewan barrelled into the foyer of O'Connell Hall and ran straight to the post-boxes that lined one of the walls. Once there, Ewan stopped, breathing deeply. If his pigeonhole contained what he hoped it would, then a whole year's worth of planning would pay off.

Since that afternoon, he had replayed the events over and over in his mind on an almost daily basis. If only he had taken a different route to work, if only he had found somebody else to accompany him. If only he hadn't had that crappy job waiting tables at the pizza restaurant.

Last year had been his first foray into the world of Kill-Soc, and he had managed to make it all the way to second place, but he had been caught out in a stupid moment of carelessness in some dingy alleyway outside his work.

Tentatively, Ewan reached inside his postbox. There was definitely something! He pulled the object out, not caring that he scraped his knuckles on the metal.

It was a plain envelope with nothing but his name and flat number. It had no stamp, which meant it had come through internally from somebody at UCE. This had to be it! Clutching the envelope protectively to his chest, he shuffled through the foyer before jogging up the stairs to his top floor flat. After fumbling with his keys, he finally managed to rush inside and power down the corridor towards his own room.

"Guess what I got this morning!" A loud and excited yell boomed through the flat just before Ewan's flatmate David popped out right in front of him. Ewan stumbled to a halt, narrowly avoiding collision as David waved an identical envelope in his face. "Did you open yours yet? Is it the same as mine?"

"I've only just got through the door," Ewan said with a roll of his eyes.

"Come on, open it!" David pleaded. Sometimes it was hard for Ewan to believe that his energetic young friend was in fact a first year Law student.

"Alright, alright!" Ewan snapped with a wave of his hand. "Let me dump my stuff first." He elbowed past David and continued along the bland cream hallway into his bedroom, chucking his bag carelessly onto the bed. Plonking himself next to it, he looked once more at the envelope in his lap. He couldn't deny that he had been waiting for this moment all year, and the anticipation had ramped up to extreme levels in the last month as Kill-Soc week approached. For everyone else it was just another week of lectures and seminars, but for the chosen hundred it was a chance for glory – so why was he suddenly hesitant to open the envelope? True, David's outburst had somewhat cheapened the experience for him a little, as Ewan had imagined that he would get his first. David hadn't played before, and Ewan had been looking forward to teaching him the rules, like a mentor – but that wasn't it.

As soon as Ewan ripped open that gum seal, something would be set in motion that he couldn't back out of. He got so far last year – what if this year he didn't do as well? What if he failed, or was barely a blip on the Kill-Soc radar, instead of a name that everybody knew like Jimmy Hale?

Even thinking Jimmy's name was enough to ignite Ewan's competitive streak with renewed intensity. None of that negative thinking, he *was* going to get just as far as last year, and then some. And if it came to another showdown with Jimmy the Kill-Soc Champion, then he would simply have to up his game…

2:16 pm

Jonny Hayes stared dejectedly at the mirror, but it wasn't his own face he was scrutinising. Since opening his Kill-Soc envelope, he had read through the rules twice and checked through the list of approved weapons. It was his first time in the game, and he wanted to make sure that he wasn't going to mess up on something simple like using the wrong kind of water pistol or something like that. Not that he was a stickler for rules, but he didn't want to get kicked out either. He was surprised to read that foam throwing stars were allowed, and Jonny immediately had visions of some black clad ninja wannabe dropping down from the rooftops and pelting him with Styrofoam.

He had spent the remaining time staring at the face of his first victim, which was now stuck up on his mirror with blu-tac. The brooding eyes had filled him with nothing but disappointment.

When he had first heard about Kill-Soc and sent his application off, Jonny had always assumed that he would recognise his victim, would know exactly where and when to ice them and be well on his way to victory. After all, as one of the photographers for the yearbook, there weren't many faces he hadn't seen before, yet here one was.

Although his assumption had hardly been a solid game plan, Jonny still felt that he had lost a part of his strategy, and that he was somehow now at a disadvantage. How was he going to make a name for himself if he couldn't even track down his first victim? He looked into his target's eyes, shadowed by close knitted brows and a scruffy goatee beard combo. He looked vaguely alternative – perhaps one of the losers that hung out at the half pipe?

With a quick glance at his watch, Jonny smiled. He still had plenty of time before he had to go to work. That left a good hour to stroll round the skate park and try to spot his target.

3:31 pm

Jimmy Hale lazily pushed open the front door, the aroma of something spicy wafting in from the kitchen. He meticulously set down his rucksack, this time filled with textbooks and notepads. There was a patch of carpet in the hallway that was worn threadbare after years of Jimmy's bag being left there. Next, he hung up his jacket on the last peg – that one was reserved just for him.

"That you, love?" Jimmy's mum appeared in the kitchen doorway. "I'm cooking you something up before I have to go to work," she stated, as if the apron she was wearing and the enticing smell wasn't obvious enough. "You can just reheat it when you're hungry."

Jimmy nodded in response, casually straightening the pencils on the side counter. His mind was already filtering through the things he had to do in his routine before he would allow himself to eat – hunger had little to do with it. First, he would organise his stuff for tomorrow – the books he would need for his lectures, as well as the clothes he would wear. Once that was done, he would complete any tasks that had run over from today, such as typing up the notes he'd made in the seminars he'd attended. Next would come a quick half hour workout, and then he would have his dinner. Any time after that would be spent rotating through computer games, websites and writing. It had been the same since Jimmy was about 11 – enforcing routines and structures to avoid having to choose anything. When faced with too much choice, Jimmy usually ended up worrying about each option until he wasted his time and did nothing at all. By turning choices into a series of unbreakable rules, he avoided those awkward situations.

"You got a letter," his mum said casually, holding up a brown envelope. Before he'd even looked up, Jimmy had factored the letter into a spot on his to-do list. It was a prompt second - after all, the letter might contain further points of action. Jimmy took the envelope from his mother and walked up the stairs, carefully avoiding catching the writing on the envelope even in the corner of his eye.

It didn't take him long to collect his books for tomorrow, as usually things tended to accumulate in piles according to what day he needed them. After taking the relevant items back downstairs and putting them into his rucksack, he was soon sitting on his bed, holding the envelope in his hands. The unknown letter filled him with trepidation - the contents might upset the routine of his life. With a deep breath, he ripped the side and pulled out the contents. Three items spilled onto his duvet: a photo of a girl, a booklet and a formal looking letter. As soon as he took in the sight of the contents, Jimmy relaxed, knowing exactly what it was. He read the letter first, just to make sure, but already his heart was beating that little bit faster with excitement.

"Dear Mr Hale,
Congratulations on your acceptance into this year's Kill-Soc widegame. Please find enclosed a copy of the latest rules and a picture of your first victim.
Happy hunting,
J Hawk – President"

Jimmy read it through three times before lying back on the bed and staring up at the ceiling, a big grin on his face. This was the time of year he looked forwards to the most, even more than Christmas or his birthday. This was the time when he stopped being Jimmy the socially awkward kid with hardly any friends – for the upcoming week or so, he would be Jimmy the assassin, Jimmy the hitman, and most importantly, Jimmy the champion.

He snatched up the rules booklet and set about memorising every new detail and change from last year.

4:44 pm

Fifteen year old Flynn Howard sat dejectedly throwing a tennis ball against the flaking paint of his brother's spare room. This week was supposed to be a treat for him – a chance to hang out with his big brother at Uni, and more importantly a chance to have a break from his constantly arguing parents. In reality, he had spent most of the week alone. Lewis had still had lectures even though for Flynn it was half term break, and in the evenings, Lewis either had lacrosse practice or had an important club night to attend – and of course, Flynn was too young to go with him.

In a way, it was almost annoying that Lewis was so *nice* about it all. He would always come back to the flat with an apologetic grin and a bag of takeaway on his wrist, and Flynn understood that Uni was meant to be this great place of self-discovery but he couldn't help thinking that if Lewis knew he was going to have so little free time, he shouldn't have invited Flynn in the first place.

The tennis ball rolled under the bed and Flynn suddenly lost all enthusiasm for the game. He glanced at the clock. Lewis said he would be back at 4. He was supposed to be taking Flynn to the cinema, but the film had already started.

With a sigh, Flynn hauled himself off the thin mattress and began to idly trace a finger through the dust on the windowsill. He thought about putting the old Xbox on, but Lewis only had Assassin's Creed, and Flynn had already completed it. That was when he heard the clang of the letterbox and the fluttering of paper hitting the fake wooden floorboards.

Twitching back the yellowing curtains, Flynn saw a young man retreating up the street, hood pulled up over his head. *Not a postman then,* he thought to himself. He looked again at the retreating figure, stick thin in skinny jeans. Probably some student supplementing their mediocre loan payments with a part time job of flyering. As he watched however, he noticed that the delivery guy didn't approach any other doors.

Curiosity piqued, Flynn ambled out into the hallway, the gloomy flat taking a moment or two to slip into focus. It was a small one and a half bedroom affair - one of many crammed into the old Edwardian building. Of the entire avenue, Flynn suspected that hardly any of the large houses remained as single dwellings. Where Flynn was expecting to see the familiar glossy leaflets screaming about how cheap various products were, there was only a single brown envelope.

He snatched it up, turning it over in his hands. It was addressed to Lewis Howard, and just the first line of an address. There was no title or postcode, and it had been written in childish biro scrawl. There was no stamp.

Temptation immediately wrapped itself around Flynn's brain, squeezing tighter and tighter until his head physically hurt. The mysterious envelope was calling to him simply because of how unusual it was. Whoever delivered it knew that Lewis lived here, and it must have come from somewhere in the city to be able to avoid the official postal service… unless the strange hoodie wearer had driven the letter in from somewhere else? And that just made it even more enticing. On the other hand, of course he knew that opening other people's stuff was wrong. Even if he hadn't had the common sense to know it intrinsically, some of the blaring rows he had overheard between his parents had forced the issues home. Countless times he had overheard his mother crying as his father yelled about respecting privacy and reading things that were confidential.

But it was his brother... what harm could it do? In the end, Flynn decided to try and pull the envelope open as gently as he could so that he could reseal it afterwards if he needed to. Easing his fingernail under the gum seal, he prised the folds of paper apart until at last it was open. He held it at arm's length, admiring his covert handiwork. *Yeah,* he thought. Unless Lewis was specifically expecting the letter to have been opened, he wouldn't notice once it was all sealed up again.

Flynn took the envelope into the boxy living room and emptied the contents out onto the table. There was a photograph of a guy about Lewis' age grinning at the camera. It was the kind of grin that was supposed to say 'I'm hard' but with the freckles and ginger mop it just made him look as if he would glow in the dark. Next was a letter telling Lewis he had been accepted into something called Kill-Soc. The thousands of questions generated by the enigmatic letter were soon answered as Flynn read the comprehensive rules booklet that made up the third item in the envelope. After reading it thoroughly from weapons list to kill protocol, Flynn breathed in excitement. This was the coolest thing he'd ever heard of! A game where people hunted each other for real! He scanned the rules again, paying particular attention to a section about recognising victims. Apparently, the ginger kid was going to be Lewis' first target, and that meant that somewhere in the city, a student had a picture of Lewis as *their* target. An idea began to form in Flynn's head.

He hurried to the end of the corridor where his brother's bedroom was. Forcing the door against the mountain of clothes that had built up against it, he snuck inside, tiptoeing around the various dirty plates and discarded boxers. At least that was one positive about living at home –

his mum would never let his room get this bad. Not entirely
sure what he was looking for, he began rooting through the
junk that littered Lewis' desk – stacks of papers and half
chewed pens, watched over by a corkboard covered in
postcards advertising the latest union nights. Next, he made
for the drawers by the bed. There was nothing on top but a
lamp, alarm clock and some boring looking textbook, so
Flynn pulled open the top drawer. He brushed aside the gum
and the condoms, making a mental note to tease Lewis about
those later, and then a grin broke out across his face as he
saw what he'd hoped to find. Lying at the back of the drawer
was a set of passport photos, one of them conspicuously
missing. Flynn would have bet everything he had that the
missing photo was the one Lewis had used for his Kill-Soc
application.

He stood in front of the mirror, holding the photo by
the side of his head, pulling his face into a close
approximation of his brother's expression. Despite there
being almost five years between them, the Howard boys had
the same straight nose, angular jaw and thick eyebrows. Even
their hair had been coincidentally cut in a similar style –
Flynn doubted that anyone would notice his was a slight
shade lighter. Flynn was glad that Lewis was clean shaven in
the photo, as any facial hair would have made Flynn's plan
impossible.

Next, he turned his attention to the clothes Lewis'
serious looking mugshot was wearing. Flynn could only see
his brother's shoulders, covered in a crimson v-neck that
plunged low in the middle of his chest. *Poser.* It didn't take
Flynn long to find the top lying in a crumpled heap on the
floor, and slip it on. Admiring himself in the mirror once
more, Flynn pulled self-consciously at the loose fabric. The
look was close, but there was no disguising the fact that he
was a scrawny schoolkid, whereas Lewis was a built lacrosse

player. Flynn tried bunching his shoulders and flexing his arms to no avail – he simply couldn't create muscle out of nowhere. Unless…

He took the jumper off, then turned to the lacrosse stick standing in the corner of the room. Prowling over, Flynn was glad to see his brother's kit discarded by the stick. All of it had the same Gryphon picture on it, and Flynn remembered that the UCE teams were named after mythical creatures. He was less thrilled at having to rifle through the grass-stained shorts and sweaty socks until he found Lewis' training shirt. It was tight enough not to swamp Flynn's slight frame, but had padded shoulders and elbows to add a bit of bulk. Pulling the shirt on, then covering it with the jumper, Flynn grinned at his reflection. He was finally satisfied that he could pass for his brother. There was a slight hint of guilt in Flynn's mind, but he shrugged it aside quickly. Lewis was always so busy, he wouldn't have time to play properly, Flynn reasoned. Really, he was doing Lewis a favour.

Suddenly, he heard keys rattle in the front door. Panicking, Flynn ripped his brother's stuff off, casting his eyes round for his own t-shirt he had removed – it must have got mixed up when he was rooting around. The front door opened, and he heard footsteps shuffle into the living room.

"Flynn?" Lewis called. "Sorry I'm late, I ran into Ellie on the way back. There was drama."

Flynn didn't have time to search for his own top. Instead, he snatched a glass of tepid water from the side and splashed it into his face. Stuffing the Kill-Soc papers into his back pocket and scooping a towel from the floor, Flynn stepped out into the hallway just as Lewis emerged from the living room.

"Hey," Flynn said breathlessly.

Lewis looked at him casually. "You ok?" he asked.

"Yeah, just had a shower."

Lewis narrowed his eyes as he looked his brother up and down. "You always put your shoes on before your shirt?"

Flynn felt his cheeks redden and the pause seemed to stretch out. What if Lewis didn't believe him? What if he could tell that Flynn had been in his room?

"Never mind, little brother," Lewis continued as Flynn breathed a sigh of relief. "Some things I will never understand about you. Any post?"

Flynn shook his head, noticing Lewis' face fall slightly with disappointment.

"Ah well," he shrugged. "So, we've missed the movie but what about bowling or something?"

"Sounds good," Flynn said, his brother's envelope nestled snugly in his pocket.

The Morning Before

11:53 am

Jodie stood back and admired her handiwork. The whiteboard that had been empty until just a couple of hours ago was now a vibrant display of photos. The hundred faces of the contestants were arranged in a large circle, threads of string pinned between them to indicate who was shortly going to be hunting who. Two hundred eyes watched Jodie, full of hope and excitement at the game about to begin any moment now. Soon, a lot of those eyes would have crosses through them as they became the first 'casualties' of Kill-Soc. Jodie smiled as she looked down at the red marker just waiting to be uncapped. Crossing the victims off was one of her favourite jobs, as each one was a step closer to the end. It was odd that after so much preparation she should be anxious to reach the end of the game, but crowning the winner and hearing about all the exploits at the after party was the most entertaining part.

"Shite, have you heard about this?" Liam sat typing at the computer. Jodie had given him the numbers of all the contestants, and he had been entering them in one by one to the text system, linking them to their corresponding pictures so that once the game was in play, they could simply click on a face to message that person. At times like this, Jodie was thankful that Liam had joined her in this. Plenty of her mates had boyfriends who would have simply left her to it whilst they went to the pub and watched sports all day. Whilst Jodie was probably capable of patching together some sort of functional system, Liam was so much better at it.

Right now, however, Liam had been distracted by a message that had popped up. "It looks like Tom's out," he said softly. Jodie scanned the board until she locked eyes with the contestant in question. She felt a twinge of sadness as she stared into the boy's face, a dark flop of emo hair hanging down from his forehead. Tom had been hit by a car a couple of nights ago and they were keeping their fingers crossed that he would be ok in time to play. Unfortunately, the message from one of his friends told them he was actually in some sort of coma and that it was more serious than they'd thought.

"It's too late to replace him," Jodie said, carefully taking the photo down. Somehow it didn't seem right to draw a cross over it.

"I'll message his hunter," Liam nodded and went back to his typing.

Jodie unpinned the string attached to Tom's photo and linked it to one of the other contestants.

"Finished," Liam said eventually with a yawn. He stretched his arms behind his head and Jodie smiled. Despite him having spent the last two days hand delivering all of the acceptance letters, and despite him spending all morning typing numbers with his nerdy glasses perched on his nose, Jodie still thought he looked cute. She stepped behind him and wrapped her arms across his chest, her hand brushing against a badge he was wearing. She glared at the red plastic thing with distaste.

"Why are you wearing *that?*" she said coldly. Last year, at the after party, an admirer had slipped the badge into Liam's back pocket, along with a phone number. She knew Liam would never call it, but seeing him sporting the crimson pin with a laser cut Kill-Soc logo was a reminder that some other bitch fancied her man.

"It's a cool design so it is," Liam defended, rubbing the shiny surface casually with his thumb.

"It's tat," Jodie chided as she untangled her arms from his. "Plus the logo isn't even official."

Liam swivelled round in the chair, grinning at her. "Aw, I think you're jealous. Come on Jode, you're my girl, you know that." Before she could respond, Liam lunged forward and kissed her, her annoyance flowing out of her as their lips touched. "Now come on," he said softly, nodding towards the screens. Jodie rolled her eyes and turned her attention back to the game.

Now that the numbers were entered, the three screens on the desk showed what they would be displaying solidly for the next few days. One was simply a directory of faces that could be clicked to contact specific players. The middle one was the main message server – everything that was messaged to either her or Liam's Gamesmaster accounts would be displayed there – all the kill notifications and the inevitable complaints that demanded her attention. Finally, the third screen displayed the homepage of the Kill-Soc website. As messages came through to her, Jodie would repost the highlights onto the website for all the competitors to see. It was a good way for them to keep up to date with how the rest of the game was going, but also in the past Jodie had seen it used as an opportunity to try and psyche out your victims, or even taunt the ones supposed to be hunting you.

"It's pretty much time," Liam reminded her. He pressed the 'select all' button on the directory, and a screen full of numbers flooded the middle monitor. Jodie took a deep breath. All the planning and preparation over the last year was about to be set in motion. She looked at Liam, who nodded with encouragement. Leaning over him, Jodie typed two simple words and pressed send.

"Happy Hunting."

Day 1

12:00 pm

The Law professor paused in his diatribe as feedback Morse-coded across the speakers he was using to spread his teachings into the furthest corners of the dark lecture theatre. The greying man looked sternly over the rim of his glasses, clearing his throat in polite emphasis.

David Hughes glanced up from his notepad, where he had already scrawled three full pages of detailed notes. He wondered why the voice he had tuned his ears to for the last hour had stopped. The interference sounded again, a buzzing dumdudumdudum, and Professor Baldwin sighed. David could tell from his silver beard and elbow-patched jacket that he was dealing with a hardcore old school teacher – one that probably did not tolerate interruptions of any kind. As David scanned the theatre for the culprit, he saw a number of his classmates shuffle awkwardly in their seats, and that was when he felt his own phone buzzing against his thigh.

Professor Baldwin coughed once more, his bushy moustache wobbling. "May I take this opportunity to inform you that anybody firing any sort of weapon in this class will be instantly failed." A ripple of sniggering spread through the room and David finally worked out what the professor was referring to. Instantly, his heart started beating faster as he reached into his pocket for his phone. Whilst pretending to rummage in his bag for a pen, he snuck a look at the screen. One message flashed up, from the number he had received in his letter. He had entered it under the name 'Kill-Soc', and the message comprised of only two words. He smiled as he read them to himself before resurfacing above the desk and staring back at his pad.

As the stuffy lecturer picked up his thread again, David put his pen down. He was aware that his notes would go unfinished, as everything that Baldwin now said about the Precedents Act was flowing straight to the back of his mind.

12:02 pm

Lewis' phone buzzed, dancing across the shiny laminate of the burger joint's table. Lewis himself was queuing at the counter, whilst Flynn idly traced his finger through a pile of upturned salt. Flynn was getting used to junk food for pretty much every meal of the day – Lewis wasn't much of a cook. At first, Flynn had seen it as a treat – a chance to eat as much meat as possible before he had to return to the strictly vegetarian cuisine his mother usually made – but now, after four days of eating crap, he was beginning to feel sick of the grease. He also thought he was getting a spot on his lip, and that wouldn't help his plan to take his brother's place in the Kill-Soc game at all. Annoyingly, Lewis had managed to fly through high school without the teenage onslaught of acne and awkwardness, and he was old enough not to have to worry about it now. Flynn, on the other hand, seemed to have inherited his brother's share of both, but he had hoped at least that spending some time way from his parents would reduce the amount of stress spots he got. Instead, it seemed they were being replaced by takeaway grease pimples. Lewis also had the advantage of regular lacrosse practice so he was still pretty trim. Flynn reckoned he'd already put on a stone since he got there.

Lewis' phone buzzed again, questioning why its owner hadn't picked it up yet. Flynn cast a furtive glance across the restaurant. Lewis was still third from the front, his attention fixed on the menus lit up on screens behind the servers. Flynn picked up the phone, for no other reason than he had nothing else to do. He wasn't usually in the habit of reading other people's texts, but because the phone had made a noise, it was at the forefront of his mind. Plus, his rules about reading other people's mail had gone out the window, so why not look at the phone? Perhaps his brother might have downloaded some fun games Flynn could use to pass the time.

The screen came to life as his finger touched it – no buttons like Flynn's own crappy hand-me-down – and Flynn couldn't help but read the message displayed there. A grin broke out on his face. The game had started!

Before deleting the message, Flynn stored the number in his own phone so he could receive any further information as the game went on. By the time Lewis arrived with the food, Flynn was just pressing the last buttons on a quick message explaining that 'Lewis' had changed his number. From this point on, any other announcements would come directly to his phone, but more importantly, they wouldn't be sent to Lewis.

1:03 pm

It had been just over an hour since Jimmy had got the message telling him the game had started. Of course, he'd known that the message would come. He had even skipped his morning lecture in order to prepare for the start of the game. Normally, this sort of routine breaking would have been unacceptable, but just like when the letter had arrived it had to be factored into place, so did Kill-Soc. It overwrote things like lectures. His rucksack had been ceremoniously emptied of the books and papers, and filled with his Kill-Soc kit, which had been put ready in the bottom drawer for over three months. Naturally, everything had its own special place in his rucksack, so that he could quickly find what he needed, depending on his situation. He had packed a variety of long-range weapons, such as the tennis ball grenades he had used last year. His kit also included a couple of water pistols and a Nerf gun, as well as numerous extras that he could fashion traps out of.

Jimmy looked once more at the photo of his first victim. He didn't think of them as targets – that made it sound like he could fail. If he called them victims, then it was as if he had already eliminated them. She was older than him – a late third year or maybe even more. She was all blue eyes and blonde hair – pretty, and by the look on her face, she clearly knew it. She looked like the kind of person who would call everyone 'Sweetie' or 'Honey', and Jimmy shuddered. He didn't like nicknames. Why wouldn't you just call somebody by their real name?

Right now, Victoria Newton should be in her Advanced Communications seminar in the John Terrence

block of UCE. Jimmy had already taken the liberty of
trawling through the UCE websites until he found a grainy
picture of her, and which faculty she belonged to. It was
amazing what you could find out if you put your mind to it.
Each faculty tended to have a group photo of each year's
students, and as soon as you knew what subject they took,
finding out when that subject ran and where was a piece of
cake. Jimmy smiled to himself as he wondered how many of
his opponents had the common sense to look in the same
place.

Of course, Jimmy wasn't going to be heading for
Victoria's class - that was far too obvious. Instead, he was
going to the main student car park. After finding out his
victim's name, Jimmy had found her social networking
profile. Amongst others, there was a photo of Victoria
posing next to a shiny new, cherry red Fiat 500 which was
parked in the UCE car park. She had even posted a comment
underneath, identifying the spot as her usual one. *Some people
made it too easy,* Jimmy mused as he shouldered his bag. He
wondered if Victoria was a first timer, or whether she
thought nobody would try to get her on the first day. Either
way, she had pretty much marked herself for elimination.

Jimmy made his way down the stairs, taking his jacket
off its hook and scooping his keys out of the dish on the
side. The trap he was going to set for Victoria was already
running through his mind as he pushed open the front door
and stepped into the sunlight.

Suddenly, something popped loudly on the concrete
path that ran across the front lawn. Looking up hurriedly,
Jimmy saw a large wet patch blossoming over the slabs
amidst tatters of coloured rubber. He only just saw the
second water bomb in time as it arced towards him from
behind the bushes that lined the street. Turning on his heels,
Jimmy ran back towards the door and threw himself inside.

He slammed the door just as the balloon exploded against the panes of glass, gleaming rivers of water spilling across the wood.

"I'll get you next time, Hale!" a voice shouted over hastily retreating footsteps. Jimmy sank to the carpet, exhilarated. He wasn't really expecting the action to start quite so soon, but secretly he was glad. Nothing could match the pounding of his heart, and the thrill of playing the game.

Already, his mind was processing this new element as he wondered how his assassin had discovered where he lived. Unless it was somebody who already knew him? No matter - this current attempt had failed. Jimmy would wait a few minutes to make sure the coast was clear, then he would continue with his initial plan.

2:34 pm

The lecture was drawing to a close, which was good, David thought, because it should have finished four minutes ago. His friends often teased him about studying law, which they considered to be one of the hardest subjects UCE offered. A lot of his time was taken up by reading extensive journals and legal documents, not to mention the often mind-numbing two and half hour sessions like the one he was currently in. It did mean however, that he was now done until tomorrow. Other students like Ewan had shorter lectures that were spread throughout the day. David at least could spend the rest of the day focusing on Kill-Soc.

It was a testament to the players that nobody had opened fire during the actual lecture, despite the professor's stern warning. Of course, the letter had clearly outlined this as one of the big rules. No attacking during official lessons, and no attacking people in their own home, unless invited in. Whilst at first glance, these rules seemed to be a hindrance, David could see the point of them. All it would take is for one complaint to get out of hand, then the game would be shut down completely, and from what David had gathered from Ewan, who had played once before, Kill-Soc was already largely frowned upon by most of the staff and UCE higher-ups.

Finally, Professor Baldwin collected his papers and stepped down from his lectern, which was the universally accepted signal that the students were free to leave. Never one for goodbyes or any other parting messages, the professor was already out the door before David had even finished putting everything back in his bag.

As the steady stream of students began to flow towards the exits, David found his way blocked by a girl, clutching a folder to her chest. She smiled at him with just the tiniest hint of embarrassment, but David was too busy staring at the cute little dimples that formed in her cheeks when she grinned at him.

"Hey," she began in a light voice. "I'm Gemma. This is really awkward, but I kind of fell asleep back there - you know how it is." She flashed another smile and David felt his cheeks redden. This girl was seriously beautiful, and a law student! The two usually never coincided.

"It happens," David replied with a shrug.

"Did you get any notes?" The girl eyed David's bag, where the top of his folder was just visible. As she said this, David's mind spiralled in a number of directions. This sort of thing didn't usually happen to him, but here he was, face to face with one of the prettiest girls he'd ever seen, not to mention that she had to at least have some degree of intelligence to have made it into the law class. David's flatmate Ewan was always boasting about some guy he'd picked up in Theatre class – it seemed to just come naturally to Ewan, but for David it was a rarity. He took a deep breath.

"I did," he began. "Perhaps we could head for a coffee and go over them?" He tried to flash her a winning smile, but having never really practiced it before, he couldn't guarantee what it looked like.

"I'd rather just get them now," she said with a smile of her own. David was certain that his half grimace hadn't looked anywhere near as cute, but he was still disappointed. He couldn't blame her though – of course a sensible law student wouldn't be in the habit of just going out with random strangers.

"Fair enough," David muttered, swinging his rucksack off his shoulder and setting it down between his feet. As he dug around for the right sheet of paper, he couldn't help but sneak a look at Gemma's legs, perfectly smooth with a hint of tan. He paused for as long as he could without it looking awkward, before straightening up and staring straight into the barrel of a gun.

Gemma pulled the trigger, sending a cascade of cool water into David's face. It soaked the notepaper he was holding and dripped down his chest and onto the gum encrusted carpet.

"I'm not even in this class, idiot," Gemma said with a huge grin.

"So you sat through a two and half hour law lecture just to get me?" David said, wiping his eyes. "Hang on, the game started halfway through the lecture..."

"Knew you'd be here, you have a perfect attendance record," Gemma shrugged. "It's Kill-Soc. You do what you have to." David looked at her in surprise. "Aw, is it your first time?" she continued after noticing his look of befuddlement.

He nodded.

"Don't worry," she consoled. "You'll see how hardcore people are this year, then up your game next time. Besides, you still get to come to the after party. Can I have your target?"

David blinked for a few seconds before pulling the photo of his intended victim out of his now damp pocket and holding it out. She snatched it eagerly.

"Ah," Gemma exclaimed. "Rick the dick! He got me last year..." With a chirruping laugh and a wink, Gemma turned on her heels and left the lecture theatre with a bouncing skip. Her phone was already in her hand, no doubt to post news of her kill on the Kill-Soc message board.

3:49 pm

The Greek warrior knelt on the ground, cradling the cloaked figure of the man he had just killed. Cold moonlight gave the scene a grey tint as he looked mournfully down at the body.

"We should not be alone," he muttered softly into the silence before bowing his head. The two men held that position for a few moments, the onlookers watching with eager anticipation and baited breath. Then both actors stood and took a bow, the house lights rising as the audience burst into applause.

Ewan loved the end of module performances, and his applause was genuine, even though technically each group was competing for coveted places on next year's advanced course. This was the final performance of the day, and although his own had gone well (a thriller about a guy with schizophrenia who invents his own brother), he thought that this one would probably win the honours.

The warrior took his helmet off and bowed once more, Leo Martin basking in the glory that he knew was his. The other actor, Jeff, gathered up the folds of his cloak and hurried off the stage. It had been a stroke of luck for Jeff to get paired with Leo the drama star for this module, as while he wasn't necessarily bad, Ewan doubted that Jeff could have carried the performance without Leo's presence.

The audience began to shuffle out of their seats whilst, on the stage, Leo began picking up the various bits of armour he had shed during the climactic battle scene. As Ewan waited for his row to clear, Jeff appeared once more from the wings. He was still in costume, the hood pulled over his face. As he strode purposefully across the boards to where Leo was crouching, Ewan saw the glint of metal as Jeff pulled a knife from somewhere within the layers of fabric. Ewan's eyes went wide. He couldn't believe what he was seeing. You often read about students going crazy and shooting up their classmates, but this was something straight out of a Scream movie.

"Shit dude, look out!" Ewan yelled. It was the only thing he could think of to do. Leo stood up and turned just as Jeff rammed the knife into his chest, the blade sinking all the way to the handle. Leo sunk to his knees and then flopped gracelessly onto his back. Ewan leaped over the rows of seats, clambering desperately forwards in order to do… he wasn't sure what exactly - all he knew was that if he didn't do something, he would never forgive himself.

It was only when he had flung himself over the final row of seats that Ewan realised Leo was laughing. Where were the screams of blood-soaked murder? The actor had propped himself up on his elbows, shaking his head jovially as he prodded the knife blade with his finger. The silver plastic sunk into the handle on some sort of spring mechanism. Ewan slapped his hand to his forehead, slick with sweat. Of course it was Kill-Soc! How could he have been so stupid? He turned back to where the last of the stragglers was watching him with barely concealed glee.

"Nice performance, Ewan. You're definitely in our group next term."

"Shut up, Will!"

As Leo clambered to his feet and brushed himself off, Jeff pulled out his phone to update the message board. Leo caught sight of Ewan's face, no doubt still blanched from the brief moment of panic.

"You ok dude?"

"Yeah," Ewan said with a guilty laugh. "I guess I over reacted a little."

"Once a drama student, *always* a drama student," Leo chuckled back. "Well that's me out of the running, struck down in the first act. Unless you want to save me, Ian?" Leo looked questioningly at the Drama Lecturer, who was busy rearranging props on a side desk. He was one of the cool ones that didn't mind people using his first name.

"Don't look at me, Mr Martin," he tutted without looking up. "Your performance, and therefore the lesson, was clearly over. It was a valid kill."

"Talis est vita," Leo sighed flamboyantly. "See you in tomorrow's class." He casually tossed the knife back to his assassin before disappearing off the stage.

"I 'spose I should return this stupid robe," the killer muttered as he pulled the hood down. Ewan stared. It wasn't Jeff. But more than that though - by a vast stroke of luck and coincidence, the guy was Ewan's own victim!

"What?" the killer questioned, noticing Ewan's stare.

"Wardrobe's back that way," Ewan said, pointing into the darkness. The assassin strode into the shadows, leaving Ewan with a hundred ideas running through his head.

3:53 pm

Jimmy stood back and surveyed his handiwork. Just as he had hoped, you would have to be looking very carefully to spot what he'd done. Just at the bottom of the driver's door on Victoria's beloved car, he had taped a piece of fishing wire. The wire ran underneath the car, where Jimmy had laboriously fastened an old school alarm clock, complete with the gleaming twin bells. That was the riskiest part of the trap – if anybody had caught him climbing underneath the car, he would have had some difficult explaining to do, and Jimmy found it awkward enough to talk to people in relatively normal situations, let alone planting a fake time bomb on someone's car.

He had prepped the clock beforehand, of course. He'd taken the timing mechanism out so the hands wouldn't move, but he'd still wound the alarm up until the key had stopped. It was this that the other end of the fishing wire was attached to. As soon as Victoria opened the door, the wire would pull the key and set the alarm off. For good measure, Jimmy had also stuck a hastily scrawled label to the face of the clock with the word 'bomb' written on it in black marker. He assumed everyone took the game as seriously as him, but there was always the chance that this girl wouldn't see the clock for what it was.

He scanned the wire and double-checked the tape one last time before sidling back across the car park. Everything was in place and secure. Now all he had to do was wait for Victoria to post her kill message on the boards – then he would undoubtedly receive his new target by text or email – that was how it usually worked when a kill wasn't face to face. Part of him wanted to hide somewhere so he could see her reaction, but Jimmy knew he would be vulnerable – especially since his hunter was already after him, judging by the earlier water bomb attack. He took a final look over his shoulder and hurried home.

3:55 pm

The racks of clothes seemed to stretch on forever, the black walls of the drama studio disguising its dimensions. Ewan stalked through the costumes, each rail holding a different theme depending on what shows had been done most recently. He padded past sailor outfits and chicken suits until he came to the back where the 'horror' costumes were kept. Grotesque masks leered at him from the shelves as he crept forwards, double checking the simple weapon he had fashioned. After rummaging around in his bag, all he could find of any use was a rubber band, which was now stretched across his fingers. All it would take was for him to lower his thumb and the projectile would shoot whichever way his fingers were pointing.

    He rounded the corner and saw his target, back turned towards the aisle. The guy was pulling the robe up over his head. Ewan let out an involuntary gasp as he saw the guy wasn't wearing a top underneath. His muscles flexed as he dropped the robe to the floor then reached over to where he'd left his t-shirt on the nearest shelf. As he stretched, the waistband of his boxers appeared over the band of his jeans. Ewan coughed, announcing his presence before things got awkward.

    The guy whirled round, instinctively holding his t-shirt across his chest, but as soon as he saw Ewan eyeing him, he smiled.

    "You drama boys are so easy," he laughed, his blue eyes twinkling mischievously.

    "What?"

"I'm not gay or anything, but I'll let you get me off."
At this, he dropped his shirt and opened his arms wide,
showing off a sculpted six pack.

Cocky bastard, Ewan thought, trying not to get
distracted. The guy's grin would have been arrogant if he
wasn't kind of cute.

"Actually," Ewan began. "I came for this." He raised
his hand and fired, recognition spreading across the guy's
face a split second before the rubber band pinged off his
chest. A red welt flashed across his skin and his mouth
opened in surprise.

"Son of a bitch," he cursed in disappointment,
rubbing the wound with his finger.

"Yeah, sorry," Ewan shrugged. "It was just blind luck
that you came in to get Leo."

"Not that," the guy said dejectedly, casting a quick
glance down his body. "I wasn't expecting you to say no."

Ewan followed the boy's gaze, his eyebrows raising.
There was always time for another notch. "What makes you
think I'm saying no?" He grinned as he jumped forwards.

4:08 pm

Jonny couldn't help feeling like the last two days had been a complete waste of time. He had staked out the skate park to no avail. He hadn't caught even the slightest glimpse of his target, and now the game had started and he was no better off. As well as visiting the skate shop *Deckers,* Jonny had even spent a brain numbingly arduous six hours trawling through every picture on the yearbook database, but that had also yielded no results. The one thing it did was confirm his initial thought about his target being part of the 'alternatives' – they usually classed themselves as outside the realm of such things as the yearbook. And lessons. And hygiene, some of them.

Now that Kill-Soc was officially under way, Jonny was spurred on by the fact that somewhere out there, somebody was hunting him, just as he was tracking his own elusive target. It felt good to constantly be on the move, it would make him harder to catch. He hadn't decided whether he was going to skip out on his Journalism classes yet – his lecturer Ms Wells was a renowned nutcracker. She taught a load of English and related subjects, and could still make Uni age guys burst into tears.

Back at the skate park once more, Jonny clutched the picture of his target in his fist as he walked up to a group of kids that were hanging around on the periphery of the concrete skating area, watching the older guys on the grindrails and the ramps. The kids were about thirteen, dressed up in baggy jeans and beanie hats. Each of them had a shiny looking Darkstar board at his feet, and one of them was even coughing on a roll up. They were the perfect wannabe skaters, lacking only the guts to try any of the tricks in front of the older generation.

"Oi," Jonny called, planting himself deliberately in the way of their view. The skater kids looked him up and down, taking in his burgundy chinos and polo shirt, before smirking to each other. It was all Jonny could do to stop himself from rolling his eyes at the display of machismo as the smoking boy attempted to blow a smoke ring, doubling over into a hacking spluttering mess. "I'm looking for this guy," Jonny continued, thrusting the photo in their faces.

"Aw, is he your boyfriend?" one of the kids leered.

"Nah, I'm too busy with your mum for a boyfriend," Jonny retorted, the universal burning power of the mum joke reducing the rest of the gang into fits of laughter whilst the lead crony looked so taken aback that he might have cried.

"I've seen him," one of the other kids piped up. "That's Mark."

Jonny turned to him, immediately tuning out the others – they were no longer of use. This kid was the smallest in the group, and instead of a beanie hat, he actually had a helmet on. "You know when he usually comes down here?"

The kid shrugged. "He just turns up whenever."

Jonny thought for a second, weighing up his options. He could continue to hunt for Mark himself, but the skater would probably be on the look out for assassins. It would be much safer, not to mention funnier, to use the kid. "How would you like to earn yourself some money?" he said, flashing the kid a mischievous grin.

"Awesome!" the boy beamed, stepping towards Jonny eagerly. Jonny indicated one of the nearby benches where they could sit and discuss their terms.

"You're playing that stupid game aren't you?"

Jonny turned back to see the gang leader scowling at him. "So?"

"So what if we told Mark that you were looking for him – that would mess up your plans." The kid put his hands on his hips in triumph whilst his minions looked between him and Jonny with excitement. Showing off in front of somebody almost twice your age must have been a big thrill.

"If you did that," Jonny began slowly. "I'd have to come back here and break your legs."

The boy's face drained. "But," he stammered. "I've seen my sister's letter. You aren't allowed to get innocent members of the public – it's against the rules."

Jonny stepped forward until his face was inches away from the boy's. He grinned cruelly. "I don't play by the rules."

5:18 pm

"You know, I didn't even get your name," Ewan said with a smile as he buttoned his shirt.

"It's Ryan."

"So…" Ewan struggled to think of something to say. It wasn't that he was embarrassed about hooking up with a cocky straight boy, it was just that he'd already seen everything Ryan had to offer – getting to know him now seemed kind of pointless.

"Is this your first time?"

"Please," Ewan scoffed.

"I meant playing Kill-Soc," Ryan said with a sly grin. Ewan blushed, aware that he had been in danger of becoming the arrogant one.

"No. I got pretty far last year – second place. I got ambushed by that douche Jimmy Hale."

"Me too!" Ryan exclaimed. "The bastard got me with a rubber knife as I was coming out of the main entrance – right in front of everyone!" Ewan couldn't help thinking that Ryan had pretty much used the same technique on Leo, but he didn't say anything. "That Jimmy guy has won the game loads of times, I heard," Ryan continued. "And he's supposed to be some total 'Beautiful Mind' weirdo."

"Uhuh," Ewan nodded casually, turning his attention to the various shelves of theatre supplies. With his clothes on, Ryan was rapidly losing most of his appeal. Although he did have a point about Jimmy. Ewan had never really seen him outside of the game, but when Jimmy was playing Kill-Soc, he was like a machine – his mind seemed to focus on nothing else, like The Terminator or something.

"Surely it's not against the rules to rough him up a little," Ryan was saying. "You know, put the wind up him a bit."

"Well you're eliminated," Ewan reasoned. "I'm not sure if you're still bound by the rules."

"We could just kill him for real," Ryan said with a chuckle.

Ewan turned to him thoughtfully. "How far would you go to win?"

"I can't win anymore, remember. But you could…"

Ewan stared at one of the props on the nearest shelf. It was a warrior's helmet like the one Leo had worn, bronze inlaid with violet. Determined. Resolute. He thought for a second. How far *would* he go to beat Jimmy? To see the tables turned on him for a change? To see the super-efficient façade crack? He smiled to himself…

10:51 pm

Jodie sat back and rubbed her eyes, the Kill-Soc screens giving her face a deathly pallor in the gloom of the office. As first days went, it had been pretty standard – the public message board had been awash with smack talk and threats, trying to goad each other into making stupid moves or presenting easy targets. The private message board had not only contained a fair number of kill notifications (which would remain private until Liam had verified them), but also the usual complaints about people's targets being too obscure, or modifications to rules. The most ridiculous had been a girl asking if she could use her actual hunting rifle, as long as it fired rubber bullets. That had been a resounding no – but at least Jodie was glad the girl had asked. Despite UCE Kill-Soc's accident free record, there was always that fear in the back of her mind that something like that could go drastically wrong. She knew that the BMU Wolf Hunt hadn't run this year because some idiot the year before fired an actual flare gun. Luckily it hadn't hit anybody, but it was enough for British Midland University to shut the game down. That was why she and Liam personally vetted each contestant, and Jodie prided herself on her ability to root out the psychos.

Her phone snapped her out of her thoughts, the cheesy pop ringtone awkwardly loud against the hum of the server unit.

"Hey handsome."

"Alright," Liam said, his voice tired. Whilst Jodie mostly stayed in the office, it was Liam's job to go around the city checking any disputes and delivering targets to those who had lost their photos or pulled off a kill with a trap. There were still the occasional contestants that didn't have regular email access or smartphones.

"Did you sort it?" A kill notification had been posted earlier, but the victim completely denied it, so Liam had gone to check it out.

"Yeah, great craic actually. It was a class trap. They'd put a fake piranha in with the other fish."

"In a fish tank?"

"Yeah, but chill – she invited the killer in. She tried to deny it, but her housemate grassed her up. Also saw her dip her hand right in. Trust me, she's dead." Jodie breathed out in relief. She knew that Liam was clear on the rules, but the last thing she needed was him okaying a kill and then having to backtrack and revoke it.

"Ok, well done."

"You ok?"

"Yeah. That was the last question mark. Hopefully the next hour will be quiet and then I'll post the first day kill notifications."

"Grand," Liam said. Jodie could tell from the tone of his voice that he was glad his citywide excursion was over. "I'll pick up a pizza on the way back."

Liam hung up and Jodie smiled to herself. At least she wouldn't have to worry about basic human needs like sustenance as long as Liam was with her. That boy seemed to eat nothing but takeaway, yet still managed to stay normal sized.

That was when she saw the message flashing patiently on the private screen. *Liam's gonna go mental if it's another dispute for him to sort,* she thought anxiously. Then she noticed that the user hadn't used the correct log in – the rules clearly stated that usernames had to be your first name followed by your contestant number. The only exceptions were her and

Liam, who simply had the prefix 'Gamesmaster'. It was easier than having to sort through endless stupid nicknames that could be from anybody. She read the message one more time:

Ki11er: Gamesmaster, we need to talk…

Not unless you're going to use the proper log on, she thought pedantically. She flicked the screen off and began to write up the kill notifications.

Day 1 Kills

Gemma006: Bless! Soaked total newbie David007 in the lecture theatre

Jen005: Just used mad ninja skills to stick Gemma006 with throwing stars
> **Jen005:** Ooh, just ran into my next target Rick008. The ninja strikes again!

Heather013: Reluctantly admitting that one of my best friends put a fake piranha in my fish tank. I guess I got eaten…
> **Jasmine012:** Come on, why would you put your hands in the water with a piranha in there??

Victoria020: Somebody actually put an alarm clock bomb under my beautiful car!

Ryan023: Knifed drama boy Leo024
> **Leo024:** You can do better than that, Ryan023! How about 'Rising Theatre Star tragically stabbed to death in front of sell out audience?'

Ewan022: After witnessing the death of my colleague Leo24, I had to take my revenge, pelting Ryan023 with the patented Deteuf Rubber Band Finger Gun
> **Ryan023:** I suppose I'll forgive you ;)
> > **Leo024:** Ewan! Call me! Now!

229

Hannah027: I love this game! Caught out sports jock Paddy028 by shouting 'catch.' He bled to death after catching my 'razor sharpened Frisbee.'

Nicola032: Took out Chris033 in the park

Adam034: Nothing like legally shooting your little sister Lucy035 with a 'poisoned' peashooter
    Lucy035: I hate you. I'm calling Dad

Stu037: Randomly came across my target Gareth038 with no weapons. Had to go tribal style and use a stick as a spear – that's allowed, right?
    GamesmasterLiam: That's fine, fella – good thinking

Andrew041: Totally embraced thug life by koshing Pete042 with some rolled up socks

Matt044: Nothing tops off breaking a new UCE freestyle record than seeing that the lifeguard is actually your target Marcus045, then smashing him with a pool noodle

Tina049: Strangled Emma050 in an alleyway. Nobody is safe – I will kill again

Becca053: Did you know that a twist of tissue makes a perfect garrotte? Ali054 does!

Ellie057: Came home to find my bed full of rubber venomous snakes. Turns out my little brother not only talks to strangers, but lets them into my room too

Suzy060: OK, somebody's been reading The Hunger Games too much. There was a papier-mache beehive stuffed into my locker. Consider me stung to death

> **Curtis059:** The Hunger Games is a book too??

> > **Sally065:** My locker had a huge toy gorilla in it

> > **Bryony066:** Mine too!

> > > **Graeme064:** Come on, I earn points for style. Nobody expects an angry gorilla in their locker

Tessa072: My cat came in with a 'bomb' tied to his collar

> **Patrick073:** The same happened with my dog. He was only out in the garden for ten minutes, then he comes back in and blows me up!

> > **Nadia071:** Jess074 didn't have any pets, so I just had to slingshot a pingpong ball at her

Helen078: Some joker filled my shed with red candles, each one labelled 'Dynamite'

> **Kirsty079:** Your shed?? I thought filling my bin was bad enough!

Phill85: Watch out, someone is laying tissue tripwires at the top of the staircases in halls. I 'fell to my death' in F Block

> **Holly086:** Yep – I also took a tumble down the G Block stairs. I guess I should have been watching where I was going

Millie091: Ok, so whoever did this deserves some serious credit. I went out for a smoke onto the balcony. It was only after I leaned on the railing that I noticed every single bar had a note taped to it saying that it had been 'sawn through' – looks like I'm now a giant mess on the pavement four storeys down

Emily093: My welcome mat had a pit dug out underneath it

Kelly095: Death from above! I managed to get two victims, Morgan096 and Nik097, by dropping pillows into the quad from my bedroom window. Was a bother to run and pick them up each time though!

<u>Day Two</u>

6:40 am

Jodie awoke on the thin mattress in the corner of the Kill-Soc office. Next to her, Liam lay face down, his breath lightly tickling her shoulder. She stared at the ceiling for a few minutes, before stiffly rolling onto the floor and reaching out for the small rucksack which contained a few changes of clothes. It was still early enough for her to get to the nearest bathroom to clean her teeth without being seen – she doubted it would look good if too many people found out she slept in the office during game week. It was also early enough for her to be sure she wouldn't have missed too much Kill-Soc action – the contestants were Uni students after all, so anything before 9am was classed as 'off peak'.

After returning with minty fresh breath, Jodie took another fond look at Liam, who had rolled over to face the wall, before plonking herself unceremoniously in the swivel chair, knees tucked up to her chin. She always liked reading through the messages that got posted after she had put up the kill notifications. If you read them carefully enough, you could work out different players' tactics, like whether they set traps or preferred a face to face kill. The cleverer contestants could also use the login numbers to try and work out who might be tracking them next. To her disappointment however, only one new message flashed up on the screen.

Ki11er: The game is changing…

A flush of anger rose up inside the Gamesmaster. How dare somebody write like they had some control over what happened here? Her fingers flashed across the keyboard.

GamesmasterJodie: Who is this?

The response came almost immediately.

Ki11er: I've caught your curiosity…
GamesmasterJodie: No, you've caught my temper. You're trying to interfere with a long standing tradition here, so back off.
Ki11er: A tradition of real people being fake assassins. It's getting old and predictable. All I'm asking is that you consider taking it to the next level. Blur the lines a little bit to recapture some of the excitement.

Jodie read the message again. It was true that a couple of students had started to comment that the game was running a little dry. Jodie had stuck with the same ideas for the last few years – it wasn't broke, so it didn't need fixing, but perhaps she had lost a little of the thrill of the game in sticking to the safe confines of success. She was normally adverse to trying something new, as she knew just how precarious Kill-Soc's position was with the higher ups, but perhaps it wouldn't hurt to hear a fresh perspective…

GamesmasterJodie: Well?

She hit enter and waited, her hand hovering over the keyboard. Nothing happened. After a few minutes, she got bored of staring at the empty screen. It occurred to her that she could check the master list to see which contestants were online, and she was just about to do so when another message appeared.

Lewis001: Hey, any chance we can meet up to talk?

Jodie thought for a second before typing her response.

GamesmasterJodie: Sure, come to the office at noon.

Gotcha, she thought as she hit enter. This time the idiot had posted without altering his log in. She would see what ideas this Lewis guy had about her game, then probably tell him to do one.

7:09 am

David Hughes had responded extremely uncharacteristically to his Kill-Soc defeat. He had gone and got wrecked. Whilst that may have been a regularity for most other students, he had been under constant pressure from his parents since the day he had started uni. They had their hearts set on him becoming a hot shot lawyer, indoctrinating him from an early age with Phoenix Wright games on his DS. As it was, he had always prioritised his work over his social life, and when he had heard Ewan going on about how cool Kill-Soc was, it had taken a lot of internal debating before he signed up for it. That only made his defeat worse.

Of course, due to his lack of experience in the drinking field, it hadn't taken much before he was completely annihilated and passing out on the actual field. Luckily, the weather had stayed dry, and when he had woken up against the bleachers wrapped in a Centaurs banner, he only had a banging headache to contend with, rather than pneumonia.

After saying a silent thanks to the UCE football team for their venue's hospitality, even if it was just a scraggy patch of grass with a ring of half height stands, he had done the walk of shame through town back to Halls. Luckily, students were rarely up this early, so he didn't have to explain himself to any curious onlookers along the way.

As he fumbled with his keys outside the door to the flat, the first thing David noticed was the sound of voices on the other side. It sounded like a lot of people, and he quickly scanned through his memory to make sure he hadn't overlooked a flat meeting, or worse, a visit from the Senior Resident. Drawing a blank, he pushed the door open and stepped inside. He immediately came face to face with Gemma, the girl who had shot him yesterday. His instant thought was that she had slept with Ewan before he dismissed that as he remembered Ewan's predilection for rugged guys.

"What are you doing here?" he managed. Even the sound of his own voice made his head pound harder and his vision wobble.

"Nice to see you too," Gemma said with a smile. "If you mean right now, I'm carrying this coffee to the front room." Only then did David register the coffee pot she was clutching. "But if you mean in general, then a few of us are here to talk about the game."

"Discussing your victory tactics are you?" David snorted, the embarrassment of how she had tricked him flaring up once more.

"Not quite. Turns out I got taken out shortly after I got you," she said with a shrug. David immediately found his anger softening. If she was eliminated too, then perhaps she might really want to speak to him. "Don't get your hopes up though Lawyer boy, I was asked here along with a load of others. Nothing personal I'm afraid." With that she bounced cheerfully into the communal area of the flat. *Mind reading bitch,* David thought acidly as he followed her.

There was quite a gathering in David's flat. As well as filling the patchy 3 piece suite, a number of chairs had been liberated from the ten bedrooms that lined the corridor in order to accommodate all the visitors. Animatedly working the room, Ewan was moving from group to group and despite the early hour, he was bright eyed and alert. As he saw David enter, he smiled, jogging over to him.

"Morning, you dirty stop out," he beamed.

David cast his eyes round the room. "How did you manage this?" he asked, avoiding Ewan's obvious reference to how rough he looked. They had a few flatmates that would not have been entirely thrilled with whatever Ewan's latest venture was.

"Most of the guys were ok with it as long as we keep the noise down," he began with a shrug. "And the ones that weren't, well…" He tapped his nose with a grin. "I'll burn that bridge when I come to it."

"So who are all these people?" Apart from Gemma, David couldn't remember seeing any of them before in his life – they also didn't look like Ewan's crowd of Theatre Studies friends.

"My bad, dude," Ewan said as he waved his arm over the group. "We have Leo from Drama, Ryan does Art, Gemma's a Media student, Victoria from Communications, Rick from Computer Science…" As Ewan continued, David zoned out. Even in a normal non-hungover state he wouldn't have been able to remember everybody's name. "This is great don't you think?" Ewan said with excitement after finishing his list.

"What exactly *is* this?"

Ewan thought for a second. "I guess you could call it a victim support group, of sorts. They were all eliminated on day one."

"And do they all know that you're still in the game?" David muttered, lowering his voice just in case they didn't.

"Another bridge that isn't important right now," Ewan said in equally hushed tones. "So will you join us? After all, I heard from Gemma that you got a bit wet yesterday." David looked again at the assembled party. *No, that was the wrong word*, he thought as he saw them arranging the chairs in a rough circle. It looked more like a meeting. He couldn't help wondering what Ewan's game was. Was he trying to get inside information on his future targets? If that was the case then David wasn't going to be part of it. Now that he was eliminated he didn't much care who won, but if Ewan managed it, it might make him insufferable to live with for the foreseeable future.

"I'm feeling kind of tired," David said, scrunching up his face childishly.

"Oh come on," Ewan said, chocking him on the shoulder playfully. "It'll be fun, I promise." He flashed David what he called his 'Pulling Smile'.

"Fine," David snapped in frustration. "Let me at least get changed first."

Ewan smiled once more, genuinely this time, as David stalked down the corridor to his room.

10:26 am

Jake Howell stood by the corner of the skate park, the giant
half pipe throwing its looming shadow over him. He
wrapped his arms around himself against the cold. He
wished he wasn't in his school uniform, as it was blatantly
obvious that he wasn't supposed to be there in his grey
blazer and blue striped tie. Unfortunately, the only way his
mum would let him out of the house in the morning was if
she thought he was going to school, so here he huddled
waiting to catch a glimpse of Mark, the guy Jonny Hayes so
badly wanted to find.

        Jake knew he could very well get himself into trouble,
after all, practically every adult ever could preach to him the
dangers of getting involved with strangers, and there was no
doubt that Jonny *was* strange (he wore purple trousers!) –
but, well, Jake's friends his own age were just so… boring.
All they did was hang around the same spot every single hour
they could, hovering on the edge of the skate park like
scavengers ready to jump in once the real skaters had left.
True, Jake repeatedly went with them because he had
nothing better to do – until now. And yes, he was well aware
that he was still hanging around the skate park, still not
actually daring to mingle with the others, but now it seemed
like it all had a purpose. He secretly hoped that once Jonny
had got to Mark, he might let Jake help him out on the next
target too.

        That was when he saw Mark strolling across the grass,
board slung across his shoulders. His beard looked scrappy
and uneven, but he still managed to look cool to Jake as he
broke into a jog before throwing his board onto the path and

jumping onto it, rolling casually up to the half pipe. It was a look that said he didn't give a shit about conforming to things like beard typicality. Jake flattened himself against the side of the structure and pretended to rummage through his rucksack.

He heard the roaring of wheels on polished wood slow to a halt, followed by the numerous slaps and shuffles that signified some complex greeting handshake going on.

"Miller!"

"Alright guys."

Jake listened intently to the inane conversation that followed, making mental notes of as much of their vocabulary as he could. He would use it to impress the peons later. It was as if the skaters were talking in some sort of secret code. Obviously, Jake recognised some of the names of tricks – like an olly was a jump, he remembered, but as well as that, they all had nicknames for each other, and ridiculous words for simple things like drink, or TV.

Next he heard the flinty click of a zippo lighter, and a strong smell of tobacco wafted across the park. It didn't smell like the cigarettes his dad smoked, and Jake assumed that the skaters were smoking something a little stronger. That was when the conversation got interesting.

"It's the Drink 'Til You Drop party at B5 tomorrow," one of them said. "You got anything to make it a bit more lively?"

"Nah man," Jake guessed this was Mark. "I've only got a half bag, and that's for me." A round of snickering rippled through the skaters. "Tell you what though, if I can get hold of a Stereotype later, I'm sure I can score you some happy."

"Yes mate!" This was followed by what sounded to Jake like a slap on the back. "Shall we say back here at 7 tonight?" Jake's ears pricked up.

"Sure dude," Mark said gruffly. "I'll T you if it falls through." *Bingo,* thought Jake. Now he knew exactly where Mark would be and when. He couldn't help grinning to himself as he shouldered his bag and sprinted towards the railings. He pulled out his crappy flip phone and dialled the number Jonny had given him the other day, excitement and pride swelling in his chest.

10:54 am

The Travel Journalism seminar had degenerated into its usual cross-table 'debate' between those with actually valid ideas, and those who simply wanted to say any old rubbish in order to score points with the lecturer. Ms Wells herself was sitting at her desk, watching the proceedings with something resembling hunger in her eyes. Seeing her students take matters into their own hands seemed to fill her with happiness.

Jonny was scribbling idly in his pad when his phone vibrated. He checked it under the desk, eyes glinting when he saw that it was Jake calling. All eyes snapped towards him as he rose from his seat, the heated topic of discussion suspended by this unexpected event.

"I have to take this," Jonny said, indicating his phone unapologetically. He was all too aware that he was risking some severe Wells wrath, but that was part of the thrill. The eyes followed him as he made his way to the door, and as it closed behind him, he heard Ms Wells tell the class that that sort of thing didn't usually happen in her seminars.

"Well?" he asked once he was safely round the corner.

"I found him!" Jake's voice rang with excitement.

"And?"

"And I know exactly where he's going to be at seven tonight."

"Go on."

Jake proceeded to explain about the conversation he had overheard at the half pipe, and Jonny couldn't help smiling to himself. His genius plan of using the kid as a spy had paid off sooner than he'd hoped "So can I be there when you do it?" Jake asked once he had finished relaying his tale.

"It will be kind of late for a school kid," Jonny replied honestly. The last thing he wanted was any suspicious questions from adults, and one thing that was likely to get them was arranging to meet a young boy at the park at night.

"So?" Jake snorted indignantly. "It won't be a problem, trust me. I'll tell my mum I'm round one of the guys' – she won't mind."

"I'm not sure…"

"Come on! I want to see what happens. I want to play when I'm older."

As he listened, Jonny felt his resolve softening. Using the boy made him sound ruthless, but *training* the boy – that was completely different. It was win-win, and surely nobody could complain about that. "Fine," he conceded. "I'll see you by the gate at half six."

"Yes!" Jake cheered before hanging up. Jonny decided not to go back to the classroom, choosing instead to slink off to prepare, head already filling with possible ways to eliminate Mark.

11:16 am

Ewan sat at the desk in his room, idly twirling the photo of his next target between his fingers. The meeting had finished and most of the guests had gone, apart from a few who had stayed around to put some last minute tactics into action.

The guy in the picture looked vaguely familiar, although Ewan couldn't place him. He had a flash of arrogance beneath his perfectly parted blonde hair, and Ewan was impressed that the guy had managed to capture it in the moment the camera had flashed. The picture was high quality too – not your average four quid photobooth job. Ewan's money was on a photography student – media studies at the very least, but he hadn't bothered to look his target's identity up. He'd made it to second place last year without wasting any time on pointless research, and he didn't intend to start now.

There was a knock on the door, and Gemma's head appeared. Ewan turned to look at her smiling at him – it seemed she enjoyed having a purpose once more. Whilst most of the people Ewan had invited over had already been eliminated, they seemed perfectly happy to help him out.

"I think we're ready to go on stage one," Gemma said brightly. "Ryan and Leo are setting up stage two."

Ewan could see why most of the other guys liked her, she seemed to shine with enthusiasm. He nodded before slipping the photo into his pocket and following her out into the corridor.

11:48 am

Since receiving the email from GamesmasterJodie outlining his next target, Jimmy had been using his time wisely. He had already found out her name, Harper, but he was having trouble finding out much else about her. She didn't seem to be active on any of the common social networks – either that or her security settings were ridiculously high.

He looked again at the photo attached in the email. A pretty girl, smiling right at the camera, long chestnut hair falling over her shoulders. There were no clues on her clothing, nothing that indicated any pastimes or club membership – it was just a plain tracksuit top. Jimmy sighed. He tried to picture her in various different scenarios: studying in the library? Cheerleading for the Centaurs? It all made his head hurt. Jimmy had always found trying to read people extremely difficult, not to mention annoying. Why should he have to work out what people were feeling? Everything in his life needed to have order, and usually he didn't bother with the chaos that was deciphering the emotions of others.

Dejectedly, Jimmy tried reading last night's kill notifications again to see if there were any clues. If Harper had made a kill yesterday, she might have let slip where it happened or at least what kind of weapons she favoured. No such luck – her first day seemed to have been uneventful.

Jimmy slammed his laptop shut in frustration. It looked as if he was actually going to have to venture outside to find out anything about his victim – something he loathed.

There was a soft knock on his bedroom door, before his mother stuck her head round. She smiled weakly as

Jimmy turned to face her. He waited expectantly for her to speak.

"Your game was on the news just now."

Jimmy arched an eyebrow. UCE itself rarely liked to publicise Kill-Soc, so it was unlikely to be anything positive. Even he could tell from the look on his mother's face that it was something bad.

"I'm worried, Jimmy. They're saying someone got hurt." She paused whilst Jimmy shifted uncomfortably. Sometimes people took it a little too seriously, but in the end it was all good fun - he just hoped it wasn't anything serious enough to get the game stopped.

"They're saying someone's died."

"What?"

Jimmy's mother took a step back, unused to the sound of her son's voice. "Apparently a body was found in the forest. They haven't said who it was or how they died."

"What's the link to Kill-Soc?" The words poured out of Jimmy's mouth before his brain's discomfort at speaking could override them.

"They found a Nerf Gun next to the body. That's one of the things you use isn't it?"

Jimmy nodded lamely. If this was true, it could mean the end of the game forever. "But…" He faltered, his stupid brain taking over. He wanted to explain that Kill-Soc gave him the only opportunity to be normal, to conquer his numerous idiosyncrasies. He wanted to tell her that he'd finally found something outside of education that not only was he good at, but that he really enjoyed. Instead, all he could manage was a shrug.

"It's not safe out there these days, what with this and that boy getting run down only the other night. You've always been independent Jimmy despite… well, just… just promise me you'll be careful won't you?"

Jimmy nodded once more, and his mother mirrored the gesture before backing out of the room. Rapidly filtering new possibilities and outcomes, Jimmy opened his laptop once more, typing in the first search engine he could think of.

11:52 am

"Well where the hell did it come from?"

Liam Brennan held the phone away from his ear as Jodie screeched at him. He had never heard her this angry before, and for once he was actually glad he was out in the city doing the donkeywork rather than being in the office with her. She sounded like she was chucking stuff around the cramped room.

"I don't know," he said, trying to placate her. He was sitting in one of the many trendy coffee bars, his laptop on the bar in front of him. It was one of those ultra modern places, walls covered in urban graffiti and nothing but ridiculously expensive fair-trade food on the menu. Even the cheese sandwiches came with grapes. Using his admin log in, he was on the Kill-Soc site, and Jodie was right to be angry. The whole message board was alive with panic over the news report, and new comments were pouring in every minute. Everyone was asking the same two questions – is it true? And if so, who died? A few contestants had already threatened to quit the game – something that had never happened since Jodie had been running things. She would be crushed.

"Anything?" Jodie asked. She was obviously trying to calm her voice, but Liam could still hear the strain. He scrolled back through the messages until he got to the first mention of the incident.

Gemma006: Has anybody seen the news? This is awful! www.ucenews.co.uk/4815162342

Liam clicked the link and was taken to the UCE News site. They had recycled the story from one of the nationals, and it was the same vague over-sensationalised reporting with little actual fact. There was no mention of the victim's name, time of death or anything, which struck Liam as odd – usually the newspapers tried to cram in as much as possible to boost their ratings.

"Not much," he muttered. "The first person to mention it is Gemma006."

"She's eliminated, right?"

"You tell me," Liam said with a sigh. Jodie's access in the office was much better than his remote access in the coffee shop. There was the sound of hasty key tapping before Jodie spoke again.

"Yes she is – find her. Find out how she heard about this."

"What about you?"

"I've got to stay here," Jodie said in exasperation. "I'm meeting that Lewis weirdo remember, the one who's on about revolutionising the game."

"Well good luck with that," Liam said with a concealed smirk. "I'll call if I find anything useful. Love you." He hung up and took another sip of his latte, before returning to the Kill-Soc site and dragging up Gemma006's profile.

11:56 am

After speaking to Liam, Jodie tried to calm down by checking her email. She immediately wished she hadn't. Not only was there already a bunch of messages asking if she was going to cancel the game because of the dead body, but she'd also received a snidy email from the Drama Lecturer about missing props. In past games, contestants had borrowed fake guns and stuff from the Performance faculty, but usually they asked first. Obviously not this year.

She looked once more at the list of missing items and frowned. Costumes? Number flags and rolls of striped warning tape? The more she stared, the less it looked like stuff that someone would use for Kill-Soc. She briefly considered firing off an equally snidy response, but thought better of it – after all, she could no more prove it *wasn't* Kill-Soc than the Drama Lecturer could prove it *was*.

Frustrated, the Gamesmaster spun her chair away from the screens and decided to wait for Lewis in silence.

254

11:59 am

Lewis Howard had been walking back from Lacrosse
practice with the Gryphons when it had happened. He had
worked up a good sweat, and his muscles ached – that was
why he'd simply watched the two girls chasing each other
and screaming, rather than intervened. Suddenly, the girl
behind had dug her hand into her pocket and pulled out a
handful of foam stars. She flicked them one by one, ninja
style - a cascade of rainbow coloured foam twirling away in
different directions. Lewis watched, fascinated as one of the
stars caught the other girl across the shoulder blades. She
instantly put her hands up and turned to face her opponent.

Although Lewis couldn't hear them from across the
street, he could tell that the girls bore no real animosity to
each other, and the victim handed over what looked like a
photo to the other girl. They were playing Kill-Soc.

As he continued along the street, disappointment
crept its way into his heart. Why hadn't he got into the game?
What set those two laughing girls apart? Why were they
worthy when he wasn't?

When he'd realised that the deadline for receiving the
invites had passed, he didn't think he was that bothered, but
now having witnessed the game in action, he wanted nothing
more than to be a part of it. He thought about talking to
Flynn, but his little brother had been acting distant for a
couple of days now. Lewis admitted to himself that he hadn't
been the best brother in the world – after all, Flynn had
come to stay with him to escape their constantly arguing
parents, and Lewis had pretty much left him on his own for
the first few nights, but now that Lewis did have a bit of

spare time, Flynn seemed to have found something else to occupy himself. Yesterday morning, when Lewis had gotten up for his 11am Sports Science class, Flynn had left a note on the table saying that he had gone into town and would be back later. Even calling Flynn's mobile resulted only in a brief conversation where Flynn stated he was fine before hanging up.

That was part of why Lewis had arranged to meet the Gamesmaster. If she could tell him why he didn't make the final 100, then perhaps he would be enlightened as to some disastrous personality failure he had, and get to work on fixing it.

That was yesterday, and now Lewis was crossing the quad, heading for the John Terrence building, where he vaguely knew the Kill-Soc office was. The four oak trees cast almost no shadows under the midday sun. Once inside, he made his way to the basement – that was the only space allocated for clubs and societies. He was vaguely aware that the Gryphons had an office down there somewhere, but like most of the other sports teams, they conducted any important meetings whilst getting blazed at the Union.

He read the names on the doors as he walked down the dingy corridor: Frag-Soc, Harry Potter Soc, LARP-Soc (he had no idea what that was), and then at the end of the corridor under the flickering light was the office he was looking for. The name Kill-Soc had been written in marker on a sticky label which was now curling at the edges. The only other door that far along was a narrow metal store cupboard, and as he got nearer, it opened, issuing forth two embarrassed looking students. The guy was in one of the other team uniforms; the girl wearing a cheerleader's top, crossed with UCE blue and gold. Both flushed and hurried off when they saw him – it was obvious what they'd been up to.

Once the two romantics had vanished, Lewis knocked quietly, the sound echoing up the corridor. He shifted his feet awkwardly as he waited. He checked his watch – he was right on time. As he stood there, he began to wonder what the girl on the other side of the door would be like. The leader of Harry Potter Soc would be a fairly obvious typicality, he reasoned, but what sort of person organised a widegame where people pretended to assassinate each other? He couldn't picture what that would look like.

"Are you coming in or what?"

The door had opened whilst he'd been thinking, and there she was. She was short, with long blonde hair that had a slight wave to it, but her viridian eyes were what set her apart. They were watching shrewdly as she took him in. If she hadn't scrutinised him through his application, she was certainly doing it now.

"Um yeah. I'm Lewis."

"Jodie," she said as she stepped aside to let him pass. It struck him how redundant the introduction was – they already knew each other's names from their logins. He cast his eyes around the small office, taking in the humming computers and the notice board covered in post it notes. He squinted, trying to catch any glimpse of information but Jodie blocked him, planting herself directly in his eyeline, hands on hips defiantly. He couldn't help thinking it was a bit of overkill – he wasn't in the game so it wasn't as if he could cheat.

"So," she said icily. "What's all this crap about changing the game?"

"I'm sorry?" Lewis frowned as anger flashed in Jodie's eyes.

"Taking it to the next level? Blurring the lines? Ringing any bells?"

"I have no idea what you're talking about," Lewis said, shaking his head. The colour seemed to fade from Jodie's cheeks as she reconsidered.

"You're not Killer? On the messageboards?"

Lewis shook his head again. "No, I'm Lewis001 – I thought you knew that?"

Jodie sank into the office chair, running her hand through her hair before regaining her composure. "Sorry, I guess I was mistaken. Take a seat. How can I help you? You know I can't tell you anything about your target, right?" Lewis plonked himself on what looked like a rolled up mattress before looking at her once more. Jodie obviously had other things on her mind, and now his reason for meeting her seemed petty and insignificant. She was watching him expectantly, and Lewis decided that asking her his question was probably more sensible than making some lame excuse and wasting her time completely.

"I'm not actually a contestant," he admitted. "I know you don't usually do this, but I was just wondering if you could tell me why I didn't make it into the game?"

Jodie frowned before spinning round on her chair and typing something into the computer. Her fingers flashed across the keyboard, and then suddenly, Lewis saw his own face staring at him from the screen.

"Lewis001. This is you." It wasn't a question. She turned to face him once more, then tilted her head towards the monitor in an over exaggerated comedy fashion, as if Lewis was some sort of simpleton who couldn't work out what was going on. She was half right.

"I don't understand," he muttered. It was definitely the picture he had sent in with his application – he remembered wearing his favourite v-neck, which he had since misplaced.

"It means you *did* make it into the game," Jodie said. "The fact that you have a functioning login should have been a big clue." It seemed to Lewis as if she was speaking as slowly as possible, as if she really believed she was talking to an actual idiot.

"I thought the login was just so everyone who applied could follow the game?" Lewis said, thinking back to the email he'd received shortly after applying.

"No," Jodie said flatly, frowning again. "Didn't you get the rules pack? Liam said he delivered them all…" Jodie's voice faded into the background as all the pieces seemed to fall into place. Flynn had started going off on his own around the same time the game must have started, and being reminded of the missing shirt only cemented things.

"Shit," Lewis breathed.

"I'll say," Jodie replied, this time with a genuine smile. "You've survived a day and a half without even trying. I'm surprised nobody came to hunt you down – we've had some pretty crafty kills already."

"It's not that," Lewis muttered. "I think my brother took my welcome pack. I think he's playing as me." Jodie turned back to the computer, clicking off Lewis' profile and bringing up the messageboard.

"Well," Jodie began thoughtfully. "Nobody's reported it, and 'you've' not made any kills either. What's he studying? We'll pull him from lectures this afternoon, but generally, I think we're ok."

"That's the problem," Lewis said, looking down at his feet. "He doesn't go here. He's only fifteen – he doesn't know the rules. He didn't even know about the game until he must have read my invite." Lewis' mind was filled with what his mother's angry rebukes would be when she found out, but when he looked back at Jodie, her face had fallen completely. "Don't worry," he said, holding out his hands.

"I'll totally accept responsibility. I'll make sure the game doesn't get spoiled or anything."

"It may be too late for that," Jodie said, ashen faced as she clicked a link which brought up a local news website. "Could your brother be involved in this?"

Lewis' mouth opened in horror as he read the headline. Someone toting a Nerf gun had been killed for real.

"Oh god," he breathed, panic rising in his throat. "He doesn't know the rules. He has no idea what he's doing – we have to find him."

12:21 pm

Jimmy had read the news article three times over before leaving the house. Sure, it was pretty vague, and nothing was concrete, but it had been enough to get his mother worried. Whilst he generally wasn't very good at reading others, he could detect when things weren't right. It was like a voice inside his head, muttering incessantly until whatever the issue was had been sorted. This made Jimmy angry. Kill-Soc was supposed to be one of the only times in his life when he didn't hear the voice. He could cast aside the systems and orders that usually controlled his life and pretend to be something else for a week or so. But now, thanks to the mysterious dead body, the voice was here, infiltrating the game.

Jimmy had tried blanking it out as he re-sorted his weapon collection, but it wouldn't stop. He would have to find out at least a little bit more in order to be able to continue the game – even if it was just the smallest scrap of information to put his mind at ease.

He didn't know if it was against the rules to visit the Kill-Soc office. After all, everybody knew where it was so it wasn't a big secret or anything. Besides, Jimmy wasn't actually looking to give himself an advantage in the game. He could simply pretend he was worried about the murder and wanted to know if the game would continue, which was partly true anyway. Whilst not the most expressive of people, if there was one emotion Jimmy could get across no problem, it was worry.

As he stalked along the Society corridor, he scanned left and right, half expecting a Nerf wielding assassin to jump

from one of the other offices. Nobody appeared. He began
to hear muffled voices, slowly sharpening into focus as he
approached the door at the end of the hall. There were two
people, male and female, and Jimmy supposed it was the two
Gamesmasters – Jodie and Liam.

"He has no idea what he's doing – we have to find
him." This was the male voice. Jimmy furrowed his brow
with curiosity. It sounded like something really had gone
wrong. Jimmy pressed himself against the wall as the voices
approached the other side of the door. Just in time, Jimmy
flattened as the door swung outwards, threatening to squash
him against the wall. Luckily it stopped a few centimetres
from his foot, and he remained undiscovered.

"He'll have access to other contestants," said Jodie
carefully. "Probably weapons too." Beyond the door, Jimmy
heard footsteps leave the office hurriedly. Inches away from
his face, fingertips curled around the wood and pulled the
door closed. Jimmy held his breath, a number of flimsy
excuses as to why he was hiding there flying through his
mind. Once again however, luck was on his side. As the door
swung away from him, the two people were already heading
up the corridor, deep in conversation. Jimmy watched them
hurry up the corridor – wherever they were going, they
obviously didn't want to waste any time. Neither of them
turned back.

Jimmy leant back against the wall as they disappeared
round the corner, his heart hammering against his ribcage.
Something had got Jodie worried, that was for sure. Hearing
the click of the office door shutting firmly, Jimmy silently
cursed himself for not having the quick thinking to jam his
foot in the door frame. This would have been the perfect
opportunity to have a quick look inside. He sighed, heading
back the way he had come, a new layer of murmuring
overlaying the voice in his head.

1:09 pm

David was pacing around the living room of his halls flat, a trail of scuff marks in the threadbare and vaguely blue carpet showing his route. The subject of Ewan's little meeting was still weighing heavily on his mind. Ewan had stated that he wanted to win the game, but surely this was taking it too far? Getting eliminated players to work for him had to be cheating surely? Once the majority of people had left, David had slunk back to his room, re-reading the information pack that had been sent before the game. There had been nothing in there mentioning something like this, but then perhaps it had never been done before?

The other option of course was to send a private message to the Gamesmasters, Jodie and Liam, and see what they said, but something was holding him back. If Ewan was in the wrong, then fair enough, but if it turned out that he was allowed to do what he was doing then David would always have the guilt of not trusting one of his friends – after all, Ewan had played Kill-Soc before, surely he knew the rules?

With a sigh, David decided to check with Ewan one final time, cursing his morality. He wondered if he would feel so strongly if he wasn't a law student? If he studied something like Computing, he didn't suppose he would give two shits if Ewan cheated his way to the top or not.

He stepped out into the corridor just as Ewan's door opened. A guy stumbled out, clutching his jacket in front of his chest. His shirt was untucked, and his cheeks were flushed. With a guilty glance at David, the guy hurried past him and out of the flat. Seconds later, Ewan emerged, grinning triumphantly and David shook his head. No matter how many random guys Ewan slept with, it was always them who wore the looks of shame afterwards.

"I thought you were strategizing with Gemma," David said bitterly.

"I was," Ewan began, stretching his arms. His shoulder cracked and he groaned theatrically. "Then I caught up with Rick. He was fixing something on my computer."

Yeah and then you fixed him, David thought as he felt his temper rising once more. He wasn't a prude or anything, but the way Ewan cut through the guys on campus was excessive to say the least. David could probably fit his entire list of hook ups into one week of Ewan's.

"How can you be like that?" he asked incredulously.

Ewan narrowed his eyes. "Like what? I'm just having fun – they know it doesn't mean anything."

"Don't you think it should?" David sighed.

"Not all the time. Sometimes it just scratches an itch… everyone goes away happy. Now do you mind, I need to shower." Ewan strolled past him nonchalantly.

"I didn't realise you were such a stereotype," David muttered.

Ewan whirled round. "I am *not* a stereotype," he hissed. "You won't catch me signing my soul away to some grand higher commitment."

"Hasn't there ever been a special one?"

Ewan paused and lowered his head. "There was one. Beautiful accent… but it didn't work out. After that I just decided all that relationship crap wasn't worth it."

"Maybe you should look him up sometime – get you back on the rails."

"You think I'm off the rails?" Ewan drew himself up to his full height, and David took a step backwards. He had forgotten how built the drama student was.

"I'm just saying, this whole Kill-Soc thing is going a bit too far, just to win, I mean."

"I always win," Ewan snarled, showing David a side he hadn't seen before. It struck him that the two flatmates didn't really know each other that well. "Why don't you go back to your case studies," Ewan continued smugly. "I think we can handle it without your help." With that, Ewan turned and stalked into the bathroom, slamming the door a lot harder than was necessary. David stood in silence, listening to the hissing sound of the shower and the rising notes of Ewan's singing. After a few moments, he went back to his own room and logged onto the Kill-Soc board. Ewan's little outburst had cemented his decision.

2:23 pm

Liam was on his third latte as he waited for Gemma to arrive. After his conversation with Jodie, he had messaged Gemma, asking her to meet him. He had deliberately kept it vague, not mentioning the article, and as he had suspected, Gemma had agreed to come. That was one of the perks of being a Gamesmaster – people generally did what you wanted.

Liam's laptop chirped, the message icon flashing in the corner of the screen. An elderly gentleman coughed politely and Liam's cheeks flushed as he muted the alert. He opened the message board, tilting the screen away as he read.

SecretAdmirer: Hey, so I'm hoping you've changed your mind. We could still work something out. There could be a lot riding on your decision…

Liam frowned for a moment, before remembering the drunken night at last year's after party. His hand went to the Kill-Soc badge pinned to his hoodie, the scarlet plastic shining under the café's spotlights. He didn't remember much about that night, after all, the Kill-Soc after party always had a free bar, but he was secretly pleased with the fact that somebody had slipped their number into his pocket. Of course he was unfalteringly loyal to Jodie, but it was always good to know that other people still found him attractive. His sister had always said that as soon as a guy got a girlfriend, he became invisible – Liam was glad that for him at least, that had proved untrue.

He turned once more to the message, re-reading it with narrowed eyes. Why now, almost a year later? An image of some psycho bitch sitting alone in her room with a load of pictures snuck on her phone flashed across his mind. He shuddered.

GamesmasterLiam: I'm sorry, I'm with Jodie – Nothing's going to change that.

His finger hovered over the enter key but something kept him from pressing it. Reading it back, it sounded weak somehow, like he was a soppy wuss. He hit delete and retyped a harsher response.

GamesmasterLiam: Look, this isn't some lame Rom-Com where you get what you want every time you pour out your feelings. And don't think you can guilt trip me because you simply 'can't go on without me' – I'm with Jodie and I always will be. Get over it.

The reply came almost immediately.

SecretAdmirer: Thanks for putting things into perspective. Good luck, Gamesmaster.

Good luck? An inexplicable chill ran down Liam's spine. Good luck with what?
    "Hey. Liam, right?"
    He looked up to see a blonde girl smiling at him. "You must be Gemma," he said as he slammed his laptop shut. "Take a seat."

3:37 pm

Flynn couldn't help grinning to himself. He felt like Alex Rider from those novels he used to read. The idea that a totally normal kid could find himself in situations where he had to avoid getting hunted down and killed seemed absurd at the time, but now here he was playing his own real life version.

It hadn't taken him long to identify his target – the ginger guy in the photo was wearing some sort of sports top, and after a quick flick through Lewis' Team Yearbook, Flynn found him. Glen Hemmings was one of the reserve midfielders for The Centaurs, UCE's football team. After a quick google search, Flynn had also discovered that The Centaurs were playing a Varsity match against the Wolves of BMU later that day.

As much as Flynn loved his brother, Lewis wasn't exactly the sharpest knife in the drawer. His wallet was left open on his desk, and surprise surprise, one of the many post it notes stuck around the edge of the computer monitor contained his credit card PIN. With only a small sense of guilt and a mental promise to pay Lewis back, Flynn had bought himself a ticket for the match, and that was where he was now, sitting amongst a crowd of roaring students on a set of freezing concrete steps.

Flynn's dad had never bothered taking his son to a football match. Lewis had always shown the interest in sports, and that was why he capitalised on 'dad time'. Flynn was usually left at home to read his favourite books or play on his computer. He had to admit that he was kind of glad, as he wrapped his arms around himself. It was almost the end of the first half, and Flynn was bored out of his mind with the game in front of him. The only thing keeping him from leaving was the thought of the secret game going on at the same time.

He had spent the first ten minutes flicking his attention between the miniscule players on the pitch, and their larger than life versions on the screens that hung above the seats. Most of them were generic jocks, looking like dumb mouth-breathers, but there were a few that stood out. The Captain, Ashford, looked like he'd walked straight out of a Hollister window, and of course Glen had the fiery ginger hair Flynn had seen in the photo. That made him relatively easy to spot down on the pitch where he sat on one of the benches that lined the grass. Whilst Flynn had little grasp of the actual rules of football other than the need to kick the ball into the opposite goal, he was well aware that the reserves didn't play all the time.

The whistle for half time finally blew, and Flynn jumped to his feet, racing down the stairs to outrun the swarms of idiots heading for the nearest bar. Jumping the last couple of steps to avoid a pool of spilled beer (at least that's what he hoped it was), Flynn whirled round and ducked into the shadows of one of the passages that ran beneath the seats. Thankfully, the security staff were all busy herding the drunkards to notice the skinny fifteen year old sneak into the depths of the arena.

As soon as Flynn was away from the public area of the building, all pretences of grandeur faded, the corridors becoming plain concrete with sickly yellow electric lights. Even though the Varsity match warranted the hiring of the large arena in the city centre, he supposed that all venues must be like this really - only looking glam and spotless for as far as the people could see.

The corridor curved gently, and Flynn assumed it ran in a big loop underneath the pitch. Occasionally, closed doors appeared but there were no sounds from behind them. Eventually he came to something promising – a slope that ran upwards onto the edge of the pitch itself. Just moments ago, he had seen the players, including Glen, jog down this slope, and that meant that they had to be somewhere close. Sure enough, Flynn heard a man's voice booming from out of a nearby room, where the door had been propped open with a muddy boot.

"Not a bad first half," the voice barked. He sounded like one of those dreaded army commanders that would bully their troops, and Flynn supposed he must have been the coach. "Marshall, pick up the pace lad! Ashford, you have to keep pushing forwards. We are *this* close. I'm not having those bastards beat us again!" This was followed by a chorus of roaring, and Flynn could just imagine the cro-mags slapping each other and banging heads as they psyched themselves up. He couldn't help but roll his eyes and wonder if Lewis was like this before his Lacrosse matches.

The testosterone-fest died down, and the grunting was replaced by the sounds of boots being re-laced, and empty water bottles being discarded. Flynn's heart raced as he realised that they were getting ready to come back out. He pressed himself against the concrete wall beside the door frame as one by one, The Centaurs marched out, each in their own wave of sweat barely concealed with deodorant. The crowd inside the stadium erupted into a mass of clapping, cheering and chanting as the first of the line, which Flynn assumed to be Ashford, stepped up onto the grass.

Finally, he spotted the ginger back of Glen's head. Flynn fumbled in his back pocket and pulled out a soft foam boomerang. It was the only thing the crappy corner shop by Lewis' place had that even vaguely resembled a weapon.

Obviously, it was crumpled from where he had been sitting on it, and Flynn flustered, desperately trying to get it back into shape. Glen was almost at the bottom of the slope, and behind him was a large out of shape man in a tracksuit. If Flynn didn't act now, Glen would be back on the pitch and out of reach.

"Hemmings!" Flynn shouted, his voice almost lost in the ululations of the crowd. Almost, but not quite. It was the tracksuited man that turned first, a frown appearing on his blotchy face. Before he could say anything, Glen stopped and turned, just as Flynn threw the boomerang.

The weapon flew in a wide arc, glancing off Glen's shoulder, his face contorting with rage. The footballer stepped forwards angrily, but the coach blocked him.

"Don't you even think about leaving this game," he shouted so loudly that his face went even redder. The coach roughly shoved Hemmings up the slope before turning back to Flynn. "I'll be talking to those bloody Gamesmasters about you, you little shit," he spat, jabbing a finger in the teenager's direction. He spat once more onto the ground before pulling a walkie-talkie out of his pocket as he strolled up the slope. "Security?" he snapped.

That was all Flynn needed to hear. He turned to run, but was struck by a sudden thought. Hadn't the Kill-Soc instructions mentioned getting the next target off your victim? How was Flynn going to do that now? If he hung around until after the game, Glen Hemmings would probably rip him to bits - if the coach didn't get him first. That was when he noticed the locker room door was still propped open. Whilst everyone else was focusing on the start of the second half, Flynn slipped inside and found the locker crudely labelled with Glen's name. He frowned as he rummaged around in Glen's kit bag, aware that he had spent far too much time lately closer to guys' underwear than he normally liked. Luckily, he found what he was looking for, and stuffed the next target into his pocket before leaving the room.

"Hey!"

Flynn froze as a torch flashed in his face - which was odd, considering all the lights were on. Shielding his eyes, Flynn could just make out the outline of a man. He was tall, with a bright green polo on, 'Security' emblazoned across the front like some flashy band logo.

"What are you doing down here?"

"Um," Flynn faltered. "I'm the kit boy?" He said the first thing that came into his head. The security guard scratched his stubbly chin thoughtfully, as if processing the existence of such a job.

"There's been a report of some kid down here assaulting players." *Assault? That was a bit harsh.* "You seen a scrawny kid with a boomerang?" The guard spoke slowly, as if still trying to work out if 'kit boy' was an actual thing. Flynn couldn't help looking behind the guard, where the fluorescent pink weapon lay on the slope.

"Nope," he said in a strained voice. "Now can I go? I have to um, sort the kit."

The guard thought for a second more before nodding his head. Flynn walked until he was out of sight around the curved corridor then broke into a jog, a grin fifty miles wide across his face. He felt like he was truly alive! He'd come to stay with Lewis to get away from his parents, but it was this now, that had truly given him the break he'd needed.

Once he had left the arena, he sat on a bench in the nearby park, watching the last of the afternoon dog walkers and joggers. A statue of a Greek Warrior cast a lengthening shadow across the grass, and the faint sound of a nearby fountain hissed in the background. Flynn's cheeks were stinging from grinning so much and he sat back, thoroughly satisfied. That was when his phone rang. Fishing the brick out of his pocket, he saw that it was Lewis' number. Without really knowing why, he let it ring out – his phone was too vintage to even have an answerphone message. As the number vanished from the screen, Flynn was suddenly glad he hadn't answered.

A string of texts from Lewis soon flooded his inbox, all of them different variations of the same message. Lewis knew Flynn had hijacked his game profile, and the fifteen year old was in big trouble.

Flynn knew he couldn't go back to his brother's. Not until the game was over.

4:35 pm

Liam sighed. Gemma had gone to the bathroom, but the meeting with her had been a total waste of time. She admitted to posting the first message about the murder report, but she couldn't remember where she got it from. According to her, she had picked up the link whilst trawling through Facebook, and that meant it was practically untraceable. Liam sighed again. It wasn't that he didn't enjoy spending nearly all afternoon tanking cheap coffee, but he was well aware that by now, the Kill-Soc to-do list was probably overflowing with disputes about false kills and cheats – and that was what Liam's real job was supposed to be.

He clicked refresh on the news site whilst waiting for Gemma to return, his eyes narrowing as the page changed. The latest update included a picture of the crime scene. Liam leaned in, scanning the grainy picture. There was a young looking police officer standing next to a taped off area, surrounded by trees and foliage. A dozen or so brightly coloured evidence markers were strewn across the ground, indicating where clues had obviously been discovered. Liam's heart sank – this certainly increased the likelihood of the murder being legit. He thought about calling Jodie, but stopped. It would no doubt ruin her day even more, and besides, it wouldn't take her to see it on her own anyway.

"Cool badge."

Liam looked up to see Gemma standing in front of him. She had her coat on and her bag was slung over her shoulder. One hand was returning her smartphone to her pocket. She was staring eagerly at the scarlet pin on Liam's top.

"Thanks," Liam muttered as he stuffed his laptop into his bag. "A fan made it for me."

"You must have lots of fans…"

Liam looked up once more, noticing that Gemma's posture had changed completely. Now she was leaning slightly forward and her eyes were wide with fluttering lashes. Her lips were pushed together into a pout.

"You know, it's the Drink 'Til You Drop party at B5 tomorrow," Gemma continued. "Maybe you could get the evening off?"

Liam began to shift uncomfortably on the stool as his mind tried to process what exactly was happening. Gemma was edging closer until she was practically leaning over him, her perfume blossoming over him and invading his nostrils. He panicked, thrusting his arms out in front of him.

"Wait," he flustered. "I'm with Jodie!"

Gemma took a step backwards, a hurt look flashing across her face. "But I thought…"

"Thought what?"

"This whole thing," she shrugged. "Calling me out here just to ask about some stupid news report?"

Liam's cheeks flushed with anger, thoughts spiralling chaotically through his mind. Had Gemma been the one at last year's after party? Perhaps she had pretended to notice the Kill-Soc badge on purpose? If it was her, then she obviously hadn't got the message when he'd replied earlier.

"Look!" he snapped harshly. "Why can't you understand? I'm happy with what I've got – you can't just swan in here with your flirty eyes and your ridiculous curves and expect something from me." Cheeks burning, Liam glared at her, her eyes shining with embarrassment. The mascara she had obviously just applied when she was in the bathroom was beginning to collect at the corner of her eyes, threatening to trickle down in dark tears.

"I just thought it was a cool badge," she murmured quietly, the background noise from the café almost drowning her out. "I didn't mean to upset you."

"Yeah, well," Liam muttered, refusing to meet her gaze.

"You didn't have to be so blunt."

Liam shrugged awkwardly, and she hovered for a moment before clutching her bag and marching towards the door, drawing an inquisitive look from the waiting staff who obviously thought this was top notch gossip to fuel their never ending shift.

4:37 pm

The heat of the sun was beginning to fade as Jimmy wistfully strode along the path, his eyes glued to the pavement. He had wandered around in this fashion for a couple of hours, unable to tie down one specific thought in the whirlwind that consumed his mind. This was not how Kill-Soc was supposed to go – it was meant to be the one time when his life was a linear process. Hunt. Kill. Repeat. But now it was threatening to become just like the rest of his existence, which was a clutter that often needed lengthy periods of sifting to avoid breakdown. Something had got the Gamesmasters worried – most probably the news report his mother had mentioned – but rather than just force it to the background and pretend that everything was ok until the game was over, they were making it the main priority. And if everyone else was prioritising it, then Jimmy would also have to.

He drew close to a group of people, instinctively lowering his head. He could already see that they were holding flyers of some sort, and that always led to awkward conversations where Jimmy was usually bullied into signing up for some stupid charity because he couldn't articulate a good enough refusal. He was just about to skirt past them when he thought he heard them say 'Kill-Soc'. Looking up, he recognised his first kill, Victoria Newton. There were also other contestants that Jimmy had seen in previous games. He assumed they were all eliminated, otherwise they wouldn't have been standing together like one huge target. Victoria caught his eye and smiled.

"Take a flyer, sweetpea," she said warmly. If she had any clue that she was talking to the one who had knocked her out of the game, she didn't show it. Jimmy snatched the brightly coloured paper from her hand and shuffled off before she could say anything else.

Once he was a few steps down the street, he looked at the flyer, his brow furrowing with confusion. It was a harshly drawn propaganda sheet depicting a Nerf gun firing a dart covered in blood. It was accompanied by the lengthy slogan of 'Stop Kill-Soc: It's no longer a game.' He crumpled the sheet and threw it into the nearest bin with disgust.

That was when Jimmy's mind finally settled. Amongst the shifting pathways and options that had stretched mazelike through his consciousness, a single route became clear and all the others blinked out of existence. That was how Jimmy's mind worked – as soon as the most obvious and logical approach was discovered, then all alternatives became obsolete. Jimmy had reasoned that if this potential murder case was distracting everybody from playing Kill-Soc, then the sooner he sorted it out, the sooner the game could resume.

He halted, catching sight of something out of the corner of his eye. A square of paper, glossy white against the thousand greys of the grit. A glimmer of recognition blossomed in Jimmy's mind, and he was certain of what the paper was, just as he was certain about the splatters of crimson that were next to it.

Jimmy nudged the paper with his shoe until it flipped over, confirming his suspicions. Staring up at him was a passport picture – a guy in a polo shirt, blonde hair meticulously parted and slicked back, and an arrogant grin flashing across his face. The photo was cut out roughly and one of the corners was bent inwards, a red stain seeping into the picture from a thumb shaped splodge. It was blood.

Looking around cautiously, Jimmy knelt to retrieve the picture, knowing in his heart that it was a Kill-Soc target photo. But why would it be here? Unless the person carrying it had been hurt?

Suddenly, a shoulder barged into Jimmy, sending him off balance. He dropped to one knee to steady himself before looking up at who had run into him. It was a girl, and even Jimmy could tell she was upset. Makeup ran in dark stormy streaks down her face, and she was sniffling through halting sobs.

"I'm sorry," she said in a broken voice. She hovered for a moment wiping her eyes as Jimmy got back to his feet. Once she had seen that he was unhurt, she hurried along her way, clutching her bag against her chest as she ran. Jimmy turned from her retreat to the door she had just emerged from, still swinging in her wake. It was one of those trendy coffee shops with confusing art splashed across the walls, and ridiculously overpriced cake. Jimmy edged towards the window, peering inside out of curiosity.

There were two guys sitting together, leaning in and absorbed in their conversation. They certainly didn't look as if they had just caused a girl to storm out. That just left one other customer. He was standing with his back to the window, wearing a simple hoodie and jeans. He was just in the process of closing a satchel and was about to swing it over his shoulder – nothing unusual or out of the ordinary. Jimmy was about to walk on, when the figure inside the café turned around. It was Liam Brennan, one of the Kill-Soc Gamesmasters, and he had a face like thunder.

Jimmy ducked out of sight as Liam pushed the door open roughly and strode down the street, thankfully in the opposite direction to where Jimmy was hiding, and in which the girl had fled. As Jimmy looked once more at the crumpled photo clutched in his palm, a couple of grating thoughts clicked together in his head. Firstly, it was obviously Liam who had upset the girl, and secondly, it was obviously *not* Liam that Jimmy had seen leaving the Kill-Soc office with Jodie – and in that case, perhaps it was Liam that Jodie and the other guy had been talking about.

Jimmy's mind fractured into two courses of action – both of equal importance in Jimmy's reasoning. One option was to follow Liam and find out what had happened between him and the girl – and perhaps also find out why Jodie seemed so intent on tracking him down. The other option was to try and discover more about the picture he'd found – if he could find out who it was of, or even better, who had it as their target, then he might be able to get closer to the root of the trouble.

Normally, Jimmy would have shut himself away somewhere, endlessly deliberating the pros and cons of each option, but as he looked up he saw that Liam had vanished from sight. One option immediately blinked out. Jimmy pocketed the photo, turned on his heels and headed back the way he had come.

5:25 pm

Now that Jake had found out where his target was going to be, all Jonny had to do was lay low until the allotted time. That way, his assassin would have no chance of getting him first.

It had started off fine, and as soon as he had returned from his seminar, he had occupied himself with various activities. But now, after doing some half-assed exercises in front of his Nintendo, watching a couple of episodes of Lost on DVD, playing about with some yearbook layouts and even reading a chapter of his current book, Jonny was bored. To make it worse, he had smoked all of his cigarettes — which, considering his flatmates' (and indeed UCE's) stance on smoking indoors, was saying something.

He still had a good hour until he said he would meet Jake, but now that he'd made the fatal mistake of actually acknowledging the time, he found himself looking at the clock in annoyingly small increments, making time crawl inexorably slowly.

He was almost tempted to run down to the off license and buy another 20 deck, but could he risk it? On one hand, the shop was literally about 50 metres along the street (close enough for him to have made the trek in his pyjamas on numerous occasions), but on the other hand, carelessness now could cost him the game.

A harsh electronic bleating shook him from his thoughts as the buzzer rang from outside. One of the others was sure to get it, Jonny thought as he tapped a brief rhythm on the edge of his desk. Seconds passed, and still he didn't hear the sounds of one of his flatmates opening the door.

Were any of them even in? Jonny hadn't bothered to check when he got home, he had just assumed that one of the five others must have been around – it was rare that the house was ever empty.

The buzzer rang again, this time making Jonny jump a little. Flustered, he got up and moved into the hallway, sticking his head around the corner of the living room door to see the room unoccupied. Empty beer cans were stacked in a pyramid on the table, but that was no sure sign of inhabitants. Jonny himself was guilty of leaving plates to pile up under his bed until they grew various types of mould.

Jonny edged closer to the window, hoping for a glimpse of whoever was at the door. As he stepped around the standard Ikea coffee table, he was wishing in his mind for the person to have left. The buzzer hadn't rung again, so maybe whoever it was had got bored. Jonny crept forwards, his breath catching in his throat for some reason.

Suddenly a shadow appeared against the glass and Jonny froze. Even through the net curtain he could tell it was human shaped. Someone was actually trying to look through the window! Jonny instantly dropped below the windowsill, pressing his back against the wall, his breath coming and short quick bursts. *Surely this was against the rules?* he thought to himself frantically as every cheap American horror movie scenario flashed through his memory. What were the laws? He was pretty certain that 'Don't answer the door' was one of them, but the others eluded him.

Outside, he could hear the sounds of footsteps crunching through the flower bed beneath the window, and as he looked out across the room, Jonny saw the shadow move across the wooden floorboards as the figure moved across the length of the window. By the looks of it, the visitor was moving around the side of the house, and Jonny's eyes flicked to the other window that was set in the left hand wall. If the person peered through that one then Jonny's hiding place would be easily visible.

Jonny lowered himself into a crouch, planting his fingertips on the floor. Silently, he slunk around the back of the sofa, carefully trying to stop himself from rising too high. He had barely managed to tuck his legs in beneath the other window ledge before he saw the tell-tale silhouette, proving that the stranger was scanning the room once more. Jonny cursed, holding his breath. What made them so sure he was definitely in there?

All thoughts of cigarettes were silenced as Jonny sat there for what felt like hours. Even after the shadow had retreated, Jonny waited, anger building. Normally he was confident, arrogant even as he lorded it over the peons. Nothing fazed him usually, but here he was, made to feel like some sort of prisoner by some jerk trying to intimidate him.

This is stupid, Jonny thought. *This is my bloody house!*

Self-assurance returning, Jonny stood up, his knees cracking as he straightened his legs. He turned to the window and let out a gasp, icy fear spreading through his body.

Someone was leaning against the garden wall, and although they were wearing some sort of visor like a paintball mask, Jonny could tell they were staring right at him. They hadn't gone anywhere at all, instead choosing to wait until Jonny revealed himself.

Both men sprang into action at the same moment. Jonny backed into the hallway whilst the stalker burst into a sprint out of sight. Was the kitchen door locked? Jonny couldn't remember ever having locked or unlocked it, but his flatmates were always in and out of the garden. He ran into the kitchen and slammed into the door, pressing his shoulder against the glass as he turned the lock. Panting, he squinted through the glass, cursing the stupid frosting that turned everything into a blur of shifting mottled blobs. It was hard to tell if the intruder was there, or if it was just the pine hedge blowing in the wind.

The buzzer rang again, and this time they held their finger on the button so the harsh alarm rang constantly, pounding in Jonny's ears.

Right, Jonny thought, pulling his mobile from his pocket. *No more dicking around.* He unlocked the screen and thumbed 9 twice. All it would take is one more 9 and he would be through to the police. He marched out into the hallway once more and resolutely picked up the plastic handset mounted on the wall, thankfully silencing the screaming siren.

"What do you want?" Jonny asked, voice shaking.

"I'm not going to hurt you," a male voice rasped. "I just want to talk."

"Is it about the game?"

"In a way."

Jonny thought for a second before reaching a decision. Screw the rules of the movies – this was real life. "Fine." He replaced the handset before ducking back into the kitchen and grabbing the first thing he could from the counter – a chunky wooden rolling pin. As he slowly approached the front door, he dropped the primed phone into his jacket pocket and held his other arm behind his back, keeping the makeshift weapon out of sight. He was surprised to see his hand shaking as he reached for the latch.

He pulled the door inwards, and was greeted by a looming shadow in a duffle coat, the hood raised into an ominous point. Jonny couldn't make out any facial features behind the cold mask.

"Jonny Hayes," the figure said gruffly. "I need you to die."

In a flash, Jonny thrust the door shut, but he was too late. The attacker already had a boot jammed in the frame.

Clearly stronger, the stranger forced the door inwards once more, and Jonny was pushed backwards, stumbling to the ground. As the attacker advanced, Jonny swept along the hallway crab-like until he felt his back hit the first step of the staircase. He swung the rolling pin, catching the figure in the side of the head. The assailant grunted but remained undeterred, catching Jonny's second swing in gloved hands and wrenching the weapon from his grip. Jonny fumbled in his pocket, his heart almost stopping when he found it empty. Casting around widely, his eyes finally settled on the phone where it lay against the skirting board after his fall, the two nines glowing prominently on the screen.

6:41 pm

Once more, Jimmy found himself hovering in the Society corridor. He had a vague notion in his mind that if he could somehow break into the Kill-Soc office, and then somehow get onto the main server, he could find out about the photo he'd found. Once he knew who it was and who was hunting them, he could get their details and... he didn't know what exactly. Help them? That was completely uncharacteristic for Jimmy, but if it meant that the game could resume normally, then he was prepared to do whatever he had to. He was aware that there were a lot of 'somehows' in his plan, but he was willing to try.

Thinking back to the various action movies he'd seen, Jimmy slipped a bank card out of his wallet and took a furtive look back up the corridor. There was nobody else around, so he went to work. Carefully, he slotted the card into the gap between the door and the frame, roughly where he thought the bolt would be. And then what? In the films, they just wiggled it around for a bit and the lock magically popped open. With a frown, he tested the card in each direction, but it only moved a few millimetres each way.

Jimmy put the card away and prepared for his second plan of attack. Unfolding one of his mother's hair clips, he had it on the good authority of many Hollywood villains that you could force the tumblers in a lock, again by pretty much just waggling it around until it clicked.

"Are you alright there fella?"

Jimmy jumped and dropped the hair clip. He whirled around to see Liam staring at him questioningly. The Gamesmaster was wearing the same indigo hoodie from in the coffee shop, a red badge of some sort pinned to the front. He had his messenger bag slung over one shoulder and he had reached up to snatch the glasses off his face. It didn't look as if he'd noticed the hairclip on the carpet, or worked out what Jimmy was actually trying to do.

"I was just…" Jimmy faltered, his brain struggling to adapt to this new random element.

Liam narrowed his eyes suspiciously. "I know you." He took a step forward, halving the gap between him and Jimmy. "You're part of the game."

Part of Jimmy's brain wanted to yell that *of course* Liam knew him – he only won the bloody thing last year, but his crippling social awkwardness kept him gawping incoherently. Another part of Jimmy's mind was flushed with anger that he could have overlooked something as simple as getting caught. If he had planned for this possibility beforehand, then he would have switched track smoothly and would have been able to talk to Liam like a half normal human being. A final feeling was a slight twinge of fear. Liam had made that girl at the café run out in tears. It was also likely that Jodie and her companion had been worrying about something Liam had done or was about to do.

"Look," Liam said in a frosty tone that didn't suit his slight appearance. "Can I help you with something?" He advanced once more, and all Jimmy could see was his personal space getting smaller and smaller, his avenues of possibility reducing by the second.

"No!" Jimmy burst out in a loud voice. "Fine!" He pushed his way past Liam and ran away down the corridor, leaving the perplexed Gamesmaster staring after him in confusion.

6:55 pm

Jonny Hayes was late, and Jake Howell was getting annoyed. The sky was pale but the sun had pretty much gone, and the air was chilly. In the usual bout of mum-angering posturing, Jake had come out without his coat, and now he was starting to regret it.

The skate equipment cast long shadows across the grass like a great spider creeping through the blades, and Jake checked his watch one more time. He was frustrated that it looked like Jonny had ditched him. Yes, Jake had badgered the student to let him come, but surely if Jonny had really not wanted him there, he wouldn't have agreed. Maybe Jonny thought he was too cool to be seen hanging out with a kid? And if that was the case, then Jake was even more disappointed. Obviously from his chinos and polo shirts, Jonny was a poser, but Jake never thought he would prioritise his image over progressing in the game – and if Jonny missed his target's little rendezvous, then he was sacrificing a major opportunity.

Jake heard voices approaching the skate park from the other side. He knew it wasn't Jonny, because he assumed Jonny would have come alone, so that left only one possibility – it was Mark and his friends about to make their 'trade'. *Unless it was the mysterious UCE killer,* he thought with a shudder. Another thing his mum had been moaning about was some news report about a body in the woods. Again, going out alone had been to show her how brave he was.

Peeking out from behind the looming half-pipe, Jake saw the familiar beanie hats and boards, although this time their whole demeanour had changed. Their voices were hushed, and they hardly took their eyes from the ground, even though there was nobody else in sight. It was as if the mere fact that they were doing something illegal meant that they had to act all shifty like they were about to get caught at any moment.

Jake turned away as one of the goons began to dig something out of his pocket. It was probably a fat wad of cash like Jake had seen on GTA, and that meant that the meeting was nearly done. Jonny Hayes was a dick, Jake decided. Screw his Kill-Soc plans! If he was too embarrassed to have Jake's help, then next time he asked, Jake would tell him to jog on. The teen kicked out angrily, his shoe catching a lump of grit and sending it flying onto the smooth surface of the half pipe. Jake followed the rock in horror as it skidded across the polished boards with a clatter, coming to a stop a few feet from the Vans of the nearest miscreant. All three of the older guys were staring in his direction, one of them clutching a small polythene bag to his chest protectively.

"What are you staring at?" Mark sneered, his patchy facial hair making his expression look gaunt and shadowed.

"Nothing," Jake said, his voice choosing that precise moment to break embarrassingly. The others laughed.

"Fuck off then."

"Wait dude," one of the cronies interrupted, and Mark turned back to see him indicating the baggie that Jake could see was filled with green leaves.

Mark slowly faced Jake with a grin. "Do you know what that is, kid?"

"I won't tell anyone, I swear," Jake stammered, fear rising as he caught the look in the skater's eye.

"I'm sure you won't," Mark chuckled. "But let's give you some incentive anyway."

Jake cast his eyes around the park in search of anybody he could call to, but the field was empty. Looking once more at the three advancing skaters, all of Jake's bravado and confidence dripped away. He cursed his desire to leave his peers behind and immerse himself in the world of Kill-Soc and the university, and not caring that the boys were going to laugh even more whilst they kicked him to the ground, Jake Howell cried.

7:11 pm

The Union bar was already starting to fill up with the
evening's revellers, but Lewis wasn't in the mood for fun.
Jodie had returned to the Kill-Soc office. They'd also
brought Liam up to speed on the situation, but he'd had no
luck tracking Flynn down either. They had told Lewis to go
home and wait for Flynn there, but his little brother wasn't
stupid. It wasn't like he was some lost child. Flynn knew
exactly where he was and how to get home if he wanted, he
just hadn't yet. And that was worse in a way, as it meant that
Flynn was being a dick on purpose. Lewis sighed as he
looked at the bottom of his empty glass. He gave a nod to
get the Firefly's attention. All the students called the bar staff
Fireflies on account of their bright yellow polo shirts. No
matter how dark it got on the dancefloor, you could always
see them flitting about collecting glasses.

"A bit early isn't it?"

"It's always beer o'clock somewhere," Lewis muttered,
looking along the bar to see a guy watching him casually. He
had a plain jumper and brown hair gelled into a spiked fringe
at the front. When he noticed Lewis looking back, he
grinned and sidled over.

"I'm Ewan," he said with a warm smile.

"And I'm straight," Lewis said, a little more harshly
than he intended. Usually he was flattered by the attention,
but tonight his focus was elsewhere.

"Meh," Ewan shrugged. "Worth a try, although," he
said as he checked his watch. "I don't really have time to pull
anyway. I've got to go kill someone."

At this, Lewis' ears pricked up. "You're playing the game?"

"You could say that," Ewan said with a wink. Lewis couldn't help wondering if he was always this cheesy, or if Ewan was employing some sort of Kill-Soc strategy.

"Aren't you worried about that news article? The killer?" It had been all Lewis had been able to think about, the idea that Flynn could get hurt eating away at his mind.

"I don't think I'm in any danger," Ewan scoffed, puffing out his chest. "Are you playing too?"

"Not really."

"Now there's an answer loaded with woe. I suppose I can spare you half an hour – oh, another pint for him, and I'll have a RadlerBomb." Ewan barely broke his flow as the Firefly was dispatched. "Thanks Adam," he said, reading the Firefly's name badge. "So didn't you get in?"

"Look," Lewis sighed. "Thanks for the drink and everything, but I'm not sure you can help."

"Try me," Ewan smiled. "And you're down to about twenty eight minutes."

What the hell, Lewis thought. Perhaps he and Jodie had been wrong about trying to keep Flynn's involvement quiet. Jodie had thought that the game would be at risk, but if everyone knew, they could all be on the lookout for him. He proceeded to explain the whole Flynn situation, watching Ewan's charm offensive transition into thoughtfulness. Once he'd finished, he watched the other guy for a few seconds as he seemed to be working things out in his head.

"Ah sorry," Ewan said after a moment. "You're right, that does seem like a reason to get drunk."

"You're telling me," Lewis shrugged. Even if Ewan couldn't do anything directly, it felt good to get the story out. Maybe Ewan would tell other contestants he met and start spreading the word. Lewis was half tempted to put a message on the board, but Jodie had hinted that if he did, she'd delete it. "Can I ask a favour? Can you keep your eyes open for him? He's like a smaller version of me. I mean, I know Liam's out there searching, but more people can't hurt."

Ewan locked eyes with Lewis raptly. "The Gamesmaster's looking for your brother?"

"Uhuh."

"That's perfect." Ewan downed his drink and wiped his mouth. "Good talking to you – I'm sure everything will work out fine." Without a second glance, Ewan scooted around a group of squawking hen night girls and left the bar, leaving Lewis watching bemusedly.

"Another pint I guess then mate," he muttered to Adam the Firefly.

7:40 pm

Jimmy sat on the riverbank amongst the reeds, throwing stone after stone into the water. Each satisfying plop was like a shake of the sieve in his mind, sorting out the ideas and the thoughts.

Plop! He'd made absolutely no progress with his attempt to sort out the mess that seemed to be delaying the game.

Plop! Whilst he'd been wasting his time in the society corridor, he'd also not been planning or hunting his next victim. Overall, he'd thrown most of the day away for nothing.

Plop! His mother would be worrying about him by now. He didn't *understand* her worries, but he knew they were there, and despite his often awkward non-communication, he didn't like to upset her.

He stood up and brushed himself off, looking up the cycle path that would lead him home. The sky was still light, but the street lamps were humming ominously, as if they were just waiting to flicker into life. As he stepped onto the tarmac, a jogger overtook him, panting loudly. As soon as she passed Jimmy, she slowed down to little more than a walk, obviously tired from her exertions.

As Jimmy continued along the path, the girl remained just ahead of him. She would jog for a few metres then stop for a moment, stretching or checking her laces with one foot propped up on the nearest bench. She was flicking her chestnut hair and bending all over the place, and any other guy would have thought she was being flirtatious, but not Jimmy. All he could do was stare at her turquoise jogging top

– a top that he had seen very recently. Jimmy couldn't believe his luck! The girl in front of him was Harper, his next victim!

He stopped in the middle of the path, hands rummaging through his pockets searching out anything he could use as a weapon. The odds of such a random meeting were thousands to one, and Jimmy didn't want to throw away such an opportunity, no matter how confused he'd been feeling just moments ago.

As his fingers scraped the bottom of his pockets to no avail, Jimmy cast his eyes frantically around the grass verges on either side of the path. As if sensing his urgency, Harper picked up her pace once more, her rest over. Jimmy began to trot lightly after her, still looking wildly left and right until he saw something he could use.

A patch of wall barley sprung up between the river and the path, universally recognised by children everywhere for their resemblance to darts. Luckily, they flew and stuck just as effectively as their metal counterparts, and Jimmy was sure that if he could hit Harper with one, then it would count.

By this time, the girl was a turquoise streak in the distance, rapidly approaching the steps that led up to the bridge leading over the river, the cycle path, and also the railway line that swung close by up ahead. Cursing, Jimmy broke into a sprint. He was much more used to lying in wait, and had very little experience of physically chasing down a victim. He was panting heavily by the time Harper hopped lightly up the steps, still too far ahead for him to catch up to.

Jimmy slowed down, his lungs burning. There was no way to catch her now. It was like the opposite of his usual thought processes. Whilst on the cycle path, there was only one clear outcome – one clear route for Harper to take. But now she was going up onto the bridge, there were far more options. She could go left or right, on either side of the road. She could even cross over and head back down the steps on the other side, although Jimmy couldn't think of any logical reason why she would do that.

Abandoning the idea of scoring a kill this time, Jimmy decided to at least watch where Harper went just in case it was a regular route – that way, Jimmy could stake out a more convenient place next time. He slunk into the shadows of the trees as he watched her reach the top of the steps and head out onto the bridge. She looked down towards him briefly before crossing the road. Jimmy craned his neck so he could keep her in his field of vision.

There was only one other person on the bridge, coming towards her over the railway line. After pausing for a second, Harper went to the right, towards the stranger.

In the distance, the horn of a train honked as the two figures on the bridge drew closer to each other. Harper in her bright turquoise top was in direct contrast with the other figure, a column of grey duffle coat with the hood drawn up. Jimmy watched as the two figures met each other, forced to do that awkward sideways dodge to get past. They both dodged the same way. Before Jimmy could react, the grey-clad stranger had grabbed Harper, shaking her violently.

The train horn blasted again, closer this time. Wide eyed, Jimmy watched in horror as Harper was forced into the railings on the opposite side of the bridge. The stranger hauled her up onto the metal, her mouth a wide, black O of surprise before he let go and she vanished over the side of the bridge.

Jimmy ran to the chain link fence next to the cycle path at the same time as the freight train roared past, the rush of displaced air buffeting him as he pressed himself against the wire. Jimmy was vaguely aware that he was yelling, but all sound was drowned out by the clacking of the wheels over the rail joints.

In a flash, the train had rumbled past, its crimson tail lights fading into the gloom. Jimmy pressed his face against the fence, trying to catch a glimpse of what had become of the girl, but the railway cutting was hazed with the dust disturbed as the train had moved through. He glanced back up, but the bridge was empty – there was no remnant of either Harper or her mysterious attacker.

It was only as he looked down once more that Jimmy saw the tattered turquoise shape lying in the grass on the other side of the rails. It had been flung far enough so that Jimmy was spared any of the specifics, but he was still aware that his eyes were damp as he turned and fled back down the cycle path.

Once Jimmy reached home, he immediately sank to the floor of his bedroom, leaning back against the door, even though his mother was at work. Tears were flowing freely down his cheeks, and part of him was mystified as to their cause. He was no stranger to crying, however it was usually when the pressures and complications of life and order became too overwhelming. This was different – he was actually feeling bad about something that had happened to somebody else, and that was a rarity.

His hand hovered a couple of inches from his mobile, and he knew deep down inside that he should be calling the police right about now. It's what anybody else would have done, but a number of voices in his head were coming up with increasingly valid reasons as to why he shouldn't. First of all, the longer he left it, the more likely they were to ask why he hadn't phoned as soon as the crime had been committed – or even *whilst* it was being committed. Secondly, Jimmy's inherent fear of talking to strangers was screaming a long protracted *nooooo!* Another fear was that the finger of suspicion would be pointed at him, after all, just as he couldn't prove who had done it, he couldn't prove he *hadn't*. Finally, and perhaps most selfishly, he didn't want to draw any more attention to Kill-Soc. So far, there had only been a tenuous link to the game, but this would cement the link and doom the game forever. There would be no way that the Uni would allow it to continue after this.

As usual, Jimmy followed the commands of his inner demons and flicked the phone away across the carpet, out of the reach of temptation. But that didn't change the fact that he needed help, from someone who would also have the best interests of the game at heart. After thinking for a moment, Jimmy had settled on the perfect person. Logically, there was only one other person who could ever be as dedicated as he was, and that was the second place to Jimmy's champion, Ewan Lloyd.

8:23 pm

Ewan had not long got in, and was now lying on his bed, propped up on one elbow, his performance notes spread out in front of him. As a drama student, he was used to marking out every specific movement and action that the actors needed to make, and he needed to ensure that everything was perfectly laid out – every timing had to be exact with minimal random variables. Every person on the stage had to be in the right place at the right time or nothing would hang together.

His laptop beeped, pulling his eyes away from his notes. Ewan saw that the message icon was flashing, red for a private communication. Raising an eyebrow, Ewan rolled off the bed and walked the couple of feet over to the desk where his computer sat, cracking his back as he did so.

As he sunk into the university standard chair and rested his elbows on the university standard desk, he clicked the message open, a smile playing across his face as he read the contents. It was a message from Jimmy Hale, the one who had beaten him last year. Just like the man himself, the message was short – abrupt even.

Jimmy019: Something's wrong. The game is in danger. We need to sort it.

Ewan laughed to himself as he read the message again. Everybody knew Jimmy was a bit spectrum, and this looked like a typical overreaction. No matter what Jimmy said, all Ewan could picture was his nemesis pointing pistol fingers at him in an alley the year before.

Ewan022: So? Go tell the Gamesmasters…

The reply was almost instant.

Jimmy019: Not good enough. They might be compromised. It has to be you.

Oh this should be good, thought Ewan, his initial hostility beginning to melt away. It couldn't hurt to meet Jimmy, he supposed, if only to hear what wild theories he'd come up with.

Ewan022: Fine, come over to halls tomorrow morning. 10am, Flat F5.

He slammed the laptop shut without waiting for a reply, then ambled back to the bed, flopping gracelessly into the yet again, university standard duvet. He picked up his pencil and began readjusting his notes.

9:43 pm

The message board had been dead for the last hour, and Jodie was fairly certain that nothing else was going to happen today. It was always the same, she mused. There was the initial rush on day one where everybody went crazy as soon as she said go, but then there was usually a lull where the competitors tended to put more thought into what they were doing, and started digging in for the long haul.

She thought back to her own day, which had been anything but lulled. She and Lewis had searched all the places that Lewis could remember taking his brother, but they'd had no luck. She had sent Lewis home, promising that she would keep an eye on the message boards for him. She had been sure that somebody would eventually notice that 'Lewis' was actually a fifteen year old boy – she was wrong. A couple of hours ago, Lewis' victim had messaged in that he'd been killed. He obviously hadn't registered the age of his killer. Whilst Jodie had been slightly impressed that Flynn had managed to score a kill so easily, she also knew she couldn't let him carry on, especially if he really was involved in the murder. But then why would Flynn kill one person, but fake-kill another? Unless it was an accident? And that still didn't explain why he'd sent her all those weird messages. Jodie shook her head, all the possibilities making her brain hurt.

Keys rattled in the door, and Liam elbowed his way inside. His glasses were propped up on his forehead and she could see dark rings forming round his eyes. He'd had a long day too.

"Any luck?" she asked hopefully. Liam had offered to go the stadium just in case Flynn was still hanging around.

"Nope," Liam said with a shrug, nudging the door shut with his foot and plonking down onto the mattress. "I did manage to speak to Glen Hemmings though."

"Oh?" Jodie said, arching an eyebrow.

"He couldn't remember anything," Liam went on, a hint of annoyance creeping into his voice. "He had trouble even recalling how it happened. Honestly, how do these jocks even function? What do they do in the real world?"

"It's all scholarships and stuff isn't it. It's all down to who you know."

"Well I think next year we should check people's IQ before we let them play," Liam said with a grin.

"If there is a next year…" Jodie said quietly, the previous moment's joviality dissipating instantly. "We have to find this kid, Liam."

"I know."

"I'm serious," she went on. "If he's the one that got the newspapers in a storm then we can kiss the game goodbye."

"And if the Uni find out we let a minor play the game, we can kiss it goodbye anyway," Liam countered.

"Then why don't we just cancel it?" Jodie said, her voice rising with exasperation. "I can send a message to everyone calling it off. If the game's doomed anyway, then what's the point?" She swivelled around in her chair, her fingers poised above the keyboard. Before she could type anything however, Liam's hand gripped her wrist softly.

"Don't."

"Why?" Jodie asked, her eyes beginning to shine. Kill-Soc was her *thing*. It was her one contribution to UCE life, and she couldn't bear to see it go down in flames.

"Surely," Liam continued, pressing his forehead against hers and looking deep into her eyes. "If this is to be the last game, we owe it to everyone to make it the best damn one there's been. We soldier on, we sort out this mess and we see it through to the end. Then," he smiled once more. "We throw the biggest feckin' after party ever."

Jodie watched him for a moment, the icy dread that had gripped her just moments before melting away. She leant in and hugged Liam tightly, pressing into him until his warmth bled into her.

"Don't worry about Flynn," Liam murmured. "I'll catch the lad."

Jodie pulled away slightly, wiping her eyes and clearing her throat, regaining her composure. "I'll post the kill notifications, then we can get an early night..."

Liam leaned in and kissed her, before she turned back to the monitors once more. She opened her inbox, seeing that an email had come through from David007 earlier that afternoon. She saw that the subject line was empty. *Nothing too important then,* she thought as she closed the window without reading the mail. Instead, she opened the day's kill notifications, ready to compile them into the end of the day summary.

Day 2 Kills

Glen002: Got killed by some D-Bag just as I was about to go onto the pitch. Centaurs rule!

Lynsey009: I'm still picking confetti out of my stuff after somebody did a drive by bombing. It's in my socks for God's sake!

Stephen018: So I don't even mind being out of the game when it happens like this… I left the house this morning to find that during the night, somebody had wrapped the entire perimeter in crepe paper flames. Should have checked my smoke alarm lol

> **Rachel017:** Glad you liked it. You don't wanna know how much money I spent in Hobbycraft for all that shit

Nicola032: There's some alliances forming here… I was running away from this one guy in a grey hood, and he chased me right into my actual assassin. Bitch sprayed me right in the face with 'acid'

> **Karine040:** I've seen the same guy sneaking around outside Griffin Hall – glad he's not my assassin
>
> > **Meriel031:** Nicola, I swear he's nothing to do with me. Just coincidence that you ran my way ☺

Andrew041: Thug Life Sock Killer strikes again! Aced Ben043 in the back of the head. These socks are lucky – but maybe I should wash them?

> **Ben043:** Trust me, you definitely should

Billie055: Took out Clark056 with a vintage cap gun. He was too busy taking selfies to notice me come in

> **Alex067:** You have a vintage cap gun?

>> **Billie055:** Yeah! I got it from The Stereotypes. Uses proper paper rolls, not those stupid plastic ring things

>>> **Alex067:** I only have a simple clicker gun. Still managed to kill Jo068 with it though!

Rob075: I should have read yesterday's messages. Went out to feed my rabbit and someone had stuck a 'bomb' to it. I'm guessing it was Nadia071...

> **Alastair087:** You're not the only one wishing they should have read yesterday's stuff. I think I found another one of Olivia084's tripwires on the B Block stairs – only noticed it after I stepped through it

Day Three

9:26 am

Jimmy had the worst night's sleep ever. Every time he closed his eyes, he saw Harper go over the edge of the bridge, and each time, his mind would add details he was sure he hadn't noticed before. Sometimes it was a scream as she fell, others it was a harsh crunching sound as the train rattled by.

To top it off, his mother kept coming in with each news bulletin to say that there'd been no updates since they'd released the picture of the crime scene. He'd never felt so updated on a lack of updates.

As it was, it was with bleary eyes that Jimmy was now making his way across town towards the Halls where Ewan lived. He had a vague conversation plan laid out in his mind, but conversations were always difficult, as you could never predict exactly what the other person was going to say, especially Ewan, who Jimmy had only really met briefly during last year's game. Jimmy was pinning all his hopes on the fact that Ewan would have equal dedication to the game as he did and so would do whatever he could to ensure its survival.

The quickest way to Halls was along the cycle path, but Jimmy couldn't bring himself to pass the spot where Harper had died. He assumed it would be crawling with police by now, and wasn't there that old adage that guilty people always return to the scene of the crime? What if the cops thought he'd done it and was revisiting his killing ground? No, it would be much safer to head around through the business district, and Jimmy had allowed himself extra time to do this.

He turned away from the greenery of the riverside and moved into the built up area, buildings rising higher and higher as he moved towards the centre. His surroundings were soon a metropolis of glass and chrome, shining in the light rain. A thousand reflections stared back at him as he strolled hurriedly past the one way windows, conscious of how people must see him from their desks on the other side.

There was no denying that he looked tired, that much was obvious by his hair sticking up in all directions and the first shades of blondish stubble appearing across his jawline, but also he noticed that he was walking stooped over, his head held down slightly. Harried, that was what he looked like, and a wave of disappointment swept over him like it had the other day. Kill-Soc was supposed to be the time where he rose above everyone else, yet here he was, forced back into his daily awkwardness by someone who seemed intent on using the game as a stage for their own evil deeds. That was when Jimmy noticed he was being followed.

They were keeping their distance, but Jimmy could see them reflected in the windows of the office block at his side. They were tall, obviously male, but wearing a large grey duffle coat that made their build difficult to make out. The hood was up, and they were wearing a helmet or visor of some sort, with Perspex goggles and a breathing grille. As Jimmy tried to watch out of the corner of his eye, he noticed his assailant pick up the pace.

Immediately, the thought tracks in Jimmy's head fractured and split – the obvious choice being whether to recognise the stranger as a threat or not. Jimmy got to a side street, hurrying across it so that he could draw level with the next building. In these windows, he saw that the stranger was now only a couple of metres behind. He was also reaching between the toggles of the coat for something in an interior pocket. The 'no threat' option narrowed and then blinked out of existence as the stranger pulled a knife from his coat, the morning sun flashing off the blade.

The stranger broke into a sprint – too fast for Jimmy to think. He was outside the revolving doors to one of the buildings, and all Jimmy could see was the constantly shifting reflections rotating with the doors. The knife was raised as the stranger ran forwards, until at the last minute, Jimmy ducked down, feeling the rush of air move over the top of his head. The stranger barrelled forwards into the brickwork, spinning on his feet just as a couple of suited men appeared in the doorway.

Jimmy panted, leaning against the wall as the businessmen cast him a dark look. The stranger hung back, the knife safely tucked inside the coat once more. As Jimmy peered through the doors, he could see another group of office workers approaching across a wide foyer. As long as he stayed where he was, the stranger wouldn't get another clear opportunity.

The attacker stepped forwards, his eyes beneath the mask creased with what looked like humour. "You're predictable," he growled. "I'll get you later." With that, he turned and fled into the tangle of side streets, leaving Jimmy wide eyed and shaken.

10:04 am

Ewan had only just got ready when the flat buzzer went. He practically sprinted into the corridor, fumbling the handset loudly. He didn't want any of the others to know that Jimmy was coming over – he didn't want anybody to get the wrong idea.

"Hello?" he asked.

"It's Jimmy."

Ewan pressed the unlock button, musing about just how much conversation he would get out of the Kill-Soc champion. He moved to the front door and waited, giving Jimmy enough time to get up the steps. As soon as he heard footfalls on the landing, he opened the door and smiled. Jimmy's hair was plastered onto his forehead, and he didn't make eye contact as he walked through the door Ewan was holding open. With a shrug, Ewan turned into his flat and cocked an eyebrow when he saw Jimmy hovering uncomfortably in the hallway. He had no idea which door to go through.

"Come on," Ewan said, tugging Jimmy's sleeve. "The front room is down the other end."

Once there, Ewan flicked the kettle on, leaving Jimmy to sit at the table. He was looking around the room with narrowed eyes, taking in the shabby sofas and the beer stained carpet. Eventually, Ewan sat opposite him.

"Well?" he began. "You were going to tell me what's wrong with the game?"

"You have blood on you." Jimmy pointed to Ewan's knuckles as he gripped his mug. Sure enough, the skin was scraped and red.

"Shit," Ewan muttered, pulling his sleeve over his hand. "I got in a fight," he continued nonchalantly.

"Me too," Jimmy blurted before launching into an extremely specific and detailed account of everything he'd seen. As he was listening, Ewan couldn't help but wonder if this was what talking to Jimmy was always like, or whether the boy was nervous. The last time they had spoken was in the alleyway where Jimmy had knocked Ewan out of last year's game. Then, Jimmy had been blunt, but now it seemed he wouldn't stop.

"Ok ok!" Ewan said, holding up his hand. Jimmy glared at him, as if breaking the flow of his narrative was a cardinal sin. "You're right, this is serious. Why didn't you go to the police?"

"They'll stop the game."

"What about the Gamesmasters?"

"They'll stop the game."

"Alright Robo-Jim," Ewan said, raising his hands once more in placation.

"I don't like nicknames."

"Noted. The problem we have is that the people you refuse to go to have all the power to actually get something done."

"Not true," Jimmy stated, his eyes fixed on a point on the wall just behind Ewan's shoulder. "We have to find who the killer is and stop them."

"Stop them?" Ewan raised an eyebrow.

"It's Kill-Soc. You do what you have to do."

"Wow," breathed Ewan. "You must really want to win."

"Don't you?"

"Point taken." Ewan thought for a moment before continuing. "So. What's your theory?"

Jimmy blinked a couple of times, then seemed to settle. "Liam."

"The Gamesmaster?"

Jimmy nodded. "He made a girl cry and I found a target picture with blood on it and he would know where everyone is likely to be because of the computers and-"

"Ok, I believe you," Ewan cut in, saving himself from another monologue. "But what's his character motivation? Why would he want to ruin a game that he runs? What made him want to hurt people?" Ewan stroked his chin in thought. "Ooh! Maybe all these years of faking it isn't enough for him any more – maybe he needs the real thing to get him off."

"Does it matter? If he did it, then he did it. Who cares why?"

"I'm guessing you're not big on feelings and reasoning then…" Ewan said under his breath. "But you could be right. Liam is always the quieter of the two. Plus he's the one that goes around town doing all the checks and stuff. Guaranteed anybody would let him in without asking any questions. It's the perfect play."

Jimmy nodded, his jaw setting as he drank in Ewan's words. It was almost as if when he turned up at the flat, he was off track somehow, and now Ewan had helped him back on course.

"So what next?"

"I assume there will be some sort of list or record in the Kill-Soc office," Ewan said thoughtfully. "It will tell you all the people that Liam has had to visit during the game. From there, you can see if any of them have been hurt – it will also give you an idea where he might be headed next – who his next target is."

Jimmy continued nodding with each statement. He stood up excitedly and headed for the door without even asking what Ewan himself planned to do. *One track mind,* Ewan thought happily beneath his expressionless face.

"Good luck," Ewan called as he heard the front door shut. A wide grin spread across his face as he was unable to believe how easy that had been. He practically skipped down the corridor and into his room, jumping onto the bed and staring at the ceiling. His cheeks were hurting, he was grinning so hard. Unable to contain it any longer, he pulled his phone out of his pocket and dialled Gemma's number. She answered on the third ring.

"Hey."

"You'll never guess who I just had over!" Ewan beamed. "Jimmy's so worked up, he came to me for help."

"Ew, you didn't...?"

"Um, no. That would kind of defeat the whole thing don't you think? Plus I'm a fan of the eye contact. Anyway, we can skip ahead a few steps now – trust me, he's ready for the final act."

"Hang on," Gemma questioned. "If you had him right there, why didn't you just end it now?"

"Tch," Ewan muttered, glad that Gemma wasn't here in person to see him rolling his eyes. "It has to look like part of the game. If the big reveal was just me and him in some scummy flat, it would lose all impact. Haven't you ever been to the theatre?"

"Alright, alright, calm down. So what now?"

"I'll start the closing scenes," Ewan stated simply.

"Good luck. I'm off to the Drink 'Til You Drop, if I can find someone to go with."

"Sounds like you need the luck, not me," Ewan countered before hanging up and looking out the window. The rain had picked up, pools beginning to form in every little turf hole that littered the quad down below. The timing was perfect, and most of the players were exactly where he wanted them. There was only one more piece to set. The final piece, but probably the most important. With a cold smile, he opened his laptop, fingers already typing a message to GamesmasterLiam.

10:41 am

Flynn was cold and wet. He'd spent the night in various 24 hour cafes, moving on whenever they'd started pestering him about buying something. As soon as it got light, he had taken to the streets, hoping for another bright May day. Instead, it had been chucking it down on and off since sun up.

He pulled out the picture of his new target, a guy with short blonde curls and a kind looking face. There were no obvious clues as to what sort of guy he might be, but Flynn was happy to try the method that had led him to Glen. He knew he couldn't go back to Lewis' place, but he also knew that the UCE library would probably have an archive of team and club pictures that would be a good place to start. Surely all students were part of some group or other, he reasoned as he made his way towards the campus.

As he trudged, his phone started ringing. Another call from Lewis. He hit decline, aware that the longer he held out, the more trouble he would be in. He hoped Lewis hadn't called their parents already, but something told him that his brother wouldn't do that. After all, Lewis was supposed to be responsible for him – it wouldn't look too good if he had to phone their parents and admit that he'd lost his charge.

Flynn smiled and slipped the phone back into his pocket.

11:06 am

Liam took his glasses off and wiped them for the hundredth time. Even with his hood up, his fringe seemed to constantly stream water onto the lenses, making it impossible to see where he was going.

He had taken a break from hunting Flynn to do a regular everyday run of the mill query check. To be honest, he was glad to be doing something simple instead of searching a whole city for some stupid kid. Leave that to the actual competitors.

His beat up converse squelched as he stepped across a sodden stretch of grass leading to the main UCE halls. He double checked the message he'd received to get the flat number then pressed the corresponding button. The intercom crackled.

"Yeah?"

"It's Liam – about the game?"

"Come on up." The channel died with a fizzle, then the intercom beeped, the door making an audible click as it unlocked. Liam stepped inside the block – a typical tiled foyer with three doors leading in the other directions, and a stairwell rising up from the middle. Before heading for the stairs, he took a look at his reflection, sighing at the image he portrayed. As one of the Gamesmasters, he liked to think of himself as the second highest authority beneath Jodie, but standing there dripping rainwater onto the welcome mat, his top clinging to his scrawny chest, he looked a tad hopeless.

Nothing I can do about it now, Liam thought disconsolately as he gripped the handrail and started up the steps.

By the time he reached the top, Ewan022 was waiting for him. Liam smiled slightly as he realised he had automatically thought of Ewan in terms of his number.

"Good to see you again," Ewan said before welcoming him inside the flat. That was another thing about being a Gamesmaster – *everyone* knew your face. Liam had no recollection of ever seeing this guy before, except for his picture on the Kill-Soc servers. Perhaps they'd met at one of the after parties, but Liam couldn't be sure. He settled for a nod as he stepped inside the flat.

Ewan showed him into the living room and sat at the UCE standard pine table. The flats were all ten-beds, but there was never enough furniture for them all to sit together. It was as if the whole Halls system was specifically designed to breed antisocialism.

"So what can I help you with?"

"Ah," said Ewan casually. "I've got a paintball gun. I wanted you to check it, see if I can use it in the game."

Liam sighed. *Was this guy for real?* "Don't need to check it," he stated. "There's no way you can use a paintball gun. Come on fella, it says stuff like that in the rules."

"Sorry," Ewan said sheepishly.

"And you could have just asked me in the message you know." Liam looked forlornly out of the window at the rain, which had conveniently upped its ferocity in the last few seconds. *I could do with a bastard hairdryer,* he thought acidly as he caught his waterlogged reflection again.

"Sorry again." Ewan was looking at him as if he was only just noticing how soaked he was. "At least let me get you a fresh top."

Before Liam could respond, Ewan had disappeared, returning a moment later with a clean jumper. He chucked it towards the Gamesmaster and Liam caught it, pressing it to his chest. It was still warm, and smelled of one of those ridiculously named scented detergents.

"Cheers, I guess." Liam turned around with embarrassment as he peeled his top off, uncomfortably aware of Ewan's gaze raking across his shoulder blades. He quickly pulled the jumper over his head, scraping his glasses down his nose in his haste. When he turned around, he could tell that Ewan was trying not to smile.

"Take this too," he said. "It'll keep the rain off my jumper." Liam eyed the garment Ewan was holding out to him. A large grey duffle coat with toggles down the front.

Once again, Flynn had been lucky. The library did indeed have an archive of team photos, and it had only taken about ten minutes to flick through and realise that his target wasn't in any of them. That was when Flynn had turned dejectedly to the back of the archive book, only to see the same face staring back at him, with the caption 'Photography by Sean James' beneath it.

How can anyone lose when it's this easy? Flynn had thought to himself after he'd asked the librarian if there was an office for photography and the like. She'd told him there was, and where to find it. From there, Flynn had waited until the office opened at 12, hanging around in the corridor waiting for the right moment. There always seemed to be people going in and out of the small office, and Flynn didn't want to risk the same sort of trouble that he'd encountered at the stadium with Glen's coach. Luckily, loitering seemed to be a fairly common student pastime, so nobody gave him a second look.

Eventually, the buzz around the office died down, and Flynn counted at least ten minutes since the last person had left – maybe an actual lecture had started. Taking a deep breath, Flynn approached the door, the makeshift sign printed on A4 paper flapping with the air-con. He stepped through into a cramped box room that still managed to contain two desks as well as a bench running the length of one wall holding a variety of cameras and lenses. Another door led off to the side marked 'Dark Room'.

Sean was sitting at one of the desks, his phone held up to his ear. When he saw Flynn, he held up two fingers, which

Flynn assumed meant something along the lines of 'two seconds.' Flynn busied himself with looking at all the pictures hanging on the walls. He noticed that there were a lot more hanging over the other desk than the one that Sean sat at.

"Jonny, will you answer your god damn phone? The Varsity negatives are here and I need your help sorting them. Call me." Sean hung up dejectedly. "My colleague hasn't come in today," he said with a shrug. "Now what can I do for you?" He looked at Flynn, noticing his age and tutting to himself. "If you're here for the high school liaison class, I'm sure that's next week." He began flicking through a day planner to double check, worry lines creasing his brow into layers of frustration.

"I'm here for this," Flynn said wryly, pulling another crappy pound shop boomerang out of his pocket. In an instant, Sean pulled a plastic gun from somewhere under the desk and levelled it at Flynn. *Did he actually have it taped there like some spy movie?*

"What now, little man?" Sean said with a smirk on his face. A brief moment of panic flashed across Flynn's mind before he settled on a plan of action. Sean had already clocked how old he looked – time to see if that led to any assumptions of his intelligence.

"Well you can't shoot me," Flynn said slowly, trying to sound as dumb as possible. "If I'm not your target…"

"I totally can," Sean exclaimed indignantly. "It says in the rules about self-defence kills. Here, I'll show you." He turned back to his desk and thumbed through the planner once more. He was just retrieving the relevant sheet of paper when the boomerang caught him across the chest. He froze mid page turn.

"You're not serious," he whined.

"Sorry," Flynn said with a shrug. "It's only a game."

"I swear you're not old enough to play," Sean said, narrowing his eyes. "I should tell the Gamesmasters."

"Well if you want to admit how easily I killed you, go ahead," Flynn countered, hoping his wits would put Sean off. If the Gamesmasters found out about him, he really would be in big trouble. To Flynn's relief, Sean seemed to sag in defeat.

"I was really hoping to show off my gun."

"What does it do?" Flynn asked, eying the weapon with a new intrigue. It looked just like any other toy, but he couldn't see any sort of dart or projectile of any kind.

"Well, I suppose you can't be killed by a corpse, however old you are," Sean said quietly. He held up the gun and pulled the trigger, a red flag with the word BANG! printed on it folding out of the barrel. "Cost me a fortune on ebay."

"That's genuinely awesome," Flynn said with a smile. "Sorry you didn't get to use it."

"Yeah well," Sean said miserably as he chucked his target photo onto the desk. "I'll buy you a Panda Pop at the after party, providing you don't get asked for ID on the door. Now get out of here before I change my mind about grassing you up."

Flynn nodded his thanks before scooping the new photo up and hurrying out of the office. It was only as he was making his way across the glistening flagstones of the quad that he realised that he'd left the boomerang behind. Again.

Flynn's phone buzzed in his pocket. He took it out, fully expecting another guilt-tripping message from Lewis. It wasn't.

Neutral meet up this afternoon at 4 – Morgan's car park. No weapons – GMJ

1:21 pm

Jodie had been half-arsing her way through the day's to-do list ever since Liam had left. She'd updated the post its and the lines that showed who was now hunting who, she'd made a number of final preparations for the after party (which was a monumental task in itself, considering nobody could ever guarantee when the game would actually end), and she'd begun on her emails, all with the thoughts of Flynn, the murder and the potential demise of Kill-Soc haunting her mind. It was hard to continue planning something that could come crumbling down at any moment.

Eventually, she got to the email from David007 that she had skipped the night before. Her face fell as she read the message:

Dear Jodie,

I'm writing about my flatmate and fellow contestant Ewan Lloyd. I don't know exact details, but he's planning on doing something to Jimmy Hale to make sure he doesn't win. He's got loads of other players involved, and the way he's been talking about it – I don't know how far he'll go to see Jimmy lose.

Please get back to me,
David Hughes

Shit, Jodie thought as she opened up the message window.

GamesmasterJodie: Are you at home?

How could she have let herself miss this? Suddenly, Jodie was filled with anger, at not only herself for skipping the email, but at David for leaving the subject line empty and causing her to skip it in the first place.

David007: Yes
GamesmasterJodie: Is Ewan there?
David007: No
GamesmasterJodie: Stay there. I'm coming over.

She thought briefly about calling Liam, but discarded the idea on the basis that the email had come to her personally, rather than the Kill-Soc server. David obviously wanted her to deal with this. She quickly brought up David's profile, noting his address before grabbing her coat and heading for the door.

As she hurried out, she collided with something tall and solid, limbs tangling amid grunts of pain.

"Ow!" Lewis said, rubbing his forehead where Jodie's elbow had caught him. Jodie herself looked up at him from where she had slid down the wall. "Are you ok?" he asked, holding out his hand for her.

She nodded, taking his hand and climbing awkwardly to her feet. She straightened her jumper, blowing hair out of her face.

"I was hoping we could do some more hunting for my brother," Lewis said apologetically.

"I was just on my way to check something out," Jodie said hurriedly, anxious to be on her way to meet David. She turned once more to Lewis, and instantly hated herself when she saw his kicked puppy face. Though he didn't say anything, she saw in his eyes a thousand accusations that she had abandoned his brother. She hadn't given up on Flynn completely, just for the moment, David's email was occupying the forefront of her mind.

"Oh," Lewis said dejectedly. "I guess I'll just head home then."

"Tch," Jodie sighed in exasperation. Before she knew what she was doing, she was digging her keys out of her bag and throwing them in Lewis' direction. "Keep an eye on the messageboards for me. Maybe you'll see something about your brother."

For a moment, it looked as if Lewis was going to hug her, but then he seemed to think better of it. "Thank you, really," he said.

"Good luck," Jodie called as she went round the corner.

2:16 pm

David had spent the last half an hour watching the front door nervously. He had taken a huge risk emailing Jodie, and she was taking her time getting over to the flat. Ewan could come back at any moment, and any chance of putting things right would be lost.

In lectures, David had been taught that lawyers had to ignore any personal feelings and remain completely detached, and whilst David was motivated by the fact the whole plan was morally wrong, he also smiled a little at the thought that this was some payback for Ewan having turned into such a dick.

The buzzer rang, making him jump slightly. He immediately thought of Ewan's return, but then quickly remembered that Ewan wouldn't ring the bell – he had keys. David picked up the handset and buzzed Jodie in, moving to meet her at the front door.

The landing was streaked with muddy footprints, the rain outside being dragged in on the feet of the various visitors of the day. As David waited, he scanned around the landing anxiously, expecting Ewan to jump out at any moment.

Finally, Jodie appeared at the top of the stairs. David felt a brief pang of sorrow for her, seeing her with her blonde hair hanging in a wet tangle over her shoulders.

"Come in," he said quietly.

"So what's this all about?" Jodie asked as soon as they were inside the flat. David looked at her, judging that she obviously wasn't in the mood to sit down with a cup of tea. He launched into an explanation of everything he'd seen and

heard since he'd returned from his crushing Kill-Soc defeat.
Jodie listened patiently until he'd finished.

"So he's called a meeting of nearly everyone who got
eliminated on day 1?" she surmised. "And they're going to
help him do… what exactly?"

"I don't know *exactly*," David admitted. "I decided it
was bullshit long before they made any concrete plans."

"Well does he want to win, or does he just want
Jimmy to lose?"

"Again, I don't know," David said with a shrug. He
knew it had been Jimmy that had eliminated Ewan the year
before, but he didn't know if Ewan wanted victory or
vengeance.

"There's not really much to go on here," Jodie
muttered critically. "Any chance we can get into his room?"

At this, David smiled. "That's easy – he never locks
his door. He thinks everybody loves him." He nodded down
the corridor, and Jodie followed him to one of the
bedrooms. As he pushed the door open, he heard Jodie gasp.
"What is it?" He noticed her eyes were wide with surprise.

"It's kind of like the Kill-Soc office…" she
murmured, half to herself. David looked around and had to
admit, he could see what she meant. He had always imagined
that Ewan's room would be like some Austin Powers style
love den, the amount of action that happened in it, however
Jodie was right. In addition to the UCE standard issue bed,
desk and chair, and a shelf laden with paintballing trophies,
there were a number of cork boards covered in notes and
pictures.

There was a map of the city with a spread of circled
locations marked on it. David recognised Halls, and the cycle
path by the river, but there were also a couple of places
marked that seemed to just be houses in the suburbs.

"Any of these places mean anything?" he asked, looking over his shoulder at Jodie. She didn't answer, as she was standing transfixed in front of one of the other boards. He moved to her side.

The board was covered in passport photos, like the ones that were sent out as target identifiers. David remembered some of the faces from the meeting he had come home to, but others he hadn't seen before. Some of the pictures were arranged into a line, most of the photos having jagged lines crossed through them. There was a preppy looking blonde boy in a polo shirt, and some sporty girl in a turquoise tracksuit, but it was the final picture in the row that had caught Jodie's attention. Jimmy Hale. Ewan had rather obviously stuck the pin through Jimmy's forehead, a bright red pin-badge with the Kill-Soc logo etched into it, making it look like Jimmy had a crimson bullet hole through his face. Jodie snatched the pin out of the wall, the photo of Jimmy floating lazily to the carpet. She looked ashen.

"How far would Ewan go?" she asked quietly.

"What do you mean?

Jodie pointed to a piece of printed paper that hung above the passport photos. "I got a few messages from some weirdo who wanted to change the game. They kept going on about blurring the lines, about making it more real."

"Right?" David looked more closely at the paper Jodie was pointing to. It was a newspaper article printed from the web. About a body that had been found. Someone had been killed around the same time the game had started. *Really* killed. His stomach plummeted as he looked again at the faces with crosses through them. Also, hadn't yesterday's kill notifications mentioned something about someone being chased by a shadowy figure?

"How far would Ewan go?" Jodie asked again, a drained sickly look creeping across her features. She felt ice prickling down her spine, making her want to shudder. David gulped, his features a perfect mirror of hers. That was how Ewan was going to change the game. He was going to kill Jimmy Hale for real.

3:18 pm

Liam had been hanging around in the coffee shop once more. This time, he had chosen to sit at the counter at the window, so he could watch the passers-by in the street outside. Not that he didn't have plenty of other things to do, but the coffee shop was perfectly situated on the avenue that led to Morgan's Car Park. He could just see the top of the multistorey poking out above the trees, and since he'd received the text message about the neutral meet up, he'd camped out here to see who arrived. Jodie must have added him to the phone list because normally, it was just the players that received them. He had to hand it to her, it was a decent plan, and he was almost embarrassed that they hadn't used it sooner. In previous games, they'd called a meet up as a way of speeding things up – particularly in games that had dragged on a bit. Sometimes you got into a situation where the final four or so were all defensive players, content to let someone else make the first move – so nobody did. The neutral meet up was usually a success because nobody could resist turning up. They also couldn't resist bringing weapons despite the warning.

Liam checked his watch – just over half an hour until the meeting time, and it would take almost twenty minutes to walk down to the building. That was another reason why it was such a solid choice. There was only the one main road that led to the car park, and despite its size, it had been usurped when the new shopping centre was built a couple of years ago, complete with a vast underground complex right in the centre of town. Hardly anybody used Morgan's any more.

He took another sip of yet another latte before slamming his cup down and practically pressing his face against the glass, earning a quizzical look from a couple walking hand in hand past the shop. There, on the other side of the road and heading towards the carpark, was Flynn Howard. Liam glanced at his laptop, open to Lewis' profile. He could see the similarity between the two brothers, even though Flynn was a lot slighter than Lewis. In a way, he was almost impressed with the kid's tenacity, and the ability to score two kills, but then he remembered the trouble he'd caused, and the possibility that he'd hurt somebody in the process.

Liam closed down the computer and stuffed it into his messenger bag, before dialling Jodie's number.

"I found him," he breathed as he hurried out of the coffee shop.

"Where?"

"He's on his way to the meet up, like you predicted." Liam couldn't help smiling to himself. This little problem was so close to being over. There was a moment's silence on the phone.

"What meet up?"

Liam slowed down his pace, tilting his head to one side in confusion. "What do you mean? A message came through about a meet up. It was from GMJ. GamesmasterJodie, right?"

There was another pause. "Liam, I didn't send that message."

"What?" Liam couldn't understand. The only people who could send messages through the Kill-Soc server were him and Jodie. "What do you want to do?"

"You catch Flynn," Jodie ordered. "I'll find out who sent the message."

"Right."

"Liam, be careful." Jodie said sternly before hanging up. Liam frowned at the odd send off. Normally, Jodie would have said she loved him, but then again, she was stressed. He put his phone back in his pocket and stalked after Flynn.

3:29 pm

Lewis had searched through computer files until his eyes started to hurt. It didn't help that he didn't really know the system, or how Jodie had organised all the different sub sections of information. Even when he'd managed to stumble across his own profile, he couldn't work out how to check if 'he' had made any posts or sent any messages or anything.

Eventually, it was his phone ringing that broke the torpor his brain had slipped into. It was Jodie.

"Hey," he answered hopefully.

"What the hell do you think you're doing?" Jodie buzzed angrily on the other end of the line.

"Um," Lewis faltered. "You said I could stay here, remember?"

"But I didn't say anything about sending messages to everyone across the Kill-Soc server. You had no right to do that!"

"I didn't do anything, I swear! I wouldn't even know how to do something like that," Lewis said, his voice rising.

"Well it wasn't me or Liam," Jodie said, making a noise like a frustrated growl. "This is doing my head in," she cried. "Someone's playing with us."

"What did the message say?"

"Some bullshit about a neutral meet up at Morgan's car park. Liam's on his way there – so is your brother. Don't worry, Liam will bring him home." Relief flooded through Lewis' mind, tinted with a flicker of uncertainty. Why would somebody create a fake meet up? It felt like they were all pieces being moved on a board, or actors being placed on a stage. The feeling of being out of control swept over him, as well as the sudden desire to find out who was pulling the strings.

"Can we use the computer here to find out where the message came from?"

"Maybe," Jodie sighed. "I didn't set the system up, some guy Rick helped me. I can talk you through what I would do."

"Ok, I'm putting you on speaker so I can type." Lewis put the call on speakerphone and then laid the phone on the desk. "Ok I'm good."

"Right," Jodie said, taking a breath. "Open up the main folder. From there, you need to find the folder labelled 'Messageboard'."

As Jodie spoke, Lewis clicked the relevant folders and files, going deeper and deeper into the workings of the server. A lot of the time, Jodie had no idea what most of it was, but she must have had to go into the messageboard history before, because each click she described took them further in.

"You're not a Gamesmaster. You shouldn't be in here."

Lewis looked up from the monitor to see a blonde kid with scruffy hair standing in the doorway. He was eying Lewis with a furrowed brow, cogs almost visibly turning inside his mind.

"It's ok, I've got permission," Lewis muttered.

"Who's that?" Jodie crackled through the speaker.

"It's Jimmy Hale," the blonde guy said, stepping into the office. "I'm looking for-"

"Jimmy," Jodie cut across him, urgency apparent in her voice. "Why aren't you going to the meet up?"

Jimmy paused mid-word and tilted his head to the side. "What meet up?"

"You didn't get a message?" Lewis asked. Jimmy shook his head. "He didn't get one," Lewis clarified for Jodie.

"Why wouldn't the message go to everyone?" she asked, urgency now being replaced with worry. "I'm sorry Lewis, but I have to go. Something isn't right here." The speaker clicked as she hung up, leaving Lewis and Jimmy staring awkwardly at each other.

3:34 pm

Jodie stared at David, who had been listening to the conversation with interest. "We have to go to Morgan's car park, fast," she stated, already moving towards the door.

"Why didn't you warn Jimmy?" David asked.

Jodie turned back to him, an exasperated look on her face. "He didn't get a message about the meet up. That means whatever Ewan has planned, Jimmy isn't part of it. Now are you coming or what?"

David thought for a moment. It didn't make sense – judging from the stuff in Ewan's room, Jimmy was the prime target, so why not lure him to the meet up? His heart full of misgiving, he nodded and followed Jodie, hoping things were about to make sense.

3:35 pm

"I'm Jimmy Hale," Jimmy repeated after a moment of silence. "I'm looking for-"

"Not now, dude," Lewis dismissed him with a wave of his hand. Jimmy took a step backwards, hovering with uncertainty.

"What meet up?" Jimmy asked again. Lewis looked at him, wondering whether he should take this guy seriously or not. There wasn't even the smallest hint of a smile on Jimmy's face to show he was taking the piss, so Lewis had to assume he was genuine, if a little weird.

"Somebody sent a message about a meet up at Morgan's car park at 4. But it wasn't Jodie, and it seems that the message only went to certain people." As Lewis explained, Jimmy's face fell. As if in a moment of realisation, Jimmy ran back up the society corridor, his head flicking left and right, wildly checking the labels on each door. Raising an eyebrow, Lewis followed him until he came to a stop outside the Archery-Soc office. Before Lewis could say anything, Jimmy was hurling himself against the door. "What the hell are you doing?" Lewis hissed, checking over his shoulder, certain that the noise would attract somebody. Jimmy turned to him, appraising his wide shoulders.

"You're strong," Jimmy panted. "Centaur?"

"Gryphon."

"Force the door open."

"What? No!"

Jimmy looked like he was about to argue, but he was halted by Lewis' phone ringing, the street tone blaring uncomfortably loud in the cramped corridor. When he answered, the voice echoed out through the speakers.

"Lewis?"

"Flynn? Hold on, I've still got it set to speakerphone." Lewis fumbled with the menu, relief flooding through his mind. Flynn must have finally got tired of hiding.

"Don't worry about that," Flynn said in a hushed voice. That was when Lewis detected the note of concern in his brother's reply. Even Jimmy had raised an eyebrow as he listened in.

"What's wrong?"

"I got a message about a meet up," Flynn continued, the sound of a car passing by drowning him out for a second. "I think someone's following me."

"Someone from the game?"

"I don't know. It's some guy in a big grey coat." As Flynn said this, Jimmy started waving his hands frantically, trying to catch Lewis' attention. Lewis glared at him in frustration.

"Wait at the car park," he commanded. "I'm coming to get you, alright Flynn? Stay there."

"Ok. Hurry will you?"

Lewis hung up, already fishing his car keys out of his pocket. He said a silent prayer for the rain, as that was the only reason he'd driven over in the first place. He set his jaw before noticing Jimmy was still acting strange. It was a cross between a small child that knew a juicy secret, and one that really needed a slash.

"What is it? You may have noticed I need to rescue my brother from some weirdo." He made to barge past the other guy, but Jimmy grabbed his arm with a strength that contradicted his slight frame.

"Wait!" Jimmy commanded. Lewis narrowed his eyes, cheeks flushing with the first spots of anger. "You heard about the body in the woods?" Jimmy continued. "The killer on the loose?"

Lewis' insides went cold. "You don't think…" He trailed off, unwilling to consider what Jimmy was insinuating.

"I do," Jimmy said flatly. "Now force this door open."

3:42 pm

Jake had waited until he could hear the theme tune to his mum's favourite show before he'd climbed out of his bedroom window. Luckily, the garage extension was below his room, so he only had to drop onto the garage roof and then drop to the ground from there.

Mark had given him many bruises, but it was the puffy and inflamed black eye that his mother had instantly pounced on as soon as he'd walked through the door. She'd gone through all the stages of mother-worry: Initial panic until she had ascertained he wasn't seriously injured, then there was anger at him for fighting (despite his many protests that he hadn't actually thrown a punch), and finally, anger at the person who'd done this. Jake had refused to give her any names, as he was well aware that in this instance, his mother's interference would definitely make things worse. Subsequently he had been confined to his room 'for his own good'. Jake wasn't sure if she wanted to keep him in whilst his eye healed, or if she was embarrassed for the other mothers on the street to see him in such a state.

Jake smiled to himself as he made his way further and further from his house. Undoubtedly he would get into even more trouble when he returned, but he had to know why he had been stood up. Obviously, he was still angry at Mark and his cronies, but dicks were always dicks – Jonny had at least seemed to be cool.

Jake took another glance at the folded piece of paper that Jonny had given him when they'd first met. It had both his phone number and his address on it. Whilst Jonny had staunchly ignored every call and text that Jake had sent, maybe he would respond to a personal visit.

Gradually, the houses changed from semi-detached family homes to the deceptively sized student terraces. Whilst they looked like rows of narrow cramped quarters, they all seemed to comfortably fit seven or eight students in. Jonny's building was at the end of the row, and for all the confidence Jake had felt whilst walking here, he now felt a tremor of nerves as his hand hovered over the buzzer. What if Jonny was angry? What if all this was some sort of trick? Jake took a deep breath and pressed the button. Not knowing was worse.

3:49 pm

Before the car had even stopped moving, Jimmy was yanking the passenger door open and jumping out onto the rough concrete. Not knowing which storey to stop on, Lewis had slowed down on the ground floor of the car park, aiming to scout each level as they went up. Jimmy however, had shouldered the recurve bow he'd taken from the Archery-Soc office and ran for the stairs.

"Wait!" Lewis called, his stomach filling with dread, but the door to the stairwell was already swinging closed.

3:52 pm

Jake saw net curtains begin to twitch in the windows of the houses either side but he didn't care. After the buzzer had been ignored, he had started to pound loudly on the front door, his fist red and stinging as he slammed it into the wood. He wasn't bothered what people thought, and he simply couldn't acknowledge the fact that Jonny might not actually be at home.

After another minute, he finally saw something moving behind the mottled glass. The random shape coalesced into a humanoid form, and the door swung open. Jonny stood there, bags under his eyes, and his usually immaculately parted hair sticking up in all directions. He looked like he had just woken up.

"Jeez," he hissed. "What do you want?"

Jake's heart sunk. It was like Jonny had forgotten all about their plans. It looked as if Jonny had forgotten all about the game itself.

"What do I want?" Jake found himself yelling. "Look at my face!"

Jonny leaned out of the door cautiously to see Jake's face in the light. After a brief glance up and down the street, he sighed in resignation.

"Come inside, quickly," he said before vanishing into the house. Jake paused momentarily on the doorstep, weighing his options. This was certainly strange behaviour. However, it struck him that he didn't really know Jonny that well, after all the university student had literally approached him out of nowhere. *Well,* Jake thought, *he can't be any worse than Mark…*

Jake followed Jonny inside, his eyes struggling to adjust to the gloom. Every curtain was closed, only faint slivers of light sneaking in through the occasional gap. Jonny led the way into the front room, before slumping into one of the ratty looking armchairs. Jake remained standing indignantly in the doorway.

"Where were you?" he demanded hotly. Despite his anger, Jake was willing himself not to cry. He wanted to show that he at least had some dignity, when it seemed that Jonny had cast his morals aside.

"I'm supposed to be dead," Jonny shrugged. If he was bothered by Jake's fury, he didn't show it.

"What the hell does that mean?" Jake cried. Was Jonny taking the mick out of him? Teasing him because he was still a kid?

Finally, Jonny's nonchalance cracked and his humanity crept through once more. "Look," he began, raising his hands defensively. "I'm sorry you got hurt, and yes in hindsight I could have messaged you, but when someone turns up offering a load of money to pretend to be dead, I'm not gonna say no."

Jake blinked, taking in the absurdity of what Jonny had just said. He'd thrown away his chance at the game for money? Jake had taken the punches because Jonny was getting paid to stay away? To pretend to be dead...

"There's no killer?" he muttered, remembering the news article he'd seen.

Jonny shook his head.

3:57 pm

The dull yellow lights gave the interior of the car park a sickly look as Flynn made his way across the third floor. As soon as he'd ducked inside one of the arches that marked each corner of the high-rise, he'd broken into a sprint, hoping to lose his pursuer in the dingy maze of Morgan's Car Park. His trainers had thumped against the tiles of the stairwell until he'd chosen a random door and forced his way inside. Now that he was out of the cramped quarters of the stairs, he took a moment to survey his surroundings. There were a number of large thick concrete pillars rising out of the floor to support the ceiling, the different ramps and layers making it look as if the building itself was sagging in defeat.

He listened for moment, straining to detect any other footsteps over his own ragged breathing, but his hammering heart and blood rushing in his ears made it impossible. He stalked forwards, anxiously fingering his phone in his pocket, half tempted to call Lewis again. But what good would that do? His brother had already said he was on his way – there was nothing Flynn could do to speed him up.

Suddenly, he heard the door creak behind him, the sound extending menacingly as it reverberated around the cavernous parking floor. He scanned the room once more, cursing himself for foolishly wandering straight into the most open part. The nearest door was in the far corner, and the nearest pillar to hide behind was a good hundred meters away. With a deep breath, Flynn turned around, hoping that his shaking knees weren't visible through his scuffed jeans.

Hovering just beyond the door was the stranger. He was tall and thin, the grey coat seeming to hang off his slender shoulders. For a second, they stood watching each other apprehensively, before the stranger lifted back the hood of the coat, blinking slightly as his eyes took in the gloomy lighting. He didn't look particularly menacing, with short dark hair and trendy geek glasses, but he was a still a stranger, and as far as Flynn could tell, had absolutely no reason for following a fifteen year old boy around.

"Flynn?" The stranger spoke in a light voice with an Irish accent, chilling Flynn's bones. How did he know his name?

Flynn took a step backwards, just as the stranger moved forwards to match him.

"We've been looking for you," the stranger continued, trying a sheepish smile. "I'm not going to hurt you."

That was when Flynn decided to run, twisted logic telling him that normal people don't need to say they won't hurt you. He spun on his heels and burst into a sprint, the stranger following suit a split second later. Flynn had easily been able to stay ahead back on the street, when he was only being followed, but now that the stranger had committed to actually catching him, his shorter legs were proving a disadvantage. It wasn't long before he could feel the tips of grasping fingers brushing against his back.

Out of nowhere, the door Flynn was making for was flung open, and time seemed to thicken around him. He flailed his arms to stop himself from crashing into the guy that was just stepping out onto the floor. *Jesus, is that a bow??*

The guy strode out of the stairwell, with a hunting bow over his shoulder. As soon as he saw Flynn, he unslung the bow, dropping to one knee. Flynn's eyes went wide.

"Get down!" the bowman barked. Flynn threw himself onto the floor, feeling the concrete tear into his elbows as he skidded. With a twang, an arrow was loosed, thudding into the stranger's chest.

4:01 pm

Lewis Howard made his way up the stairs, hoping that the door to the third floor would offer something other than the deserted parking floors that the two previous doors had yielded. Third time lucky, although what greeted his eyes was a scene from a nightmare.

His little brother was lying on the concrete, forearms scraped raw from where he'd fallen. Lewis could already see red patches seeping through his jeans on his thighs – Flynn must have hit the ground hard. That was when he saw Liam Brennan with an arrow in his chest. The grey duffel coat he was wearing was darkening as a halo of crimson bloomed around the shaft of the arrow, a discarded poppy dropped face down on the chest of a fallen soldier. He turned to where Jimmy was standing, eyes wide.

"What did you do?" Lewis asked, his breath catching in his throat. "He's not a killer, he's a Gamesmaster!"

Jimmy gingerly laid the bow on the concrete, blinking rapidly. "What if he's both?"

Lewis shook his head before pulling his phone out of his pocket. He was already dialling 999 as he knelt down beside Flynn. Whilst he told the operator what happened and where they were, he hoisted Flynn to his feet. He looked at his brother questioningly, and between sobs, Flynn nodded that yes, he was ok despite everything that happened. That was when Jodie and David arrived.

Jodie bustled in from the stairwell, David following closely behind. She strode with a purpose, like she was expecting to see something like this, but she halted when she saw Jimmy staring blankly at her. She blinked a few times. If

Jimmy was ok, then Ewan's plan had surely failed? Lewis was
there hugging what must have been his younger brother –
was that all the loose ends tied up? They'd won then? The
game was saved? Over her shoulder, she heard David gasp,
and finally she saw the body on the floor. Not a body. Liam.

"No!" Jodie screamed as she ran forwards, dropping
to her knees. Liam's eyes were closed behind his glasses, and
he didn't respond when she grabbed him. "How did this
happen?" she shrieked as she shook her boyfriend, trying to
jolt him back into action. She looked around at the others,
tears welling up in her eyes, desperate for someone to explain
this to her. All that met her was a series of blank expressions.
Flynn pressed his face into Lewis' shoulder, David stood
with his hand over his mouth, and Jimmy was staring at the
ceiling almost as if he didn't understand what was going on.
But he did have a bow at his feet. "You!" Jodie yelled,
springing at Jimmy like a wild animal. The boy raised his
hands in front of his face, crying out as Jodie beat at him
with a hail of blows, releasing all of her anger and grief,
pouring it through her fists. Her only thought was that it
should be Jimmy on the floor instead of Liam.

She didn't stop even as the emergency services roared
up the ramp and screeched to a halt before them. There was
an ambulance flanked by two police cars, the car park now
flashing with blue and red – the disco of crisis. The
paramedics rushed to help Liam whilst a horde of black clad
police officers swarmed over the others like beetles. They
pulled Jodie away from Jimmy, who was now wailing to
himself, the chaos proving too much for his ordered mind.

David watched the proceedings, sickness bubbling
inside his stomach. He wasn't sure whether he was disgusted
at the sight of Liam's wound, or the disintegration of morals
and humanity that had led to it. Liam was being loaded into
the back of the ambulance, Jodie already perched on the

bench that ran along one side of the vehicle's interior. Jimmy was in cuffs, being led towards one of the waiting police cars. The rest of the officers were talking to Lewis and Flynn, notebooks in hand. David had no doubt that they would want to speak to him too, and in his head, he began running through everything he should tell them. Behind him, the door to the stairwell opened once more, this time revealing Ewan Lloyd.

Ewan's usually confident façade dropped instantly when he saw the carnage stretched out across the parking floor. "What happened?" he stammered.

David rounded on him savagely. "I hope you're happy now!" he spat.

"What do you mean?"

"Jimmy shot Liam," David snapped, waving his hand across the disaster scene, including the pool of Liam's blood on the concrete.

A tear fell down Ewan's cheek. "I only wanted to scare him," he said, voice cracking. "I thought that if Jimmy reckoned there was a real killer, it would distract him from the game and I could win."

David looked over his shoulder to where a couple of police officers were heading their way. They seemed to have finished with the Howard brothers, as Lewis was now leading Flynn away, a blanket draped across his narrow shoulders.

"Tell it to them," David muttered unsympathetically.

The Day After

3:46 pm

Jodie Hawk had had a long day. She'd spent the first few hours with the police, and then the rest of the time at the hospital by Liam's side. Liam's parents were flying across from Dublin but wouldn't arrive until later that evening.

At different times, David and Lewis had been to visit – Flynn had been immediately fetched and whisked home by his angry parents. The only other thing that she'd done was to make a brief trip back to the Kill-Soc office.

There'd been an envelope waiting on the carpet for her when she'd opened the door. It wasn't a cheap crappy brown envelope like she used to deliver invites, it was a crisp white one with the UCE official stamp on it. Even though she knew Liam couldn't hear it, she'd taken it to the hospital so she could read it to him, unwilling to give up on the fact that he had always been there to support her through the bad times, as well as share all the good ones.

Dear Miss Hawk,

After yesterday's tragedy, we are hereby notifying you of the dissolution of the UCE Kill Society. You have two days in which to clear the office. At the end of this time, you will be expected to return the keys.

It is also my duty to inform you that with immediate effect, you are prohibited from organising and participating in any current or future UCE Society events.

Yours sincerely,

E. Saunders – Head of Extra Curricular, Sports and Societies

There was a quiet cough in the doorway, and Jodie looked up to where a nurse was standing, an awkward expression on her face. It suggested the nurse would have rather been anywhere else in the whole hospital instead of this room.

"I'm sorry, but it's time for you to leave," she said nervously.

"But," Jodie began to protest. "I can't leave him."

The nurse's face softened a little, but she didn't give in as she had on all her previous attempts. "You have my sympathies, but I'm afraid…" she faltered, taking a breath. "I'm afraid we need to take the body to the morgue. Leaving it here has been most uncharacteristic."

Jodie turned back to where Liam lay. The body. It. He wasn't her boyfriend any more, he was a cold and pale *thing* that just happened to have his face. Even that looked different after the doctors had taken his glasses away. Liam Brennan had passed away in the night, but Jodie had refused to leave him until now. It was as if the nurse's bluntness had lifted the veil from Jodie's eyes, and only now could she see the truth. Liam was dead.

Jodie let herself be led out of the cramped room, along a sterile corridor with gleaming tiles and into the foyer.

"Do you need anything?" the nurse asked. Jodie shook her head, suspecting it was one of those questions like 'how are you', where you aren't supposed to answer truthfully. The nurse gave a nod of barely concealed relief before pressing a clear bag into Jodie's hands and disappearing back into the bowels of the hospital.

Jodie stood aimlessly for a few moments before stepping through the automatic doors into the car park, the crisp air making some small effort to revitalise her after the tortuous night. Her life was empty, all purpose had died with Liam. She didn't want to go home alone, and she couldn't go back to the office even if she wanted to. Where did that leave? She settled for the nearest bench, staring out aimlessly across the tarmac, watching the cars coming and going. There was a girl sitting alone on the other side of the car park, and there was a constant flow of vehicles in and out. She noticed that everybody arrived with the same face – a distinct look of concern for whoever the injured party was. It was only the departure that differentiated them. There were those that seemed to glow from the all clears and the getting betters that they received, and there were those that like Jodie, had the meander of loss, whether it was immediate, or simply the knowledge that it was coming and unavoidable.

It was only now that Jodie brought herself to look through the bag the nurse had given her. It was the items Liam had with him when he died. A bag that contained his life, boiled down into a wallet, a phone and some pocket junk. She fished out his phone and flipped it open, suddenly desperate to leech any extra memories of him from inside. Before she could stop herself, she was sifting through his old messages, her mind reading them out in his voice, recreating every nuance and characteristic that made it his. His phone was set up to receive Kill-Soc posts too, so she could cover every aspect of his life.

SecretAdmirer: Hey, so I'm hoping you've changed your mind. We could still work something out. There could be a lot riding on your decision…
GamesmasterLiam: Look, this isn't some lame Rom-Com where you get what you want every time you pour out your feelings. And don't think you can guilt trip me because you simply 'can't go on without me' – I'm with Jodie and I always will be. Get over it.
SecretAdmirer: Thanks for putting things into perspective. Good luck, Gamesmaster.

Jodie's heart fluttered as she read Liam's staunch defending of their relationship. Before she could stop herself, she was weeping, the message emphasising how much she had lost. Even when Jodie had been too busy with Kill-Soc proceedings, bossing him around and giving him orders, he had stuck by her, not once thinking of anyone else.

Just then, a shadow crossed in front of her, stopping so that all she could see was the elongated form of a vaguely human shape. She looked to the side to see Ewan Lloyd hovering awkwardly by the side of the bench.

"May I?" he said quietly, indicating the empty spot on the bench at Jodie's side. She considered everything that the police had told her: how Ewan had been so intent on getting back at Jimmy for defeating him the year before that he had orchestrated the whole trick. How he had convinced Gemma to create the fake news report about the body in the woods to start the panic. They'd even mocked up the crime scene with stuff they'd taken from the Drama department. From there, all they had to do was stage a few fake 'deaths' and make sure that Jimmy saw all the clues. Using the eliminated players for a fake flyer campaign also helped to get Jimmy worked up. The final straw had been convincing Rick to clone the Kill-Soc server that he had helped Jodie set up all those years ago. He'd put a copy on Ewan's computer so that Ewan could send the messages about the meet up. It was Ewan's fault that Jimmy was now facing a manslaughter charge, and technically, it was Ewan's fault that Liam was gone.

The fact that Ewan was here and not in custody showed that the police believed his explanation that it had all been a joke that went too far. After all, could anybody really have predicted what Jimmy would do? They said that Liam had been in the wrong place at the wrong time, and that Jimmy had thought he was trying to hurt the kid, Flynn.

What good would holding a grudge do now anyway? Jodie sniffed, then nodded, Ewan sitting down beside her.

The two of them didn't speak for a few minutes, each in their own thoughts. Jodie reasoned it must have been difficult for Ewan too, knowing that his joke had caused so much pain.

Eventually, Ewan spoke. "I want you to know something."

"You don't have to do this," Jodie said, a small part of her wanting to spare Ewan the grief, but mostly because she knew if he went into too much detail, she might end up crying again.

"Yes I do," he replied, a note of determination rising in his voice. "You have to understand."

"I get it," Jodie snapped, thrusting her hand into the hospital bag once more, grounding herself in Liam's stuff. "It was an accident. I actually thought you were going to kill Jimmy for real. It was a stupid trick that went wrong."

"Did it?"

Jodie's insides went cold. She stared at Ewan, who was now wearing a twisted smirk. "What do you..?" At that moment, her fingers brushed against something familiar in the bag. She looked down and saw the scarlet Kill-Soc badge that Liam had been given at last year's after party. A badge she had seen very recently in Ewan's room. "You gave it to him?"

Ewan watched, his eyes glinting as she discovered each layer.

"You weren't just after Jimmy…" Jodie muttered, thinking back to the messages on Liam's phone. "You set him up because he wouldn't *sleep* with you??" She was incredulous now, wishing that she was wrong, that Liam hadn't died for something so petty.

Ewan only nodded. "Two birds, one stone," he said. "Or should I say arrow."

"You won't get away with this," Jodie declared hotly. "I'll tell the police everything."

"They'd never believe you."

Jodie opened her mouth to respond but all she could manage was a choking gasp. Ewan was right – all he'd done was talk and type – everything else pointed to Jimmy, the autistic kid that they would accuse of not knowing the difference between the game and reality. Ewan leaned in, his lips millimetres from her ear and tear streaked cheek.

"I always win."

Epilogue

To: Stereotypes@UCE.net
From: JHawk@UCE.net

I know you will have heard about what happened to my
boyfriend Liam Brennan during this year's Kill-Soc game.
Although Jimmy Hale fired the arrow, he wasn't responsible.
A Drama student called Ewan Lloyd orchestrated the whole
thing on purpose. He explained everything, but the police
won't believe me – in terms of actual proof, it still looks like
Jimmy's fault.
You guys are my last hope of getting justice for Liam…
Yours desperately,
Jodie Hawk

To: JHawk@UCE.net
From: Stereotypes@UCE.net

Jodie,
Mission accepted.
We will contact you shortly regarding payment.
The Stereotypes

THE STEREOTYPES

Prologue – The Meeting Room

The meeting room was dark, matching everything about the clandestine gathering that was about to take place. Dark because of the ominous prearranged time of midnight. Dark because the room was hidden deep underground. And dark because nothing bright and benevolent was ever discussed there.

With a click, a single light flickered on, turning some of the blackness into grey. As more and more humming lights twinkled into existence like constellations, vague shadows became objects of certainty. There was a long black table, with leather chairs arranged around it like a corporate boardroom. Along one wall was a sideboard with a set of ghostly monitor screens as well as a printer and a phone.

One of the monitors buzzed into life, a string of start-up code clicking across, sending laser light trails into the furthest corners of the room. Eventually, the machinery settled, the lights dimming once more, throwing the room back into the gloom. A red digital time display lit up above the computer desk, gilding everything in cherry embers.

Midnight.

Almost instantly, a shuffling came from outside the only door, which slid open without sound. A large silhouette blocked the doorway, a different shade of black to the rectangular void behind it. Like spectres, eight figures glided into the room and sank into the seats around the table. The darkness didn't bother them – they knew exactly who was sitting where, without having to see their faces.

Nobody flinched when the printer rattled – they were all used to the procedure by now. They would periodically be

summoned to the meeting room to receive new instructions.
It had happened so often that they had stopped asking the
fundamental questions, like how the printer knew that
everyone was there before it started printing. Once it had
finished, the figure closest to the desk leaned over, hazing
into crimson existence briefly as he passed in and out of the
glare from the digital clock.

The torch app on a mobile glared fiercely, throwing an
angular face with high cheekbones into a silver halo as he
scanned the printout. As they were all expecting, it was a
message from their enigmatic leader.

> Good evening, Stereotypes,
> Prepare to be tested. Here you will find everything you
> need to recruit new members to our little enterprise.
> Further instructions to follow.

Suddenly, a spotlight clicked on, throwing a single beam into
the centre of the table. A box was waiting there, previously
unseen in the gloom. Tentatively, the figure at the head of
the table reached over and lifted the lid. Everyone leaned
forward to inspect the contents: a stack of flyers – plain
black with a simple question in white – *Are you a stereotype?*

In the warm glow of the spotlight, the Stereotypes
looked at each other with wide eyes. Since the group had
formed, they'd only replaced members who had graduated
and moved on – it had never been forced upon them before.

Collectively, they gulped.

Chapter 1 – The New Boy

The coach shook gently as it bounced along the motorway, fields and trees slipping past in the darkness. For the past three hours, Lee Radley had been lounging in his padded seat, legs stretched out in front, making the most of the Gold Standard seat that had been booked for him.

There was hardly anybody else on the coach, and Lee had been alternating his time between checking his emails, reading some fantasy novel he'd chucked into his bag, and losing himself in the various clickbait articles that littered his Facebook newsfeed. That and making eyes at the girl who brought the coffee round, of course. He'd found himself, in his eternal boredom, wondering what her job title actually was. She wasn't a waitress… maybe a steward? Lee resolved to ask her if she came round again, although as the evening had gone on, her trips up the aisle had become less frequent.

Lee peered out the window, trying to pick out any geographical details that could tell him where he was, but instead all he could focus on was his reflection in the darkened glass. He wasn't that bad looking - quirky, people used to say as they took in the kink in the bridge of his nose, and his slightly off centre grin with the full lips. He patted furiously at the wedge of sandy hair that had stuck up from where he'd been pressing his head against the glass during the journey, then smiled when he caught the coffee girl's reflection watching him with a smirk. He winked back and she turned away, pretending not to have noticed whilst blushing furiously.

Just then, a sign flashed past on the side of the road, a streak of blue lightning in the coach headlights. It had been too fast to read, but the fields rapidly gave way to fences and houses – the suburbia that surrounded the cities like satellites. Lee pressed his face once more against the glass and squinted, trying to scan the road ahead. Sure enough, a cluster of bright lights was rapidly coalescing into the familiar shapes of high rise buildings.

"Ladies and gentlemen," came the voice of the steward girl crackling over the intercom. "We are just approaching the city limits, which means that in about ten minutes' time we will be arriving at our penultimate stop tonight – UCE main campus. If you're planning on leaving us at UCE, please make sure you have all your personal belongings with you."

Pity, thought Lee. Another twenty miles or so, and he could have easily got the steward's number. As it was, he stuffed his laptop into his messenger bag, and collected the detritus from his travel snacks into one single heap. He kept his phone in his hand, twirling it between his fingers as the buildings by the side of the road got bigger and brighter.

After a moment of contemplation, he tapped the phone's screen and thumbed through his contacts until he reached his father's number.

No answer.

Next, Lee tried 'Dad Office', this time greeted by the classical tones of the company's hold music.

"Good evening, Radley Incorporated, how may I direct your call?"

"Hi Paula," Lee said. "Is my dad around?"

"Good evening Lee. If you'll hold one moment, I'll check."

Lee sat back as the orchestral symphony struck up once more. What his father's PA meant was that she would ask if he could be bothered to talk to his son or not.

"I'm sorry Lee, but Sir Radley is in the middle of something very important right now."

Denied. The excuses weren't even that good any more. When Lee had started Uni, his father had always been busy with meetings or paperwork – now it was just 'something important.' He couldn't even be bothered to make something up.

"No worries," Lee sighed. "Thanks for trying."

There was a pause on the other end of the line. "I really am sorry Lee," Paula continued quietly. "I understand this is a strange time for you."

That was right, Lee thought. Not many students transferred so close to the end of the year. He felt a strange connection with Paula, who had at least acknowledged the changes he was having to make, even though they'd never met. Lee still felt like he knew her better than he knew his father.

"I'm sure if you needed help sorting things, your father wouldn't mind you using some of his security retinue. I'll email you the contact details."

"Thanks Paula, I'll bear that in mind."

"Would you like to leave a message for Sir Radley?"

Lee considered for a moment. "Tell him I've arrived safely, and I'll…" he stopped. What exactly would he do? Try phoning again later for another stellar chat with Paula? "Just tell him I got there safely."

"I will do Lee. Have a good evening."

"You too Paula."

By now, the bus had come off the main roads and was weaving its way through the more urban streets to its destination. Slowing down, the vehicle pulled in alongside a row of blocky buildings, the occasional classical front still standing, protected by historical listing – obvious University buildings.

"Ladies and gentlemen, this is the UCE Campus stop," the steward chirped. "We'd like to thank you for travelling with us tonight, and we wish you all the best with your continued journey."

Lee climbed to his feet and jumped down onto the tarmac, flashing a final cheeky grin at the steward as he left. The driver was already heaving bags out of the luggage hold, and Lee quickly snatched up his hiking rucksack and pulled it over his shoulder. He'd had to pack rather hurriedly, cramming as much as he could into the bag, and trusting that his father would dispatch a squad of minions to deliver the rest of his stuff later.

The coach engine growled and the vehicle lurched off amidst a spluttering cloud of exhaust. The few others who had gotten off had dispersed into the shadows of the campus, but Lee stood where he was, staring through the black gates before him. On the other side was a spacious quad – largely grass but with a few pathways stretching across it, connecting the various surrounding buildings like veins or tendons. In each corner stood a tall oak tree, filled with wide leaves that shone verdantly as they caught the security lights. Attached to the side of the opposite block were a set of huge glowing letters, a whole storey's height, announcing that this was the centre of UCE, the University of Central England.

It was obvious that the buildings surrounding the quad were solely academic, purely by their lack of activity. Student Halls would be alive whatever time it was. Lee flicked his phone on, bringing up the map function with a brush of his thumb. Once the GPS had located exactly where he was, it didn't take him long to spot O'Connell Hall on the sprawling campus.

After checking he had the key that UCE had sent him in advance, Lee readjusted the rucksack on his shoulder and walked into the darkness.

Chapter 2 – First Impressions

Lee awoke to the sound of whispering. He blinked a few times, taking in the blank room he'd snuck into when he'd arrived. He'd been dog tired by the time he'd got there, so had just pulled a blanket out of his bag and flopped onto the bed without even turning the light on. It had been late enough that even the rest of his flatmates had been asleep, or at least holed up in their rooms, so he hadn't met anybody yet.

"I'm telling you, someone's in there…" A female voice from the other side of the door.

Lee stretched before setting his bare feet noiselessly onto the carpet. The room was pretty similar to the one he'd had at his previous uni, all pine and well meaning blue trim. There was a blank notice board and empty cupboards, all waiting for Lee to put his mark on them, but that would have to wait until his dad sent the rest of his stuff over.

"I'm not knocking," another voice hissed. "You knock!"

Lee stood up, scanning the floor for where he'd chucked his t-shirt, then smiled to himself. Why not give the girls outside something to remember? He padded silently over to the ensuite, pausing in front of the mirror. With a smirk, he pulled the waistband of his Calvins down just enough so that they were revealing the first hints of hair. Next, he splashed a little water down his chest so his skin shone slightly.

"What was that?" the first voice rose upon hearing the tap. "I don't like it, maybe we should wake up the boys?"

Lee leapt into action, yanking the door open as fast as he could and leaning casually against the frame, ignoring the girls' panicked squeals.

"Can I help you?" he asked silkily, noticing both the girls glance down towards his shorts. One was tall with long blonde hair, the other shorter with close cut brown hair - a pixie, or a page boy or something, Lee remembered. Both were attractive, and Lee could instantly see he was going to enjoy himself here.

"We weren't sure if someone was in there," the blonde began. "The room was empty you see."

"Well I'm in here now," Lee said with a grin, throwing the door open as if to show off a luxurious apartment, despite there only being a rucksack and a pile of clothes in the middle of the floor.

"We can certainly see that," the pixie muttered slowly, eyes fixed somewhere around Lee's flat stomach.

"I'm Sarah," the blonde said with a beaming smile. "She's Kelly."

"Lee, pleased to meet you," Lee introduced himself, holding out a large hand to shake.

"You too," Kelly nodded, still not quite making it as far as Lee's face.

"Well," Sarah went on. "We'll leave you to get sorted. We usually go for breakfast at The Union if you want to join us? They do a solid hangover cure."

"Yeah cheers," Lee smiled. "I'll think about it." He turned slowly, being sure to give them plenty of time to check out his ass, then he noticed something scratched into his door. Caedo Tu. "What's this?" he asked, scraping at the letters with his finger. It was etched deeply into the wood, the blue paint flaking off round the edges. He turned back to see Kelly and Sarah shifting uncomfortably.

"Um," Sarah faltered. "The guy that had the room before you... He..."

"That should have been cleared up by now!"

All three of them turned to look up the corridor, a tall and thick set guy in a bright red polo shirt lolloping towards them. He sidled up to them, leaning against the wall and panting slightly. Lee read the words 'Senior Resident' embroidered across the guy's polo.

"I'm Harry, good to – oh!" Harry stopped and stared, as if only noticing Lee's current lack of clothes. "Don't… don't you want to get dressed?"

Lee winked at the girls. "Nah, I'm good."

"Right, well um…" Harry faltered whilst the girls giggled. "As I was saying, I'm Harry. Yes. Senior Resident for this block. If you need anything then I'm your man. Once again, apologies about the door. The boy who lived here before had… issues. He's… gone now. Anyway, if you don't mind, I've got to go through fire safety and all that stuff."

"Go for it," Lee said, deliberately reaching into his shorts and having a good scratch.

"Look," Harry snapped. "I really would find this easier if you put some clothes on. I'll wait in the living room." With this, the Senior Resident turned and marched back up the corridor, disappearing into one of the doors on the left.

"What's his deal?" Lee asked the girls, the feeling that he'd teased a little too much beginning to dawn on him.

"He's not really into, well *anything* us students get up to," Sarah stated bluntly.

"I heard he's Christian," Kelly muttered, as if that explained everything. "And we know they don't worship idols."

"Wow," Sarah said flatly, giving her friend a playful shove. "We really should leave you to it – besides, looks like this bitch needs a cold shower. It really was good to meet you. Think about breakfast, yeah?"

"I will," Lee nodded as he watched the girls head back up the corridor, already whispering to each other mysteriously.

It didn't take him long to dig out a fresh t-shirt from his bag and pull it over his head. His jeans from yesterday were still viable, and within a few minutes, Lee was hopping up the corridor, straightening his socks before he found the living room.

It was a large open plan room, with one end carpeted in pale blue, and one end covered in cheap cream lino. The carpeted end played host to a variety of mismatched chairs, roughly facing a wall mounted flat screen, whilst the other end was a kitchen filled with off-white appliances and cupboards with name labels on. Lee couldn't help smiling – whichever uni you went to, somethings were always the same. *Universal,* Lee thought to himself with a smile.

Harry was sitting at a long wooden table that marked roughly halfway between kitchen and living room. He had a folder full of printed sheets laid out carefully in front of him.

"Ah," he said, looking up at Lee's now clothed form appraisingly. "Take a seat."

"Sorry about before," Lee muttered. "I was only teasing. Just playing up for the girls, really."

"Yes well," Harry mumbled, straightening his folder. "There's no need to be such a… a…"

"Stereotype?" Lee suggested.

"Why would you say that?" Harry's face seemed to drain, beads of sweat forming on his brow.

"Sorry," Lee said, raising his hands in platitude. "I thought you were having trouble finding the word."

"Don't joke about stereotypes," Harry breathed quietly. "Besides, the word I was looking for was *twat.*"

"Ok," Lee said slowly. For someone who hated stereotypes, Harry was certainly being a stereotypical weirdo. "Let's just get on with this safety bumf shall we?"

"I think that's best."

Harry proceeded to read through each one of his meticulously printed sheets, outlining what to do in the event of fires, floods, earthquakes, and even hurricanes. He spoke in serious monotone, like he was a machine delivering data.

"What, no zombies?" Lee joked once Harry had finished.

"I hope you were paying attention to all that," the senior resident chided.

"Come on," Lee snorted. "When was the last time a hurricane hit the city?"

"That's not the point."

"Alright, alright. Yeah I was listening. It's mostly the same to my last place anyway."

"Ah yes," Harry said, clasping his hands together. "They don't tell us Senior Residents why people like you get transferred. However, I wouldn't count out some sort of mischief on your part. Let me tell you, I take my job very seriously here, and I won't have someone like you spoiling things."

Lee bristled for a second before playing it down – he was still touchy about having to transfer. "Aw come on Harry, anyone would think you don't like me."

"Well you haven't exactly made a very endearing first impression."

Lee pouted petulantly. "Is it because you saw my junk?"

"I think this introduction is at an end Mr Radley," Harry flustered, collecting his sheets. "I've arranged a buddy for you – he's on your course so he can show you the ropes better than me. Here's his number – he'll be expecting a call. Good day."

Lee watched silently as the senior resident left the room hurriedly, slamming the door slightly harder than was necessary. *Meh,* Lee thought. *Can't appeal to everybody.* At least Kelly and Sarah seemed to like him, and Lee would much rather have their attention, even if that did make him slightly shallow. He sat back and added his buddy's number to his phone, before firing off a quick greeting message, made more difficult by the fact that Harry hadn't actually mentioned his name.

Whilst waiting for a reply, Lee noticed a chalk board hanging from the wall that had his new flatmates' numbers jotted on it. He added those into his phone too, just in case.

Chapter 3 – Buddy System

An hour later, Lee was showered and dressed properly, waiting on the steps outside O'Connell Hall. His buddy had messaged back saying he would meet him here, and more importantly, that his name was Dan.

Sure enough, Lee soon saw someone striding purposefully towards him, even giving a nod when their eyes met. Dan was tall and angular like one of those Easter Island statues, although he had a smile that softened the image.

"Alright mate," Dan said warmly, gripping Lee's hand in his huge palm. "You must be Lee."

"Yup," Lee replied. "Good job really, otherwise that would have been awkward."

"Ha yeah," Dan chuckled. "Coach says we have to come across as nice – it's this new image thing he's trying out."

"Ah, so you're on a team?"

"Centaurs," Dan nodded. "UCE's finest footballers. Anyway, I was thinking we could do a quick lap of campus, then hit the pub - sound good?"

"Sounds great," Lee nodded, glad that unlike Harry, Dan seemed to have his priorities straight.

As they walked, Dan filled him in on everything they'd done in Business class this year, and Lee was relieved to hear that it wasn't vastly different to what he'd covered at his old uni.

"No offence," Lee grinned. "But I wouldn't expect a footballer to be doing Business."

"Meh," Dan shrugged. "I'm no stereotype. I'm fairly realistic about my chances as a sportsman. Business is hopefully for a career, football is just exercise and a laugh."

They continued to meander around the various blocks, with Dan pointing out various bits of interest –

mostly places in which he'd pulled, or his teammates had done something hilarious. Lee didn't mind – at least it showed that UCE had character.

Eventually, they made it to the quad where Lee had got off the bus the night before. It looked completely different in the morning sunlight, the dark grey shadows of the evening now bursting with summer greenery, pinpricks of white and yellow littering the grass where meadow flowers were growing through. Not only were students crossing the quad on the concrete paths, bags slung over shoulders and notepads clutched to chests, but a fair number were also lounging on the grass, sipping coffee or hair of the dog beer cans. Lee took a deep breath, revelling in the sun and the freedom – this was uni life at its best.

Lee's attention was drawn to a statue that stood next to one of the paths, glinting in the light. It was either very meticulously cared for, or it was new. It was a male figure in gleaming bronze, head tilted to where his outstretched hand clutched a polished orb of pearl. His features were vague and generic – not of anybody in particular, but his expression was serious and tinged with sadness.

"What's that?" Lee asked, walking over to the statue to read the plaque on the side of the plinth.

"Ah," Dan said, his voice suddenly solemn and quiet.

As Lee approached, he could see various trinkets laid out around the statue's plinth: a blue and gold sports scarf, a pair of geek glasses and a shot glass, as well as various flowers and cards. It was obvious that it was a memorial statue, and Lee shivered awkwardly, caught moving in a direction he no longer wanted to pursue. He was the new guy – he had no right or desire to take interest in UCE's past tragedies, but he also didn't want anybody to see him physically turn away – that would make him seem heartless.

He slowed his pace, the words on the golden plaque clarifying into a set of names and a dedication.

Liam Brennan
Jack Dyer
Alex Marshall

Spirits and Stars

Suddenly, Lee felt a large hand on his shoulder. Dan gently turned him round, an apologetic look on his face.

"Come on, let's get that drink," he said softly. "I'll fill you in en route."

Lee nodded, letting Dan lead the way across the quad towards one of the corner passages. As they walked, Lee became fully versed in UCE's recent losses - the poor boy that got taken out for real during the fake assassin game, and the two guys that had killed themselves at the same time, one of which happened to be a player on Dan's football team.

"That's part of the reason why Coach wants us to change our behaviour," Dan said ruefully. "We didn't really treat Alex like we should have."

"What's the other part?"

"Hmm," Dan said with the ghost of a smile. "You'd have to ask our Captain Luke about that one. But it's not all doom and gloom. There were two guys that woke up from comas, so you know, UCE heals too. Anyway, here we are."

From the outside, The Union was nothing more than a set of glass doors set into a bland concrete façade. It could have been anything – a car park or even a warehouse, however once they had stepped inside, its true purpose was obvious. The foyer was plastered in flyers and posters, as well as the mandatory warnings encouraging students to take regular water breaks and never to leave their drinks unattended. An unmanned desk stood before them, and Dan explained that at night, bouncers would conduct searches and ID checks from there.

"The club side is through there," he said, pointing to a row of closed doors. "It's your typical bar and dancefloor situation, but it doesn't open 'til later."

Instead, Dan headed left, into a bright open area with lots of booths and sofas. Flatscreens dotted the walls, and there were a couple of pool tables at one end. There was still a bar, however coffee machines and displays of cakes and cookies were interspersed with the traditional beer taps.

Dan headed straight for the bar, ordering them a pint each, cocking his head to a clock that hung from the wall when Lee raised an eyebrow. The clock had no numbers, just the slogan *It's always beer o'clock* emblazoned across the middle. Lee couldn't help smiling as he sipped the froth from his beer and scanned for a place to sit.

As he'd hoped, he spotted Kelly and Sarah sitting in a booth, perusing a couple of menus. He and Dan slid into the seats opposite them, picking up menus of their own.

"Dan, good to see you," Sarah beamed. "Been showing Lee around?"

"Uhuh," the footballer nodded. "You ordered yet?"

"Not yet," Sarah said, glancing down at the menu.

At this moment, an employee in a bright yellow polo shirt came up to the table, a notebook clutched in his hand, pencil poised eagerly.

"Two hangover cures please," Kelly said with a grin.

"Same," added Dan.

The waiter turned to Lee, who shrugged. "Why not?" he said. "Another hangover cure."

"Cheers Firefly," Dan said as the waiter went back to the bar.

"Firefly?" asked Lee.

"They're yellow," Kelly said, leaning in like she was about to reveal a huge secret. "You can see them in the dark."

"Fireflies and Centaurs? I'm sensing a theme here…"

"The Lacrosse team are called Gryphons," said Sarah.

"I prefer the Hydras," Kelly said hungrily. "It's the little trunks they wear." This earned her another shove from her friend.

"What do you call the Senior Residents?" Lee asked, thinking of Harry's less than warm welcome. "How about Warthogs? They're fat and red."

The others laughed, whilst Lee excused himself to the bathroom. When he returned, four plates piled high with fried greatness had been delivered from the kitchen. His three companions were already tucking in, and Lee could tell from the satisfied way that the conversation had been instantly halted that the food was good. He dived in.

Once they'd finished, they all sat comfortably lolling in the post grease contentment until Dan checked his watch.

"I should get going," he muttered, stretching his arms across the table. "I need to burn some of this off before practice later. You know how to get back to O'Connell from here?"

"We'll take him," Kelly said cheerfully, reaching across to grab Lee's arm. "He's our new flatmate, after all."

"Well if you need anything else, just ask. Otherwise, I'll see you at The Business End tomorrow morning."

"There is one thing," Lee said slowly. "What are The Stereotypes?" He looked at his companions, noting their discomfort. Sarah had become absorbed in the menu once more, whilst Kelly seemed fascinated by a loose thread on her top. Dan checked his watch again. "It's just that I saw something on the toilet wall," Lee went on. "It mentioned stereotypes with capitals, like they were important or something."

"It's nothing," Dan muttered. "Just some stupid message. So I'll see you tomorrow. Bye girls." With that, the footballer headed for the exit.

Lee, Kelly and Sarah sat there for another ten minutes or so, but every conversation he tried to start seemed to fizzle into nothing. Eventually, the girls made their excuses and offered to walk Lee back to O'Connell hall.

"It's ok," Lee said, faking chirpiness. "I remember the way. I'll grab another drink then go for a wander."

"Fair enough," Sarah nodded. "See you at home." She stood and shouldered her bag, then waited for Kelly to do the same. With a final wave, they left in silence, with Lee trying to figure out exactly what he'd said wrong.

Once the doors had swung shut behind the girls, Lee leapt to his feet and rushed back to the toilets. Doing his hair at the mirror whilst waiting for the current guy to finish at the urinal, Lee reviewed the information in his head. The first time he'd mentioned stereotypes had been an accident, but Harry had still reacted badly. The second time he'd done it on purpose, and it had the same effect. Even Dan had said earlier that he was 'no stereotype.' Lee knew that The Stereotypes were more than just some random toilet vandalism, and what had really piqued his interest was the fact that they seemed to have a reputation.

The other guy left without washing his hands, and Lee shook his head in disgust before stepping up to the row of urinals, scanning the endless amount of scrawled abuse that was written there. The mother of someone called Glen seemed to fare particularly badly amongst the slurs, and Lee couldn't help smiling as his eyes roved over the immature and often illiterate comments. There was also a missing poster for someone called Ewan, although why they would have stuck it in the toilet, Lee could only guess. When Lee finally found the message he was looking for, he took a deep breath and checked over his shoulder to make sure nobody else was about to come in, then took a snap of it on his phone before leaving.

Back in the booth, which had now been cleared by the staff – Fireflies, he reminded himself - Lee gazed at the picture with wondrous eyes. It was a simple message, written in thin cursive hand – perhaps that was what had caught his eye, as the person who wrote this could obviously spell.

Are you a Stereotype?

The message was then followed by a mobile number, and it was this that Lee now typed hastily into his phone. He thought for a moment, then smiled to himself as he typed a message of his own.

I could be...

Lee pressed send.

Chapter 4 – The Lay Of The Land

The remainder of Lee's first week passed quickly. The rest of his stuff still hadn't been delivered, and he was a little tired of recycling the same three outfits in various different combinations, but still he didn't phone his father. Sir Michael would hardly see Lee's belongings as a high priority.

Despite his lack of possessions however, Lee had settled in to his flat with ease. Kelly and Sarah had soon forgotten the 'breakfast of awkwardness', and Lee had met the rest of his flatmates and found them just as agreeable. Even his Business lectures weren't too bad, although he did have to prepare a presentation for next week. He'd found there was a good mix of things he'd covered already (so he could show off and look clever), as well as things that were new to him (so it wasn't a complete waste of time).

One thing Lee did prefer over Northern was the fact that everything at UCE seemed to have a nickname, even the buildings. The technology block was called The Red Shed, and the building where Lee took his classes was lovingly referred to as The Business End. It had helped Lee to get his bearings quickly, not to mention giving him some top quality pun potential.

Nothing came of the text message, and Lee began to think that perhaps Dan had been right – maybe it was just a stupid piece of graffiti, or perhaps it meant something years ago, but not anymore? The busier Lee got across the week, the less he'd had time to think about it.

Now it was Friday, and the flat was buzzing with excitement. Everybody had somewhere to be, whether it was out on a date or hitting the clubs. Dan, Kelly and Sarah had promised to take Lee to The Union so he could experience it in all its Friday glory, and Lee was certainly curious to see what the other half of the building was like.

There was a knock on his door. "I'm coming in, make sure you have pants on!" Dan strode in, beaming at his humour. From his already rosy cheeks, Lee guessed he'd been pre-drinking. "I bought some emergency shirtage, as requested," he announced, holding up a pair of slightly creased garments. One was a dark blue check, and the other was a hideous tropical print with palm trees and sunsets. Lee immediately grabbed the check shirt, leaving Dan to drop the other one unceremoniously on the floor.

"Cheers," Lee said gratefully, pulling the shirt over his black vest.

"It sucks you still haven't got your stuff," Dan said, looking around the blank room.

"Yeah," Lee mused, giving himself a quick spray of aftershave. "My dad's a busy guy, I guess."

Kelly and Sarah appeared in the doorway, their hair and makeup immaculately styled. Both were wearing breezy summer skirts and strappy tops, although Kelly had gone for a much shorter version of each than Sarah.

"Ready boys?" she purred.

Dan visibly gawped at the girls whilst Lee snatched his wallet and keys off the side. They hurried out of the flat and into the still warm evening.

The walk across campus was spent sneaking sips from Kelly's hip flask, though Lee was unable to identify exactly what was in it. Kelly called it 'party spirit'; Sarah said it was better left a mystery.

"The bouncers *never* search that high," Kelly said with a wink as she slipped the flask back into a garter beneath her skirt.

Once they were past the doorman and the ID checks and searches, they hovered in front of the doors that led to the club side. Lee could feel the bass pumping through the floor.

"Ready?" Dan asked with a grin. He pushed the doors open and the volume instantly doubled. They stepped out onto a raised balcony, looking out across the pulsing lights. Steps led down into the throng below, and the bass seeped into Lee's core like it was trying to replace his heartbeat. For tonight, his body would run on a different system. Sarah led the way down the steps, clutching the rail as she tottered on giant heels.

The Union was alive as they descended into the seething mass of bodies, pulsing with neon passion. To one side, the dancefloor flashed and hummed, slowly melting into the slightly calmer and more chilled section with the comfy chairs. Running through the centre was the bar – the backbone around which everything hung. The Fireflies flitted behind the counter, never really making a dent in the crowds that jostled there.

"Oh look," Sarah yelled to Kelly, pointing vaguely across the dancefloor. "There's Marie!"

"Aww," Kelly cooed. "Poor lamb."

Without another word, the girls bustled into the dancefloor, elbowing their way through the swaying silhouettes to get to their friend. Lee hovered awkwardly on the periphery before Dan pressed his mouth against Lee's ear. His breath was warm and beery.

"Drink?"

Lee nodded. "Drink."

They skirted around the edges of the dancefloor, Dan using his height to pick out the easiest route, Lee clinging to the back of the footballer's shirt like a small child.

Once they got to the bar, Dan snagged a Firefly and ordered two pints, before turning and leaning back against the glossy counter and surveying the scene.

"Ah, there's the Captain," he said loudly over the music as he nodded over to one of the booths. A typical football pretty-boy was sitting there, his arm around the shoulder of another guy that looked to be the exact opposite. Small and slight, this guy looked like he'd recently had the crap kicked out of him. There was bruising around his eye, his nose looked broken, and Lee thought he could even see bandages round his wrist. An odd couple, he thought to himself.

"I should probably just check in quickly," Dan continued with an apologetic shrug. He slid around the back of the waiting customers, and Lee soon saw him fist bumping and back slapping with his Captain. Lee turned back to the bar just as the Firefly set the drinks down. Before Lee could even fish out his wallet, the barman was already leaning towards the next in line.

"Hey," Lee called. "How much?"

The Firefly turned to him with a look that suggested Lee was challenged in some way.

"Dan Madden's drinks go on the team tab," he said with barely concealed contempt before taking the next order. Lee was already forgotten.

Win, Lee thought, wrapping his hand around the cool glass.

"Looks like your friends have ditched you."

Lee turned, eyebrow raised as he watched a stupidly beautiful girl sidle up next him. She was blonde, hair pulled back into a ponytail, with just enough tan to look gorgeous rather than tacky. She wore a slinky black one-piece, much classier than most of the halter tops and mini-skirt combos that Lee could see twisting across the dancefloor. With a confident smile, she took Dan's pint and sipped it elegantly.

"I'm Rebecca."

"Lee."

"You look…"

Lee smiled, his chat up protocols flowing into his brain. "I know, I know. You're trying to work out if I'm fit or not, right? Most girls just go for 'quirky'." He flashed his most lopsided grin.

"Actually, I was going to say unfamiliar. You must be new."

"Oh," Lee said, flushing with embarrassment. "Yeah I'm new. Transferred at the start of the week."

"I see," Rebecca smiled mischievously. "Well come on then quirky, let's go find somewhere quiet. We can get to know each other."

Lee grinned with relief as he took her hand. His charms hardly ever failed him before, and he was glad the girls of UCE responded to them too.

She led him through the labyrinth of dancers until they came to the row of booths along the side wall. All were filled with groups of students playing drinking games, or couples wrapped in each other's arms. Lee's face fell.

"Don't worry," Rebecca said, catching his disappointment. "I know somewhere else. We'll just duck outside for a bit."

Lee paused for a moment, feeling a pang of guilt. This was meant to be his first big night out with his new friends, but here he was, on the verge of ditching them. He scanned across the room, seeing Dan and some of the other footballers on the stage with their tops off. A ring of revellers were cheering and pumping their hands in the air. As Lee watched, they sprayed their chests with Lynx and held lighters up, a series of flames blooming towards the ceiling with a loud whumpf. A celebratory yell erupted from the stage, mixed with a round of applause from the onlookers. Dan and his teammates swaggered off the stage in triumph, to where a tray full of shots was waiting. Their image reboot was obviously not complete yet, and it was clear that Dan would be just fine without Lee. His guilt faded as he turned back to Rebecca.

"Well?"

"Yeah, sorry," Lee muttered, transfixed by her eyes. They were blue, so pale that they caught every coloured flash and strobe from the dancefloor, making her look like her eyes were constantly changing kaleidoscopes. "Let's go."

She took his hand once more, leading him around the edge of the room towards the fire exit, propped open to relieve both the heat of the evening and the cravings of the many smokers. Stepping through the clouds of smoke and vapour, they were soon trotting along an avenue lined with hedges. Academic buildings rose up on either side, their huge windows giving faint glimpses into the seminar rooms and lecture theatres beyond.

They came to a set of steel steps leading up the outside of a large rectangular building, and Rebecca hopped lightly onto the first step.

"Don't worry," she laughed playfully, noting Lee's apprehension. "This is the exam hall. I come up here to think sometimes. The view is pretty cool, and we won't be disturbed."

Lee smiled and followed her up, their tinny footsteps echoing off the red bricks. The steps zig-zagged all the way to the top of one of the corners where there was a raised block almost a whole storey above the vast flat roof – an expanse of grey lining broken only by a skylight looking down into the hall below. Around the edge, a wooden lining stood out against the greyness, although it was splintered and broken after years of exposure to the elements. Up there in their little square parapet, Lee felt like he was a god looking out across the world, artificial stars of office block and house lights merging in the blackness with their astral counterparts. Faint noises of the Union drifted up like ghosts.

"There," Rebecca said silkily as she sat herself on the ledge that ran around the tower. "This is much better. So you say you transferred – where from?"

"Northern," Lee said, tearing himself away from the view.

"By choice or... other?"

"Isn't it always a choice?" Lee replied, avoiding the question.

"People rarely *choose* to get expelled." Rebecca was watching him intently, trying to work him out by his reactions.

"No," Lee countered, enjoying the badinage. "But they obviously choose to commit the misdemeanours that *get* them expelled."

"So did you?"

"Ha, in a way," Lee said. He looked at the girl in front of him, watching her expression. He was fairly certain that there was nothing there beyond natural curiosity – after all, why wouldn't you want to find out about the new kid? "You really want to know the story?"

"Sorry, I didn't mean to press," Rebecca said innocently. "I was just being nosy."

"No it's fine," Lee shrugged. "You can hear all about my tragic fall from grace at Northern."

"Can't wait," Rebecca said with grin.

"There's not much to tell really," he began. "I had this mate, Charlie, and well, let's just say he wasn't that into rules. Nothing major, just a bit of drugs here and there, but he had a nice long list of marks against his name. Anyway, there was a halls inspection and quite a lot of drugs were found. I figured if Charlie took the hit for it they'd kick him out, but I had a clean record so I said they were mine."

Whilst Lee had been talking, Rebecca's expression had remained neutral, however now she frowned. "But if you had a clean record, why did they expel you?"

"Well technically they didn't," Lee said wistfully. "My dad found out about it, so he took the liberty of pulling me out and transferring me here. He didn't want everyone to know that I was associated with drugs. He's kind of big on reputation and stuff. UCE is a fresh start I guess."

"Except you just told me all about it," Rebecca said thoughtfully. "What if I told everyone else?"

"Would you do that to the new kid?"

"I've got a better idea of what I'd like to do to the new kid," she said with a smirk that made Lee's eyes light up. "Why don't we go back to my place, and I'll show you?" She stood up and held out her hand.

Lee was split. His head was telling him that he should return to his friends, even if they had seemingly abandoned him first, whereas obviously, his trousers were telling him to go with Rebecca. His trousers won out, and he took Rebecca's hand.

Soon enough, they were at Rebecca's student house — a tall and narrow terrace somewhere across town. Her room was all candles, fairy lights and coloured silks, although Lee did catch a glimpse of a few cheerleading trophies lined up on a shelf before they tumbled onto the bed, locked at the lips. Her hand was already jammed down the front of his jeans.

"Wait," Lee mumbled, pulling himself away for a second. "I don't have any... you know."

"Top drawer," Rebecca breathed before lunging for his mouth once more. Lee reached into the drawer behind him whilst Rebecca freed him first from his trousers, and then his shorts.

Chapter 5 – Stereotypical

Lee awoke on his back, the aches in various muscles a testament to how good the night had been. He glanced to his side to see Rebecca sleeping with the sheets wrapped round her. She looked serene, resting lightly on the pillow, her hair splayed out around her, lips slightly parted. It was a pity he was going to leave her.

As stealthily as he could, he slipped out from under the covers, casting his eyes around for where his pants had ended up. Typically, they had been flung to the other side of the room. Gingerly stepping across the floorboards, Lee snatched his shorts up and pulled them on before looking for more of his clothes. He'd managed to track down his vest and one of his socks when Rebecca stirred from her slumber.

"You sneaking out on me, Radley?"

Lee turned back to her guiltily. She'd propped herself on one elbow, a disappointed pout on her face. Back at Northern, Lee had perfected his escape plan, but he appeared to have let his standards slip a little.

"I… uh…" That was when he paused, replaying her initial comment in his mind. "Hang on," he said in a measured voice. "How did you know my surname?" Lee was certain that he hadn't mentioned it over the evening – in fact, he usually avoided mentioning it at all, so people wouldn't associate him with Radley Incorporated, his father's company.

Now it was Rebecca's turn to shuffle awkwardly as she realised her mistake. "I… uh…" she echoed.

"What is this?" Lee challenged. "Did you know who I was before you met me?"

Rebecca paused, studying him whilst she worked out what to say.

"You know what?" Lee snapped. "Forget it." He scooped up his jeans and his shoes and made for the door.

"*You* texted *us,*" Rebecca stated as she pulled a top over her head. "You started this."

Lee whirled on her, dropping his clothes to the floor again. "I started *what?* And I didn't text you. I've never even met you!"

"You mean you don't think you could be one of us?" Rebecca said slyly, an eyebrow raised.

Lee froze, mouth open as he realised what she'd quoted. "You're a Stereotype," he whispered. "How did you...?"

"There's a camera in the toilets," Rebecca began. "Your face doesn't match anyone on the student database, and there were no visitors signed in that day. The only logical explanation was a new kid that hadn't been added to the files yet. A quick search and we found you: Lee Joseph Radley, 20 years old, studying Business at Northern until last Friday." Rebecca smiled, proud to show off the power of the Stereotypes.

"You can do all that?" Lee asked in wonder.

"That's nothing," Rebecca snorted. "We can do pretty much anything. People usually come to us with a specific request, however lately we've been on a bit of a recruitment drive. Your response was... interesting."

"You were sent to scope me out?"

"We were curious," Rebecca shrugged. "What kind of person would message a random number they saw written on a wall?"

"So what happens now?"

"Now," Rebecca said casually, looking at the clock on her bedside table. "Now, I have to get ready and go to class."

"But what about me?" Lee demanded petulantly.

"You need to make a choice," Rebecca replied, finally leaving the bed and moving to the wardrobe. "I wasn't kidding when I said we could do almost anything – grades, protection, sex, drugs, you name it. When you work out if you want to be part of it, we'll be waiting." She picked a pair of leggings out of the wardrobe and began to pull them on, whilst Lee finally donned his own trousers.

"Why are people so afraid of you?" Lee asked, thinking back to everyone else's reaction when he mentioned The Stereotypes.

"None of it's free," she shrugged. "Sometimes we have to collect payment."

Once she was ready, Rebecca led Lee downstairs and out the front door. "Don't take too long, ok?" she said, patting him on the arm. Then, with a playful wave, she hopped off the pavement and jogged up the street, leaving Lee with his mind whirling.

His thoughts were no less clear when he made it back to O'Connell Hall about twenty minutes later. When he pushed the door open, a loud cheer roared out from the living room, and he gingerly stuck his head round. All of his flatmates were there, wolf whistling and clapping at his return, and they took great pleasure in pointing to another chalk board entitled 'The Pull Chart', to which they had added his name, along with a single tally mark. Lee noticed that Kelly was ahead by miles. He gave them all a cheeky salute before heading along the corridor to his bedroom, desperate for a shower and some time to think.

A hand grabbed his wrist and he turned round, jumping slightly. Sarah was beaming at him mischievously.

"Well, who was the lucky girl? Or guy?" she asked.

"Ha," Lee laughed. "Her name was Rebecca."

"Ooh, Rebecca? I wonder if I know her?"

"Um," Lee shrugged. "Blonde, ponytail, maybe a cheerleader?"

"Rebecca Carter? She's the *head* cheerleader. Tell me you didn't…"

Lee flashed her a grin in response.

"Oh Lee, this is bad."

"It was pretty good if you ask me."

"No," Sarah sighed with exasperation. "Who do head cheerleaders usually go out with?"

Lee thought for a moment. "Ah shit."

Interlude – The Meeting Room

Rebecca Carter walked through the dark corridor, fiddling with her phone as she went. The glow from the screen bathed the plain and slightly damp walls in eerie neon. It made the sheens of moisture look as if they were some sort of radioactive slime. No matter how many times she checked the screen, there was still only the same two messages displayed - the first from Lee where he had decided that he wanted to join The Stereotypes, and the second one summoning her to this meeting.

She wasn't nervous - it wasn't as if she hadn't been called to these meetings before, having to drop whatever she'd been doing and excuse herself to their secret lair. This time she'd been in the middle of a particularly thorough makeover, and whilst she hadn't finished the all-over tan she'd been hoping for, she was thankful the message hadn't come when she'd only had one eyebrow done.

She felt a slight flutter in her chest, because she was certain that the meeting was about the potential new recruits they'd all been collecting. Last meeting, they'd sent the Leader a list of names, and this was going to be when everyone found out the reply – she couldn't wait to see the looks on the others' faces.

Rebecca reached the door at the end of the corridor and pushed it open quietly. She was the second to arrive, Rick O'Reilly already lounging in one of the chairs that surrounded the conference table. The Techie looked bleary eyed and half asleep as he leaned forward over the glossy tabletop.

"Ready for judgement?" Rebecca smirked.

Rick looked at her, his face falling. "What do you mean?"

"Well," Rebecca began as she sat opposite him. "If you submitted a duffer, then you'll have to deal with the consequences." She rested her head back confidently. Somehow she knew that Lee would be extremely valuable to The Stereotypes in the long run — she had nothing to worry about.

"What consequences?" Rick asked, trying to reassure himself. "It will either be a yes or a no — it's not like I'll have to sacrifice blood or anything... right?"

"Who knows?" Rebecca shrugged. She was playing him now, winding him up before the rest arrived. "Are you starting to wish you put more effort in? What exactly have you been doing anyway — staying up all night playing Minecraft again?"

"Actually," Rick said, rising to the banter with mock indignance. "Me and Drew were trying to work out how to type this..." He paused and made a gross wet sound with his mouth, like moistening his lips in an over exaggerated way.

"What?" Rebecca asked incredulously.

"That noise," he continued, making the sickening sound another couple of times. "If you were to write that down, how would you do it? We were thinking like a 'tmp' sound."

"Why are you even thinking about shit like that?"

"Ah," Rick chuckled. "We're trying to think of a new insult when we're typing to noobs on the message console. You know, stuff like 'I totally tmped you' or whatever."

"Marvellous," Rebecca sighed.

"Come on, where is everyone?" Rick moaned, jumping out of his seat and beginning to wander around the room restlessly. "Hey have you seen this photo?"

Rebecca looked over to where Rick was standing by one of the noticeboards. He was holding an old photograph, the colours faded. It was a group of men, all dressed in smart blazers and ties.

"It's the original Stereotypes," Rebecca explained. "I found it in the store room. I thought I'd put it in here so we could try and be more like them. You know, sophisticated and stuff."

"Ha, this dude even looks like you. Same jaw."

Rebecca was about to chastise Rick for being so immature when the door opened again. They both swivelled to see the rest of The Stereotypes filter into the meeting room. The grin immediately vanished from Rick's face, nerves taking hold once more, and Rebecca shifted in her seat, straightening her dress.

One by one, The Stereotypes took their seats and waited for the familiar clicking of the printer. True to form, it was less than a minute after the last person sat down before the machine began spooling paper. It was a short communication.

Message received re: New Recruits
All may join if they can prove their worth.
Further instructions to follow

So Rick had been wrong – instead of a yes or a no, it was the dreaded maybe. It seemed they were going to hang in the balance for a little bit longer. Rebecca looked to the head of the table, eyes meeting with the intense ones that were watching her there.

"Bring them in…"

Chapter 6 – Inner Sanctum

Lee was sitting at his desk trying to start the first paragraph of his Business presentation when he got Rebecca's message. It was the first he'd heard from her since the other morning, and he felt a jolt in his chest when he read it – a jolt that was half nerves and half excitement. Lee's mind was full of snatched images of their night together, but with the added buzzkill of Sarah's mention of a boyfriend. Had Lee really been the 'other guy'? Was he that bothered if he had?

Lee got up from the desk and stretched, glad to have a diversion from his work. 'The Perfect Business Model' would have to wait. He gave his pits a quick sniff, and after deciding that he wasn't too fusty, headed out into the corridor.

He stuck his head into the living room, where Kelly was lounging in her dressing gown, a glass bubbling with alka-seltzer gripped between her palms.

"Morning," she said as she looked up blearily.

"It's like 2 in the afternoon," Lee replied, rolling his eyes. In the short time he'd been at UCE, he'd seen Kelly go out almost every night, but only make two of her Psychology seminars. "So," he began. "Do you know where the Society Corridor is?"

"Why?" Kelly asked, narrowing her eyes. "Thinking of joining a club?"

"I might see what's on offer – looks good on a CV and that."

"Well have fun," she mumbled, returning to her hangover. "All the Soc stuff is in John Terrence."

Lee nodded his thanks before hurrying out of the door. It was a short walk to the quad from O'Connell, and Lee remembered that John Terrence was the block that had the glowing UCE letters on the side.

He jogged across the grass, weaving in and out of the groups of students lounging with cans of beer, folders and notebooks half-heartedly spread out around them. The doors to the John Terrence block were open, the June warmth seeping into the foyer, the sunlight embossing the tiles with gold.

There were two main corridors leading off from the foyer, as well as a large spiralling staircase that rose up from one corner. After a quick peep through the right hand doors, Lee could just about make out classroom numbers, so he tried left.

The left hand corridor was much more promising. A single flight of stairs led down to a basement level. It was narrow and carpeted, lined with doors that had name labels rather than class codes. There was no sign of Rebecca.

As Lee moved down the Society Corridor, he read the different signs: Frag Soc, Ultimate Frisbee Soc, Cropper Soccer Soc and Harry Potter Soc (he smiled to himself as he read that one). He approached the end of the corridor, the last few doors becoming shabbier. The Archery Soc door looked busted, covered in tape and hastily attached bolts and padlocks, whereas the door at the end had a large cross scribbled over the sign. Lee could just make out the words Kill-Soc beneath the marker scrawl, and he remembered Dan's explanation about the memorial statue – no wonder Kill-Soc had been shut down.

The only other door was a thin metal one with a grill at the top, almost like a locker door. There was no name label. Lee was about to turn around when it struck him. If The Stereotypes were as mysterious as they were made out to be, then surely they *wouldn't* have a sign advertising their location.

Smiling, Lee threw open the door, reaching for a light switch. His grin faded as a tiny store cupboard was thrown into glaring light from a naked bulb. One wall held a rack of shelves, stacked high with packs of paper towels, plastic cutlery and trays. Opposite, a similar rack held bottles of disinfectant, window spray and a few cans of paint. The cupboard was so narrow that as Lee walked in, his shoulders grazed the shelves on either side. On the back wall was a small grimy sink, and a bucket with mop handles sticking out of it. The only other thing was a notice reminding cleaning staff to wash their hands after dealing with the various chemical cleaners, complete with crude hand graphic.

Dejected, Lee shuffled backwards out of the store cupboard – there wasn't enough room for him to turn round – and came face to face with Rebecca. She looked completely different from the last time he'd seen her, now in her Cheerleading outfit. Blue and gold lines criss-crossed over her tight white top, also forming a double hem of her short black pleated skirt. As she moved closer, she swung her hips, causing the skirt to ripple with each step.

"Having a cheeky one in the cupboard before I got here?" she asked, grinning mischievously.

"No!" Lee flustered, his cheeks reddening. "I thought you might be in there."

Rebecca raised an eyebrow. "Umm…"

"Not doing anything weird," Lee protested, holding his hands up.

"Relax, quirky," Rebecca said, shoving him playfully in the side. "Besides, you're half right." She took Lee's hand and led him back into the store cupboard.

"There's nothing inside," Lee said flatly. "I checked."

Rebecca tutted. "You looked, but you didn't *see*. Stereotypical student guy." She strode to the back of the cupboard and placed her hand over the outline on the cleaning notice.

"No way!" Lee gasped. "A handprint scanner??"

Rebecca turned to him with a sigh. "This isn't a spy movie, Lee – you just have to push it." She grunted as she did so, but the wall swung inwards, revealing another stretch of corridor ending in a staircase descending into the darkness.

"That's almost as cool," Lee breathed.

Rebecca turned, placing her hand firmly on his chest. "Whatever happens down there, you're sworn to secrecy – you know that, right?"

"I swear."

"Oh, and don't mention our hook up."

The cheerleader smiled as she forged on into the gloom.

"I thought The Stereotypes knew everything," Lee whispered.

"We don't spy on each other, stupid!"

They went down the stairs, turning back on themselves until they were in a shorter hallway that seemed to run directly underneath the Society Corridor. The passage ended abruptly in yet another plain door.

Rebecca turned to Lee once more. "Ready?" she asked.

He nodded in response, thinking it odd that she kept pausing. Was she trying to give him a chance to back out? Well no way. He stepped past her and pushed the door open.

The meeting room was long and wide, with a large conference table in the centre. On the back wall was a bank of screens, some desk equipment and a glowing red digital clock. Every sleek leather chair bar one was filled. A group of nervous looking students huddled in the far corner next to a noticeboard. Lee thought he saw a list of names but no matter how he craned his neck, he couldn't read it.

Next, Lee scanned the seven faces before him, but he couldn't say that he'd seen any of them before. The six guys and one girl were all watching him intently. To further cement the awkward 'Apprentice' style vibes, Rebecca slid past him and sank into the empty chair.

"Um hi," Lee began sheepishly. "I'm Lee Radley."

"We know who you are," said the guy at the head of the table.

Lee cursed himself – Rebecca had already said they'd found out who he was before even making contact.

"It's like this, Mr Radley." The guy was stocky and slightly brutish looking. He was unmistakably a musclehead, but the opposite of Dan. Lee's buddy's face was softened by his warm smile, whereas this guy was almost perfectly handsome, but seemed to have all the charisma and appeal of a brick. "Our leader says you can join us if you prove your worth."

"Which one of you is the leader?" Lee asked, looking around again to see if he could distinguish anything that set one of them apart. There was nothing.

"Our leader is elsewhere. We receive communications from him as necessary. I usually coordinate things in his absence."

Lee nodded, mentally filing away the information. "So how do I prove my worth?"

The jock smiled. "If you'll wait with our other recruits, you'll find out in due time." He nodded his head to the group in the corner. "Rick will take you next door."

At this, one of the guys from the table stood up. He was kind of short, with brown hair that was hanging over his ears. He was wearing a t shirt covered in green binary code like something from The Matrix.

Under the fierce scrutiny of The Stereotypes, Lee made his way across the meeting room to join the other recruits. Rick led them to a side door which opened into a slightly more comfortable looking den type room. Complete with a naked light bulb hanging down over a couple of threadbare armchairs, the area looked like a typical student hangout rather than the headquarters of a secret club.

"We won't be long," Rick said solemnly, before leaving the recruits on their own. Lee was surprised to hear the click of the door being locked, and he wondered if The Stereotypes were always this serious, or if they were putting it on to scare the newbies.

Lee looked around the room at the others. What were they? His companions? His competition? There were five boys and two girls, and none of them had moved since Rick brought them in. They stood in a cluster in the centre of the room as if the furniture might jump to life at any moment and devour them.

Shaking his head slightly, Lee slumped theatrically into one of the armchairs, a small cloud of dust billowing from beneath the cushion. As soon as he was seated, the others seemed to relax. They took the other seats, perched on the arms or leaned against the walls until they were in a rough circle.

"I guess this is ok," one of the guys said tentatively.

"You actually think we'll get marked down for sitting on the furniture?" This was one of the girls - a redhead with a band t-shirt on and spiked wristbands. She spoke with such disdain that Lee found himself drawn to her and her 'no bullshit' attitude.

"How do you think we prove our worth?"

"I heard you had to kill someone."

A ripple of laughter swept through the circle. As this suggestion was shot down, Lee sat back and listened, taking everything in. It was clear that some of the recruits knew more about The Stereotypes than others. It was also blatantly obvious that the guy who had spoken first, who'd since introduced himself as Brendan, knew practically nothing. None of the others had given their names – obviously going for the top secret element.

Just when the group seemed to be getting comfortable, Rick reappeared, and everyone immediately stiffened up again. Without a word, Rick held the door open with his arm, and the recruits shuffled back into the meeting room. The jock was standing at the head of the table, so they filtered round until they were all hovering awkwardly before him.

"Right," he announced. "Time to find out how to prove your worth. And don't worry, you don't have to kill anybody." He looked pointedly at the boy who'd suggested that, who lowered his eyes awkwardly.

Lee couldn't help grinning at the fact that The Stereotypes had been listening in on their inane chat.

"There are eight of you, and eight of us," the jock continued. "So you'll each get one of us as your guide. We each work in different areas, so you'll have an opportunity to help us out. From that, we'll decide whether you make the cut or not. Any questions?"

Lee wasn't surprised to see that nobody ventured a query. Perhaps they were all feeling awkward about having been overheard. Some of them had said some pretty stupid things after all.

"Right then. Amy Gibson, you'll be working with Rick."

Rick caught the eye of the punky redhead and nodded. The jock continued to pair up the recruits, and Lee was matched with Sam, a skinny boy in black with a beanie. When he'd finished, he dismissed the potential candidates with the promise that their mentors would be in touch soon.

"Actually," he said after a brief pause. "Radley and McCarrick, you can stay here."

Lee exchanged a quizzical glance with the short blonde kid who'd been paired with the jock - Niall McCarrick. The other recruits left the room, leaving Lee and Niall standing apprehensively before the conference table. All The Stereotypes were watching them with blank expressions, although Lee noticed Rebecca deliberately trying to avoid his gaze.

"As it happens," the jock stated. "We have business tonight. A party that requires our services in town. Sam, it will be your team and mine."

Lee's mentor nodded. "I'll make the necessary arrangements."

"You can come along," the jock said, turning back to Lee and Niall. "I'm sure there'll be an opportunity for you to show us what you've got. Meet us at the main gates at 9."

Lee hovered awkwardly, waiting to see if anything else was coming. He tried to catch Rebecca's eye once more, but now she was staring intently at the table.

"We're done here," the lunkhead said, a half smile playing across his lips.

"Oh," Lee said softly, his cheeks reddening with embarrassment. He and Niall turned and left the meeting room, hearing the dull murmur of voices pick up as soon as the door closed.

As they stalked back up the corridor and into the store cupboard, Lee reviewed the brief encounter. The Stereotypes had played it very close to the chest. Apart from Rebecca, he had only learned two other names – Sam and Rick. Everybody else had managed to snag their recruits using pronouns only. The head guy hadn't even explained what services The Stereotypes were providing for the party: they'd given Lee and Niall as little information as possible, so that they couldn't give anything away. Except they now knew where their secret lair was – something that was surely more powerful than names.

Smirking to himself he turned back to the wall, which had swung shut after they'd passed through. He placed his palm over the hand print graphic and pushed. The secret door didn't move. He braced his other hand on the wall and pushed with all his might. Still nothing. Rebecca had obviously lied about how easy it was to gain entry. *Well played.* All they'd really given him was a ticket to the mental asylum if he tried to tell anyone there was a secret room behind the store cupboard wall.

"Hmm," he mused.

"I guess I'll see you tonight then," Niall said quietly.

Chapter 7 – Worthless

Lee had been ready for hours, even with the agonising 'what to wear' crisis he imagined most girls went through every morning. He had no idea what he was supposed to be going *as* – should he be a party goer in Dan's emergency shirt, or was the operation darker than that, calling for an all black 'up to no good' outfit?

In the end, he had settled for the middle ground, wearing a half respectable pair of jeans and a simple long sleeved black jumper.

"Ooh, where are you going? Did you join the Dockers' Club?"

Lee looked up to see Kelly hovering in the doorway. She looked remarkably bright eyed, considering the state she was in earlier. "Ha no," he laughed. "Just some party in town. And anyway, wouldn't it be called the Dock-Soc?"

Kelly frowned, holding her fingers up to her forehead as if attempting some sort of psychic connection. "Hmm, I'm not aware of any party tonight."

"Come on," Lee scoffed. "You can't know about every single party in the whole city."

"Well I've managed to tune out the kids' birthday parties, but it took time," she grinned. "Have fun then, and remember not to talk to any strangers."

"I will...or I won't... you know what I mean."

Kelly laughed again, giving a little wave as she headed back to her own room.

With a breath of trepidation, Lee gave himself one final glance in the mirror then left the flat, bracing his shoulders in the cooling air.

Before long, he was approaching the gates by the quad, their shadows elongated into a spider's web crawling across the tarmac. Sam and Niall were already there, and as

Lee approached, he also saw the jock standing a couple of metres away. To the casual observer, it would seem like they had nothing to do with each other. The jock was checking his watch every few seconds, despite now clearly being able to see Lee hurrying towards them. Lee wondered why Niall was standing with Sam and not his own mentor.

"Alright dude," Sam said with a smile when Lee arrived. He was dressed in black skinny jeans and a band t-shirt, his thin pale arms hanging by his sides. A beanie was jammed over his head, but Lee could see a few tufts of blonde sticking out the bottom.

Niall also gave a nod of greeting. He had come in full on party mode with a fitted shirt and new looking white trainers.

Without a word, the jock started walking, hands jammed into his varsity jacket. Niall eagerly started to follow, but Sam held an arm out, a knowing look on his face. When the jock was about twenty paces ahead, Sam nodded and started to move.

"What are we doing?" Lee asked, shaking his head.

"Jud's the Jock," Sam reasoned, saying it with an unmistakable capital letter. "He's too good to walk with us. Especially as I'm a lowly second year."

"Even me?" Niall protested, his eyebrows tilting towards kicked puppy. "But I'm his recruit. I'm like his padawan."

Sam laughed to himself. "Jud's no Obi Wan. To him, there's only people who matter, and people who don't."

"I thought the Coach was making them you know, not be douchey," Lee said, dredging up the fact he'd got from Dan.

"Ah," Sam said with a smile. "Coach Williams is in charge of the Centaurs. Jud however, isn't a Centaur. He's a

Chimera – a triathlete," he added when he caught Lee's raised eyebrow.

"What about you?"

"I'm the Skater. I'll walk with anybody."

The three of them walked for a few paces in silence – Lee lost in thought, and Niall looking forlornly after Jud, whereas Sam seemed to be nodding his head to a rhythm only he could hear. Occasionally, he would glance upwards to make sure they were still on the right route.

After a minute or two, they rounded a corner into an alleyway to see Jud standing with a group of guys. They were all similarly tall and built, and from the shoulder punching and general homoeroticism, Lee assumed they were yet more jocks.

"Go on then Anakin," Sam said, gently nudging Niall forward. He jogged forwards and mingled into the crowd of muscle, which was suddenly acceptable now that Jud wasn't on his own.

Sam and Lee hovered at a respectful distance as the athletes finished their greetings and began to continue along the alleyway as a group.

"He's sure enthusiastic isn't he?" Sam chuckled, watching Niall repeatedly get denied a high five or a fist bump.

"So how does this work now?" Lee muttered, keeping his voice down below the echoing footsteps of the marching jocks.

"Right," Sam began with a deep breath. He switched to a business-like tone. "We all represent a social clique at UCE: like Jud is the Jock, I'm the Skater, Rebecca is the Cheerleader, and so on and so forth."

Lee nodded as he listened, again filing the information away.

"We're each responsible for a certain thing, or providing a certain service, and we each have a team to help it run smoothly."

"So Jud's the Alpha Jock and these other guys are like his minions?"

"Yeah I guess," Sam said with a wry smile. "But I wouldn't say that to their faces."

"What makes the alphas better than the rest?" Lee wondered aloud.

"Most of us have connections," Sam shrugged. "Like my dad owns the Darkstar skate brand. Jud's father won gold in the javelin at the Olympics. It was pretty solid of Rebecca to snag the heir of Radley Incorporated."

"Yeah. So what's your team for?" Lee asked, changing the subject before he was forced to talk about the legendary Sir Michael Radley.

"Ah," Sam nodded his head. "You're about to find out."

Lee looked ahead to where the Jocks had paused in the street, silhouettes in the street lamp spotlight. Niall was lost in the crowd somewhere, although Lee thought he could make out a slightly shorter shadow tiptoeing and weaving to try and see past the others. They had stopped next to a beaten up baby blue Volkswagen camper. Whereas before, Sam had held back and deferred the lead to Jud, here he strode forward with confidence, banging a fist on the back window of the van.

The door swung open, releasing a cloud of smoke and the tinny beat of some punk metal album screeching out of an iPod dock. A squad of black clad, beanie wearing, pierced and tattooed youths lined the sides of the van's interior, and the floor was piled with crates of beer, bottles of spirit and boxes of snacks. As Lee watched, Sam went round his team of skaters, handing each of them a couple of small baggies –

one containing the unmistakable green/brown of weed, the other bulging with some sort of pills. Lee turned to see that Jud's jocks had spread out around the van, with some of them branching to each end of the street to keep watch.

It struck Lee that The Stereotypes knew exactly what they were doing, and that this was obviously not their first party situation. Sam and his team would provide the booze and the highs, whilst Jud's men would act as bodyguards. Lee couldn't help wondering how much you had to pay to benefit from this service.

When all the skaters had been supplied, they began to clamber out of the VW, pouring out of the vehicle as if it were a clown car. They each picked up a box from inside and stood in a group, the jocks surrounding them in a loose circle, shielding them like Roman Legionaries. Once the last skater was out, Sam closed the door and thumped the window once more. The engine roared to life and the van disappeared down the street.

"Why not just take the van to the party?" Lee whispered.

Sam leaned in. "Party people would see it. The last thing I want is for my crew's wheels to be called The Stereotypemobile or something. This way, we could have come from anywhere."

As one, the skaters and their escort of sportsmen trooped along the pavement, with Lee bouncing around in the middle like a loose ball bearing in an otherwise well-oiled machine. Niall seemed to have settled down now that all he had to do was walk. The group turned one more corner and then halted in front of a tall narrow house.

"This is it," Jud grunted.

Sam surveyed the dark windows and the noticeable lack of music. "It doesn't look like a party. Are you sure?"

"Of course I'm fucking sure," Jud growled. "Who's the boss round here, huh?" He glared, and Sam lowered his head. "We'll go inside and see what's going on," Jud stated. He pointed at two of his jocks. "You two stay here and guard the skaters. Radley, you're coming inside. It'll be good practice."

Lee looked awkwardly at Niall, feeling like he had usurped him somehow. The two of them turned to Sam, hoping he would speak out. Instead, the Skater pulled a cigarette out of his pocket and shrugged. You obviously didn't argue with Jud.

Jud placed his hand firmly on Lee's shoulder and steered him up the steps. Lee could feel Jud's muscles tensing in his forearm as it rested behind Lee's neck. For some reason, Lee couldn't stop cold beads of sweat forming on his forehead.

"Um, the door's open," Lee murmured as he saw the distinct strip of pitch black between the peeling wooden door and the frame.

"See," Jud growled. "We're definitely in the right place." He gave Lee a rough shove so that he fell forward through the doorway, landing on his knees. Dust billowed up from where Lee hit the floor boards.

"What the hell was that for?" he hissed angrily as he climbed to his feet, casting a wary glance around the room. There was no furniture, no wallpaper and no lightbulb attached to the dangling wire in the ceiling. The place was a derelict. "There's no party…"

"You catch on quick."

"But Sam…"

"He has to think it's real, just like all the others."

At this, Lee turned around, his stomach filling with lead. The jocks had spread into a rough semi-circle, all watching him intently. One of them reached up and bolted the door, whist another cracked his knuckles ominously. Jud took off his jacket, folding it and laying it reverentially on the windowsill.

"Did you really think you could be a Stereotype?"

Lee was about to state that he had been invited, and the leader had approved the list of recruits, but Jud was already advancing.

"Did you really think you could sleep with my girlfriend?" he said quietly.

"I-"

Crack! Jud's fist hit him like a brick to the face. Lee stumbled back, the shock flooding his brain. Despite his brash attitude, he'd actually never been punched before – he considered himself too charming to get beaten up. He was about to be proved wrong. Crack! Jud's left swing was just as powerful as his right. Lee was knocked to the ground, and that's when the others pounced, leaping forward like a pack of hyenas. Lee shielded his face as feet pummelled his gut, his crotch and his legs. Anything left exposed was kicked or stamped on.

Suddenly, there was a pounding at the door. The jocks stepped back from where Lee cowered, covered in a layer of dust mixed with blood from his split lips.

"What's going on in there?" Sam called through the door. "Jud?"

Jud looked down at Lee and smiled. "The party's cancelled," he barked over his shoulder. "Disband!"

"But what about-"

"Take your Skaters home, Sam!" Jud snapped angrily.

There was the unmistakable sound of Sam and his team shuffling off the front steps, the noise rapidly fading to silence.

"You see," Jud smirked. "I call the shots around here. Consider your application terminated."

"But the leader said…" Lee sobbed.

Jud aimed another kick to the boy's ribs. "I don't give a shit what some printer tells me. If he asks, I'll just say you couldn't prove your worth, and that'll be the end of it. Laters, Radley."

As the jocks left the empty house, the adrenaline and shock of the fight began to ebb from Lee's system, leaving him with nothing but the rapidly increasing sting of his various wounds.

After he was certain that they'd left the street, Lee pulled himself to his feet and shuffled towards the door of the abandoned house. As he pushed it open slowly, the cool night air sent electric tingles through his open cuts.

To Lee's surprise, Niall was sitting on the wall that surrounded the overgrown patch of grass that served as the house's front garden. He had his arms folded across his chest and he looked up glumly when he heard Lee's dragging footsteps on the concrete.

As Lee approached, he could see a streak of what looked like spit running down Niall's shirt. Despite his beating, Lee felt a pang of sympathy for the other boy.

"They left me behind when I said we should wait for you," Niall said apologetically. "I didn't know what was happening until they came back out. Sam and the Skaters had already gone. Are you ok?"

Lee shrugged as he sat stiffly next to Niall. "I think I failed recruitment," he said with a wry laugh.

"Me too," Niall said quietly. "Turns out disagreeing with Jud is a big no – hence the spit. Come on, I'll walk with you."

Lee nodded and prised himself off the wall, the two failed recruits walking dejectedly into the night.

Chapter 8 – Reparations

"I told you," Lee groaned as the nurse stuck the final butterfly stitch to his cheek. "I was mugged."

The greying woman looked at him sternly over the rim of her glasses. "Next time, I'd just hand it over." She glared pointedly at where the top of Lee's phone was peeking out of his pocket. "You're lucky your nose wasn't broken, that's a common one round here."

"Yeah, well I put up a good fight," Lee lied.

The nurse appraised him once more. "I've got three grandchildren," she tutted. "You think I can't tell when someone's hiding something?"

"Can I go now?" Lee snapped.

"I'm done," the woman sighed. "You need to come back in a couple of days to get those stitches looked at." She tore a slip off her pad and handed it to him. "In the meantime, no strenuous activity, no sports, no swimming, no operating heavy machinery. And cut out the booze if you can."

"No pissed tractor ball then," Lee muttered under his breath.

"Heard it all before," the nurse said before stepping aside so that Lee could leave the consultation room.

He hopped off the bench, scribbled a hasty signature on a form the nurse waved under his nose, and headed into the foyer. The room was quiet, with just a couple of people hunched over in the waiting room. Despite it being large and airy, with potted plants and background music that was just on the verge of becoming a lift jingle, the waiting patients seemed to be huddling under a storm cloud, arms wrapped around themselves and misery written all over their faces.

Niall had offered to wait, but Lee had sent him home, figuring he would probably want to put the night behind him as quickly as possible.

With a shudder, Lee stepped through the automatic doors and into the carpark – a vast expanse of grey tinged with halos of light: white from the hospital floods and yellow from the street lamps on the road. After a quick scan of the skyline to get his bearings, Lee stalked off in the direction of O'Connell hall.

As he walked, the cool air blowing onto his raw skin and the faint thump of weekend party music washing over him, Lee's aches and pains dulled. His rage however continued to fester. It wasn't the first time he'd ended up in hospital – back at Northern there'd been the time he'd fallen over drunk and punctured his elbow, and another time he'd snapped a tooth face planting the kerb – but those times it had been down to him. He'd drank too much and he'd lost control. This time however, he'd been put there by others, and he couldn't reconcile with that fact. Any scars he bore from the night's encounter wouldn't be his to brag about, they would stand on Jud's mantelpiece – trophies for the jock's strength and masculinity.

Soon, the lights of O'Connell rose before him, and all Lee wanted to do was climb into bed and picture all the grotesque punishments he could inflict on Jud. As he approached the door, reaching into his pocket for his key, a figure emerged from the darkness. Lee's face fell with distaste as he recognised who it was.

Rebecca Carter was dressed immaculately, as if she had just stepped out of a showbiz party. Her makeup was subtle, eyebrows arched slightly to make her seem like she was perpetually intrigued and astounded by whatever was before her.

When she saw Lee, she hurried forwards, concern flashing across her face. She grabbed his shoulders, taking in the stitches across his cheek.

"Oh my god, Lee!" she cried. "What happened? When Jud said the deal had gone bad, I was worried about you!"

Lee grimaced, squirming out of the girl's grip. "Gone bad?? That's rich. Just leave me alone."

"What do you mean?" she asked. "Jud said there was a rival dealer and you had to split before things got rough."

Lee looked at her incredulously. Did she really believe the shit that Jud had fed her? "The only rival was Jud and his gang," he spat. "They did this to me."

"Lee, I had no idea." She reached out to him once more, but he backed way. Lee noted her complete lack of surprise. She might have had no idea, but she definitely knew what Jud was capable of.

"This is your fault too," he said, his voice rising in frustration. "You led me on. You took me home. You had a boyfriend."

"But," she faltered. "The Stereotypes… the recruitment."

"And sleeping with me was a vital part of the process was it? What did you do, take notes?"

"It wasn't like that." Rebecca lowered her head, her voice dropping.

"Well how did Jud find out?"

"I don't know. Maybe we were seen leaving the Union."

"You know what? I should have expected it," Lee said angrily. "You're the Cheerleader. *Stereotypically,* this is what you do."

"That's not fair."

"Whatever," Lee muttered. "Screw your stupid Stereotypes."

"What about joining?"

"Didn't Jud tell you? I failed recruitment. Niall too, if you give a shit."

"But that's not right!" Rebecca said indignantly.

"Well unless you're going to personally ask the Leader to give us a second chance, I guess Jud's word goes."

Rebecca opened her mouth as if to respond, but seemed to think better of it.

"Thought not," Lee muttered acidly. He pushed past her, jamming his key forcefully into the door and pushing it open. He slammed it behind him before she could say anything more, and stomped up the stairs.

The flat was dark and quiet, but as soon as he closed the front door, a light flickered on. Sarah's head appeared out of her room, a slight scowl etched on her face.

"Finally," she grumbled. "Your one night stand's been ringing the buzzer for the last hour. Naturally, we ignored her, but seriously, you need to sort that out before-" She trailed off as Lee crept forwards into the glow from her doorway. "Ah," she murmured quietly as she took in his battered features. She made to step forward, but Lee held up his hand.

"It's ok, don't worry about it." He didn't feel like explaining everything yet again, even if Sarah would probably be the most sympathetic listener.

"Ooh, this will cheer you up," Sarah said, suddenly beaming. "You had a delivery this evening. Some guy in a suit..."

"You mean my stuff?"

Sarah nodded. "It's all in your room."

Lee smiled, giving Sarah a quick but painful hug before running down the corridor to his room. It was crammed with taped up boxes and suitcases, and despite everything, Lee couldn't help feeling his mood lift. Already he was looking around his scant bedroom and seeing it as it would be after he'd finished, mapping out which poster would go where, sorting his clothes into the various drawers and sections of the wardrobe, and seeing his computer and stereo all set up on his desk. If he moved the bed to the other wall, he would have the perfect angle to watch the screen. Lee tugged at the bands of tape surrounding the first box, glad to have something to distract him from The Stereotypes.

Interlude – The Meeting Room

Stereotypes
Congratulations on recruiting some new members. It
is time for phase two. You each need to use your areas
of expertise to earn as much money as possible. The
one who earns the least will be punished.
You will also find that attached are your new exam
schedules. You will see that you have all been enrolled
in a new class – 'Deconstructing Stereotypes'. All you
need to do is turn up to that exam. Information to
follow.

Jud finished reading the message to the others, slamming the
paper down onto the table.
"What the hell?"
In the past week, they had whittled down their eight
recruits to just three, and Jud had messaged the leader with
the names. He'd thought that would be the end of it, but
now out of nowhere there was a phase two! Jud couldn't
help wondering exactly how many phases there were, and
precisely what they'd done to deserve this sudden shake up
of their order.
A slender boy with quiffed hair leaned in to whisper
frantically to the girl next to him. She was wearing eyeliner, a
tie-die dress and a necklace of flowers. After a moment, the
boy stood up, placing his hands defiantly on the table top
and clearing his throat.
"Jud, this is totally unfair," he announced with a
theatrical wave of his hand.

"Just shut up. We're all in the same boat here, Joe," Jud muttered dismissively.

"Not so," Joe replied indignantly. "You guys provide a service – something people pay for." He pointed to himself and the flowery girl. "Me and Emma work *for* the group. How can we generate money from cover ups and representation? We're being set up to fail."

"What do you think the punishment is?" This was Stephen, the Academic. He had jam jar glasses, fiery ginger hair, and freckles splashed haphazardly across his cheeks. He and his team ran grade fixing and essay cheat scams – there was no way he'd lose the competition, but true to his stereotype, the mere mention of a punishment was enough to have him on edge.

"I don't know," Jud murmured, his mind whirling through all the ways he could profit with his muscle for hire.

"Because I'm on track for a First," Stephen continued, pushing his chest out. "And I don't want anything to ruin it."

"Why is this happening now anyway?" Joe shrieked, getting himself more and more worked up.

"Isn't it obvious?" Emma countered. "We recruit new members, and then we're suddenly hit with a competition to rank us? The Leader obviously wants to replace some of us."

"Well that's fan-bloody-tastic," Joe wailed. "We might as well just give up now. It's not fair Jud! What if I just quit now? What would our glorious Leader do then huh? Jud?"

"I don't know!" Jud yelled, slamming his fists down. The table jolted, scattering the pens and mugs that were on there. Everyone stopped bickering momentarily, staring at the Jock with the red cheeks and the heaving chest.

"We could just refuse," Rick said, folding his arms. "We don't play."

"I think that's a bad idea," Rebecca stated. "The Leader won't like it."

"Well are you going to tell him? Because I'm not," Rick replied, making the wet lip smacking sound to finish.

"Did you just tmp me?" Rebecca glared. "Because if you did, I swear to god-"

"The Techie's got a point," Jud cut in loudly. "We make a pact here and now. None of us raise any money. None of us try to win. We can't all be punished."

Silence.

"Come on, hands in. Swear it," Jud commanded fiercely. He held his large hand palm down over the table. One by one the others placed theirs in, until only one was left. "Stephen?" Jud growled with a hint of menace. Reluctantly Stephen added his hand to the stack. "There. It's settled. Nothing to worry about."

Chapter 9 – Punishment

Lee stepped back and surveyed his room. Once he'd got his computer set up and connected to the Intranet, he'd spent the rest of the week meticulously unpacking and sorting through his belongings. He'd also been to get his stitches taken out, and generally was feeling a lot less pathetic.

"A bit gay isn't it?"

He turned to see Kelly grinning at him from the corridor. She was looking at the massive *Topman* display poster that hung on the far wall. A handsomely chiselled model was pouting seductively whilst tugging at his vest as if about to rip it off.

"It's not adoration," Lee chided. "It's motivation. He keeps me going to the gym. Besides," he grinned. "Girls seem to like him."

"Well this girl prefers a real man – I like something I can grab hold of."

"Brilliant – so does your visit have a point or are you just here to lech?"

"Both, obviously. I really want to go and sit in the sun, but Sarah's in a seminar and all the others are boring. Do you fancy it?"

Lee paused for a moment.

"Please?" Kelly begged, batting her lashes and sticking her bottom lip out.

"Yeah alright, but I might have to bring my laptop."

"Yay!" she shrieked, clamping him in a quick hug. "We can road test this new skirt I've got – you can tell me if I look frumpy."

"Joy," Lee muttered sarcastically as she dragged him out.

Soon enough, they were strolling through the park after Kelly insisted on buying them ice creams. Her brightly coloured billowing gypsy skirt certainly didn't make her look frumpy, and so she was skipping happily along, filling Lee in on all the best party locations, and times she'd been so wasted she couldn't remember getting home. She made it sound like she'd definitely made the most of her time at UCE.

"Lee, hey!"

Lee tore himself out of Kelly's life story and looked up, shielding his eyes against the glaring sun. Niall was waving to him from where he was sitting on the grass. He certainly looked more cheerful than the last time they'd met.

"Who's this?" Kelly asked with a mischievous grin. "He's kind of cute. Bit short though."

"Niall. He's a Star Wars fan."

"Meh, I could look good with buns."

"You mind if I go and say hi?"

"Not at all."

Lee jogged over, Niall standing up to greet him. Whilst the two boys shook hands, Kelly sidled up behind Lee, a look of vague interest on her face.

"You remember Amy, James and Elliott, right?" Niall waved his arm over the people he was sitting with. Lee nodded, recognising them all from the Stereotypes recruitment.

"Let me guess," Lee said. "You guys didn't make it either?"

James and Elliott shook their heads, whilst Amy scowled.

"Rick axed me because I rewired his laptop," the punk girl said bitterly. "I improved its speed by like 20% but couldn't help going through his files – did you know he has a whole clone of the old Kill-Soc servers on there?"

"Hmm," Lee mused. "So what are you guys up to?"

"We're just hanging out," said Elliott. He had dark spiked hair and piercing grey eyes, which Lee thought made him look almost ethereal. "Bitching about those jerks in their stupid dungeon."

At this, Lee became painfully aware that Kelly was listening intently to everything that they said. He hadn't told anybody else about his encounter with The Stereotypes, and he was suddenly afraid that Kelly would judge him for wanting to be part of the clandestine group with the shady reputation.

"Well, catch you later I guess." Lee said, desperate to move on before Elliott gave anything else away. "Good to see you."

"You too," Niall said. "Oh, here – take my number in case you feel like joining our little group of rejects."

Lee typed Niall's number into his phone, then steered Kelly away. Thankfully, she didn't comment on anything she'd heard, only how pretty Amy was, and how highly she rated her over the likes of Rebecca Carter.

They curved round the lake, pointing out the shadows of the gigantic fish moving beneath the surface, until eventually they came to the top end of the park. There was a wide stretch of grass on one side, with a statue of a Greek style gladiator in the middle surrounded by flowerbeds. On the other side was the various ramps and rails that signified the skate park – the afternoon buzzing with the dull roaring of wheels on lacquered wood.

"Here'll do," Lee said, flopping down onto the grass and squinting at the skaters zipping over the ramps. He thought he could make out the stick figure of Sam the Stereotype standing atop the half-pipe.

"Oh," Kelly pouted. "I thought we could sit by the bandstand." She pointed over to the other side of the park. "There's some cute guys that do yoga there sometimes."

"Tough," Lee said with a grin as he pulled his laptop out of his messenger bag. "I like it here, and I think you'll find that when I'm settled, I'm very difficult to move."

"Unless you get kicked out and have to transfer," she countered playfully, smoothing her dress out as she sat beside him.

"Ha bloody ha." Lee's fingers began to dance across the keyboard, his eyes fixed on the screen.

"What are you working on?"

"Just sending a quick email," Lee replied without looking up.

"Boring!" Kelly began ripping up clumps of daisies, popping the heads off one by one and firing them into Lee's lap.

"I did warn you," he muttered. He scanned the email one last time and hit send. "Done now anyway."

They lay back, staring up at the clouds, shifting clumps of cotton wool rolling across a pastel blue background. The longer Lee stared, the more tranquil he felt.

"This is the life," Kelly sighed happily. "Forget lectures and qualifications and all that. This is what it's all about."

Lee began making a story out of the shapes he could see. There were four long blobs that could just about pass as humanoid, and the one at the front had a long tendril snaking out of it, leading to a large roundish looking blob. Where the tendril touched the sphere, smaller fingers of fluff branched out so it looked like the tendril was breaking the shell. It filled Lee's head with fantastic stories of angry Gods and far off worlds.

Suddenly, he felt an elbow sharply in his ribs. "Ow! What?" He sat up, glaring at Kelly and rubbing the spot where she'd jabbed him.

Kelly was sitting up, looking over at the skate park, her brow furrowed with curiosity. As Lee followed her gaze, he realised she was focusing on what was *beyond* the half pipe and the grind rails. A black SUV was speeding along one of the park tracks, plumes of sandy dust rising from the tyre treads. As they watched, it veered off the track and started ploughing across the grass.

"What the?" Kelly wondered in bewilderment.

By now, some of the skaters had noticed the car heading towards them. Starting with those closest and highest, but spreading like a ripple across a pond, they began to hop off their boards, flick them into hands or let them roll to a halt, and turn to face the behemoth chugging their way.

Kelly jumped to her feet as the car pulled up in the shadow of the half pipe. All four doors opened, spilling suited men onto the grass. All of them had sunglasses and walkie talkies, and Lee even thought he caught a glimpse of a pair of handcuffs shining in the sun. The men marched forwards through the massing crowd of alternatives, their leader pointing up at the group still huddled at the top of the half pipe.

"Wait!" Lee called, Kelly already out of his reach. "Bloody hell," he muttered as he followed her. She came to a halt by a row of bushes that bordered the skate park. The crowd was less than a hundred metres away, and from here, Lee and Kelly could hear the increasingly foul profanities issuing from the angry group.

Three of the men spread out, acting like a barrier to stop the skaters from following the fourth man as he climbed up to the launch platform. He muscled his way past the skaters until he came to Sam, the Stereotype's scarecrow arms folded defiantly across his chest.

It looked like the two of them were talking, but no matter how hard he strained, Lee couldn't pick out what they were saying. After a moment, Sam seemed to nod in resignation, holding out his hands in front of him. The suited man reached under his jacket for his cuffs, and that was when Sam struck. He thrust his palms into the man's chest, not even pausing to see the impact. He whirled on his heels and sprinted to the other side of the platform. Where would he go? Would he vault the railing and jump the six metres to the ground?

Suddenly, the man was behind the Skater – Sam wasn't going to make it to the rail. Out of nowhere, a baton extended into the man's hand and he slammed it between the boy's shoulder blades.

Kelly gasped as the thud resounded across the grass to their hiding place. Lee's face was set grimly as he watched.

Sam fell to the ground, and the large man was on his back in an instant, pulling his arms behind him. The rest of the skaters were helpless behind the suited barrier, and Lee noticed that the other men had also flicked batons out and were brandishing them menacingly.

"This is awful," Kelly said softly, tugging at Lee's sleeve. "I want to go now."

Lee nodded, taking her hand. Together, they hurried away from the skate park in silence.

Interlude – The Meeting Room

"Leave us," Jud commanded. The recruit Brendan jumped slightly before scuttling out of the room. Jud scrunched the newspaper he was holding tightly in his fist. "Explain to me once more how the fuck this happened?" His eyebrows were creased into a permanent V of anger.

Joe Nichols scanned the headline once more. 'UCE Student Leads Drugs Ring'. There was a picture of their fellow Stereotype Sam Street being forced into a police car, along with most of the front page columns filled with information.

Joe gulped, wishing that it wasn't just him and Jud in the meeting room. There was nobody to rely on to back him up, not that Brendan could have done much. From what Joe had seen, the boy was bright, but soft as shit. "I don't know," he muttered flatly.

"You're in charge of cover-ups!" Jud roared, banging his fists ape-like onto the surface. "Your specific fucking job is to make sure that shit like this stays buried!"

Joe stepped back until he was pressed against the wall, as far away from Jud's fury as possible. "This didn't come from the The Rag," he said defensively. "I can see everything they're about to print before they print it. They didn't write this."

Too enraged for words, Jud jabbed his finger onto the page, where the name 'UCE Rag' was clearly visible.

"Yes I can see that," Joe stammered. "But I'm telling you, The Rag office didn't print this."

"So what does that mean?" Jud growled.

"Well," Joe began thoughtfully. "Either they printed this at a different office, which doesn't make any sense because... just why would they?"

"Or?"

"Or someone's out-hacked us. It could be someone at The Rag who got around our spyware, or it could be someone completely different *pretending* to be The Rag."

"Could they do that?"

Joe thought for a moment. "Those idiots at the newspaper? Doubtful. But someone else... I'd have to check with Rick."

When it was clear that Jud wasn't going to reply, Joe nervously ducked out of the meeting room and vanished into the darkness.

Alone, Jud stared at the treacherous newspaper, the implications grinding around in his mind. On an obvious note, with Sam in custody, The Stereotypes would lose a huge chunk of revenue, but that wasn't Jud's only concern. If someone else really had printed this under the guise of The Rag, then that meant someone was deliberately targeting them.

He glanced over at the printer that usually delivered the instructions from their enigmatic leader, and for the first time since he'd joined, Jud Hunter thought about sending something back. Obviously, they'd sent messages to the leader when they'd been told to, but never spontaneously like this.

He went over to the wall of screens and pressed the only button he could see. With a click and a hum, the central monitor started to glow. There was no load screen, no operating system or any icons to click on, just a dark green background with a single flashing input marker.

Jud hurriedly typed a brief message explaining what had happened to Sam. He kept looking at the door, anxious to finish typing before anyone could come in. He didn't want them seeing him messaging the leader and thinking he was rattled.

He hit enter, the input marker shifting down a line with another click.

The reply came almost instantly.

Re: Sam Street
The Skater was the first. If you continue to avoid competing, another one of you will fall. I have records of everything you've ever done, and will hand them to the authorities if necessary.
Time to up your game.

Chapter 10 – Canvassing

"So," the lecturer went on. "An effective business model can be the difference between a multimillion pound deal, and the bus fare home." Dr Stroud was tall and willowy, seeming to flow gracefully up and down the aisles.

Lee had quickly learned not to follow the lecturer with his eyes, as that soon led to neck sprains. Instead, Lee usually sat back with his eyes closed and let the tide of information wash over him.

"Mr Radley? It's your turn to present."

Lee opened his eyes and grabbed his notebook. Sliding his chair back, he moved slowly to the front of the room, noting the expressions his classmates wore. About half the class were sitting back with feigned interest, their presentations already delivered. Most of the others were trying to sink into their chairs, making themselves as small as possible because their turns were inevitably coming up soon. Finally there were about two or three faces that were watching Lee with rapt attention, pens already poised to note down any gems of worthiness he might disclose. Lee wasn't generally bothered about speaking in front of the class, after all, if there was one thing that his father had managed to instil in his son during their scant time together, it was the art of the boardroom confidence. Lee took a deep breath, about to begin when a knock rapped against the door.

The lecturer turned to peer through the glass panel and Lee followed his gaze. Standing in the corridor was a tall guy in a tailored shirt, a pencil tie dead straight down the middle of his chest. He had close cropped brown hair and glasses. If he didn't have the youthful features of a late teenager, Lee would have assumed he was staff.

"You can start, Mr Radley," Dr Stroud said before opening the door and letting the visitor inside.

"I've been focusing largely on the testing element," Lee began. "If you want your company to be self sufficient, then you need to make sure they can handle anything that comes their way. In light of this, I would propose setting up a scaled down version of the business and trialling it with a small test group, effectively creating a cell that can generate income whilst trouble shooting any issues that arise. A clever manager might set up multiple independent groups all contributing profits to the business as a whole." He stopped, waiting for some sort of acknowledgement from the lecturer for his efforts. Dr Stroud however, was leaning towards his visitor, whispering emphatically. *Great*, Lee thought sourly. He could handle his classmates switching off, but surely the lecturer should pay attention? Grades were riding on things like this after all. "I'd also propose crack and hookers," he added loudly, earning a couple of sniggers from his audience.

This at least seemed to catch Dr Stroud's attention. He readjusted his glasses guiltily. "Yes. A sound plan, thanks Lee." Another round of laughter peaked, and Lee took a bow, earning a confused look from the lecturer. "Right well, I think we'll end it there for today."

Back in his seat, Lee glanced at the clock, seeing that there was still almost twenty minutes of the lesson left. He turned around to his classmates, but they were already shoving their belongings back into rucksacks or tucking folders under arms, Lee's moment in the spotlight already forgotten. None of them seemed bothered by Dr Stroud's visitor, and Lee wondered if this was a regular occurrence.

Dr Stroud let a group of students pass before drifting casually back towards the visitor. An odd sense of familiarity nagged at the back of Lee's mind until he realised where he'd seen the newcomer's face before – in the shadows of the meeting room. He was a Stereotype!

Out of curiosity, Lee slowed down his packing away. Normally, he would just shove everything into his bag and sort it out later (if it was lucky), however, now he was meticulously placing each item into his pencil case, taking extra care to straighten the papers in his folder.

"It's only one set of essays," Stroud murmured, sounding harangued. "I can manage it perfectly well on my own."

"Are you sure? I mean wouldn't you rather take the pressure off a little? I'm sure we can come to some sort of-"

The Stereotype halted as Lee's pen clattered to the floor, rolling across the tiles excruciatingly loudly in the now silent room. Both men turned to look at Lee, who shrugged sheepishly.

"Ah, Lee," Dr Stroud flustered, his cheeks reddening. "I didn't realise you were still in here."

There was a brief flash of recognition as the other guy met Lee's eyes, and without wasting a second, the visitor strode forwards, hand outstretched confidently.

"Conrad Jackson," he smarmed, grasping Lee's hand before it was offered. "Undergrad TA."

"I bet," Lee muttered so that Dr Stroud couldn't hear. It was obvious that Conrad was making a show of pretending it was the first time they'd seen each other.

"Well, if you don't mind, Dr Stroud and I are in the middle of an important meeting. See you later… Lee, was it?" Conrad grinned, a row of perfectly straight gleaming teeth shining for a split second.

Lee looked to Dr Stroud for confirmation, but the lecturer seemed to be intently picking at a loose thread on his cardigan. With a pointed glare, Lee left the room.

The sun was shining out in the quad, and the lawns were once again full of students lounging around. As the end of term got closer, the amount of folders and notebooks decreased, but the amount of beer cans and bottles seemed to rapidly replace them.

Lee was heading for the Union because Harry had called a block meeting, and whilst the early finish of his Business seminar gave Lee plenty of time to get there, he still wished he could flop down onto the grass and join the others for an hour or two.

"Hey dude, you need anything?"

"Nah man, I'm clean." Lee looked up, expecting to see a gaunt, snaggle-toothed addict face. Instead, his way was blocked by a smartly dressed kid in a woollen tank top, thick rimmed glasses perched on the end of his nose.

"I was talking about grades," the kid said. "Any subject, any lecturer – I can get all the assignments."

Lee was astounded, standing with his mouth open. "Um," he faltered after realising he'd been gawping for some time. "No thanks."

As soon as Lee had refused the offer, the kid was instantly scanning the quad for someone else to accost.

By the time Lee had traversed the central hub of UCE, he'd also been offered a mobile phone upgrade, as well as admin access to the university network. It was as if the quad had been suddenly requisitioned as an illicit bazaar.

Hurrying away from the various hawkers, Lee jogged the rest of the distance to the Union. When he arrived, there was a fairly large group of familiar faces spread across the various tables and benches. Niall and Elliott gave him a quick nod from one of the tables, Elliott's eyes gleaming like sunlight on water. After a quick bout of meerkatting from the steps, Lee soon spotted Kelly and Sarah sitting in one of the booths with bored expressions across their faces. He bounded down the steps and slipped into the booth beside Sarah.

"Any idea what this is about?" he asked.

"God knows," Sarah replied sullenly. Her tone said she would have rather been anywhere else.

"Knowing Harry, it will be something totally lame," Kelly chipped in. "Do you remember that stranger danger thing when we started? There were puppets for God's sake!"

Just as Lee was horrifically imagining Harry re-enacting a puppet assault, there was a harsh throat-clearing cough and the background chatter died down. Harry was standing at the front of the room, flanked by four other students in red polos. Despite being different shapes and sizes (one was even quite pretty), Lee couldn't stop imagining the Senior Residents as a row of fat sweaty warthogs, thanks to his first encounter with Harry.

"Thanks for coming today," Harry began in his whining, reedy voice, his companions nodding in unison like dashboard dogs. "As we're nearing the end of term, I'd like to use this meeting to express UCE's views on any shenanigans you might be planning. Any unruliness will not be taken lightly." At this, the subordinates changed their nodding to disapproving head shakes.

Lee's heart sank as Harry proceeded to run through various activities that UCE apparently would not tolerate, failing to realise that he was merely providing the students of O'Connell Hall with a bucket list of mischief.

Harry soon moved on from acts of vandalism (fire extinguishers are *not* toys) to blatant disregard of health and safety (mouldy rice is *not* a suitable basis for a competition) and Lee felt his attention wandering. He began to scan around the room, people watching. Obviously there were students he knew from his floor, but there were others he'd never even passed on the stairs, and Lee began to amuse himself by inventing names and backstories for them.

He was just padding out the life of a particularly arrogant looking guy with blonde hair pulled back into a ridiculous man-bun (his name was now something pretentious like Layton, and he was saving up to go backpacking round Mongolia or somewhere), when he felt something brush against his knee.

Looking up, Lee saw Kelly wink at him mischievously. He peered under the table, where she was pressing her infamous hip flask against his leg.

"You know there's a bar like right there," he whispered.

"This is more fun."

"What's in it this time?"

"See if you can guess."

With an apprehensive grin, Lee took a swig, feeling the chemical burn of cheap tequila scorch a trail down his throat. With a shudder, he passed the flask to Sarah, who took the hit without flinching.

Soon, the three of them were rosy cheeked and giggling at most of Harry's outdated slang, the words 'jackanapes' and 'tomfoolery' earning both raucous laughs from them, and fierce glares from the Senior Residents.

After a particularly arduous section about animals (no livestock is permitted in UCE Halls), Lee excused himself to the bathroom. Harry paused mid-sentence, his eyes following Lee as he strolled jovially in front of him.

"Sorry old chap," Lee drawled. "Do continue." He heard Harry tutting loudly as the doors to the toilets swung closed.

Head starting to ache slightly, Lee stepped up to the urinal and paused, eyes roving across the graffiti wall. He quickly located the message that had drawn him in earlier, but this time it was surrounded by lots of other messages. Lee took a step back and realised that they were all offering some sort of service, from hook ups to beat ups. Snapping a quick picture on his phone and finishing up, Lee strode out with a grin on his face. Something had got The Stereotypes worried.

Chapter 11 – Cry For Help

That evening, Lee was lying on his bed, staring at the ceiling. After the block meeting, he, Kelly and Sarah had stayed at the Union for a couple more drinks, which were now mixing horrendously with the tequila from Kelly's hip flask. The girls themselves had decided to stay on until the club night unfolded, though Lee had no idea how they would be able to stay awake or even functional after drinking for so long.

For now, Lee was content fixating on a scuffed patch in the plasterwork, a classic concerto CD playing softy in the background, lulling his brain into a soothing state of disengagement. Overall, his new life at UCE wasn't so bad. He'd quickly got himself settled in and found a decent group of friends in Kelly, Sarah and Dan. He was doing ok in his Business class, and since he'd got his stuff sent over, his other side projects and hobbies had also been picking up. He still hadn't spoken to his dad, but that wasn't exactly anything new.

Lee was jolted from his life assessing by the harsh bleating of the flat buzzer. He waited for a moment to see if any of the others would address it, but when the noise came again a minute later, he assumed nobody else was in. Was he really the only one out of ten to be staying in? Did that make him some sort of loser?

The buzzer rang again, for longer this time. It was probably one of the girls, unable to find her keys in her inebriate state. With a sigh, Lee rolled off the bed, his tequila head following a split second behind. He moved out into the corridor and fumbled with the plastic receiver mounted on the wall.

"Finally drank your limit huh?" he said wryly.

"Lee?" the reply crackled over the intercom. It was Rebecca.

"What do you want?" Lee sighed irritably. It was as if simply hearing her voice had upgraded his slight fuzziness to full on tequila headache.

"Can I come in?"

"I don't see why. I made it pretty clear last time that I don't want anything to do with you."

"Please," she begged. "I need your help."

It was then that Lee noticed the slight crack in her voice that suggested she was crying, or had been up until very recently. He cast a glance up and down the corridor, double checking that nobody else was around.

"Fine," he muttered, satisfied that they would be alone. He pressed the button to open the door down below.

A few moments later, there was a soft knocking at the front door, and Lee ambled over. Rebecca was standing there, and just as he had guessed, her eyes were puffy with streaks of mascara that had been hastily wiped away.

"Well?" Lee questioned bluntly. He didn't want to let on that he still found her attractive after everything.

Rebecca pushed past him with a brief flicker of distaste as she scanned the scuffed blue carpet and off white walls of the corridor. She stopped by the door to the living room, obviously unsure if anybody else was in there.

"We'll go to my room," Lee said, indicating one of the side doors.

Rebecca went inside, immediately sitting on the edge of the bed. If she was intrigued or even bothered by the giant posters, she didn't say anything. Lee plonked himself down into the office chair and spun it round to face her.

"So…?" Lee asked impatiently. Rebecca had begged to be let in, and now she was just sitting there sniffling quietly to herself.

"It's this challenge from the leader," she began. "We each have to earn as much money as possible, using our specific areas. The loser has to be punished."

"Sounds a bit harsh."

"Anyway," she continued. "I'm losing." She paused for dramatic effect, but Lee remained nonplussed.

"And?" he challenged. "What's that got to do with me?"

"You don't understand," the cheerleader whined. "You know what happened to Sam?"

"I watched him get taken down."

"That was because we refused to play. The leader targeted Sam on purpose, and set him up for all the drug stuff. He has dirt on all of us, which he can use if we don't do what he wants."

"Sounds like a smart chap," Lee mused. "And I still don't see why I should help. Is all the dirt the leader has on you true?"

Rebecca nodded.

"Then it's your own fault. You knew the risks when you joined The Stereotypes."

Rebecca laughed to herself acidly. "You know the myth that if a lecturer is over ten minutes late, the students can go home?"

"Uhuh," Lee nodded, wondering why Rebecca had changed the subject. He remembered at college when his entire History class had hid in the library from their teacher who had turned up late. They had eventually been rounded up and told how stupid they were.

"Well how about this one?" Rebecca continued. "If someone dies in the exam hall, everybody automatically passes."

"Right," Lee said slowly.

"We've all been entered for a new exam," Rebecca stated. "If we don't pass it, we fail our degrees, but it's a subject that we haven't studied – I don't even think it *is* a subject."

"Look," Lee sighed. "What are you saying?" He was getting tired of all the build up.

"I'm saying that the loser of this competition is going to have to die so that everyone else can pass. And currently, that's me."

Chapter 12 – Change Of Heart

Lee woke up, guilt instantly flooding his mind. He lay still for a few minutes, watching the sunlight stripe across his chest as it filtered through the blinds. He didn't want to turn his head because he knew he would still see the vague imprint signifying where Rebecca had lain until just a few hours ago.

They had talked into the night. At first Lee had been sceptical, until Rebecca had read the Leader's actual message to him. The Leader had made it perfectly clear that the only way to get through the fake exam was to score a pass through a death in the exam hall. They'd spent hours going over various possibilities to get Rebecca out of the game, but in the end it all became fruitless. She was stubborn. She wouldn't refuse to play and risk getting a criminal record. She wouldn't risk not passing the year either. It seemed that the only option she would even consider was to pick up the pace and win the contest legitimately. She had said on more than one occasion that she didn't care if one of the others lost – as long as it wasn't her.

By then it was extremely late and the cheerleader didn't want to go home, so Lee begrudgingly let her stay, with the express condition that there would be no inappropriate conduct (he'd even set himself up on the floor).

Of course it hadn't taken long before he'd felt a hand snaking its way up his thigh and into his shorts. He'd tried to resist but once again, by then it wasn't his brain that was in control. The lips that followed the hand only cemented things, and he'd jumped into the bed as if his life depended on it.

During the night, he hadn't given two shits about Jud, The Stereotypes or anything else – his body had existed solely for pleasure – but now that Rebecca had snuck out, all the thoughts of responsibility and shame came back, the weight of them dragging Lee from the euphoric cloud he'd been lounging on.

In this clandestine hook up, he was effectively wrecking a relationship – something which he'd already been beaten up for – and there wouldn't be much stopping Jud from doing it again if he found out. But it was more than that, Lee reasoned. He'd always considered himself as a decent person. Yes, he had his flaws, but he wasn't mean about it. Every time he could have been accused of using somebody else for his own gain, well, they got gains too. Nobody really lost. But what he'd done to Jud? That was a bit of a dick move, and maybe Lee *did* deserve the pounding he'd got from the jocks.

Then there was the issue of The Stereotypes. Like Rebecca, he couldn't really say he would be that bothered if one of the others was losing. After all, they'd all signed up to follow the instructions of their mysterious leader hadn't they? They'd *chosen* to get involved, and now they might end up paying the price. Also, on a personal level, evidently none of them had bothered to question his dismissal from the recruitment. If Jud lost the competition, then Lee didn't suppose he would bat an eyelid. But Rebecca? That was different. He hadn't ever thought she could be at risk. Maybe it was because the others were just names on a bit of paper, pictures on a screen, or in Jud's case a total douche regardless. But Rebecca, she was *real*. She was soft, and beautiful, and- Lee shook himself, sloughing off the compliments before he got too warm and fuzzy.

That was the crux of it right there. He'd slept with Rebecca and now he actually kind of *liked* her. Maybe that was why she'd instigated it again – to seal the deal. But what could Lee actually do about it? He could sabotage the others so that Rebecca won and somebody else had to take the fall

– but that would be Lee personally choosing someone to die, and he wasn't sure he could do that.

That was when Lee hit on a possible solution. Instead of choosing who won or who lost, perhaps he could mess the game up so completely that it couldn't be played. The Stereotypes wouldn't be responsible so they wouldn't be punished by their leader – surely that was a win-win solution?

Lee jumped out of bed, suddenly infused with rebellious energy. He grabbed his jeans from the previous day and rummaged through the pockets, pulling out his phone. He fired off a quick message asking Dan to come over, then got dressed and waited.

Within half an hour, Kelly, Sarah and Dan were sitting around the table, watching Lee expectantly. Whilst Kelly had complained loudly at having to actually get up, Dan hadn't raised any objections to coming over before practice.

Whilst he had their attention, Lee proceeded to explain about The Stereotypes ("I knew it!" Dan said, punching the air jubilantly), and the competition they had been drawn into. Lee was thankful that nobody asked him any awkward questions that he couldn't answer, after all, he was aware that there was lots he didn't actually know about the intricate workings of the secret organisation. He was also glad that his friends didn't berate him for getting involved in the first place.

"Let's just say that all this really is going on right under our noses," Sarah began sceptically. "How are we supposed to stop this? Why don't we just talk to campus security or the police or someone?"

"Because Rebecca will go down too!" Lee hissed.

"No offence, but do we care about her now?"

"Didn't Jud break your nose?"

"It wasn't broken," Lee defended. "And besides, you saw what happened to Sam Street at the park." He rounded on Kelly. "It's not just about Rebecca. If we get involved then we're potentially saving them all from something they can't control."

"Even Jud?" Dan asked.

Lee paused for a moment, watching the faces of his friends. They were watching him eagerly, awaiting his decision. "Even Jud," he conceded.

"So how're we going to do it?"

Lee smiled to himself, holding his phone out for the others to see. Glowing on the screen was the picture he'd taken of the graffiti wall in the Union toilets, covered in The Stereotypes services.

"How's that supposed to help?"

In response, Lee dialled a number and held the phone up. "Alright Niall," he said with a knowing grin. "Fancy a bit of revenge?"

Interlude – The Meeting Room

Rebecca Carter slipped into the darkness of the meeting room, head spinning with confusion. She sunk into her usual seat and thunked her forehead onto the glossy table. On one layer she knew she had to keep her mind focused on The Stereotypes, but Lee's face kept flashing up in her mind. She racked her brain trying to remember how she'd felt when she'd first got together with Jud – the excitement and the electricity, but now all of that was gone. She'd never thought twice about cheating on him, and she was certain that he slept around too, but for some reason, her two encounters with the quirky Lee Radley had stuck with her, whereas all the other times it had just been a bit of something different to mix things up.

"Where have you been?"

Rebecca snapped upright, her eyes scanning the gloom in panic. As she stared, Jud materialised out of the shadows, his broad shoulders looming over her. As he got close enough so that she could smell his beer breath, the cheerleader reached tentatively behind her for the light switch.

All of a sudden, the meeting room was bathed in light, throwing Jud's blotchy face and slightly unfocused eyes into harsh detail. There was a number of empty beer cans strewn around the floor, and Rebecca couldn't help wondering how long her Chimera boyfriend had been waiting for her. She regarded him with apprehension – this wouldn't be the first time that his sports aggression had been released through alcohol – but to her relief, he sank into the chair next to her.

"You've been with him again haven't you?" he spat. Rebecca's silence gave her away.

"What is it about this guy?" Jud slurred. "I mean look at me: I'm fit, rich, and connected – what else do you need?"

At this, a swathe of answers raced through Rebecca's mind. Perhaps someone who was actually kind and considerate? Maybe someone who knew more than three moves in bed? Ooh, what about a guy that actually cared more about her than his stupid teammates? Luke, the captain of the Centaurs had pretty much rocked the status quo by prioritising a *boyfriend*, but the sentiment didn't seem to have rubbed off on any of the other UCE athletes.

"You think he can save you, is that it?"

Rebecca looked at him furiously. Did Jud think that this was solely about the competition? Sure, she'd gone to Lee for help, but what had happened after – that had been a result of real feeling hadn't it? Lee certainly hadn't complained.

"He might not be able to save me," she began pensively. "But at least he can't hurt me." Jud opened his mouth to retort, but she cut him off. "I just need something that's not connected to The Stereotypes right now – something normal."

Jud banged his fist half-heartedly on the table. "You're wrong," he stated flatly. "You need someone who's in the thick of it. We can work together – get through this as a team."

"And have the leader stitch another one of us up with the police? He's made it clear that we have to follow the rules – and I don't think he'd appreciate a team up. No," Rebecca reasoned. "Lee's outside the influence of the leader. He's my respite."

As she watched Jud's head lolling, she got up from the table, confident that he was too drunk to cause any more trouble. She made her way to the door.

"You'll see," Jud growled. "You'll see there's nothing special about Lee fucking Radley."

Rebecca shook her head and disappeared into the corridor.

Chapter 13 – The Anti-Stereotypes

"So we're all clear?" Lee asked as he looked around the table. As well as Kelly, Sarah and Dan, Lee had invited Niall, Amy, Elliott and James over, and they now occupied the living room of Lee's flat. Lee had just finished explaining his basic idea about sabotaging each service The Stereotypes provided so that their competition was a bust.

"This is awesome!" James enthused, his grin unbreakable. With his chestnut curls and little ears he looked like some sort of mischievous imp, bursting into life now that he had a nefarious purpose to work on.

"To think, we wanted to join The Stereotypes," Elliott said. "But now we're going to save them. They were just in it for the money, but we're so much better. We're like… noble and stuff."

"We're the Rebel Alliance," Niall added, earning a groan from the others.

"Nah, it's more like The Matrix," Elliott challenged. "Eight Stereotypes to sabotage, eight of us to do it. Providence and all that."

"I hate to rain on your parade, Morpheus," Amy said flatly, her flaming hair and dark eyeliner making everything she said seem angry. "But I'm not sure this is going to work." She looked pointedly at Lee. "I'm sorry, but some of what you're suggesting is going to need access to The Stereotypes lair, as well as stuff like who's doing what, where and when. I've got some pretty good computer skills, but I'm no Trinity."

"We need an inside man, like Cypher!" Dan yelled, pleased to contribute to the geek off.

"A Stereotype of our own?" Kelly asked. "And if anyone else makes a Matrix reference, I'm leaving."

"Fair play," said Lee. "You're right, this is serious. And Amy you're right too – I hadn't thought about that."

"Can't you just ask Rebecca?" Sarah suggested. "Surely she'll do it for you?"

"No, she can't be involved," Lee stated, ignoring the raised eyebrows from the others. They didn't know the details of his relationship with the Cheerleader. "She doesn't want me to ruin the game, she only wants herself to win. It's for her own good that we do it this way, but still, she might not see that, and try to stop us."

"Then this is all for nothing," Amy sighed. "None of this will work, and I'll never get my own back on Rick the dick." She stood up to leave, disappointment crawling across her face.

"Wait," Lee said. "There's someone else we can try, but I'll need a bit of time." He watched anxiously as Amy hovered for a second, then sat back down. Lee breathed a sigh of relief. "For now, you each know what you're doing, so start making the necessary preparations. I'll be in touch when I've got our insider sorted."

The others nodded and Lee instantly felt a pressure lift in his chest. He'd progressed from everyday grunt to group leader in very short space of time, and he was glad that he hadn't failed miserably in getting the others to follow him. *I'm totally Ripley in Aliens,* he thought wryly, glad he hadn't said it out loud and incurred Kelly's movie reference wrath.

One by one, Dan and the failed recruits left the meeting, until it was only Lee, Kelly and Sarah.

"I hope you know what you're doing," Sarah said, a note of concern in her voice. "There's a reason why people act funny about The Stereotypes. Their name is thrown about whenever somebody gets beaten up or goes off suddenly. They're not good people to piss off, Lee."

"Trust me," Lee replied. He walked down the corridor to his bedroom, leaving his flatmates to exchange a quizzical glance behind his back.

Once in the confines of his room, Lee pulled out his phone once more and dialled.

"Good evening, Radley Incorporated, how may I direct your call?"

Lee paused for a moment, knowing how the next few lines of conversation would unfold. He'd ask for his dad, pretending there was a chance, then Paula would pretend to check and come back with some flimsy excuse. Instead, Lee decided to cut right to the chase.

"Paula, it's Lee. I need some money from my father. Can you arrange a transfer?"

"I'm sorry Lee," Paula sighed. "You know Sir Radley's thoughts on the matter. He's been especially clear since your relocation to UCE."

"Perhaps if I explained?" Lee pleaded. "Just let me talk to him."

There was silence on the line, and Lee could almost picture Paula thinking it through. He wondered if she had children of her own. Was his predicament with his dad pulling at the heartstrings?

"I'm sorry Lee, I really am, but there's nothing I can do."

"Great," Lee snapped petulantly. "Thanks for nothing."

"If it was up to me," Paula murmured softly, trying to placate Lee's frustration. "But as I said, your father has been most insistent." She said this last part with a measured quality as if she was trying to say something more.

"What exactly did he tell you?" Lee asked, dreading the answer.

"I told her not to entertain any of your stupid schemes," a gruff voice crackled over the line, self-important and authoritative. "Goodnight Lee. Paula, my office. Now."

The line went dead, and Lee felt a pang of guilt. Paula was probably going to be in trouble with his father – he just hoped that the punishment wasn't too severe. With a sigh, he thought about Sir Michael's stance on money - the one Paula had mentioned. His father strongly believed that no matter how rich the parents, the children had to earn their way, same as everyone else. This meant that fatherly handouts were rare. Lee had hoped that since he'd changed University, his dad might have taken pity on him, but no. Apparently, his father had hardened his heart even more so. Lee couldn't blame him really – what had happened at Northern didn't exactly earn Lee any honour points – and that was as good as currency with his father, but still, it didn't stop anger bubbling away in Lee's head.

It was a good job his mother had also known Sir Michael's staunch policy, and left Lee a backup before she'd died. That was one of the fondest memories he had of her, sneaking him pocket money so he could go and buy sweets after her husband had said no. Lee jumped up from where he'd been sitting on the bed and rummaged in his bag for his wallet. He tipped out the contents, scattering various student cards, receipts, pennies and lint onto the duvet. Once it was empty, Lee stuck his little finger inside the lining and used it to worm out one final card that was hidden there – a credit card that his mother had set up for him. He'd deliberately kept it out of sight and made it hard to get to so he wouldn't just burn through it – after all, his mother had stated that it should only be for emergencies. It was a wonder that he hadn't caved sooner, with all the financial denials his father had dealt him over the years. He didn't even know how much was on there, but he hoped there would be enough. For emergencies. Surely this counted, didn't it? He thought back to what Elliott had been saying about saving The Stereotypes and being noble, and was suddenly sure that his mum would approve of his selfless actions. All he had to do was wait for the morning when the banks would open.

Chapter 14 – Bail

Lee sat awkwardly in front of the glass barrier, nothing but an old style phone handset before him, connected to the wall by a coiled wire. He'd only been there for about ten minutes and the plain wooden stool he'd been given was already sending his backside numb. He cast a glance either side, thankful that he'd arrived early enough to be only one of two people at the Police Station visiting room. He didn't know why he felt so weird about it. After all, he hadn't done anything wrong, but there was still the association of knowing somebody who had.

There was movement behind the glass, and Sam Street shuffled into the room on the other side of the barrier. He looked completely different, as if everything that made him The Stereotype Skater had been stripped away. His piercings were out, and he'd lost his beanie so that his tufty straw hair hung down around his shadowed eyes. To complete the image, he was wearing a grey jumpsuit, like something a janitor might wear.

When Sam saw who was behind the glass, he frowned in confusion, picking up his phone handset.

"Lee? What are you doing here?" he asked as he sat on an equally uncomfortable looking stool on his side.

"Didn't they tell you?"

"They mentioned bail, but they didn't tell me who it was. I thought maybe the leader, but… I can't believe it's you! I thought you were done with us."

Lee nodded awkwardly. "Well, it's not as simple as that. I need something in return."

Sam raised an eyebrow.

"I need you to get me into The Stereotypes' lair. Secretly."

"No way." Sam shook his head stolidly. "They're bound to be working on how to get me out of here. I'm not going to sell them out by sneaking you in – for whatever reason."

At this point, Lee explained what Rebecca had told him – about how Sam's arrest was their punishment for not playing in the Leader's competition. He watched his former mentor's face fall. "It seems *they* sold *you* out," he concluded solemnly.

"But they wouldn't…" the Skater muttered quietly.

"Come on," sighed Lee, before explaining how Jud had beaten him up after Sam had left the supposed party.

"But that's Jud! He's a complete dick, but the others… the Leader…"

"Do you even know who the Leader is? How can you make any judgement on what they would or wouldn't do? He told you to do all these drug deals and then personally got you arrested for it because you wouldn't do what he said? Sounds like a great guy. Face it Sam, the Leader used you."

"And what are you doing then?" Sam asked, his cheeks colouring with frustration. "You're prepared to bail me out on this one condition? Sounds like you're using me too."

"That's different."

"How?"

Lee sighed. He'd hoped he wouldn't have to go into this next part – he figured Sam would have been too overjoyed with freedom to ask any questions. He'd obviously underestimated the Skater's loyalty to The Stereotypes. He went on to reveal the next level to the Leader's twisted plot – about what really happened to the loser at the exam. "So you see," he said defiantly. "I might be using you, but if I can find anything in that lair that helps me stop this stupid game, then I'll be saving you too."

"Sounds like I'm safer in here," Sam said flatly.

"I wouldn't count on it," Lee replied, thinking on his feet. "How much revenue has the Skate team drummed up whilst you've been in here, do you think? Enough to keep you off last place? You think being arrested means you're out of the competition?" He watched as Sam thought things through. Lee had absolutely no evidence to suggest that any of what he'd just said was true, but he really needed Sam to think it was. He just hoped he'd painted a bad enough picture of the Leader for Sam to think it was plausible. "It's your choice," he said finally. "You come out with me now and help me stop all this, or you wait in here and take your chances. Maybe they'll let you miss all your exams. Maybe not."

Sam thought for a second more. "When you put it like that…"

"Excellent!" Lee beamed, only a few steps away from actually punching the air. "I'll go and sort it out. See you in reception."

The next couple of hours was spent arduously filling in stacks of paperwork, including Lee's own criminal record check. There was a tense moment of panic about Lee's transfer from Northern, but luckily no charges had been pressed so he was technically clear.

When Sam finally emerged into freedom, he was back to his Skater self, piercings, beanie and black outfit all in place. He'd collected his personal effects and even the smile he was wearing went some way to erase the harrowed look he'd worn earlier.

They stepped outside into the sunlight, and Sam stretched his arms, taking a huge breath. He closed his eyes and sighed with contentment.

"I hate to be a buzzkill dude," Lee said, tapping the Skater on the shoulder. "But time is kind of crucial here…"

Sam's eyes snapped open. "Ok, let's get this over with," he said with a nod. "Then I'm laying low for a while."

The two of them walked across town, and Lee felt a thrill building in his chest. Whilst everyone else was busy going to work, shopping, meeting friends and just being so… normal, he and Sam were embarking on something that was the complete opposite. It was like a whole secondary layer existed beneath the normality, with the underground society, the nefarious plots and the courageous attempts to foil them.

Sam turned off the main street and stepped through the iron railings that signified the boundary to the park. They were at the corner near the bandstand, the racing green coloured structure standing empty in the centre of the grass. In the distance, Lee could make out the angular shapes of the children's play area contrasted with the smooth curves of the skate park on the opposite side.

"Shouldn't we be heading for John Terrence and the Society corridor?" Lee asked.

"Nah," Sam said with a grin, more of his old chirpiness building up the further he got from the Police Station. "My way is better."

Soon, the two of them were in the shadows of the half-pipe. Sam had given a few greetings to the skaters that were there, before ducking under the support struts. Tucked against the back wall was a narrow green shed, the council logo stencilled on the side.

"It used to be storage for park supplies," Sam explained. "Gardening stuff and shit. Mostly we use it to get high out of sight. Nobody will bother us." Sam reached forward and slipped off the padlock over the door. It wasn't clicked into place, but you'd have to have been looking closely to notice.

"Um…?" Lee questioned, wondering what exactly they were doing here. He knew Sam had been locked away for a while, but now really wasn't the best time to stop for a joint.

"Trust me," Sam said, eyes glinting before he stepped into the shaded interior. Wheels roared on the halfpipe overhead, and Lee slipped inside after his friend, being sure to close the door behind them.

The shed was exactly as Lee had expected. An old lawnmower with its engine panel open and parts strewn across the concrete occupied one end, whilst the other end was piled high with rolls of turf. They'd been well and truly neglected, and the grass was brittle and yellow. The whole place smelt musty – like damp tinged with old smoke.

Without speaking, Sam pushed a couple of turf rolls to the side, revealing a trapdoor cut into the floor. "Tadaa!"

"This was where you were aiming for when you ran from the police!" Lee said in awe.

"Oh, you saw that huh?" Sam muttered with a hint of embarrassment. "But yeah. I wasn't counting on them being so... dedicated to law enforcement." He reached for the dusty ring set into the hatch and pulled it up, revealing a square of pitch black descending into the depths of the earth. A ladder was fixed to one side, and Sam lowered himself onto the top rung. "Pull the hatch down after you, and the turf will fall into place."

They climbed down through the darkness in silence, and Lee lost all sense of time and distance. It was as if he had been swallowed up and now existed as nothing – just a consciousness without a body. After a few minutes (or possibly hours) he heard the sound of Sam's feet hitting solid ground. There was a second of fumbling, followed by a click. Lights flickered on, revealing a plain concrete corridor stretching off into the gloom.

"The word is that UCE was used as an evacuation centre during the war," Sam explained with a hint of pride.

"The tunnels were built as a quick getaway in case we got invaded. Good job we won."

"How many are there?" Lee asked, filled with wonder. Even though the corridor was nothing but grey stone, he couldn't help looking in every direction as they walked along, like something new and fantastic might pop out at any moment.

"Most of us have access to one somewhere," Sam mused. "The best one is Jud's. There's an old locker in the changing rooms with a false back."

Despite that sounding incredibly cool, Lee refrained from commenting. He didn't want to praise anything associated with Jud the Jock.

They carried on walking, their footsteps echoing through the passage. Eventually, they came to a junction and turned into a new corridor that Lee recognised. The other branch was the one that led to the cleaner's cupboard in the society corridor in John Terrence. They'd cut across town completely underground.

"Wait here," Sam whispered. "I'll make sure it's empty."

Lee nodded as Sam slipped forward, disappearing into the meeting room. There was a minute of nothing but Lee's breathing whilst he imagined Sam checking the other rooms, then the Skater appeared in the doorway, flashing him a thumbs up and a cheeky grin.

Lee stepped forwards into the meeting the room, remembering the last time he'd been there. Despite being full of promise and potential, he realised that even then, Jud had been making fun of him. This was Jud's domain and Lee had been the know-nothing newcomer. He smiled to himself, almost wishing Jud could see him now. The first thing Lee did was walk over to the noticeboard and snatch the roster he'd spotted last time. He smiled as he read it – a list of names and duties.

Emma Blunt – The Artist
Rebecca Carter – The Cheerleader
Stephen Curtis – The Academic
Jud Hunter – The Jock
Conrad Jackson – The Staff Liaison
Joe Nichols – The Performer
Rick O'Reilly – The Techie
Sam Street – The Skater

"You know," Sam said, snapping Lee out of his wishful thinking. "This would be easier if you told me what we were looking for."

"This place isn't bugged is it?" Lee asked, scanning the walls and ceiling for anything out of place.

"Ha, no," Sam laughed. "We don't bug *our own* house. Just everywhere else."

Lee thought for a moment, before explaining his sabotage plan.

"I like it," Sam said with an appraising nod.

"What we really need is to do as much of it around the same time, to give The Stereotypes less time to fix it. To flood them with problems all at once. Any ideas?"

Sam's face lit up. "I know just the thing," he beamed. He practically skipped over to the cabinets next to the computer monitors and began rummaging around in the drawers whilst Lee waited eagerly. "Bingo!" Sam cried, waving a thick folder full of papers.

"What is it?" Lee asked as Sam brought the file over to the table.

"Every year, UCE has a summer carnival to mark the end of study and the start of exams."

"So?"

"So it's always prime business for The Stereotypes. Pretty much all of us get involved."

"Ah!" Lee gasped, catching on. Most of The Stereotypes were going to be working at the carnival. All at the same time.

"This file is an outline of what everyone's going to be doing. It's all here." Sam puffed his chest out with pride.

"Come on then," Lee grinned. "Grab it and let's go!"

"We can't take it," Sam chided. "The carnival's coming up – The Stereotypes will be checking it regularly – it would be noticed too quickly."

"Oh," Lee muttered, disappointment dampening his initial excitement.

"Don't worry, my little recruit," Sam said knowingly. "I believe the printer has a copy function."

"Yes mate!" Lee was instantly energized again as Sam took the folder to the printer. Everything was starting to work out. They were going to hit The Stereotypes at the summer carnival.

Chapter 15 – Groundwork

"I don't even want to know how you got this," Lee said, holding the tiny glass vial delicately between his thumb and forefinger. He held it at arm's length as if the contents would jump down his throat in an instant.

Kelly grinned, taking the bottle and slipping it back inside her bag. "Let's just say I know a guy with access to the sample cases in Biology."

"Excellent," Lee said. "Here's your targets." He handed Kelly a list of names he'd found in The Stereotypes file – they were all going to be involved in one of the ventures at the carnival.

Kelly took the list and scanned it, rolling her eyes. "Not surprised, she's a slag. Slag. Slag. Ooh really? I'll tease her about it afterwards. Slag. Slept with him. And him. Slag. Slag. Slag."

Lee glanced awkwardly at the others, who shrugged. "Do you think you can get them all?" he asked, once Kelly had finished running down the list.

"Easy," she nodded confidently. "There's nobody on here that I can't legitimately cross paths with for some reason or other. Wish me luck!" She shouldered her bag and headed towards the door.

"Remember, only one drop each," Lee called. "We don't want to hurt anyone!"

"Yes boss," Kelly replied sarcastically before leaving the flat to begin her mission.

Lee turned to Amy, who had been watching Kelly with interest. Amy's red hair was pulled into two pigtails, and she'd gone all out on the eye makeup. It was a look that said she was out to cause trouble.

"What about you?" Lee asked.

Amy held up a USB drive. "The code is written and ready to go. All I need to do now is get it onto Rick's computer."

"I can help with that," Sam said, lurching forward from where he had been leaning against the wall. Despite saying he wanted to lay low, he'd obviously been enticed by Lee's plan. "Rick keeps a server in The Stereotypes den. It links to his personal one by wi-fi or something computery like that. Anyway, what you change on one of them automatically copies to the other. I'll take you in - you won't even have to go near him."

"Pity," Amy said bitterly. "I'd like to see his face."

"I'm sure you'll see it at the carnival," Lee consoled. "You ok to go now?"

"No problem," said Sam, whilst Amy nodded in agreement. They also headed for the door, and Lee wondered whether Sam would take Amy through the same tunnel at the Skate park, or whether he would use a different one.

Finally, Lee turned to the last remaining pair he'd called over. Sarah and Elliott had one of the hardest jobs so far. Kelly and Amy just had to start a ball rolling, and the rest would happen as a matter of course. These two however, had to try and convince people to actually *do* something. Their targets were perfectly free to choose not to do it, and thus put the plan at risk. If it paid off though, it would be a real boon, affecting multiple layers of The Stereotypes' workings.

"So how's it going?"

Elliott and Sarah looked at each other before answering.

"It's been difficult," Sarah admitted. "For the last few days we've spent every bit of spare time hanging out near the staff room – except when that smarmy git's there."

"Conrad," Elliott clarified.

"Yeah, him," Sarah continued. "You know he and his team do practically everything for the lecturers? Marking, planning, you name it. I even heard him saying that he delivered a Geography seminar once when the lecturer was ill."

"For a price, obviously," Elliott said.

"Makes sense," Lee mused. "I guess some lecturers are just as lazy as the students are."

"Anyway, as I was saying. It's been difficult to convince the staff they're overworked when they've got Conrad and his minions ready to take the load off."

"Although they don't all use him," Elliott said, picking up the thread. "Have you encountered Ms Wells? She's vehemently against Conrad Jackson and his cronies. She was quite vocal about it – in fact, I think she's our most secure candidate so far, and not even for the reason we're going for. I think she'll do it to help our actual cause of messing up Conrad's enterprise."

"What about the others?"

"Well, we've done everything we can," Sarah said with a sigh. "Every pigeonhole has a flyer from the ATL in it about the proposed action." She said this last part with quotation fingers – after all, the action was purely fictional, aimed at UCE staff only. The rest of the Association of Teachers and Lecturers knew nothing about it. "Elliott also leaked an email to all the teaching staff that's sure to cause some ripples."

Lee turned to Elliott with a raised eyebrow.

"I basically faked an email from some high up governor I found on the UCE website. It outlines a load of proposed changes to working hours and stuff like that. It's nonsense really, but it's enough to get the staff annoyed."

"The best thing," Sarah continued. "Is that if anybody goes to the Dean, he'll just deny it. But that's exactly what he'd do even if it was real, so we can't lose. If anything, it will just make the lecturers even angrier."

"It's fingers crossed time now, to see how it plays out," Elliott said hopefully.

"But I think Elliott's right about one thing," Sarah concluded. "If a powerhouse like Wells gets on board, then most of the others will follow."

"Well done," Lee said happily. "This all sounds great."

Sarah and Elliott nodded before leaving the room. Lee couldn't help grinning to himself. Everything was coming together nicely.

Interlude – The Meeting Room

Conrad Jackson sat pouting whilst Stephen read the flyer
he'd brought in. He started drumming his fingers anxiously
on the table top, beginning to get more and more frustrated.
Considering he was The Academic, it was certainly taking
Stephen a long time to read.

Eventually, Stephen lowered the piece of paper. "I
don't get it," he said slowly. His cheeks flushed, combining
with his ginger hair and freckles to make it look like he was
actually going to burst into flames. He spoke as if it
physically pained him to admit he didn't get something. "So
the staff might strike, big deal. I mean, yeah it sucks for you.
No staff means no work for you to do, but you're ok." At
this, he nodded his head to one of the whiteboards on which
somebody had drawn out a ranking for the competition.
Conrad was currently fourth, and therefore pretty secure.

"No staff means no work for you too," Conrad
huffed. That was the trouble with these brainiac types – yeah,
they could recite pi to god knows how many decimal places,
but they had absolutely no common sense or logic. "If
there's no staff setting work for the students, what exactly
are you and your team going to do?"

"Ah," Stephen said, brow furrowing. He was currently
sixth in the ranking, and could still slip down into the danger
zone.

"And look at the dates," Conrad said, jamming his
finger onto the page. "That's carnival time. If we're out of
action then, the others are going to get a huge boost ahead of
us. But that's not the worrying part," Conrad continued,

straightening his tie. "This was sent out around the same time as the strike flyers." He handed Stephen a print out of the accompanying email, once again resuming his finger drumming whilst The Academic read.

"They're not going to like this," Stephen surmised.

"It's not real!" Conrad snapped, his voice rising. "Rick hooked me up so I can monitor all the staff communications. Whatever it says on that email, it wasn't sent by the governors."

Stephen looked up, mouth open. "The same happened with The Rag, you know, the article about Sam. That somehow got past Joe."

At that moment, the main door opened and Jud walked in, engrossed with his phone. Conrad and Stephen watched as The Jock made straight for the score chart, adding another £100 to his tally. He was currently sitting in third. As he turned away from the board, his phone chimed.

"Aha!" he yelled after reading the message.

"Good news?" Conrad asked flatly.

"You know that jerk Lee Radley?" Jud enthused. "He told Rebecca that he got transferred for taking a fall for one of his mates, Charlie."

"Brilliant Jud, but there's something more important-"

"But guess what?" Jud asked, cutting across The Staff Liaison. "There's no such person as Charlie at Northern. Or Charles. Just a long list of misdemeanours committed by Radley himself. He's been lying!"

"Wow," Conrad said sarcastically. "People lie, big surprise. But Jud, you really need to hear this."

"I have to go and tell Rebecca," Jud said with a triumphant laugh. Ignoring his colleagues at the table, Jud strode out of the meeting room.

"Well that's just magical," Conrad sighed.

Chapter 16 – Carnival

Lee looked out over the UCE summer carnival, butterflies not just flittering in his stomach, but full-on trying to escape. He was standing on the sixth floor of the John Terrence building, behind the giant C attached to the wall outside. Below him was the quad, which had been transformed over the last couple of days. Streams of bunting were hung between the oaks that stood at each corner, all linking up to a flag pole in the centre of the square. Mounted on the pole were a number of shields, representing the many sports teams of UCE, each one decorated with a mythical creature. There were two concentric squares of stalls and games forming aisles that people could walk around in a loop, as well as two temporary bars set up, one at each end. A stage was set up along the wall opposite the main gates, and Lee had heard there was a pretty decent line up of student and local bands playing later on in the day.

The sun was almost reaching its zenith, the colours of the flags, stalls and streamers at their brightest in anticipation of the carnival opening at noon. As it was, the quad was currently closed off to everyone except those involved, and as Lee watched, he could see people scurrying ant-like between tents, and flaps of canvas rippling as people made last minute preparations within.

Inside John Terrence, the atmosphere was calm; the corridors deserted. Thanks to Sarah and Elliott, the majority of the lecturing staff had been on strike for the last couple of days, and were planning to make it last the rest of the week, effectively crippling Conrad and Stephen's progress in The Stereotypes' competition.

As soon as the carnival opened, Lee would be able to find out if the rest of the initial groundwork had been successful, then put the final phases of the plan into action. By tomorrow at the latest, he was confident that The Stereotypes would be well and truly stuck – unable to compete so the Leader surely had no option but to cancel the whole thing.

Lee checked his watch – it was almost time. He stepped away from the window, the butterflies increasing their ferocity within him. Once down on ground level, he left the block by the back exit, so he could walk around and join the queue at the main gate like everyone else. He had to look like just another carnival visitor, so when the time came, he paid his money and got his wrist stamped before moving into the quad.

Being inside the carnival was completely different to the bird's eye view Lee had seen it from before. All the tents and stalls were open now, each with their own lights, music and smells. Each section was an individual set of senses that drifted outwards so that as you walked along the aisles, you were swirling through a mix of different sensations. Lee pictured it like drops of oil in water, each person that moved between the stalls creating their own swirl.

A burst of bubbles blew across Lee's path, followed by a laughing girl with daisies in her hair. He couldn't help smiling at her happiness, after all, this was the celebration to signify that lectures and seminars were pretty much done. There was now a week of revision (drinking) before exams started.

That was when Lee saw Rick. The Techie was walking along just a few paces in front, hands stuffed into his pockets and head lowered. He was a stark contrast to bubble girl, and

Lee thought he could guess why – he just needed to follow for a bit to make sure.

Rick wove his way through the East side of the quad, popping into stalls to half-heartedly pick up trinkets or leaf through some posters, and Lee was always right behind him. Luckily The Techie seemed so self-absorbed that he didn't look round once.

Just as Lee was beginning to get bored, a group of guys stepped forwards, blocking Rick's path. Lee immediately dropped to one knee, employing the age old shoelace tying delay. As he fumbled with his laces, not really doing anything productive, just moving them around a bit, Lee watched out of the corner of his eye.

"Excuse me," Rick muttered without looking up. The guys didn't move. They were an eclectic mix of friends: one was tall and gangly, acne raging across his pointy face, another was short with long straggly hair and glasses that probably came from the NHS, and the third was squat and fat, like a Buddha statue in baggy jeans. Lee could imagine them all in the Frag-Soc, or whatever it was called.

Buddha leaned in, and Lee had to strain to hear over a spontaneous ukulele chorus that had broken out.

"That upgrade you sold me melted my hard drive," Buddha hissed.

Rick finally looked up. "Yeah," he muttered. "Sorry about that. I'm in the middle of working on a patch, but it will take time. Next upgrade's free, how about that?" From his manner, Lee guessed this wasn't the first complaint he'd had.

Techie? Tick! thought Lee. Amy's bit of code had obviously done its job – Rick's reputation would be damaged, and no one would be likely to go to him for more software now.

"Not good enough, dude," Buddha continued. "Do you have any idea how much stuff I lost? I had three gigs of hentai on there. I want my money back."

Lee finished playing with his laces as Rick fumbled in his pockets for his wallet. The last thing Lee saw was The Techie desperately counting loose change whilst the geeks around him continued to bemoan their gargantuan porn loss.

Next, Lee scanned the rest of the carnival, looking for a particular tent. After a moment, he spotted an array of pink and red hearts sticking out above the height of the surrounding stalls. This was where Rebecca and her enterprise would be based. From the files they'd retrieved from the lair, Rebecca was running some sort of kissing booth. The understanding was that people in the know could pay extra and get extra – Lee wasn't clear on exactly *what* you could pay for or how far you could go, but the whole thing made him shudder slightly. He just hoped that Kelly's part of the plan had been successful so the brothel booth would have to stop.

Lee did feel a little guilty about sabotaging Rebecca's plan, but he'd decided long ago that making her win wasn't the way. They all had to lose equally.

Lee approached the lurid pink tent, cringing slightly at the hearts and cupids that adorned the front. There was a row of six seats behind a counter upon which hung two signs: 'Girls' and 'Boys'. There was the beginnings of a queue forming in front of the tent, but Lee was pleased to see that all the seats were empty.

Earning a look of outrage from one of the fuglies waiting for a smooch, Lee slipped down the side of the tent, peering around the back.

It was like looking at a sleazy calendar brought to life. There was a collection of girls in bikinis and the buffest guys imaginable wearing the smallest shorts. All were tanned, oiled and perfectly presented until you looked at their faces. Lee had to stifle a snigger when he saw that nearly all of them had sores around their mouths. There was the full range, from red welts to cracked, oozing, crusty yellow blotches. Kelly had come through!

"We thought we could just use concealer," one of the bikini girls whined in a typically airheaded voice.

"Are you actually as stupid as you look?" Rebecca appeared through a gap in the bronzed flesh. She was dressed as a burlesque host, all feathers and frills, but the image was tainted by the look of disgust on her face. "How did this happen?"

"Most of us were at Kristian's party the other night," the bikini girl continued, voice catching like she might burst into tears. "We played spin the bottle and..." she trailed off into sobs.

If only they knew the truth, Lee thought, impressed with Kelly's efficiency. He wondered if she had also been at the party, or if she had got them one by one.

"Oh for God's sake!" Rebecca spat, rolling her eyes. "Nobody's going to want to come anywhere near you!"

"Couldn't we like... blindfold them?" one of the pretty boys said, as if coherent speech was a challenge for him.

Rebecca didn't even justify him with an answer, shooting him down with just a narrowing of her eyes. "Go and put some clothes on," she ordered. "We'll have to think of something else."

Job done, Lee grinned. It would take at least another week for their infections to clear up. Rebecca's roster was out of action until after the exam and the end of the competition. He turned to sneak back along the row of tents.

"Lee?"

He stopped mid step, his mind flitting between pivoting on his heel, and the ridiculous option of continuing and pretending he was someone else. He pivoted. Close up, Rebecca looked stunning in a blood red corset and suspenders. He was thankful that Kelly hadn't dosed her too.

"What are you doing here?" she asked.

"I was um… checking to see when the kissing was going to start," he blushed.

"Well, slight problem with that." She waved her hand across the now empty space. "Nobody turned up," she lied, oblivious to the fact that Lee had seen all the kissagrams there a minute ago. "Ooh," she purred. "Jud gave me an important message earlier."

"Was it with his mouth or his fist?" Lee said acidly before he could stop himself.

"That's not funny," Rebecca said, anger flashing across her face for a split second. "Anyway, he's not the only one with flaws. He found out some interesting information. About you."

Lee's heart sank into his feet. This could be it. This could be the end of everything. Jud had somehow discovered the sabotage plan.

"He told me *you* did all the stuff you blamed on Charlie. In fact there's no such person as Charlie at Northern. It was you all along."

"Oh," Lee muttered, relief flooding through his system that he had to conceal.

"Well?" she demanded. "Is it true?"

Lee shuffled his feet. "Yeah."

Rebecca looked at him as if reassessing his character and Lee felt the sudden need to defend himself.

"I don't have the best relationship with my dad," he explained. "I thought that by playing up a bit, it would force him to take notice."

"Understandable," Rebecca said, her expression softening. "Did it work?"

Lee laughed bitterly. "No. I got a letter from Northern saying I was being transferred at my father's request. He didn't even tell me in person."

"Well I'm glad you transferred." She leaned in and kissed him, catching him by surprise, the entire carnival, the plan, The Stereotypes – everything disappearing for that one moment in time when it was just them entwined. She pulled away then whispered in his ear. "I know you'll help me in the end." With that, she slinked out of the tent, leaving Lee with flushed cheeks and the need to wait a moment for his desire to subside before he re-joined the carnival crowds.

Once calmed down and back in the fresh air, Lee wished he could have told Rebecca that he already *was* helping her, but that was all about the heroic aspect wasn't it? It wasn't about the recognition, doing it was enough – that's what Niall would probably say anyway.

Lee took a breath, pride beginning to rise in his chest. Everything they'd planned so far had worked: the staff had gone on strike, ruining Conrad and Stephen's chances, and thanks to different viruses, Rebecca and Rick were also out of the running. The rest would come later.

Checking his watch, Lee made his way to the centre of the quad where the flag pole rose, displaying the team shields with pride. The memorial statue stood off to one side, a couple of girls spinning brightly coloured poi on the grass in front. Further along, Lee spotted the rest of his team sitting on the grass, the beginnings of a pile of empty cans already forming in the centre.

As he approached, Niall looked up. "Are we good?" he asked.

"Oh, we are good," Lee beamed happily. "Did you hear that guys? Thumbs up for later!"

"What do we do until then?" Elliott asked, crunching an empty can and adding it to the heap.

"It's a carnival!" Lee yelled, arms outstretched. "Eat, drink and be merry!"

The assembled group raised their drinks and cheered before splitting up and heading off to explore the festivities. Only Sam hung back.

"Everything ok?" Lee asked.

"When I was at the lair with Amy, I noticed a score chart they're using to track how much money they've collected for the competition."

"Right..."

"Well even if we sabotage everything now," Sam said in a measured voice. "Surely they'll just use the rankings as they stand to decide their winners and losers."

"Ah crap," Lee muttered, his mind already spinning with potential ways around this new barrier.

Sam grinned mischievously. "I was kind of hoping you'd ask me to do something about it."

Lee looked up, a fond smile crossing his face. "You're loving this aren't you?"

"Way more fun," Sam admitted.

"Then, Sam Street," Lee began, officiously clearing his throat. "I would be honoured if you would wreck the shit out of the The Stereotypes scoreboard."

"It would be my pleasure, Mr Radley, sir." Sam bowed with a flourish before vanishing into the crowds.

Lee smiled to himself and cracked a can of his own before sinking onto the grass.

Interlude – The Meeting Room

After leaving Lee, Sam went straight to the Society Corridor. He passed through the cleaner's cupboard and into the meeting room. He was hoping that it would be empty like all the other times he'd snuck in, however this time he was disappointed.

As soon as he opened the door, Emma Blunt looked up from where she was sitting at the table. She was wearing a loose blouse, again with her necklace of flowers and billowing skirt. Of all The Stereotypes, she looked the most like she belonged at the carnival, yet here she was hiding in the secret lair.

"Sam," she called, jumping to her feet. "When did you get out? How are you?"

"Oh you know," The Skater shrugged. "I'm ok. I don't really recommend prison though. Doesn't live up to the hype."

Emma gave him a quick hug whilst he stood there, arms by his sides. "I take it you've heard about the competition?"

"I have indeed," Sam replied wistfully, looking over at the scoreboard on the far wall.

"Yep," Emma said, following his gaze. "That's the shitlist."

"That the only one?" Sam asked, trying to sound as subtle as possible.

"Uhuh," Emma nodded. "Jud wanted to keep it central so people always had to come here personally to update it."

"Rebecca's doing well," Sam said, noting The Cheerleader's second position.

"Yeah," Emma replied with the tiniest hint of jealousy. "She's never been out of the top three."

"Hmm," Sam mused. He was sure Lee had mentioned something about Rebecca being at risk – perhaps he'd heard it wrong. "So," he said, changing tack. "How come you're not at the carnival? I figured you'd be selling beads and shit."

"I'm on my way," she said with a quiet laugh. "I'm just waiting while Michael gets the stuff from the supply room."

"Michael?"

"Yeah, my recruit."

"Ah." Suddenly, an opportunity opened up in Sam's mind. "I've just come from there, it's rammed already."

"It is?" Emma's smoky eyes suddenly flared in panic. "I was hoping to get a good place." She hovered awkwardly for a moment, deliberating. "You think Michael will be ok on his own for a bit?"

"He passed recruitment," Sam reasoned. "I'm sure he's a big boy. But you could always leave him a note just in case."

"Good idea."

Sam couldn't help smiling to himself as Emma scrawled a note explaining where she'd gone, tearing the page from the pad on the desk. She set it carefully in the centre of the table where it was sure to be seen, then she hurried to the carnival with a little wave to Sam as she left.

As soon as he heard the door close, Sam jumped into action. He slipped into the other corridor, past the lounge room that Rick had left the recruits in before. At the end was another door leading to a large storage room. There were shelves and shelves of boxes and crates containing everything all of them could possibly need. Sam peered round the edge of the door, seeing the back of a guy with a stripy jumper. He was whistling to himself as he checked various boxes on the shelf in front of him. There was a small pile of boxes that he'd already decided to take to the carnival.

Easy, Sam thought to himself. Michael was the typical inept guard that you always saw in the movies, busily occupied with some menial task whilst James Bond snuck into the secret base behind his back.

Padding silently back to the meeting room, Sam grabbed Emma's note and crumpled it into his pocket before tearing off another page from the pad and writing his own.

Michael – I had to go ahead to grab a decent pitch. Bring the stuff over when you're ready. Also, just got new instructions. The Leader wants everything from the noticeboard destroyed to maintain secrecy – use the furnace in the generator room.
See you in a bit – Emma

Sam carefully set the note where Emma had put her original, then snuck back out, a huge grin on his face.

Chapter 17 – Breaching The Peace

Evening had drawn in and the carnival was now awash with light. Neon strips wound around everything, flashing in time with the beat of the band jumping around on the stage. Firebrand were the last act of the night, and were the closest thing UCE had to celebrities. Apparently they'd formed at the University and just stuck around after they'd graduated. The lead singer was currently screaming into the microphone whilst jets of flame shot out over the audience. It was a good job that loads of staff were on strike, Lee thought to himself. Otherwise health and safety would have had a fit.

Lee was standing towards the back of the crowd, the seething mass getting tighter and more energetic the closer you got to the stage. He was half-heartedly nodding his head along to the music, but his mind was elsewhere. He was running through the final stages of the plans, his palms sweating. This was the riskiest part not only in terms of getting caught, but also in the fact that he was relying a lot on booze, high spirits, and of course *stereotypes*.

"Are we ready?"

Lee jumped slightly, turning to see Niall standing beside him. He couldn't have said when Niall had appeared. He looked bulkier than usual, and Lee remembered that he was wearing extra clothes in preparation for his part in the plan. Mischief glinted in the other boy's eyes.

"Ok guys," the band's singer yelled. "This is our last song, 'Bastard Hairdryer.'"

"I think this is it," Lee said, almost wishing it weren't true as the band erupted into yet more screaming.

"We'd better get into position then. Good luck."

Before Lee could voice any reluctance, Niall was twisting away through the crowd. Lee took a deep breath and turned towards the flagpole. Luckily, everyone's attention was on the stage, and nobody gave him a second glance as he pulled his hood over his head. This time, he had gone for full on ninja outfit – as black as he could get so that he would hopefully blend into the night sky.

He reached the pole and looked up, the point stretching into the darkness, the shields only faint outlines in the night.

This is going to work, this is going to work, he repeated in his head as he coiled the draw-rope round his hand and began to shimmy upwards, the pole clamped between his knees. When he was about halfway up, he reached the first of the team shields, giving him more hand and footholds to get him to the top.

Finally, nestled amongst the shields clustered around the pole, Lee reached into his pocket for a Sharpie and carefully reached for the closest shield - a golden dragon curled around a volleyball, set on a sky blue background.

The music from the stage rose to a crescendo then exploded into silence with a final blast of flame.

"Thank you and goodnight," the Firebrand singer called across the crowd.

Lee hurled the shield into the audience and then huddled behind the others still attached to the pole. Clinging on with one arm wrapped around the pole, he fished his phone from his jacket pocket and sent a group message that he had written in advance.

Go

With a loud thud, the shield landed on the concrete and cracked in two, the crowd spreading out to form a circle around the projectile. There was a second or two of stunned silence as people took in what lay before them: a broken Dragons shield with the slogan 'Centaurs Rule' scrawled across it.

As Lee hoped, he could soon hear the cries of dissent from those loyal to the UCE Volleyball team, as well as protests from those who supported the Centaurs, maintaining that they had nothing to do with it. Lee smiled as the first shoves were dealt, distracting those who had turned to stare up at the flag pole, trying to work out how the shield had fallen with such ferocity. He knew that at the same time, after receiving his text, Dan would be busy smashing up the equipment in the printroom, and James would be similarly decimating the art supplies, thus ruining Joe and Emma's cogs in The Stereotype machine. With the strike, and the brawl developing in the quad, Lee doubted the acts of vandalism would be noticed until the morning.

"Centaurs rule! Centaurs for the win!"

Lee looked out across the sea of tents to see Niall on the far side of the quad. He was wearing a blue and gold Centaurs training kit, screaming football propaganda at the top of his voice.

"Fuck you!" he yelled once he'd gained the attention of enough carnival goers. Niall ran to the nearest table, stacked high with bottles of booze waiting to be stocked into the nearby bar. With all his might, he heaved the table over, sending the bottles smashing to the ground in a fizzing bubbling froth.

Before anybody could react, Niall sprinted full pelt behind the nearest tent. From his vantage point up the flag pole, Lee could see Niall frantically pulling off the Centaurs top and shorts, revealing a white jersey with padded

481

shoulders and a giant red Gryphon on the front, complete
with matching red shorts – the uniform of the UCE Lacrosse
team.

He popped out on the other side of the tent, jumping
up and down like a crazed ape. "Gryphons could take
Centaurs any day!" he cried, before yanking the tent over to
the side so the flaps of canvas billowed into the path and
covered his escape. Lee saw him already pulling the jersey
over his head as he ran, and Lee knew he was wearing as
many different uniforms as he could fit. Just as they'd hoped,
more and more people were getting involved in the scrap
that was quickly getting out of control. The Dragons and
their supporters were after the Centaurs for their sacrilege
against the shield and the alcohol, whereas the Centaurs were
busy defending themselves against the Dragons, whilst at the
same time trying to catch the Gryphons for their slanderous
comments, and all the while Niall was running around
causing havoc and bringing a new team into the fray with
each outfit change.

Lee took the chance amongst the confusion to climb
down the flagpole, jumping the last few feet to the concrete.
He hopped over a couple of cheerleaders who were pulling
hair and scratching each other whilst rolling across the floor
and then ran for the gates, ducking under a folding chair
being swung by a gigantic brute in a muscle vest.

Once out of the gates, Lee didn't look back until he
reached the shadows of Van Ristell Hall – their prearranged
meeting rendezvous point. He saw that Dan and James were
already waiting there, leaning against one of the giant
ornamental flower urns that marked the entrance. Dan was
grinning insanely, whilst James seemed to be covered in
paint.

"That. Was. Awesome!" James said as Lee approached, chest heaving and panting for breath. Lee noticed that even James' hair had flecks of green paint in it.

"The Stereotypes certainly won't be printing anything for a while," Dan smiled, before proceeding to recount precisely what he'd done to each bit of equipment in great detail.

After a few moments, the battle cries coming from the quad were drowned out by the wailing of police sirens. Lee looked up to see a pair of patrol cars race past in a flash of blue and red.

"Time to leave," James said. "I'll see you at yours in the morning." He turned and disappeared into the shadows.

Dan and Lee were also beginning to trudge across the grass when they heard a call from behind.

"Wait for me!"

They turned to see Niall running towards them, wearing nothing but a pair of black swimming trunks, a turquoise Hydra curling across the hip. He caught up with them, leaning hard against Lee's shoulder as he regained his breath.

"I'm not going to ask what you did in that outfit," Lee muttered with a smile.

"Don't let Kelly see you in those," Dan chuckled, pointedly looking down to where the tiny trunks outlined pretty much everything Niall had to offer. Niall caught his gaze, and reddening intensely, he hastily moved his hands over his crotch.

"Do you think it worked?" he asked.

Lee looked around, cocking his head and listening to the sounds of multiple cases of resisting arrest. "Yes my friends," he nodded. "I think we're good."

Chapter 18 – The Morning After

Lee awoke, staring at the ceiling as usual. There was something about the ceiling that seemed to prepare him for the day ahead, as if the uneven pattern of the nobbly artex could somehow contain the answers to all the day's potential dilemmas.

A light snoring drifted up from the floor, where Niall was lying on his front across a load of cushions that Lee had snatched from the sofa in the living room. The blanket had rolled off and Niall was stretched out, only the miniscule Hydra trunks covering his behind. That had been the major flaw in Niall's plan: in wearing all the different sports uniforms, he'd forgotten to keep any of his own clothes. Understandably, he'd not wanted to do the walk of shame alone in the middle of the night, and seeing as he would have been coming back to Lee's flat the next morning anyway, Lee had let him crash on the floor.

Gingerly tiptoeing around Niall's shoulders, Lee stepped over to the wardrobe and pulled out a t-shirt. After slipping it on, he scanned the rest of the contents for something suitable for Niall. He chose a simple pair of boardies, and was deliberating which top he could sacrifice for a couple of days when a garish flap of material caught his eye from underneath a pile of crumpled shorts discarded at the bottom of the cupboard. As he retrieved it and shook it out, he realised it was the hideous emergency shirt that Dan had brought for him before their trip to the Union. Perfect.

He left the clothes along with a towel in a folded pile next to Niall's head before grabbing a quick shower and then heading to the front room.

Sarah was sitting at the table, her laptop open in front of her. On his way to the kettle, Lee saw that her browser was open on the UCE Intranet, and every few minutes, she was hitting refresh.

"Anything?" Lee asked.

"Not yet," Sarah replied. "But it's still early."

"Tea?"

"Win."

Whilst Lee went about making the tea, Sarah continued alternating between the Intranet and some cheesy gossip site. Just as the kettle was boiling, the buzzer went and Sarah jumped up to answer. When she returned, she was accompanied by Dan, Elliott and James. The boys looked tired, stubble crawling across their jawlines, but Elliott's eyes were still glinting with excitement despite the early hour.

"Doing the tea?" Dan asked. "Good man. It's exhausting work, smashing shit up."

"I can't believe you guys had so much fun last night," Elliott said with a hint of disappointment. "All I got to do was talk to the teaching staff."

"Which worked fantastically, by the way," Lee said over the whistling of the kettle.

Sarah gave him a nod of thanks before hitting refresh again. "Still nothing," she muttered.

Lee set a bottle of milk and a bag of sugar on the table before passing out the mugs of tea. James immediately grabbed one and clamped his hands around the mug, breathing the scent in almost reverently.

"Got one of those for me?"

Lee looked up to see Amy leaning against the door frame. She'd somehow found the time to put a flourish of dark streaks through her hair, and her lipstick was a deep carmine.

"Sure," Lee said with a smile, returning to pour another cup. Amy sidled round the table to sit opposite Sarah, whilst the boys had comfortably slipped into a conversation about the latest sports results. As Lee leant back against the worktop watching the three guys chatting and laughing, he couldn't help smiling warmly. Although Dan was a jock, Elliott was the unmistakable film geek and James was the quiet one, they'd all effortlessly settled in with each other like they were old friends. They were undeniably their own set of stereotypes, but they were united through common goals and friendship, rather than selfish money-grabbing and ruthless competing. Lee couldn't picture Jud Hunter engaging in such an absorbing conversation with his fellow Stereotypes.

"Ugh," Kelly grunted as she entered the room, wrapped in a fluffy dressing gown.

"Fancy a brew?" Lee asked.

"Don't be stupid," Kelly responded disdainfully. "Tea is for losers. Hair of the dog, mate." She pulled her hip flask out of the folds of flannel before taking a sip amongst a round of cheering and hooting from the boys.

At that moment, Niall appeared, hair pressed against his scalp and skin glistening. In the Hawaiian shirt and board shorts, he looked like he'd just stepped off the beach. He shook his head like a dog, sending droplets of shower water sprinkling onto the carpet.

Dan started laughing hysterically as he recognised the shirt.

"No offence dude, but you look like Gordon Tracy," Elliott said with a grin.

"At least I'm not John," Niall countered, seamlessly picking up the pop culture reference. "Stuck in space all day, I bet his life is totally boring."

"Probably just jacks off all the time," James chipped in with sly smile.

"Yeah," Dan roared, cheeks burning. The laughter had brought tears to his eyes. "It's like 'Sorry hurricane victims or whatever, International Rescue can't help right now, I'm busy at the moment.'"

"Eurgh, this control panel is all sti-"

"Update!" Sarah called, cutting through the banter. The boys stopped giggling and straightened up, Dan sniffling guiltily.

"Well?" Lee prompted, leaning forwards anxiously. Sarah's face remained inscrutable. "What does it say?"

Sarah cleared her throat before reading from the screen, all eyes fixed on her. "Following the events at last night's UCE Summer Carnival, and the numerous complaints received as a result, we hereby announce that all student activities, including Societies, Parties, Sports Fixtures and Rallies will be discontinued for the remainder of the year. This includes any gatherings in Halls, as well as off-campus Student Housing Properties. In accordance with sub-section 7 of the Universities Charter, Campus Security will be exercising their right to enter any Student Property suspected of breaching these restrictions. Blah blah blah, E Saunders – some woman from UCE." Sarah looked up, a pensive expression on her face. "That's good right?"

"It's the best we could have hoped for," Lee confirmed, at which Niall jumped forward to give him an awkward fist bump. "Whilst they'll never be able to stop absolutely every party, it will be a big enough dent to mess things up for Jud and Sam's team too."

"Where is Sam?" Amy asked, looking around the room as if The Skater might have snuck in whilst everyone was focused on Sarah. He hadn't been seen since his trip to destroy the score chart.

"Would you believe, he's been called to a Stereotypes meeting," Lee said with a chuckle. "He said it would look suspicious if he didn't turn up."

"Makes sense," James reasoned. "He'll be ok won't he?"

"I'm sure he'll be fine – he knows the inner workings better than any of us, remember." Lee paused before continuing. He'd been gearing up to make a big leader-like speech, and now seemed like the perfect moment, but he was worried it would sound cheesy. Making plans and giving orders was easy because there was a purpose – a mission to complete – but this was different, it was a show of emotion in front of a group of people that really despite everything, Lee didn't know all that well.

As if reading Lee's mind, Dan started banging his now empty mug onto the fake marble counter that lined the kitchen wall. "Speech! Speech!"

Feeling his cheeks begin to burn, Lee moved to the open space in front of the table. "I just want to say well done," he began sheepishly. "You've all done excellently and I think we've done something good. The Stereotypes will have to stop their stupid competition, and maybe, just maybe this will give everyone else the break they need to realise that they don't need to rely on The Stereotypes for stuff. They might be able to break away."

"Not to mention you'll probably get the girl," Sarah said with a wink. Despite Lee trying to hide it, everyone had soon realised that this all led back to Rebecca in the end.

"Well yeah," Lee laughed. "I'm a *stereotypical* guy. What can I do? Anyway, I just wanted to finish by saying thank you. None of you had to help me with this, but you've gone beyond the measure to do so. So from the bottom of my heart, thanks."

Dan erupted into a round of applause, the others following suit. Lee looked around the room, certain that he'd made a solid a group of friends for the rest of his time at UCE. Except Kelly wasn't clapping.

"What's wrong?" Lee asked, heart sinking. Had he forgotten something crucial?

"Are you kidding?" Kelly said, a look of outrage flashing across her face. "Parties have been cancelled! What am I going to do now?"

Lee looked at her, horrified, before she burst into raucous laughter which soon spread to the boys like wildfire. Before long, everyone was joining in and Lee leaned back once more, contented.

Interlude – The Meeting Room

Michael Wheeler stood before the conference table, which
was full. All of The Stereotypes were watching him, barely
disguised vehemence pouring out of them. He looked to
Emma for support, but she just glared at him. Even the
other new recruits, Shannon and Brendan avoided his gaze.

"The note said to destroy it, I swear," Michael
murmured, looking over his shoulder at the empty
noticeboard. Before the carnival, he'd taken everything down
and burned it in the incinerator like he'd been told.

At the head of the table, Jud seethed. "Get out," he
ordered so low that his lips barely moved.

With a jump of fright and a whimper, Michael
practically fled out of the room.

"That's it?" Stephen The Academic said, mouth open
in wonder at Jud's leniency. "You're just going to let him go?
I thought you'd deck him."

"I think we have more important things to worry
about," Joe reasoned. He looked over to the notice board.
Yesterday it had been the focus point because it held the fate
of one of them in the competition scores. Now it drew their
attention because it signified the hopelessness of their
predicament. The game couldn't continue, and they couldn't
use their previous scores. There was no way to see who
would have to pay the price at the end – and yet somebody
had to otherwise they would all fail their degrees. As Joe
looked around the table, he couldn't help but picture each
member's wealthy connections, each of them oddly wearing
a sinister look of disapproval. Failure was not an option for

any of them, even him. His mother was a once famous soap actress - how would it look if the son of Serena Nicholls, star of the small screen, failed Uni?

"I just don't get it," Rick mused. "Yeah the noticeboard was down to Emma's twatty recruit, but everything else is just bad timing, right?"

"Maybe it's Lee?" Rebecca said, giving Jud a knowing look. "He promised he would help..."

"How is this helping?" Stephen wailed. "Instead of one of us being screwed, we're all in the shit. Yeah, big improvement."

"Lee Radley did *not* do this," Jud snapped menacingly. "He couldn't have."

"What about the Leader?" Conrad asked.

"Why would the Leader sabotage his own business?"

"I meant that we should ask him for help," the Staff Liaison sighed. He'd never heard The Stereotypes referred to as a business before, but in the end he supposed that's what it was. A slice of their profits always went to the Leader, so he reasoned it must be a lucrative deal to keep going. Well now they were screwed, he hoped the Leader's business model had a contingency plan.

Conrad sat back, taking his glasses off to polish them with his sleeve. With them off, the faces around the table became a blurred mess of colours, but he liked to think that his hearing somehow improved whilst his eyes degenerated, like Daredevil. Everyone was calling out theories or suggestions, shooting down and stomping all over the opinions of everyone else. Some were still advocating Lee, whilst others were still trying to convince Jud to message the Leader. As Conrad listened, the words began to overlap and blend into each other.

"Lee!"

"Leader!"

"Lee!"

"Leader!"

And suddenly a thought ignited in his mind, so strong that it eclipsed everything else — a memory of a visit to Dr Stroud's Business class. Suddenly excited, Conrad caught Jud's eye and nodded towards the other room.

Excitement bubbling away inside, Conrad led Jud into the den, leaving the others to argue out their frustrations over the conference table.

Chapter 19 – The Calm

A week had passed since the UCE carnival, and as Lee had hoped, there had been a distinct lack of Stereotype action. Whereas before, the quad had been filled with teamsters trying to hawk the services of the secret group, the last few times Lee had traversed it, he had remained unaccosted. Most of the signs from the Union toilets had been removed, and things were back to normal.

Lee was currently stretched out on the grass, can in hand. Kelly sat beside him, trailing her hand lazily through the daisies and buttercups. Lee had recently finished his only Business exam, and Kelly had also just come out of one of her own. For both of them, it was their final exam and marked the end of the current year at UCE. Soon, the flat would begin to empty as people went back to their various parts of the country for the summer. Lee thought of his own holiday arrangements. No doubt he would be allowed the use of one of his dad's townhouses, although he doubted it would be the one his father was actually residing in at the time. Lee imagined that Sir Michael could think of nothing worse than eight weeks with his son. Maybe Lee would get in touch with some of his old mates from Northern – if they hadn't forgotten about him that is.

"Well," Kelly said. "You've certainly shaken things up since you got here."

"Yeah," Lee laughed. "Not exactly what I had planned. All I really wanted was to just settle in – maybe talk to my dad a bit more now we're in the same half of the country."

"And instead you saved the world."

"Ha, something like that."

"Do you think it worked?"

"Well," Lee mused. "We certainly ruined their contest. I guess it all depends on what the Leader decides to do."

"Have you seen Rebecca?"

"No." That was slightly annoying. She'd come to Lee for help, and whilst he hadn't actually publicly taken the credit for what happened, Rebecca could have given him an update. As it was, Lee couldn't help feeling a little bit used.

"Maybe she's just waiting for it all to end," Kelly reasoned. "When's the exam they're all supposed to go to?"

"This afternoon," Lee replied quietly.

"What?" Kelly smacked him in the arm. "What are you doing here? You should go and see what's going on!"

"What for?" Lee protested. "They'll just be sitting in the exam hall. I won't be able to talk to anybody."

"Still," Kelly said thoughtfully. "If anything is going to happen, it's going to be there."

Interlude – The Exam Hall

Jud Hunter peered through the grimy window of the exam
hall. The glossy wood tiled floor was covered in individual
desks set into rows and columns. Despite being able to seat
at least three hundred students, he could see that only the
front row of eight seats had paper on them.

A sense of dread was lying like a knot at the bottom of
the Jock's stomach. They had no idea what awaited them
once inside the hall, after all, it was an exam that the Leader
had made up, and one that they had no hope of passing. It
had been made clear that the only way any of them would
pass this year was through a death during the exam.

He turned around and scanned his companions. All
looked similarly nervous, but there was one face missing.

"Where's Rebecca?"

Nothing but shrugs.

"Ugh," Jud growled. "I'm going to look for her."

"But the exam starts in ten minutes!" Stephen cried,
the thought of missing an exam absolutely abhorrent to him.

Shrugging off the Academic's protests, Jud strode
away along the wall of the exam building. He already had a
rough idea of where Rebecca would be – she had a spot she
liked to go to think and be alone. Soon enough, he was
climbing the metal staircase up to the roof of the hall, his
feet clanging against the steel.

About half way up, Jud's phone vibrated. Pausing on
the stairs, he answered the call.

"It's blank!" Stephen shrieked on the other end of the
line. "The exam's blank!"

"What?"

"The invigilators aren't here yet. Emma snuck in for a look. It's just blank paper! What are we going to do?"

"Just go in, I'll sort it I promise." Jud hung up, a cold lump forming in his chest. He'd read the Leader's message just like everybody else, but still he'd clung to the possibility that the exam might have been passable. Obviously not. He continued up the stairs.

As he'd expected, Rebecca was in the small tower that rose up in one corner. She had her back to him, her hair blowing over her face as she leaned over, staring down at the concrete below. True to her designation, she was wearing her blue and gold cheerleading outfit, even now.

"You're going to miss the exam," Jud said harshly, not in the mood for any of is ex girlfriend's silliness. If the outcome hinged on them all being in the room below, then he was prepared to drag the Cheerleader down the stairs if he had to, even for a blank exam.

"I'm not going," Rebecca said, finally turning around, her lips pressed firmly into a pout.

"Yes you fucking are. I'm not risking anything because of you."

"No Jud," she protested, her voice cracking. "There's no contest any more. The Leader is going to kill one of us, I'm sure of it."

"Ah," Jud said, conviction rising in his voice. "I've got a theory about that. I think I know who the Leader is."

"What?" Rebecca said, her eyes suddenly widening.

"Think about it," Jud continued. "All of this started at the same time as Lee Radley arrived. I already told you that he faked the reason for his transfer from Northern. I found out something else too. You know that his dad is the boss of Radley Incorporated? Well it turns out he's one of those hard ass 'earn your own way' types – he's even said it in interviews and stuff. He doesn't give Lee any money at all, so where does Lee get it from? Also, Conrad heard Lee presenting in Business and you know what his plan was? To form a small test group that were completely separate from the management that earned all the money. He even went on about setting up multiple observation groups. Don't you see? That's what The Stereotypes are – a focus group under observation! I'm telling you, Lee Radley is our mysterious Leader. And there's no way he'd hurt you."

To the Jock's surprise, Rebecca laughed.

"You couldn't be more wrong," she spat with disdain.

"What are you on about?" Jud asked in confusion.

"Honestly, all this time hearing you call the Leader Him and He, when you've been completely misled. You never even considered the possibility that the Leader could be female."

"You know who it is?"

"It's me, you hopeless prick!"

Jud stood gaping at her, mouth open. "But…?"

"You know my father went to UCE."

Jud nodded. Just like every other member, Rebecca was well connected. Her father was a UCE graduate, contributing a lot of money to the new library a couple of years ago.

"Well he founded The Stereotypes," Rebecca said proudly. "Back in those days, secret societies were all the rage. It went from strength to strength until it became what it is today, with me in charge."

Jud could feel his temper rising, colour flooding his cheeks. "Then what the fuck is all this about?" He waved his hand over the roof. Looking down through the skylight, he could just make out the others filtering into the exam hall and taking their places.

"I spoke to my father, learned what the old group was like."

"That stupid photo," Jud muttered, pieces falling together inside his dense head.

"I realised that compared to them, we were a disgrace. Hence the recruitment drive. The contest was a way of filtering out the weak links – Emma was right about that."

"Putting aside the fact that you're a lying, conniving bitch," Jud said, clenching his fists. "Why did you make the contest fatal? Why have it end like that?"

"Ah well," Rebecca shrugged innocently. "That was down to you. You beat Lee up. You needed to be punished."

"You punished everyone because of what I did?"

"Did I?" Rebecca leaned over the edge, peering through the skylight. "Look at them - do they look punished?"

"Sam got arrested."

"True – he was Lee's mentor. I assumed he was in on it. I'll admit I was wrong about that, but someone bailed him out so no harm done."

"You put out that fake Rag article about him?"

Rebecca nodded smugly.

Jud stepped forward confidently. "Well your little plan failed. The contest got ruined so now nobody can die. Whatever your intentions, you screwed everyone in the end anyway. Nobody's going to pass the exam. Nobody's going to pass the year."

"Maybe," Rebecca smiled sweetly. "Maybe not."

"Pah," Jud scoffed. "You can't kill me."

"I don't need to," Rebecca said, looking over the ledge of the building and smiling at something she saw down below. "I just need to make you angry."

Chapter 20 – Deconstructing Stereotypes

Lee smiled when he saw Rebecca up on the roof of the exam hall. She leaned over briefly, as if she'd wanted him to see her. After Kelly's words on the quad, the notion had grown and grown in Lee's mind until he'd had to excuse himself and jog across campus to the exam hall.

He checked his watch, brow furrowing as he saw that the exam was due to start at any moment. What was Rebecca doing up on the roof when she should be inside? Maybe the exam had been cancelled? But no. Lee could clearly see Sam's blonde mop sitting at a desk near the window.

That was when he heard a scream from above. Rebecca was in trouble! Lee sprinted round the corner to where the steps led up to the roof. The whole staircase shook as he took them two at a time, emerging onto the roof seconds later, panting.

Jud had Rebecca by the shoulders and was shaking her violently, her neck jolting back and forth.

"Get off her!" Lee shouted, advancing.

Jud turned to face him, eyes wild. "Fuck off Radley," he spat, jabbing Lee sharply in the chest. Lee tumbled backwards onto the grit covered surface amidst the splintered edging. "This is between me and her. Stay out of things you don't understand." With that, Jud turned his attention once more to the cowering Cheerleader.

Vision full of sky, Lee fumbled around, his hand skittering across the gravel until his fingers closed around part of the wooden edgework. Years of rain and wind had made the wood weak, and a length broke off in his hand. He scrambled to his feet, brandishing the timber like a bat.

Lee saw Jud with one hand on Rebecca's throat. The Jock was screaming at her, his voice snatched away on the breeze so that the meaning was lost to Lee's ears. Rebecca was grabbing at his arm, twice as thick as her own – it was futile.

"Jud!" Lee yelled furiously before swinging the wood into the side of Jud's head. There was a sickening crack and the timber splintered into jagged strips hanging loosely from the handle end that Lee gripped.

Rebecca raised both hands to her mouth as Jud released her. He turned slowly to Lee, a trickle of blood running from his temple. Splinters of wood were matted into his hair, rapidly soaking with scarlet. As Lee watched in horror, the corner of Jud's mouth dropped, the eye on the side Lee had struck rolling up into his skull.

"You...don't..." the Jock slurred. With a look of disbelief on his ruined face, Jud tumbled over the parapet. There was a split second of silence before the Jock crashed through the skylight. His body plummeted into the exam hall amidst a rain of glass. Screams poured up through the jagged hole before the agonising crunch of splintering wood and bones as Jud slammed into the desks below.

Chapter 21 – Pass And Fail

Lee stood paralysed. He was staring down through the skylight into the exam hall. Jud gazed emptily back up at him, body twisted amongst shards of glass and smashed desks. A ring of overturned chairs surrounded him, as well as a growing crowd of Stereotypes and exam invigilators. As he watched, someone held up a mobile phone, camera clicking to catch Lee's guilt.

The flash of the camera jolted Lee out of his stupor, and he stumbled away from the ledge. He turned to where Rebecca was watching him, a blank expression glazing her eyes. All of this had been for her, and now Lee couldn't even read a single mote of gratitude on her face.

"Um," Lee began, trying to clear his mind. Every time he blinked, he saw Jud's face going over the edge. "You should go down."

"What?"

"In all the confusion, people won't realise you weren't there from the start. If you go down now, you should still get a pass."

"What about you?"

"It's too late for me," Lee sighed, thinking back to the cameraphone. "They saw it was me. Now hurry before someone comes up here. You need to be in that exam hall."

Rebecca nodded and moved to the stairs. Hovering with one foot over the first step, she turned back, her pleated cheerleading skirt rippling. "Lee?"

He raised an eyebrow.

"Thanks." Then she vanished in a flash of blue and gold.

Lee watched the empty space she'd occupied for a couple of seconds. The space between the railings opened up into the sky, the first hints of cloud beginning to form as the afternoon drew on. He sat down, leaning against the concrete ledge that surrounded the perimeter of the parapet. His mind was a daze, constantly flitting between Jud's fall and Rebecca's departure. Thanks. That was it. Surely, *stereotypically*, she would have offered to stay behind with him – to take the fall together, but no. That would have been too 'romance movie'. All they'd shared was a couple of nights of lust, nowhere near enough to base a relationship on.

Sirens rose from below, and Lee soon heard the screeching arrival of a number of vehicles. He thought about leaning over to see what was going on, but he suddenly felt drained of energy. What was the point? He couldn't help feeling cheated, especially after the elation of seeing the sabotage plan come together so perfectly. He'd done what he set out to do hadn't he? He'd stopped The Stereotypes' competition and saved Rebecca – what he hadn't bargained on was the price. Lee thought he could get away with it, but now he was a killer – something far worse than the reputation of any Stereotype. Nobody gets out for free.

The first of the police officers appeared at the top of the stairway. He paused, eyeing Lee warily as if he was unsure how much resistance he was going to meet. Unmoving from his position against the wall, Lee obviously posed no threat whatsoever. The officer stepped up onto the roof, flicking his cuffs out as he approached.

"You're not going to try anything, right kid?"

Lee shook his head blankly, allowing the officer to cuff his hands behind his back. The policeman helped him to his feet before gently guiding him down the stairs.

The next few hours passed in a blur for Lee. There was the descent into the sea of gawping faces and flashing cameras before being pushed into the back of a police car. Lee had tried to spot Rebecca in the crowd of curious onlookers, but he couldn't find her. Hadn't she even stuck around long enough to see what happened to him?

After that, there was a seemingly endless amount of waiting around in rooms of increasing gloom and depression. Lee hadn't seen this side of the police station when he'd come to bail Sam, and he felt an explicable pang of sadness for The Skater, even though it was Lee's turn now.

Lee had filled out numerous forms, and he had also repeated his story at least five times to five different people. He'd kept it simple – saying that he'd seen Jud and Rebecca grappling on the roof. There'd been no point denying the fact that he'd hit Jud, but at least he'd got the point across that he was trying to save Rebecca. He definitely hadn't meant for Jud to fall. He thought about telling them about The Stereotypes, but Lee realised that it would do far more harm than good. Not only would all The Stereotypes come under fire, so would everyone that had helped Lee's sabotage plan – and considering he'd organised that himself, it wouldn't help his case against premeditation.

Each time he told the same story, he was met by the same blank stare as the listener made notes. Lee guessed they weren't allowed to show any signs of judgement, but at least a nod of understanding or something to show they could see where he was coming from would have helped. He wondered if each time he told it, he was progressing up or down the ranks of police.

Eventually, they seemed to tire of Lee's story, and left him alone in a grim looking room, bare except for a couple of plastic chairs and a shoddy folding table. There wasn't even the standard panel of glass that was a mirror for Lee, but a window for whoever was on the other side. Instead, the only thing that broke up the featureless walls was a difference in the shade of green it was painted. Around waist height, the olive colour changed to more of a mint green, making it look as if the whole room was sinking into sludge.

After what felt like hours of thumb twiddling, the door opened and another officer, female this time, cleared her throat.

"Someone here to see you," she announced in monotone.

Lee's eyes lit up as Rebecca Carter stepped into the room. She had changed into jeans and a jumper, but she looked exhausted.

"Lee," she breathed, clamping him in a hug that set his heart skipping. "They grilled me for hours!" She released him from her embrace and then moved around the tiny table to sit opposite him. The police officer watched them grimly for a moment before stepping outside and closing the door.

"What did you tell them?" Lee asked quietly, mentally crossing his fingers.

"I told them exactly what happened."

Lee's heart started beating even faster as he thought through all the truths Rebecca could have spilled.

"Jud was going to hurt me, and you came to the rescue. Everything else was an accident."

Lee let out a breath. She hadn't mentioned The Stereotypes, or any of the sabotage or anything that could get her into trouble.

"In fact," she continued. "You kind of did me a favour, getting rid of Jud. He wasn't the best boyfriend in the world."

"You make it sound like I did it on purpose," Lee said, an uneasy feeling growing in his stomach. "Or worse, that you're glad Jud fell."

Rebecca smiled sweetly. "Well it is a pretty big coincidence," she said. "You turning up like that. It was as if you knew exactly where I'd be."

"Only because…" Lee faltered, pieces beginning to click in his mind. "Because you showed me." He thought back to the night at the Union, where Rebecca had insisted on taking him up to the roof, showing him her special place. And then she'd slept with him. Had it really been that simple? That one event that had secured everything? That night would make Jud angry enough to get violent, whilst at the same time ensuring Lee would do anything he could to protect Rebecca. "You…" Lee gasped, his mouth hanging open with disbelief.

"Like I said," Rebecca said with a flicker of eyelids. "A big coincidence."

She stood up, all the exhaustion and trauma she'd been displaying sloughing off her like an old snakeskin. Lee cast his eyes around the room, searching for a camera, or microphone or anything that could have recorded the hints The Cheerleader had dropped. There was nothing.

"Goodbye quirky," she laughed before swanning out of the door.

Lee jumped to his feet to follow as the officer reappeared.

"Someone else," she muttered, halting Lee in his tracks. All the sudden anger that had flared up at Rebecca melted away as a shadow filled the doorway a split second before Sir Michael Radley stepped into view.

He was wearing an immaculate white suit, his silver hair swept back into a lion's mane around his head. Lee couldn't help rolling his eyes when he spotted that his father was holding an actual cane, gripping it so tightly that Lee could see the tendons popping in his father's knuckles.

Lee fell back into his seat, searching his father's face for any sign of emotion. He thought about telling him everything, about The Stereotypes, about Rebecca, about why he got himself kicked out of Northern, but he couldn't.

When faced with the man he'd craved the attention of for so long, he was suddenly rendered speechless.

"Are you going to bail me out?" Lee managed after a minute. Whatever the amount ended up as, it would not make so much as a dent in Sir Michael's funds. "They haven't charged me yet, but it's probably going to be manslaughter," Lee continued, a tear forming in the corner of his eye as he said it out loud.

Sir Michael shook his head in disgust, looking down at his son with contempt. He turned and walked out.

"Dad?" Lee cried, the tear finally falling. "Dad?" After everything, this was the worst. Any amount of punishment could have been tempered by acknowledgement from his father, yet here it was, denied. "Dad!"

Epilogue – Cellmates

Lee pulled at the sleeve of his grey jumpsuit. It seemed to have been designed with maximum discomfort in mind, as it was tight in all the wrong places, yet hung loose in the most embarrassing areas. Despite keeping himself fairly trim, the jumpsuit made him feel like a sumo wrestler stuffed into a leotard.

The guard that was marching him along the corridor had one hand firmly gripped around Lee's upper arm, steering him along. They passed rows and rows of cells, and Lee couldn't help staring into each one through the open hatches in the doors. It was the same morbid fascination that kept people staring into the wards of a hospital – Lee was dreading the kind of company he would be forced to keep, and was anxiously searching out a face that didn't scream child killer at first glance.

"Almost there, Radley," the guard said, with what Lee imagined to be a hint of smug satisfaction.

Lee gulped, looking into the nearest cell. A bald head leered out at him, shrunken features, a pale cracked mouth and too few teeth suggesting years of drug abuse. As Lee passed, to his horror, the gaunt man blew him a kiss.

"I bet you're good with those lips," he croaked, before cackling with hoarse laughter.

Lee jumped back, colliding with the guard's solid chest. Despite chuckling to himself, the guard didn't break stride, nor let go of Lee's arm. They walked on for another few paces in silence, before Lee could take it no more.

"Please," he begged, squirming in the guard's iron grip. "Who am I in with? It's not anyone... like *that* is it? I've not done anything near as bad as most of these guys."

"A criminal's a criminal," the guard said flatly, causing Lee's knees to shake. "But don't worry. As it happens, you'll be in with a fellow student. You've got quite a bit in common – maybe you two know each other?"

Lee racked his brain as they continued towards the end of the corridor, but he couldn't think of who his cellmate could be.

"Here we are then," the guard said happily.

Lee peered through the hatch to see a plain cell with two low beds, rough blankets draped over thin mattresses. There was a tiny window set high in the wall, casting a rectangle of dull grey light onto the tiled floor. Sat huddled on one of the beds, knees drawn up, was a skinny guy with scruffy blonde hair and wide eyes. His few personal effects were laid out in geometric shapes on the blanket in front of him.

"Lee Radley," the guard announced as he unlocked the door and pushed it open. "Meet Jimmy Hale."

COMING SOON
SHARDS

The Gods have delivered their Sufferance.
All that remains are shards of memory – broken remnants of lost worlds.
The Elements have no choice but to try and piece these shards together, to work out what happened, what they've lost, and what to do next.

ACKNOWLEDGEMENTS

Nichala, Miguel, Lexie and Little Jess – UCE belongs to you this time around

Hannah Gadd – This is the voice of The Beautiful People. We know that you can hear us…

Ms Wells – I know I make you out to be a battleaxe, but it's hero worship, honest!

Ross – The only one that dared. Never again.

Smith – Don't think, just do it – you're a daddy now!

The Boys Of B5 – We never did get that hockey set back. Also, the mouldy race would have been awesome if the cleaners hadn't confiscated it

Pigeon – Smell the ozone

The Gs – Thanks for being on the message board

Liam, Nik, Mark and Dan – Fellow Drink Olympians

Bunty and Cassie – Cheers for proofing!

Trigger Street – Who's laughing now?

The Current 250 – Victory is yours

The Kenches – For not grassing up my vandalism

Cassie – Cheers for generally bigging me up in the USA

Pete – Red Red Red Red Red Red Red Red Red Red Red

Universities everywhere that play assassination – Best fun in the world

Danny Dyer – Jimmy stole your foibles (and some of mine!)

My Facebook Friends – I borrowed your names for most of the Kill-Soc players

Beeve – Love your car! It started with just the name, but Victoria Newton became more like you the more I wrote

P-Dog – Thanks for showing me how to fire a rubber band

Drew – For Jimmy's explanation and the tmp!

Patrice – Thanks for sharing the RadlerBombs. They were not nice. Not nice at all

Tubbs – Nice title

Burge – Drama all the way
Pizza Express High Wycombe – It wasn't always crappy, honest!
G2 – Competing for English points was awesome – can't remember who won though…
Aunty Jessie – Did you spot the coat reference?
The Girls of Rohan - For the Exam Hall Death plan
Burleigh History A-Level Class – For the hide and seek
Owen Bowkett – For the change in The Stereotypes culprit
G4 – We saved your tooth
Flat 29 – For The Shitlist
Allen – UCE needs its staff
Topman High Wycombe – Thanks for the giant posters. Art project, my arse...

Thanks for everything

About The Author

Philip T McNeill currently teaches English and Drama in a Gloucestershire Secondary School. He can often be found writing or drawing when he should be paying attention in meetings. Right now he is on a train currently heading towards Newport. Shudder.

Check out his web comic 'Clamp Oswell's College Years' at www.clamposwell.com

Leave reviews!
Post Book Selfies!

@philiptauthor
@clamposwell

Facebook – The Locte Chronicles
Facebook – Clamp Oswell's College Years

Printed in Great Britain
by Amazon